THE
FALL OF
NESKAYA

BOOK ONE OF
The *Clingfire* Trilogy

A Reader's Guide to
DARKOVER

THE FOUNDING

A "lost ship" of Terran origin, in the pre-Empire colonizing days, lands on a planet with a dim red star, later to be called Darkover.
DARKOVER LANDFALL

THE AGES OF CHAOS

1,000 years after the original landfall settlement, society has returned to the feudal level. The Darkovans, their Terran technology renounced or forgotten, have turned instead to free-wheeling, out-of-control matrix technology, psi powers and terrible poi weapons. The populace lives under the domination of the Towers and a tyrannical breeding program to staff the Towers with unnaturally powerful, inbred gifts of *laran*.
STORMQUEEN!
HAWKMISTRESS!

THE HUNDRED KINGDOMS

An age of war and strife retaining many of the decimating and disastrous effects of the Ages of Chaos. The lands which are later to become the Seven Domains are divided by continuous border conflicts into a multitude of small, belligerent kingdoms, named for convenience "The Hundred Kingdoms." The close of this era is heralded by the adoption of the Compact, instituted by Varzil the Good. A landmark and turning point in the history of Darkover, the Compact bans all distance weapons, making it a matter of honor that one who seeks to kill must himself face equal risk of death.
TWO TO CONQUER
THE HEIRS OF HAMMERFELL
THE FALL OF NESKAYA

THE RENUNCIATES

During the Ages of Chaos and the time of the Hundred Kingdoms, there were two orders of women who set themselves apart from the patriarchal nature of Darkovan feudal society: the priestesses of Avarra, and the warriors of the Sisterhood of the Sword. Eventually these two independent groups merged to form the powerful and legally chartered Order of Renunciates or Free Amazons, a guild of women bound only by oath as a sisterhood of mutual responsibility. Their primary allegiance is to each other rather than to family, clan, caste or any man save a temporary employer. Alone among Darkovan women, they are exempt from the usual legal restrictions and protections. Their reason for existence is to provide the women of Darkover an alternative to their socially restrictive lives.

THE SHATTERED CHAIN
THENDARA HOUSE
CITY OF SORCERY

AGAINST THE TERRANS
—THE FIRST AGE (Recontact)

After the Hastur Wars, the Hundred Kingdoms are consolidated into the Seven Domains, and ruled by a hereditary aristocracy of seven families, called the Comyn, allegedly descended from the legendary Hastur, Lord of Light. It is during this era that the Terran Empire, really a form of confederacy, rediscovers Darkover, which they know as the fourth planet of the Cottman star system. The fact that Darkover is a lost colony of the Empire is not easily or readily acknowledged by Darkovans and their Comyn overlords.

REDISCOVERY (with Mercedes Lackey)
THE SPELL SWORD
THE FORBIDDEN TOWER
STAR OF DANGER
WINDS OF DARKOVER

AGAINST THE TERRANS
—THE SECOND AGE (After the Comyn)

With the initial shock of recontact beginning to wear off, and the Terran spaceport a permanent establishment on the outskirts of the city of Thendara, the younger and less traditional elements of Darkovan society begin the first real exchange of knowledge with the Terrans—learning Terran science and technology and teaching Darkovan matrix technology in turn. Eventually Regis Hastur, the young Comyn lord most active in these exchanges, becomes Regent in a provisional government allied to the Terrans. Darkover is once again reunited with its founding Empire.

THE BLOODY SUN
HERITAGE OF HASTUR
THE PLANET SAVERS
SHARRA'S EXILE
WORLD WRECKERS
EXILE'S SONG
THE SHADOW MATRIX
TRAITOR'S SUN

THE DARKOVER ANTHOLOGIES

These volumes of stories, edited by Marion Zimmer Bradley, strive to "fill in the blanks" of Darkovan history and elaborate on the eras, tales and characters which have captured readers' imaginations.

THE KEEPER'S PRICE
SWORD OF CHAOS
FREE AMAZONS OF DARKOVER
THE OTHER SIDE OF THE MIRROR
RED SUN OF DARKOVER
FOUR MOONS OF DARKOVER
DOMAINS OF DARKOVER
RENUNCIATES OF DARKOVER
LERONI OF DARKOVER
TOWERS OF DARKOVER
MARION ZIMMER BRADLEY'S DARKOVER
SNOWS OF DARKOVER

THE
FALL OF
NESKAYA

BOOK ONE OF
The *Clingfire* Trilogy

MARION ZIMMER BRADLEY

AND

DEBORAH J. ROSS

DAW BOOKS, INC.

DONALD A. WOLLHEIM, FOUNDER
375 Hudson Street, New York, NY 10014

ELIZABETH R. WOLLHEIM
SHEILA E. GILBERT
PUBLISHERS
http://www.dawbooks.com

First printing, July 2001

1 2 3 4 5 6 7 8 9 10

DAW TRADEMARK REGISTERED
U.S. PAT. OFF. AND FOREIGN COUNTRIES
—MARCA REGISTRADA
HECHO EN U.S.A.

PRINTED IN THE U.S.A.

Rose, this one's for you!

ACKNOWLEDGMENTS

Heartfelt thanks to the usual list of suspects: Betsy Wollheim, Ann Sharp, Elisabeth Waters, Susan Wolven and especially Dave Trowbridge, for mcguffins, military insight, and so much more.

DISCLAIMER

The observant reader may note discrepancies in some details from more contemporary tales. This is undoubtedly due to the fragmentary histories which survive to the present day. Many records were lost during the years following the Ages of Chaos and Hundred Kingdoms, and others were distorted by oral tradition.

AUTHOR'S NOTE:

Immensely generous with "her special world" of Darkover, Marion Zimmer Bradley loved encouraging new writers. We were already friends when she began editing the DARKOVER and SWORD & SORCERESS anthologies. The match between my natural literary "voice" and what she was looking for was extraordinary. She loved to read what I loved to write, and she often cited "The Death of Brendan Ensolare" (FOUR MOONS OF DARKOVER, DAW, 1988) as one of her favorites.

As Marion's health declined, I was invited to work with her on one or more Darkover novels. We decided that rather than extend the story of "modern" Darkover, we would return to the Ages of Chaos. Marion envisioned a trilogy beginning with the Hastur Rebellion and the fall of Neskaya, the enduring friendship between Varzil the Good and Carolin Hastur, and extending to the fire-bombing of Hali and the signing of the Compact. While I scribbled notes as fast as I could, she would sit back, eyes alight, and begin a story with, "Now, the Hasturs tried to control the worst excesses of *laran* weapons, but there were always others under development . . ." or "Of course, Varzil and Carolin had been brought up on tales of star-crossed lovers who perished in the destruction of Neskaya . . ."

Here is that tale.

Deborah J. Ross
March 2001

BOOK I

1

Coryn Leynier woke from a dream of fire sweeping down from the heights. The dream had begun peacefully enough, but with an unusual vividness, as were so many of his dreams since his body had begun changing with adolescence. At first, his glider hovered beneath Darkover's great Bloody Sun, its silken sails spread wide over fragile wooden struts. Last summer, his eldest brother, Eddard, who was heir to the mountainous Verdanta lands, had shown him how to ride the air currents for short distances. In his dream, Coryn soared freely. He felt no fear of the height, only pleasure in the limitless heavens.

Summer lightning flashed in the distance, across the Hellers. The air crackled with energy. Smoke curled skyward from a grove of resin-trees. Coryn tensed. Since he could remember, he and his brothers had kept watch for forest fires, sometimes competing to be the first to sound the alarm.

In his dream, Coryn struggled to turn the glider, to head back to Verdanta Castle with the news. But the wood and leather apparatus would not respond. It fought him like a living thing, twisting and turning in his grasp.

Coryn noticed the starstone, a chip of brilliance, lashed to the cross-beams. It looked just like any other starstone, bestowed on each child according to family tradition on the Midwinter Festival following their twelfth birthdays, but this one he knew was his own. As he gazed at it, blue light flared within, as if in recognition. He'd heard that with such a stone, a trained *laranzu* could send a glider wherever he wished, not just where the uncertain winds took it. The idea stirred something in him, a wordless longing.

To go where he chose, not where chance carried him. . . .

Coryn gazed into the starstone and pictured the glider turning back toward home at his command. Blue fire flickered in its depths. His nerves prickled and his stomach clenched, as rebellious as the glider. Still, he kept his eyes fixed on the starstone, trying to go deeper, ever deeper.

The fire shifted, pouring down the hillsides, leaping over the firebreaks which were strangely overgrown with neglect. In a matter of moments, it enveloped brush and copse, sweeping over everything in its path. Grass went up in puffs of smoke. Resin-trees blazed. As the pockets of flammable sap ignited, the trees exploded, one by one, showering live cinders in every direction. Smoke, dense and acrid, billowed from the forest.

Far in the distance, alarm bells sounded, over and over again as every holding in the Hellers, from Aldaran to the Kadarin River, was roused.

In the next heartbeat, he was sitting up in his own bed in Verdanta Castle, shivering as if it were deep snow season and not the height of summer, with alarm bells ringing in his ears.

✦

Coryn scrambled into his boots and bolted headlong down the stairway. Tessa, his oldest sister, hurried along the corridor with a tray of cold meat buns. She wore an old gray dress, several inches too short and patched with scraps of even older garments. She'd tied a white kerchief over her hair, so that she looked more like a scullery maid than her usual demure self, the lord's eldest daughter. Coryn grabbed a bun and stuffed it in his mouth while he pulled on his shirt. For once, she did not object.

In the courtyard outside, dawn cast muted shadows across the bare-raked earth. A fitful breeze carried the hint of the day's heat to come.

The yard seethed with movement. Everyone old enough to walk was here, all hurrying in different directions, carrying shovels and pitchforks, rakes and sacks and buckets, folded blankets and threadbare linens for bandages. Yardfowl squawked and fluttered, raising more dust. One of the castle dogs scampered by, barking. Men struggled to lash shovels and rakes to the saddles of pack *chervines*. Padraic, the castle *coridom*, stood on the rim of the largest watering trough, shouting orders.

Coryn paused on the threshold, heart pounding. For an awful moment, the yard seemed to slip sideways. He gulped, tasting bile, and swayed on his feet.

Not again! he stormed inwardly. He could not, *would* not be sick. Not now, when every able-bodied male over the age of ten, be he family or servant or guest, was needed on the fire-lines.

"You're with me on the firebreaks, lad." Eddard stepped into the yard, gesturing for Coryn to follow. "Get the horses ready!" Eddard was dressed for riding in supple leather pants and boots, and he carried two message rolls wrapped in oiled silk. "Petro!"

Coryn's next older brother, Petro, had already mounted the sleek Armida-bred black which was the fastest horse in the stables. His face was flushed and his black hair, so unlike Coryn's bright copper, jutted in all directions, giving him the aspect of both fear and excitement.

Eddard thrust one of the message rolls into Petro's outstretched hand. "This one is for Lord Lanil Storn, a direct request for his help."

"Help?" Petro asked, incredulous. "From *Storn?* Are we that desperate?"

"We've asked under fire-truce. This one looks to be the worst within memory," Eddard said, clearly uneasy. "Only a fool would let his neighbor's house burn and think his own safe."

Fire-truce, Coryn repeated silently. But would it hold? Verdanta and Kinnally had been raiding each other's lands for so many years that few recalled the original squabble. He believed it had had something to do with the ownership of a nut-tree grove which had long since died of root blight dusted accidentally over the hills by aircars from Isoldir.

"Father also asks for your passage to the Tower at Tramontana. If Lord Storn grants you leave," Eddard said with a twist of the mouth that indicated how unlikely he thought it, "you are to give this second roll to the Keeper, Kieran. Also give him a kinsman's greeting, for he is Aillard, related to Grandmama's family."

Petro tucked the rolls into his belt, his eyes stormy. "If *Dom* Lanil believes he can gain some advantage over us by waiting while we spend our strength on this fire or by blocking Tramontana's aid, then no more scroll of parchment will change his mind."

"Mind you bide your tongue," Eddard said with a trace of sharpness, "and repeat only what you have been given and not one of your everlasting speeches. Your mission is to ask the man for help, not to lecture him on the evils of modern society."

Petro subsided. "I will do my best. After all, Father says that if you treat a man as honorable, he is more likely to behave that way."

"Good speed, then, lad, and may Aldones bless your tongue as well as your horse's heels."

Petro nodded and spurred his horse through the gates at breakneck speed, scattering yardfowl.

Eddard gestured to a man halfway across the yard, struggling with the harness on a *chervine*. "No! Not like that!"

Lord Leynier's bay stallion, massive enough to carry even a legendary giant, whinnied and danced sideways, ramming one shoulder into the scullery lad clinging to its bridle. The boy sprawled in the dust as the horse reared, pawing the air.

Coryn grabbed the reins before the beast could trample the boy. White ringed the horse's eye and its body reeked with the smell of fright. He put one hand over its nose, pulling its head down. "Easy, easy," he murmured. The horse snorted, eyes less wild.

"Here, now." Lord Beltran Leynier, tall and grizzled, yet still powerful across the shoulders, took the reins from Coryn and swung up into the saddle. "First party, with me!" He galloped for the road, mounted men and pack animals close behind.

Stepping back, Coryn stumbled into the kitchen boy. The boy's cap went flying, to reveal pale red hair, twisted into clumsy braids and wound into a crown. *Aldones!* It was his baby sister, Kristlin, dressed in some servant's castoffs. She was only eight, too young to be assigned to anything more interesting than rolling bandages or chopping onions. From the look she gave him, he'd find spiders in his bed if he said a word to anyone.

"Coryn! Where are those horses?" Eddard yelled from across the yard.

Within the dusty closeness of the stables, the few remaining horses stamped and nickered. The groom had just finished cinching the saddle on Eddard's raw-boned gray mare. Coryn checked girth, breastplate and crupper strap on his own dun-colored Dancer, for they would be scrambling over rough terrain and a slip of the saddle could be fatal.

"You be careful out there, you young rascal," the groom said. "I've not seen a fire this bad since Durraman's donkey was foaled."

In the yard, Coryn scrambled on to Dancer's back and caught the lead line for the pack *chervines* from Padraic. He and Eddard clattered down the strip of road in the brightening day.

A plume of smoke rose from the forested hills, still many miles off. Coryn *sensed* the acrid lightning tang, the greasy feel of smoke from half-burned soapbush, ash across his face.

The world reeled, sky and green-gold hills blurred . . . melted. . . . Acid stung his throat. He swayed in the saddle, retching.

With a fistful of sandy mane in one hand and the other clenched on the pommel of his saddle, Coryn struggled to keep his seat. Eddard, riding ahead of him, had not noticed. The spasm of dizziness passed, leaving a sour film in Coryn's mouth.

Coryn's hand went to his neck, where his starstone lay insulated in the pouch of thick silk which he'd stitched himself. He felt its inner light as a wave of heat through his fingers.

He thought miserably that if only he knew how to use starstone and glider, as he'd dreamed, there would be no need to send Petro racing to Tramontana, or be at the mercy of High Kinnally. He, Coryn, could go aloft and drop the precious *laran*-made fire-fighting chemicals directly on the blaze.

With that thought, he pressed his lips together, dug his heels into Dancer's sides, and galloped on.

✦

Coryn, along with his brother Eddard and three of the smallholders from the rough borderland along the Heights, labored through the day, working their way along the established firebreaks and cutting new ones. Last summer's fires had been smaller than usual, but the winter had been mild. Dense foliage, much of it flammable soapbush, overflowed every open space and gully.

By the next morning, it was clear that the men were spread too thin, the land too vast to clear containment breaks of everything that could burn. As yet, there was no word from High Kinnally. Perhaps it was too soon.

Eddard brought them to the southern hill above the fire to spy out its direction. Timas, the oldest of the smallholders, studied the wind, the dryness of the underbrush, the slope of the hills. He had worked Verdanta's fire-lines since he was a boy.

"Tha'," he pointed up the slope, "and tha'. D'ye see it, m'lord, how the land sits to channel the flame upward, toward the grove?"

Coryn, munching on a handful of nutbread smeared with sour *chervine* butter, followed the old man's gesture. The wind blew fitfully and at an angle. If it held steady, Timas said, the fire would follow the steeper path to a protected valley where resin-trees and firecone pine crowded together. But if it changed direction . . .

The other way, the shallow, easy slope, bore nothing but grass. A spit of bare rock separated the two paths.

Coryn's sight wavered and he *sensed* the streams of ghostly fire. Images came to him—the wind freshening, shifting. Narrow tongues of fire lapped at the curling grass; it caught, flames racing faster than a galloping horse. Seeds sent tiny embers aloft as they popped, leaping ahead of the main fire. He saw them land on the rocky spit and as quickly go out. The fire left a crust of black behind it as it leaped along the easy slope.

Coryn's sight raced ahead with the fire. More embers landed on the rocky divide. Beyond his line of vision, the spit narrowed, the rock weakened by years of alternating summer heat and winter freeze. A spiderweave of minute cracks gave rooting to windweed and other quickly growing grasses which sprouted in the spring rains and died as quickly in the heat. A single spark landed—he felt it catch, the sudden flare of the dried windweed tendrils. In the next heartbeat, the fire burned on both sides of the barrier, lapping toward the resin-trees.

If the resin-trees go up, we will lose the entire mountainside. . . .

Coryn blinked, realizing that a long moment had gone by.

"— but it will be worse if the fire heads due south," Eddard was saying. "We must not risk the trees."

The old man shook his head, eyes cast down before his lord's heir. "Ye canna' trust the grass," he said stubbornly.

"Timas is right," Coryn said, a bit surprised at how steady his voice sounded. "The fire—it will start with the grass but it won't stay there. Up there past the outcrop . . ." Quickly, he described what he had seen. The other men fell silent, listening to him.

"Aye, that's the way of it," the old man said, nodding. "I've seen sparks leap ten feet or more. Rock, river, fire-break. But you, young lord, how did you know?"

"I—I *saw* it. It happened just like you said."

"Nay, lad, I said only how the fire *could* go. One way or t'other, at the beck of the wind."

Coryn lifted his chin and faced his older brother. "It *will* go that way. I saw it."

"You believe you did, *chiyu*." Eddard raked back his dark-red hair, leaving it just as unruly as before. "But if we choose wrongly and leave the resin-trees unprotected —"

"Lord Eddard!" One of the men, who had gone down halfway toward the fire, shouted and pointed. "The wind!"

"Zandru's curse!" Eddard spat. The wind had shifted, whipping the flames into miniature firestorms, burning even hotter and faster than before.

Toward the grassy slope.

"Let it have the grass!" Eddard shouted, swinging up on his horse. "Downslope, where Coryn saw it leap the rock! With luck we'll be in time!"

◆

Coryn could not remember being so numb with exhaustion, so drained in every muscle and nerve fiber, as when he and Old Timas stumbled into the makeshift camp on the third night of the fire. They had worked without stopping all that night and the next day, cutting new, wider firebreaks, clearing away grass and underbrush.

They saved the resin-trees, only to lose the next two hillsides and part of a nut-tree grove. Coryn saw the fear in the eyes of the smallholders who depended on what their children could gather in the forests to feed their families during the lean seasons. The next few winters would be hard, until the nut trees which had not been too badly burnt could bear again.

Lord Leynier was a generous man. In times of need, the castle would slaughter some of its livestock, the older and weaker animals, to distribute the meat and lessen the demand for feed grain.

Now, toward the end of the third day, a young boy on a pony brought orders from Lord Leynier that the men who'd gone out in the first groups were to rest. A handful of replacements had come from the small estates to the south and east. But they could look for no help from High Kinnally.

Lord Lanil Storn had refused both men and Petro's passage to Tramontana.

At the news, a cry of dismay rose from the smallholders. Ash-streaked faces turned paler.

"*Vai dom,*" said one man, "how can they not send help against—against *fire?*"

Eddard's jaw set tight, and for a moment Coryn saw his father's eyes flash in his brother's face. "I know not if he means to let us waste our strength against the fire and then strike when we are weak, or if he is fool enough to think the fire will stay on our lands only."

Coryn thought of the old proverb, *Fire knows no law but its own.* Then he remembered that Kieran, the Keeper at Tramontana, was a distant Aillard cousin. The obligations of blood ran strong in the Hellers. "Perhaps," he said in one of those quicksilver leaps of thought which came all too often now, "he fears that the Tower may give us other things besides fire-fighting chemicals."

"You mean weapons?" Eddard looked grim. "If only they would! That is, if there is anything left of us once this fire is done."

Eddard turned toward the waiting horses, but Coryn remained for a moment with Timas. The old man's eyes watered as if smoke still blew across them.

"It's a rough business," Coryn blurted out, aware of his own awkwardness. Without knowing why, he wanted to say something, to ease the other man's unvoiced distress.

"Aye, lad, that it is." Timas's voice was gravelly from smoke, but Coryn felt the emotional resonances beneath the words. "But fightin' fires isna' like warfare. Then it's the lords that get all the glory and it's us poor folk that pay for it."

"But," Coryn said, repeating words he'd head his father utter, "would you not suffer even more under an unjust ruler? Not every lord takes care of his people as my father does. Storn would let your children starve while he sits in his castle and feasts, or so I've heard. Isn't that worth fighting for?"

Sighing, Timas shook his head. "How little you know of it, lad."

✦

"Eat as much as you can and then sleep," Eddard said as they reined their plodding horses into the makeshift headquarters. The camp lay on

flat, rock-strewn ground, set on a hillside that had burned a dozen seasons before, so that only brush and saplings grew. A spring yielded water
for cooking and bathing burns.

The women and younger children of the Castle had set up picket
lines, an outdoor kitchen, and a few tents. Tessa and the next youngest
sister, Margarida, moved briskly between the tents, carrying bandages
and salves for burns, basins of washing water, and poultices for pulled
muscles. In the absence of Lady Leynier, for their mother had died at
Kristlin's birth, Tessa assumed the duties of supervising the household
staff and dispensing herbal remedies to everyone on the estate. In her
plain dress and kerchief, her sleeves rolled up to the elbow, she issued a
stream of orders for the care of the injured. Margarida followed in her
wake, a wide-eyed shadow.

Men who had come in earlier, their faces and garments grimed with
ashes, hunkered over cups of meat-laced porridge or sprawled exhausted
on blankets.

Coryn slipped to the ground and gratefully handed over Dancer's
reins to one of the Castle people. The smell of the food sent a wave of
nausea through his belly. He followed Eddard to the rough table where
Lord Leynier sat, poring over maps with his *coridom*. At his left side, a
stranger stood, watching silently. The hood of his dark gray cloak masked
his features.

"We have arrested the fire along these lines," Padraic said, tracing
them on the map. "But we cannot guard this entire front, even if we
could get there in time. If we push on, if we try to save this part of the
forest, then we risk losing even more in other places."

Tired men are careless, Coryn repeated to himself what his father had
said so many times. *And fire is unforgiving.*

"If we permit the fire to burn itself out," his father said unhappily,
"who knows how much more it may consume? There will be even greater
hunger and cold in the winters to come."

Coryn felt a rush of pride for his father and how he cared for the
lands and people under his stewardship.

"The Tower folk will arrive in time to save your forest," the stranger
said.

"Father," Eddard broke in, frowning. "We received word that Petro
could not get through to Tramontana. I understood that we could expect

no help from that quarter, or from the six-fathered *ombredin* at High Kinnally."

"It is our good fortune that *Dom* Rumail arrived early," Leynier said with a deference that surprised Coryn. "And that he has the skill to contact the Tower through his starstone."

"I could do no less." The stranger lifted the hood of his cloak back from his face, revealing a face so long and seamed, it might have been made from leather. Coryn thought him the homeliest man he had ever seen, yet the deeply shadowed gray eyes burned with an inner fire.

"It is in my brother's interest to protect the lands of his future daughter-in-law," *Dom* Rumail said.

Laranzu! Coryn caught the glitter of a starstone at the man's throat. He had never met a *laran*-gifted sorcerer before and now stared, entranced.

"Come on, young pup," Eddard threw one arm around Coryn's shoulders. "We'll starve, standing here. Let's eat!"

Coryn lowered himself to the folded blanket in between two sleeping men, his brother Petro and one of the stable hands, and accepted a cup of stew topped with dried fruit from Kristlin, who was still wearing those castoff boy's breeches.

With the first tentative bite, Coryn felt ravenously hungry. He wolfed down the whole portion. Someone else brought him another plate and also a tankard of watered ale. He dimly felt his head drop forward, someone take the dish and cup from his hands, and then he felt nothing at all.

◆

Shouting woke him, and for a dizzying moment he wondered if the last three days had not been yet another dream. He struggled upright, blinking in the cloudless daybreak. Another man, not Petro, snored at his side, but the rest of the camp was already roused.

"They're here!" Margarida, Coryn's middle sister, raced through the camp, shouting. "Tramontana has come!"

Coryn threw his head back, searching where she pointed. Across the clear, empty sky, four—no, six—gliders moved swift and silent as hawks. Silhouetted against the eye-searing blue, the figures appeared swollen by the sacks of fire-fighting chemicals they carried.

In the camp, the gray-robed stranger stood apart from the others. Lips moved, although no sound came from his mouth. Something in his posture pulled at Coryn, drew him near. The man's hands cupped something which glowed faintly blue. He stared into it with an intensity that both fascinated and repelled the boy. Aloft, the group of fliers divided, some heading toward the two most desperately pressed firelines.

"It's all right, I don't eat children." *Dom* Rumail looked up. A fleeting smile lightened his features. He lifted the hand that held the starstone. "Nor will this harm you. It's not wizardry, you know."

"Y–yes, I know that," Coryn said, suddenly shy. "I have one, too. All of us except Kristlin, who is too young, were presented with starstones at the Midwinter Festival of our twelfth years."

"May I see it?"

Coryn couldn't think of a reason to refuse, but he slipped the starstone reluctantly from its silk pouch around his neck and held it out. To his relief, the *laranzu* made no attempt to touch it, but merely bent over the lightly flickering gem, studying it.

"Yes, you've keyed into it, albeit roughly. Who showed you how to do this?"

"N–nobody. Father's been too busy. And Eddard —"

"Eddard!" *Dom* Rumail snorted, as if it might as well have been Coryn's horse. "And the wrapping—did you do that, too?"

Coryn blushed. His older brothers and sisters wore their starstones bare against the skin, when they wore them at all. Margarida, complaining that her stone gave her a rash, had wrapped it in a scrap of velvet from the late Lady Leynier's Midwinter gown. Coryn had gone to his sister for advice when, several weeks after his birthday, he'd awakened from nightmares. He dreamed that shadowy figures were impaling his chest on a sword of molten blue steel. When he tried the velvet, it made his nightmares worse. The circles under her eyes showed that it hadn't helped her either. It had been his idea to try silk, although Margarida had been the one to pilfer the scraps, cut from their grandmother's wedding gown and destined for a patchwork comforter.

"Your stitches betray you, boy," *Dom* Rumail said in a voice less gruff. "Put it away for now and don't let anyone touch it. From now on, only you or your Keeper may handle it safely. I must speak with your father."

Relieved, Coryn went back to his work. The gliders from Tramontana had dispersed, each to unload bags of fire-retardant chemicals in a different front line of the fire. Already, the smoke had changed in color. Coryn joined some of the other younger people, his brother Petro among them, up a little way on the hill above the camp. From here, he could see the billows of rust color streak the charcoal clouds.

There would still be more work to do, backbreaking and long, slow labor sifting through the ashes, making sure no live embers lingered to spring to life again. But the larger battle had been won.

2

When at last the ashes had been combed through and every lingering ember extinguished, when those who had labored so hard against the fire had time to rest and their burns and bruises were tended, Lord Beltran Leynier held a feast of celebration. He included not only his own household but every man and woman on the estate and every smallholder and his family, a gesture of unusual magnaminity.

That evening, the great hall of the castle glowed with candlelight. Tessa and Margarida had bedecked the hall with wreaths of late summer lilies and garlands of brown and blue, the Leynier colors. Padraic the *coridom* had arranged every serviceable table in the castle into a long-stemmed T, with Lord Leynier properly at its head and Rumail at his left hand, in the place of honor.

Coryn sat a few places away, sandwiched between Eddard and his young wife on one side and Margarida on the other. His mouth watered as one succulent dish after another was carried out, the slow-roasted bull calf, the barnfowl stuffed with nuts and apples, the loaves of fresh-baked bread redolent with rosemary and garlic, the last of the winter gourds glazed with honey. He had no idea food could taste so good. In addition to the grueling physical work of the last week, the nausea had receded, leaving him ravenous.

After the platters of dinner meats had been removed and the honey cakes reduced to crumbs, Lord Leynier called for another round of wine for each guest, even the children. Rising to his feet in the expectant hush, he lifted his own goblet.

"At this time of thanksgiving, we offer our hospitality and our deepest thanks to our honored guest. Rumail of Neskaya, your presence here and your actions in fighting the worst fire of many years bring new meaning to the phrase, *S'dia shaya.* You lend us grace."

Rumail nodded and replied formally, *"S'dei par servu.* For myself, I am glad to have done what I could. My brother, Damian Deslucido, who wears the crowns of Ambervale and Linn, believes that with great power comes even greater responsibility. I could offer no less than my full assistance in such a time of need. Like my brother, I believe that the gift of *laran* confers an obligation of service. In fact, some say there will come a time when those in the Towers will dedicate their talents only to peace and never to war."

"War is terrible enough when fought with sword and arrow," Beltran Leynier said grimly. "But no man can stand against these devil-weapons unless he commands them himself."

Padraic had told Coryn the story of how his eldest brother, who would have been heir to Verdanta, had been killed in the last battle with the Storns of Callarma. His uncles, Beltran's two surviving brothers, had died in an ambush which had come under the guise of a truce negotiation. As certain as next winter's snows, his father was right. Neither Callarma nor High Kinnally nor anyone else would dare to challenge Verdanta in the face of superior *laran* weapons.

After the faintest pause, Rumail continued, his voice shifting into formal, mellifluous cadences, "In the name of Damian Deslucido the Invincible, King of Ambervale and Linn, I convey to you warmest greetings and salutations. He sends these gifts as a token of his high regard."

Padraic, acting in his role of *coridom,* handed Rumail a parcel the length of a man's forearm and half its height, wrapped in a cloth which was dyed deep blue and bore the sheen of costly spider silk. Rumail grasped the parcel so that the iridescent fabric fell away, revealing a casket of beaten copper. Murmurs rippled around the table at the sight of such riches, for copper was the most precious of all Darkover's rare metals.

With a single swift movement, Rumail tipped the casket open, releasing a cascade of spice packets, lengths of embroidery-covered lace from Dalereuth, strands of Temora pearls, and a magnificent piece of polished amber carved in the shape of a cloud leopard. Margarida, who loved beautiful things, clapped her hands in delight, as did Eddard's wife.

Lord Leynier, clearly astonished, offered thanks in equally formal language. Rumail went on to present his primary mission, which everyone at the table already knew: the offer of marriage of King Damian's heir, Prince Belisar, to a Leynier daughter. What he did not say aloud, everyone also knew, which was that the marriage hinged on the girl's ability to bear children of exceptional *laran*. When the first proposal had arrived, Tessa, the only daughter of marriageable age, had been indignant.

"I will not be *barragana* to any man's accursed breeding schemes!" she said in an unusual display of temper, for she was normally the most conventional of the girls.

"It is an honorable marriage *di catenas*," her father corrected her, "and not an unfair bargain." Although he had the power to force the marriage, he rarely used his authority when his children were truly unwilling. "You would trade what you contribute to the royal bloodline in exchange for a life of comfort and relative safety."

Eddard's wife of less than a year, now visibly pregnant, had brought a sweet temper as well as a dowry of prime farmland to the marriage. Her condition had kept her away from the fire camp, but it was only a matter of time before she stepped into the role of Lady of Verdanta. Tessa would eventually have to marry to find a household of her own.

"You'd be Queen," Coryn reminded her. That seemed like a grand enough thing to be.

"Nobody's asking *you* to—" Tessa broke off, blushing furiously.

"We marry where we must, not where we will," Beltran said. "Love between a man and his wife comes later, or not, as the gods will it. Meanwhile, we each do what we can for family, for nothing is stronger than the ties of blood." He left unspoken the thought in everyone's mind, that alliances uncemented by fruitful marriage too often proved worthless. The value of such a union spoke for itself, in the names of the smaller estates now under fealty to King Damian.

In the end, her temper having run its course, Tessa said she would marry this Belisar as was her duty. If, that is, he were kind and tolerable to look at.

"You have several daughters here," Rumail said, his eyes sliding from

Tessa, darkly lovely and poised with her hair coiled low on her neck in a silver butterfly clasp, to Margarida, with her freckles and snub nose, dressed in a smock she'd embroidered herself, and then for an instant up to the gallery where Kristlin watched along with the other young children. "My brother asks that I be allowed to examine each of them, to determine the strength and suitability of each girl's *laran*."

Coryn glanced at Margarida. She kept her eyes downcast, yet he caught her flicker of dismay. She was barely fourteen—

"I had assumed the testing would be only for Tessa." Beltran said, frowning. "For she is not only the eldest, but of the most fitting age for marriage."

Rumail's expression remained bland as he said, "Yet the most fitting age may not be the most fitting match. Let us at least resolve the question of the *laran* potential of each girl before we proceed further with negotiations."

"If it is truly necessary, you are free to examine them in any way which is seemly for a maid and an unmarried man who is not her relative," Beltran said, with a trace of heaviness in his voice.

"It is necessary," Rumail said. "*Laran* may lie dormant, or be blocked, or may simply remain as a potential for the next generation." Coryn could tell from the shift in the man's voice that now he spoke with the authority of a trained *laranzu*. "I assure you, what I do will in no way compromise your daughters' honor, nor will there be any pain. And you, *damisela* Margarida, may have your nurse present if you wish."

Margarida lifted her eyes and said with spirit, "I no longer require a nurse, *vai dom*."

"*Dom* Beltran," Rumail continued, leaning forward slightly, "it was not my mission to test your sons, but I would like permission to examine young Coryn. I believe he may also have the *donas*, the gift."

Beltran nodded in assent and signaled for the tables to be cleared away and the evening's entertainment to begin. Tessa played the *rryl* particularly well and had a light, sweet voice. Petro, who had no singing ability, accompanied her on lap drum and Margarida on a small reed flute.

As Coryn set out a cushioned chair for Tessa, he felt *Dom* Rumail's eyes on him. A little thrill went up his spine. Perhaps this *sense* of his was a kind of *laran*. He might be able someday to pilot a glider with his starstone. Images of hovering, soaring, looking down on forest and

meadow from eagle's height, surged over him. Fervently, he prayed to
Aldones it might be true.

◆

Dom Rumail was given the small chamber used for hanging linens to dry
during the winter for his testing. All through the next morning, he examined the girls, beginning with Tessa. Coryn didn't see her until that evening, for Eddard sent him out to ride the boundary lands around the fire,
searching for any deeply-buried embers. Dinner was informal, as was
usual on work days, with hot meat pies, aged *chervine* milk cheeses and
dried fruit bars, nutbread and bowls of oat groats with savory sauce laid
out in the kitchen. Coryn found the two younger girls and Petro here,
chattering away.

"It was like—" Margarida lifted her hands in a fluttering gesture,
"—like dancing on a cloud."

"Do you mean he made you go to sleep?" Petro said, scowling.
"What's so grand about that?"

"You're jealous 'cause you got left out," Coryn said.

"Am not," Petro said. "I just don't want some old wizard poking
around in *my* mind. Who knows what he'll do once he's in there? He
could read your thoughts . . . all your nasty little secrets. How'd you like
everyone to know about the time you set fire to Tessa's hairbrush and
then dropped it down the latrine?"

Coryn landed a punch on Petro's shoulder while Kristlin giggled, "So
that's what happened to it. She was mad as Durraman's donkey for a
tenday, thinking she'd lost it."

Before Kristlin could ask exactly how Coryn had set the hairbrush on
fire, Margarida said, "It was rather nice, what *Dom* Rumail did. In a
dreamy sort of way."

"Well, *I* didn't like it," said Kristlin, sticking out her lower lip. Her
brows knitted, stormy. "It felt . . . I don't know, like the way a snake
sounds over dry leaves."

"You? What do you know?" Coryn grinned. "You don't even have a
starstone yet. You're just a little girl, running around in boy's breeches—
whose were they, anyway? Fra' Domenic's?" he jibed, unable to resist
teasing her.

"What do you care, so long as they weren't yours?" she said, darting
away when he reached out to tickle her.

One of the house servants came in and said that if Master Coryn had finished eating, could he please attend *Dom* Rumail? With a tingle of excitement dancing in his stomach, Coryn made his way to the linen rooms. The air smelled faintly of cedar and goldengrass, used to sweeten the sheets and keep away moths. A handful of candles filled the little chamber with gentle light. Rumail sat on a stool, hands loosely folded in his lap. Folded blankets cushioned a low table and formed a pillow.

"Am I to lie down?" Coryn asked.

"Not just yet, young master. I have a few questions for you. I have already studied your lineage, so we need not go into that. How long have you been having attacks of dizziness and disorientation? Has the nausea made it difficult for you to eat? Have you had visual disturbances, where things were not the right shape or color or would not hold still?"

"I didn't—" Coryn bit his lip. He'd thought he'd done a good job masking his weakness. Eddard hadn't noticed anything on the fire line, or hadn't seen fit to mention it. "It's excitement, that's all. It has nothing to do with, well, anything." But even to his own ears, he sounded unconvincing.

"It has very much to do with the awakening of *laran*." Now a steely certainty rang in *Dom* Rumail's voice. Coryn felt something darkly powerful emanate from the *laranzu*. "And it is not a thing to be either ashamed of or taken lightly. These are the symptoms of threshold sickness, which often comes when *laran* powers awaken at puberty. Often, the stronger the sickness, the more powerful the *laran*."

"Th–this means I really do have it?" Coryn blurted out. Eagerness quivered along his nerves. *"Laran?"*

"That may well be, *chiyu*. It is what we are here to discover. Tell me, what happens when you look into your starstone? Take it out and show me."

Coryn unwrapped the stone, his eyes resting on the flickering blue light in its heart. He had the curious sensation of falling into it, going deeper and deeper. After only a few moments, the sense of giddy whirling which was now sickeningly familiar came over him. His stomach clenched and he broke out in a cold sweat.

"Enough! Look away now!"

Coryn's fingers shook as he tucked the starstone back into its silken pouch. Haltingly, he answered Rumail's questions about the symptoms which, he admitted, had been growing steadily worse over the last season.

"Is it very bad, this threshold sickness?"

"It could become so if it is not treated," *Dom* Rumail said. "Yet I have seen young people enter the Tower with far worse cases than yours and grow to the fullness of their talents."

"What—what must I do?"

"For the moment, simply lie down and relax as best you can. Leave the rest to me."

When Coryn lowered himself to the padded bench, the dizziness intensified. Closing his eyes as he was bid, he felt the touch of a fingertip between his brows. The world steadied. Shortly after, he felt warmth in the pit of his stomach, creeping up his spine. His arms and legs felt heavy and then light. He seemed to be floating on a gauzy, sunlit cloud. His muscles melted as if he had been soaking in a hot spring, like the one Eddard had found on Cloudcap Mountain. Thoughts drifted pleasantly through his mind, as insubstantial as ghosts. No wonder Margarida had enjoyed it, for she was given to daydreaming fancies.

Once or twice, Coryn became aware of the sound of Rumail's voice, although he could not make out any words. From time to time, also, it seemed as if the inside of his skull had turned into his bedchamber and there was someone else moving about in it. Man or woman, he could not tell beneath the cloak of misty gray. He felt only a dreamy indifference and no sense of intrusion.

The visitor drifted across the room, picked up the comb of carved shell from its place on the shelf, pulled a strand of coppery hair from its teeth and placed the hair in an unseen pocket. Then it stooped to open the chest at the foot of Coryn's bed.

Coryn watched, now from the vantage of his head upon his own pillow, as the visitor took out every piece of clothing, one by one—his holiday tunic of Dry Towns linex, his best winter cloak of tightly-woven blue wool trimmed with cloud-leopard fur, vest and pants in supple crimson-dyed leather which had once belonged to Eddard and no longer fit him, a dagger with the tip broken off, a box of soapwood scratched with his initials and filled with childish trinkets—poor quality river-opals in a bag stitched by Tessa for his sixth birthday, a stick horse and rider, a handkerchief embroidered with cherries which had once been his dead mother's.

The visitor carefully folded and replaced all the items except for the dagger and the handkerchief.

What did this person want with him, with the things that it had taken, the hair and the dagger and the handkerchief? Coryn could only watch in horrified fascination as the visitor spread the handkerchief on his chest, over his heart, and placed the coiled hair in the center.

The figure reached up to its hooded head and, with a sharp jerk, drew out one of its own hairs. This it twisted together with Coryn's hair and wrapped in the handkerchief.

This wasn't right, *couldn't* be right! Coryn struggled to move, to turn his head, to shout aloud. Dom *Rumail, help me!* But his voice and body remained locked, as if encased in a block of ice.

The faceless visitor picked up the dagger and held it over Coryn's belly. Light glinted on the tip, now whole and needle-sharp, the broken bit filled in with blue glass which glowed eerily from within.

Coryn glanced around wildly, hoping for something he could use to defend himself. In an instant, he was no longer in his bedchamber. A vast gray emptiness, more barren than anything he could imagine, stretched out endlessly in all directions. He felt neither warmth nor chill, nor any substance beneath him. Overhead stretched an equally formless sky, lighter gray and unchanging as far as he could see. The place was empty except for himself and the gray-robed visitor.

The tip of the dagger slid into his body with only a pinprick of pain. He felt it pierce his skin, his muscles, right down to his spinal column and deeper still. In that instant he knew it would not kill him, yet every nerve, every fiber of his body rebelled. With that new ability, he *sensed* a wrongness beyond words. His vision went white.

With a twist and a slash, the dagger sliced open his belly. He could not see, but he felt something being placed in his very depths.

The handkerchief! With my hair—and whose? Why? Why?

Bits of thought and memory swirled around him, as if he had been caught in a shower of embers from an exploding resin-tree. Something deep within him tore loose from its roots.

Coryn screamed soundlessly and tried to arch away. Anything, anything to get away, to not feel that terrible wrenching *wrongness.* He hurled himself this way and that, blind in his desperation.

A corridor appeared suddenly before him. He bolted down it. The walls folded themselves around him, surrounded him on all sides. A soft gray blanket settled over him, as he became one with the substance of the walls. At last, he was safe. If he could not get out, then no one and nothing could enter. Nothing could reach inside him.

The next moment, the dagger was gone. Hands pushed the edges of his wound together. Unearthly warmth surged along the cut, fusing the edges. He drew a deep, shuddering breath. There was no pain. For one long moment after another, there was nothing except his own breathing. Silence and numbness bathed him.

Dimly, distantly, he felt the hands withdraw. In a body which was no longer his, the fiery streams faded into coolness.

The hooded figure bent near, until a breath whispered on his cheek. *"You will say nothing of this. Nothing."*
NOTHING . . . NOTHING . . .
Then true darkness took him.

3

Bright sun woke Coryn the next day. He opened leaden eyelids and studied the slant of the light. It must be well into midmorning. Why had he slept so late?

He heaved himself up on one elbow and wondered for a wild moment if he had been abed with lung fever, which he'd had when he was six. Sour cobwebs lined his mouth. He was where he should be, in his own bedroom with the same gray-and-pink smooth-cut stone walls hung with the same ancient tapestries of the legend of Hastur and Cassilda. Ruella, his old nurse, said they were woven by Great-aunt Ysabet, who never married and lived to be ninety-two, enough years to supply a castle twice this size with tapestries.

He lay in his own familiar bed, with the running stag which was the Leynier emblem carved into the headboard, wearing his own nightshirt. Yet . . . he had no memory of having gotten here.

Someone had brought in a folding table bearing a platter of fruit and drybread, a bowl with two brown eggs, and a tankard of lukewarm water laced with tonic herbs. He suspected Tessa's hand in the bitter-tasting water. She'd think it just the kind of wholesome thing to give someone who'd been sick last night—

Last night!

Coryn's hands flew to his abdomen. When he pulled the shirt up, he saw no trace of a scar. He touched only whole, healthy skin. Had it all been a dream? The formless gray plain, the intruder, *the dagger—*

He bolted across the room for the dark wooden chest. Throwing himself on his knees, he jerked the lid open. He pulled out one familiar item after another. Yes, there was the cloak, the festival shirt. His fingers touched hard metal—the dagger. The tip was as blunt as ever, a blade deemed safe enough to give to a boy for practice.

Coryn pawed through the chest until he found the soapwood box. The bag of river-opals was there, as well as the stick toys, but no handkerchief.

Coryn's stomach plummeted like a stone. He started shaking, bone-deep shivers like those of a man caught in a killing cold.

His hands moved of their own accord, pushing aside the remainder of the chest's contents. He took out the cheek strap from the bridle of his first pony, wrapped in a scrap of the animal's blanket, the vest of age-softened crimson leather which Eddard had passed down to him. And there, shoved into the far corner, a scrap of white. . . .

He drew out the handkerchief with its tiny embroidered cherries, smoothed its wrinkles. The fabric, delicate to begin with, had worn almost through in places, giving it the weight and feel of gauze. What had possessed him to rumple it so carelessly?

No matter, it was here. Everything was here. Last night's nightmare had been just that, a fevered vision borne of too much wine after the stress of so many days on the fire-lines. He'd also been suffering from threshold sickness, that's what *Dom* Rumail had called it. No wonder he'd had bad dreams. Now, with the handkerchief safe in his hands, everything made sense.

A tap sounded at his door, more mouse scratching than a real knock. He tucked the handkerchief inside the soapwood box and scrambled to his feet, heart beating unaccountably fast, just as the door swung open. Kristlin stuck her head in.

"Wait till I say to come!" Coryn flushed, acutely aware that he was standing there in his nightshirt with his legs bare to the knees. Then he saw her face and broke off.

Kristlin's cheeks were pale as milk, except for two spots of vivid color and crimson ringing her puffy eyes. Today, as she had since the fire, she wore boys' breeches, this pair fairly clean, patched over the knees and seat, and a shirt two sizes too big for her. She sobbed and threw herself into Coryn's arms.

He sat her down on the bed. "What's the matter, *chiya*? What's happened?"

"No! No! I don't want to go!" Her words dissolved into sobs. She buried her face against his chest.

"Nobody will make you do anything . . ." His words sounded hollow to his own ears.

"Papa says I have to—have to—go away. To Ambervale," She pulled away from him, her eyes snapping with her old spirit. "To marry that stinky old Belisar! I told Papa I never, ever want to get married! Not to anyone!"

Coryn sat back, bewildered. Just when things started to make sense, the world turned itself upside down. Kristlin, his baby sister, to be wife to the heir of King Damian Deslucido? She must have misunderstood. Surely it must be Tessa, who was grown up enough to be married and certainly looked like a Queen, or even Margarida, who had complained so much about the rash from her starstone—surely that meant she had *laran*. But *Kristlin?*

"There has to be some mistake. Just let me get dressed and I'll talk to Father. We'll sort it out, you'll see—" He disentangled himself from her arms. When he rose, his knees threatened to buckle under him. He caught himself on one hand on the bedpost, blinking back sudden grayness.

"I think you better have some breakfast first," Kristlin said with one of her quixotic shifts in mood. She'd obviously decided that the matter was settled now that her favorite brother was taking her part. "You slept in all day yesterday, lazyhead."

"I did what?"

"Well," she counted on her fingers, "it was two days ago *Dom* Rumail tested you, and he said to put you to bed afterward, because you'd had a bad spell of threshold illness, and the next day you didn't get up, so he gave you some *kiri—, kirian*, well, anyway, stuff to help you, and wouldn't let any of *us* try it, not even Margarida and was *she* mad 'cause she says she gets revulsions of the stomach just as bad as you, and then Tessa got bossy and said you'd need something to eat when you *did* wake up, so here you are." She folded her hands in her lap. "If you aren't hungry, can I have your eggs?"

Coryn thought that if he had to put up with any more of her chatter, he'd pack her off to Belisar himself, but she left him cheerfully enough. He devoured the entire breakfast. It all tasted wonderful, even the ripened *chervine* cheese.

The food steadied his stomach. He pulled on his boots and the cleanest shirt and pants he could find, and went in search of his father.

✦

Coryn made his way to the eastern tower, where Lord Leynier met with Padraic to go over the estate accounts and conduct other business early in the day. The room resembled a solarium with its thick glass windows along the curved outer wall, bright in all but the stormiest winter mornings. As a young boy, Coryn loved to sit on the pinewood floor and play quietly while his father worked. He'd even sneaked in uninvited once or twice alone, although that was strictly forbidden, until one day Petro got caught doing the same thing and spent a week scrubbing out the latrines.

Petro had a talent for getting into trouble, not so much for what he did but how he'd always argue why it was right and necessary when he got caught. Sometimes he'd even convince his father, or at least so entertain him as to receive a lesser punishment, which only encouraged him. If it had been Coryn caught in the eastern tower room, he'd have had a month at the latrines, not just a week.

Coryn paused in the small connecting chamber and lifted his hand to knock on the inner door. Voices reached him, his father speaking the name of a Tower. *Neskaya.*

". . . for the sake of the boy's health and sanity," rumbled a bass voice. *Dom* Rumail. ". . . there should be . . . no delay . . ."

Coryn held his breath in the silence that followed. Above the pounding of his heart, he heard his father's quiet words, *sensed* the fear and love behind them.

"You are sure Coryn is at risk? That sending him to a Tower is his only hope?"

"Nothing is certain but death and next winter's snows," the *laranzu* replied, his voice rising in forcefulness. "But this much I can swear to you, *vai dom*. In all my years, I have never seen a child suffer threshold sickness this severe . . ." His voice lowered, the words muffled. ". . . without skilled care. Perhaps, if he had been taught from early years by a household *leronis* . . ."

Rumail's words trailed off and the silence lengthened. Coryn's hand ached from the tension of clenching his fist. His mind jumped and darted from one thought to another—his promise to Kristlin, the vague uneasiness from last night which even now stirred once more, and now this news, that he himself must be sent away—that he had *laran*—

Unable to contain himself any longer, Coryn rapped on the door, startling at the loudness of the sound. At his father's word, he lifted the latch and went in. The scene was much as he expected, his father sitting behind the big burlwood desk, *Dom* Rumail in a cushioned chair.

"Ah! There you are!" His father gestured for Coryn to come in, just as if he'd been expected.

Coryn lowered himself on the bare stool, wiping damp palms on the thighs of his pants. He kept his eyes fixed on his father's. He did not want to look at *Dom* Rumail.

"It's about Kristlin," he began. His words spilled out as he stumbled through her story.

"She is indeed the one who tested strongest for the *laran* qualities King Damian is looking for in a match," Beltran said gravely. His brows, black shot through with gray, drew together briefly. "So it is for her that the marriage offer is proposed."

"But she's only—" —*eight!* Coryn bit off his words, *sensing* his father's distress. He did not need to be reminded how badly Verdanta needed this alliance. It was not so long ago that children even younger than Kristlin were forced into matings in order to breed exotic new strains of *laran*.

"*Dom* Rumail assures me that no true marriage will take place until Kristlin is of a suitable age, which will not be for some years," Beltran said. "Today she will be handfasted by proxy and the contract signed, nothing more."

Coryn caught the edge of his father's thought, *A handfasting is not a marriage. I pray this one will hold until the alliance can be made irrevocable.*

"She—I'm not sure she understands that, Father," Coryn said.

"But in time, she will," his father said. "If things were otherwise, I would have done my best to make a good marriage to someone else for her. She would have had to leave her own home for her husband's. That is the way of things in this world. As it is, this is a far better match than she could have ever hoped for. With a future Queen for a sister, the other girls may look in higher places for their own marriages, so everyone benefits from the match."

Rumail turned and Coryn could not evade his glance.

"And I—I am to go to a Tower?" He posed it as a question, although he already knew the answer.

"I thought you might have heard a word or two while you waited outside," his father said. One corner of his mouth quirked upward, as it did when he was trying not to smile. "*Dom* Rumail has already told you that you may be gifted with *laran*—"

"Not *may be*," Rumail interrupted, with a resonance in his voice which bespoke his years of Tower authority. "He has a powerful gift. We must not lose it, or him."

Beltran went on without missing a breath, "—and that for your own health, you require the care of people who know how to treat threshold sickness, how to teach you to use your *laran*. If you truly do not want to leave home," he went on, ignoring Rumail's pointed frown, "it might be possible to arrange for someone from Neskaya or Tramontana to come here."

"I *do* want to go to a Tower," Coryn blurted out. His voice shook, but perhaps only he could hear it. *But not to Neskaya.* He knew nothing of the Tower, beyond that was where Rumail served. He shifted uneasily under the *laranzu's* gaze.

"I thought you might look upon it as yet another adventure," his father said, sighing. "And I much prefer this be of your own choosing. When you knocked on the door, we were just discussing the matter of which Tower."

"I am, of course, most familiar with Neskaya," Rumail said. "The workers are highly skilled, and have great matrix screens capable of almost any *laran* work which can be imagined. But when I left, several new commissions required their combined attention. With those priorities, they already have all the young people they can properly train. I am not returning directly there, so I could not escort Master Coryn in any event. But Tramontana is just as qualified to begin his training. I will be happy to arrange it."

Tramontana . . . Relief, like a cool breeze in the stillness of a sultry summer night, swept through Coryn.

"Yes, that makes sense." Beltran nodded. "To get there, you must take the longer route to avoid crossing into High Kinnally lands, but the weather is mild, so that is not a problem. In addition, we have distant kin at Tramontana, and it would be well to cement those ties, come next fire season."

"When I have learned to use my powers, *I* will summon Tower gliders and their chemicals," Coryn said. "We will have no further need of outsider help."

Rumail looked at him sharply, but Beltran chuckled and said, "That is true enough, should you still want to return to us after seeing the wide world. Now, go and find your little sister, so we can explain to her that she need not leave home quite yet."

✦

The doors had been thrown open to the warm summer night. Coryn stood at the threshold, looking out over the empty courtyard and wondering when he would see it again. It seemed a century ago that he'd watched the frenzied activity of the firefighters. Here Padraic had shouted out orders in that bellow of his, and there Kristlin had fallen on her backside, almost trampled by Beltran's unruly bay stallion.

Kristlin . . .

He'd hardly recognized her when she'd come downstairs for the handfasting ceremony, wearing a dress that rippled as she walked, blue trimmed with ivory lace at the high neckline and tied about her slender waist with a matching ribbon. Ruella had brushed her unbound hair until it shone like polished brass. At least, Kristlin looked like the child she was, although a pretty one. No one could reasonably assert that she was old enough to be married.

Tessa had worn her good dress, the same as at the banquet after the fire, but she wore no jewels, looking more like a somber young matron than a still-eligible *damisela.* Margarida practically giggled with relief that she had not been chosen. She wore her hair in a child's braids over a smock she'd embroidered with her own designs of butterflies and windflowers.

Unlike the previous celebration, there had been little rejoicing past the simple proxy ritual. Petro disappeared into one of his black moods and Tessa refused to sing without him, claiming a delicate voice. Eddard's wife excused herself early to take to her bed. Although she had not complained, her skin was ashen with the fatigue of her pregnancy. Coryn worried that Kristlin would mind, but she seemed happier to have the whole thing over with.

"Brother . . ." She'd come up so silently he hadn't heard her. "Are you sad?"

He shook his head, startled. Had she *sensed* his mood? "Not sad, just—just wanting to remember this." He swung his arms wide to the yard, the estate grounds, the mountains with their forests and wild streams beyond.

He hugged her hard, feeling her wiry arms tighten around him.

I'll miss you. The words formed in his mind, so that he could not be sure who had said them. In their separate ways, they were each bidding good-bye to childhood. She would stay at home for a handful of years and then go on to her place as *di catenas* wife to a king, maybe the mother of kings even greater. His way led to a Tower, to Tramontana, to the secrets of the starstone and *clingfire* and things he could not yet imagine. He shivered, wondering if he would ever see her again.

Coryn would have preferred to leave for Tramontana without either breakfast or fuss, but *Dom* Rumail departed the same day, so the household stayed up half the night preparing an unusually elaborate meal, everything from cinnamon-flavored apple twists to fat sausages. He'd eaten far more than he wanted, mostly because Rumail kept lecturing him that loss of appetite was one of the danger signs of threshold sickness. He would rather have Tessa fussing over him with her herbs.

Then, while still at the table, Beltran gave yet another speech thanking Rumail, and then one for Coryn's special benefit. Coryn had heard all the phrases before: "family honor" and "noble deportment." His body wouldn't sit still, no matter how hard he tried. He wanted to be away, off to the adventures which surely must await him.

Kristlin sat at her usual place, having defied Ruella and dressed in an old smock and underskirt. Her eyes looked red and she sniffled. Rumail took her small hand in his and said, "Let the joining of these children bind our lands in enduring goodwill and prosperity. May this union be a harbinger of a new world, one in which brothers no longer make war upon one another, but live together under one King, all obeying the same just rule."

"Peace and happiness for our children and their children is our dearest wish," Beltran replied.

"The question is," Petro muttered as they left the table, "which King and whose version of justice?"

Coryn, his stomach churning with the too-rich food, turned to his brother. They had drawn a little away from the others and spoke in lowered voices. Usually he paid little attention to Petro's rambling, but now he asked, "Do you mean King Damian—or *Dom* Rumail—would be— would be—" He couldn't quite force out the words, *would be tyrants?* He knew little of King Damian Deslucido, but Rumail filled him with an uneasiness he could not put words to.

"I don't know," Petro answered. "*Dom* Rumail has been our good friend and I know nothing against this Damian. My objections apply to any King. If one rules over so many, who must *he* then answer to? If an ordinary man is treated unjustly—if a farmer starves because royal soldiers steal his crops or a woodsman has his hand chopped off for not bowing quickly enough to suit the King—what can he do but take up arms? And then what will stop the King from turning against his own people? But these are dangerous thoughts, little brother. Keep them to yourself. Promise me."

Coryn gulped and nodded, thinking of his own formless distrust of Rumail.

The party proceeded to the yard, where Rumail's horse and pack animal stood waiting, alongside Coryn's dun Dancer, and a *chervine* laden with everything a young man entering a Tower might want, from down-stuffed quilt to soothing winterberry lotion, tins of candied figs and rock sugar, even a set of reed pipes to while away the long winter nights.

Coryn's escort, a livestock handler named One-eyed Rafe, waited beside his own mount. No one knew how he'd lost one eye, although the other looked as pale as if all color had been burned out by gazing too long at the sun. Coryn didn't know the man well, had barely exchanged a few sentences with him. Castle gossip had it that Rafe had been a mercenary soldier in his youth and he looked capable of single-handedly fighting off a small army. The long-knife strapped to his thigh in a well-worn leather sheath had done ample service.

As the final round of well wishes and good-byes drew to a close, Rumail bent to speak to Coryn. "If I alarmed you with my frank talk, it was to prevent you from taking serious symptoms too lightly."

Rumail's nearness sent prickles up Coryn's spine. With relief, he turned to accept one last hug from Margarida. Then he moved toward Dancer, gathering up the reins in preparation for mounting.

Rumail restrained him with a single feather-light touch on the back of the wrist. "You are feeling better *now*, I can see that. The *kirian* sometimes has a lasting beneficial effect. But travel, for even a few days, can upset that fragile balance."

He gestured to Rafe. "If the young master should experience any recurrence of threshold sickness, you must make sure he eats well and is kept warm. If he becomes disoriented—doesn't know where he is, doesn't recognize you, seems confused, or cannot eat—then you must give him this." Rumail held out a small glass vial half-filled with colorless liquid. He placed it in a pouch of wool-lined leather and handed it to Rafe. "Only a spoonful at a time. If he can still ride, make all speed to the Tower. Under no circumstances must you leave him. Do you understand?"

Rafe placed the wrapped vial in his saddlebags without a word, his expression as blank as ever. Clearly, he needed no foreign wizard to teach him his duty.

Kristlin threw herself into Coryn's arms. For once, he had no words of easy reassurance for her. Just as he was beginning to squirm, she drew back. Rumail reached out to stroke her head, but she shied away.

"You are not to touch me." Kristlin lifted her chin, her eyes flashing. "It is not *you* who is my promised husband, but Prince Belisar, he who will be King."

"Nevertheless, you must speak politely to *Dom* Rumail, who will be your kinsman," Tessa, who had been following behind, said primly. "And a Queen must be courteous to everyone, especially a *laranzu* of great power."

"When Coryn comes back from the Tower, we'll have *him* and then we won't need anyone else!"

Tessa flushed, stammering out an apology for her younger sister's behavior. Rumail waved her words away, saying, "She is but a child, already missing her big brother. I leave her to your care and tutelage, *damisela*."

Coryn swung up on Dancer's back and took a last leave of his father. As he rode out of the yard, with Rafe in the lead, Kristlin darted after him. She clung to his stirrup.

"I would take you with me if I could, *chiya*," he said.

Her lower lip trembled, but she shook her head. "I don't want to go to a Tower, not even with you. I want to stay here forever."

On impulse, he said, "At the bottom of my chest is a carved soap-wood box. Will you keep it for me? Then, whenever you are missing me, you can hold it and know I am thinking of you."

She brightened, nodded, and released his stirrup. His hand went to the inner pocket of his vest, where his mother's handkerchief lay safely tucked. As long as it was safe, so was he.

✦

By the time Rafe called a halt for the midday meal, sun and fresh air combined with the exercise of riding to dispel the queasiness from the over-rich breakfast. They were still riding through Verdanta lands, but as the hours wore on, the shape of the hills grew less and less familiar. The trail wound past rock formations pocked with caves, through meadows of sun-parched grass, and down valleys lush with ferns and brambleber-ries. They stopped to let the horses drink and rest beside a stream.

Coryn sat on a fallen log, picking at the yellow-flecked shelf fungus growing along its length and nibbling the last of his nutbread and cheese. Once this narrow stretch of forest had been wide and deep, and trailmen were said to have roamed it, but the river had become a mere stream and no one had seen the elusive creatures in living memory. Maybe he'd come back some day and look for them. He wouldn't be staying at the Tower forever . . . would he? He sighed, stretched, and went to get another apple from his saddlebags.

"You've a good enough appetite," Rafe said.

"Yes, I'm fine." Coryn took a bite from the apple. It was last fall's harvesting and had lost its crispness. He'd been searching for the right time to speak all morning. "Rafe . . . you're my father's man, are you not, and not *Dom* Rumail's?"

The old soldier's mouth tightened at the corners. Coryn had guessed right, that he didn't like being given orders by a foreign *laranzu.* He'd handled the wrapped vial of *kirian* as if it were tainted with wizard's magic.

"And we both know I don't need a nursemaid," Coryn went on. "I think . . . I think it would be less insulting to both of us if I took the *kirian*, the vial he gave you, and used it when I need to. Instead of you having to watch over me and the trail at the same time."

He half-expected Rafe to protest, but the man nodded, fetched the leather pouch from his saddlebag, and handed it over.

Coryn waited until Rafe had gone off into the ferny undergrowth to relieve himself. Crouching beside the stream, he unstoppered the vial. A faint lemony smell rose from within. He dumped out the contents, rinsed the vial twice and refilled it with fresh water. Except for a bit of dampness, no one could tell by looking that anything had changed. He tucked the wrapped vial inside his vest, next to the folded handkerchief.

Mounting up once more, Coryn felt as if a great weight had been lifted. He'd broken free of Rumail's hold. He was going to a Tower, to be trained in *laran*, to learn to fly a glider with his starstone and maybe learn the secrets of talking to other Towers at a distance or making *clingfire*. He sang and made jokes as the day drew on. Although Rafe wasn't much for conversation, he smiled now and again.

✦

Late into the fourth day, Coryn and Rafe left the forested slopes for barren, rock-strewn hillsides. Haze covered the sky. The air turned icy, with a metallic taste. Thunder rumbled, soft and blurred. The horses jittered on the narrow path and the usually placid pack *chervine* shook its antlered head nervously.

Coryn pulled his horse to a halt at Rafe's signal. The old soldier lifted his head, turned to the north. "From up Aldaran way, I reckon. Ages ago, they worked weather-magic there. Mayhap they still do. We'd best find shelter."

Dancer whinnied and pawed the trail, pulling at the bit. Coryn nudged him on. Clearly, this was no ordinary storm—the taste of the rising wind, the sudden chill, the prickly feeling along the back of his neck—all bespoke some kind of *laran* at work. He'd never heard of weather-magic, and Aldaran, though fearsome, had always seemed far away.

They urged the horses around the curve of the hill. Hooves clattered on loose rock, sending a rain of chips downslope. The thunder took on a sharper tone.

Coryn lifted his eyes to the featureless white sky, but saw no lightning. "Rafe—"

But the older man, in the lead, wrestled his mount to a halt. The horse pranced and swished its tail. In an instant, Coryn's heart fell. The entire hillside lay covered beneath a rockfall. Instead of a narrow trail bounded on either side with barren soil pocked with boulders and scrub brush, steep but passable, they faced a pile of jagged boulders, many of them chest-high to the horses. Upward, the entire cliff face had fractured and fallen away. In the V-shaped crevice at the bottom of the hill, a small copse of brush and a few straggly trees still stood.

Lightning flashed across the sky and thunder cracked again. Clouds, gray and swollen, billowed out from the north, building visibly from one moment to the next. The wind, even colder now, whipped across Coryn's face.

"Which way?" he called to Rafe, raising his voice above the wind.

The old mercenary's mouth twisted as he brought his horse to face downhill. The horse squealed, refusing for a moment until Rafe reined him in a tight circle and clapped his heels into the animal's sides.

The horses stumbled down the rise, following the rockfall. Even the surefooted pack *chervine* lost its footing once. After a few minutes, Rafe signaled for them to dismount and lead their animals.

Dark, angry-looking clouds now stretched from one horizon to the other. Lightning kindled the sky, followed almost instantly by ear-splitting thunder. Dancer whinnied and pulled back, ears pinned flat against his neck. Coryn patted him and urged him on. The horse moved forward, reluctance in every tense line of his body.

Wetness spattered Coryn's face: huge, icy drops. Within moments, the rain increased to a downpour. He pawed through the *chervine's* packs for his hooded cloak. By the time he managed to pull it out, his shirt and vest were soaked through.

Coryn shouted to Rafe, who'd wasted no time in donning his own cloak. "We've got to get out of this!" Through the downpour, he could see the copse at the valley floor. It wouldn't offer much shelter, but it was more than they had here.

Then he saw—*sensed*—an invisible river tumbling down the V-cleft, gaining power with each passing moment, carrying away everything in its path—men and horses as well as straggly trees.

"Flash flood!" Coryn cried.

Rafe already had brought his horse and pack animal to face upslope. Dancer and the *chervine* turned eagerly, as if they realized the danger also.

Climbing back up was harder than Coryn imagined possible. His boots slipped on the loose rock, now slick with rain. A stone tipped and slid away as he stepped on it. Pain shot up the outside of his ankle.

A few minutes later, Dancer lost his footing and slid backward in a hail of stones. The horse's forehooves pawed the slope frantically. From below, Rafe cursed; one of the stones must have struck him. Coryn dropped the reins rather than risk them snapping. He watched, his heart pounding, as the dun horse slid another few feet and came to a stop, hindquarters bunched. White ringed its eyes.

Coryn clambered down to Dancer and gathered up the reins. "Easy, easy," he murmured, stroking the horse's hide. The horse quivered under his touch. He felt the animal's fear as a battering wave. The more he reassured the horse, the more calm he himself felt.

Rain came down in a torrent, making it impossible to see more than a few feet. Wind blew steadily, driving the droplets deeper into the folds of Coryn's cloak. Step by agonizing step, Coryn led the horse up the slope to where his pack *chervine* stood, shaking its antlered head to send sprays of water in all directions.

"No point in going on," Rafe said as he brought his own two animals level with Coryn. "Stop now, wait it out."

Rafe was right. It would take hours to work their way to the top of the rockfall and find some way across. Even then, they might find themselves in exactly the same situation without adequate shelter, only wetter and more exhausted.

Rafe, not waiting for a reply, moved toward the rocky barrier. This close, the barrier gave a slight but perceptible shelter from the wind.

"There!" Rafe said.

Coryn couldn't see what the old soldier pointed to, but as they approached, he made out a rough overhang where a huge flat shard extended like a tabletop beyond its supporting boulders. It was barely deep enough for the two of them, but the ground underneath looked relatively dry.

"Saddlebags—there. Blankets—there." In a few terse commands, Rafe organized the little shelter. "In!" He half-pushed Coryn to the back of the overhang. "Out of those clothes!"

"But—" Coryn bit off his protest. His shirt and vest were soaked to the skin, and now that he was no longer climbing, chill seeped through. It was better here, out of the wind, but not much. Even as a child, he

knew wet clothes would steal body heat even when the outside temperature wasn't that cold.

He set aside his cloak, which was thick enough to be dry on the
inside. Shaking, he tugged off his boots and wet clothing. A sudden gust
cut across his bare skin like a knife edge. The next moment, Rafe shoved
a bundle into his hands—his winter-weight shirt and pants of soft thick
wool, which Rafe had somehow dug out from the bottom of the *chervine's*
pack.

By the time Coryn had pulled on his dry clothes, Rafe crawled in
beside him and forced the *chervine* to lie down, its body blocking the
worst of the wind. The horses, tethered close to the opening, assumed
postures of sullen endurance with their heads down and tails clamped
against their rumps.

Thunder sounded again, shivering through the rockfall. Coryn
couldn't tell its direction. The rain redoubled its strength; the sound
shifted to a harsher note.

Hail.

Coryn caught a glimpse of the pellets of ice over the *chervine's* shoulder. He began to shiver again.

"Ah, there," Rafe said gently, drawing his own blankets around
Coryn.

A sudden deafening noise, louder than thunder, jolted Coryn. His
eyes focused on gray light outside. The din increased, as if some giant
were slamming boulders into the hillside above them.

Rafe sat bolt upright, grabbing for the *chervine's* reins. The animal let
out a terrified bleat as it struggled to rise. Rafe grabbed the *chervine's*
head, using it as a lever to force the animal back down, on to its side.

Coryn caught a glimpse of rocks pelting down the hillside. Their impact quivered through the boulders around him, through the very earth
itself. Rain sleeted, now straight down, now gusting to spray his face with
half-frozen droplets.

The outer edge of the overhang splintered with a resounding *crack!*
One of the horses screamed, suddenly cut off. Coryn flinched and gathered his feet under him. Every fiber in his body shrilled to *get out now!*

As Coryn scrambled for the opening, Rafe reached out with his free
arm and grabbed the neck edge of his cloak. Coryn spun around under
the power of the older man's grip. For an instant, he struggled as mindlessly as had the *chervine*.

"No chance out there." Rafe jabbed his thumb back at the avalanche and shouted over the racket. "Only hope—wait it out."

Coryn's eyes focused on the hillside beyond. There was no sign of the horses. Some of the hurtling stones were small as pebbles, others massive. If one of those struck him, or even the fist-sized stones, a lucky blow to temple or spine, a slip on the wet ground . . .

He shuddered, drew his knees up, and crossed his arms over his bent head. A moment later, he felt Rafe hunker down beside him, placing his body between Coryn and the hurtling stones.

Help . . . Help . . . ran through Coryn's mind. The syllables pulsed in time with his racing heart. Without thinking, he reached for the pouch which held his starstone. His fingers pushed through the folds of silk to grasp the crystal. It warmed immediately under his touch.

Help . . . Help . . .

For an instant, Coryn thought he felt a response, but could not be sure. The uproar outside seemed to lessen. A short time later, he made out the sounds of individual stones from the differences in pitch.

He lifted his head. Rocks blocked three-quarters of the entrance. In the gloom outside, he saw that the rain had dropped to a drizzle, then a mist. For seconds at a time, no stones rushed past.

When several minutes had gone by in silence, Rafe straightened up, handed the *chervine's* reins to Coryn, and clambered toward the opening. He had to push aside a heap of rocks in order to climb through. Widening the opening did not, however, bring any more light into the little cave.

Coryn crawled forward, enough to see that dusk had come upon them. A stray gust brushed his face with icy fingers. The temperature was falling fast.

Rafe came back a few minutes later. Even in the gathering darkness, Coryn felt him frown.

"Not good. Whole hillside's slid down on us. No way around now. Take us hours just to climb out." He reached for the saddlebags with their trail food and handed a packet to Coryn. "Stay here tonight."

"The horses? Are they—"

Rafe shook his head, barely visible. "No sign."

Dancer . . . And Rafe's two mounts, innocent beasts they had ridden into danger. Coryn's heart tightened into a knot of pain. They could have escaped, he told himself, but he did not believe it.

Although he was not hungry, Coryn managed to eat some jerked meat and fruit-nut bars, along with sips of water. His stomach tightened ominously, but eventually, his tired young body relaxed. He drifted into an unsettled dream of wandering naked across a sheet of ice under a featureless sky, of lying helpless while a shadowy cloaked figure drew near, of fire. Fire racing across the forested slopes, fire raining from the sky . . .

Fire lapped at him, strange blue flames. Shivering, he tried to avoid it, but as he moved away, the flames rose even higher, closer. Tongues of brightness consumed whatever they touched. From his outstretched fingers, the blue fire ran up his arm. The flesh of his hand crisped, leaving blackened, smoking bones.

"Help! Fire! Help me!" he shouted as he tried to smother the fire with his good hand. Instantly, it, too, caught fire.

The flames slowed their course as they worked their way inward, into one shoulder and deeper, toward the core of his body. He screamed in earnest now, his own terror crystallizing into sound. His cries reverberated in his skull. In the distance, someone called out a name which he vaguely recognized as his own. The more furiously he beat at the blue flames, the faster they burned. If he ran outside, the rain might quench them—

"Coryn! Coryn, lad, what is it? Be no fire here! No harm, see?" A shadowy figure reached for him, blurred fingers closing around his arms. His charred bones splintered under the pressure.

"No! No!" Coryn threw himself backward, desperate to break away. Horrified, he watched the blue fire creep up the hands of the figure. Any moment now, the very walls of the shelter would catch fire, too.

Then he was held immobile, clasped in an embrace as unyielding as stone itself. A glass vial was forced between his teeth and liquid gushed into his mouth. He sputtered, swallowing a little but spitting more out. His stomach twisted sickly. Turning just in time, he vomited, heaving again and again until there was nothing more to come. His eyes watered, and acrid saliva filled his mouth.

He heard a voice, so low and resonant that he could catch only a phrase or two. "Holy St. Christopher . . . Bearer of Burdens . . . Protector of children . . . Into Thy care . . ."

He looked down at his hands and saw, as if the images were painted on layers of gauze, his hands, whole and unharmed, and his other hands, his dream hands. Bits of heat-blackened flesh clung to splintered bones.

Pain shrilled along his nerves. And still the fire burned, eating through the muscles of his chest, his ribs, his heart. . . .

Evanda and Avarra, Aldones the Son of Light, even you, Zandru of the Forge—help me! Help me!

As if from an immense distance, a voice whispered through his mind. It reminded him of tiny silver bells, sweet and full of light. *Who are you?*

Who was he? For a panicked moment, he could not remember his name.

The fire! The blue fire! Help . . .

Hold fast, little brother. We will send help . . .

Though the voice faded into silence, though the words were few, a sense of immense calm flowed through Coryn. His muscles softened and grew heavy. His body sagged in Rafe's arms, in some other, invisible arms. The blue flames flared once more, then receded. Finally, he slept. This time, no dreams came.

5

The sour smell of vomit filled the little cave. Coryn rubbed gummy residue from his eyes and sat up, finding himself alone. The opening had been cleared away, except for drifted rubble, and the light outside shone clear and bright. Both the older man and the *chervine* were missing.

"Rafe?"

Where had he gone? Crept away in the night to save his own skin? No—the saddlebags of food and warm clothing were still in the cave.

At first, Coryn could barely recognize the landscape outside. Loose rocks, varying in size from boulders to pebbles, lay heaped with long-dead branches and trees torn from their moorings on the heights. Wetness gleamed like fresh-spilled blood in the slanting morning sun, pools and rivulets, even piles of quickly melting hailstones.

There was no way through the debris plugging the valley floor. Already, water had pooled upstream and every few minutes a tree branch would be dislodged to go swirling downriver. The reservoir kept rising, fed by the water draining off the hillsides.

The *chervine* stood downslope, browsing placidly on splintered branches which still bore fresh foliage. It whuffled a greeting as Coryn approached through the debris and streams. He patted the animal's neck, checking for injuries. Low on the near foreleg, scraped skin and clotted blood marked a swollen joint.

Coryn left the *chervine* and climbed upslope for a better view. He couldn't see much, even when he stepped up on the nearest large rock-pile. Then he caught sight of a patch of brown hide marked with dark, almost black streaks, half-buried in a stack of heavy dark stones. He couldn't tell which of the horses it was, as both of Rafe's were bays. At least it wasn't Dancer, who was a dun.

A breeze, ice-tipped, ruffled Coryn's hair. He shivered and for an awful moment, the hillside seemed to ripple and heave. Acid rose in his throat. His knees wavered under him. He caught himself against the nearest rock, a waist-high boulder. When he closed his eyes, the swaying sensation intensified. He opened them and focused on the rock, the pattern of old weathering split by fresh, razor-sharp chipping. It felt solid under his hand. Gradually, his vision and his stomach steadied.

"Rafe?" He called. "Rafe!"

Coryn's voice reverberated off the hillsides. A moment later, he heard a faint response. Echoes distorted its direction. He scrambled on top of the boulder, waving his arms above his head so he could be more easily seen.

At last, Rafe emerged from behind one of the bigger piles upslope. He led the other bay horse, which limped heavily.

Rafe waved, sunlight glinting off his broad smile. Coryn gulped, shamed that he had for one moment imagined the old soldier might have deserted him.

In his usual terse phrases, Rafe outlined their situation. Their assets included the contents of the saddlebags, two lame pack animals, plenty of water, and the fact that neither of them was seriously injured. The worst of the storm had clearly passed, although snow remained a danger. On the other hand, they could not follow their planned route. The only alternate involved even rougher territory with limited supplies and uncertain weather. But even worse, it would take them through lands belonging to the Storns of High Kinnally.

Coryn talked as they began pulling the blankets and saddlebags from the shelter. "When things were so bad last night, I—I don't know, I called out for help. And someone answered."

"Laddie, it was a rough night to put visions in any man's mind. You screamin' about fires everywhere—and the old wizard's medicine only made you wilder."

"But it wasn't—" No, better keep quiet about what he'd done. And why.

"But Holy St. Christopher, Bearer of Burdens, *he* answered our prayers," Rafe added in the low voice of a man who has witnessed a miracle.

It was useless to discuss the matter any further.

They loaded the animals and made their way back the way they had come. The horse favored its injured leg, but they could not leave it behind.

As morning wore on into midafternoon, the sky hazed over again, obscuring the huge red sun. Several times, as they entered a sparsely wooded area where fire had raced through the underbrush some years before, Rafe climbed the tallest trees to take his bearings. Coryn's father told stories of men gifted with the sense of always knowing where they were, but whether this was common sense and experience or some minor form of *laran*, he never said. Whatever skill or talent Rafe possessed, he looked satisfied as he descended from his last climb.

"With luck, we'll stay clear of the boundary," he said, meaning the edge of High Kinnally territory. "Not that would make any different to the Storn devils, should they find us out here." His hand moved toward the long-knife strapped to his thigh.

"Well, if they have any sense, they're home right now, warm and dry." Coryn struggled to suppress another shiver. They'd been coming more frequently all morning, even as the day grew warmer. He was not cold enough to shiver, and he knew it. It was better that Rafe believe he was all right, that the prayers had worked.

✦

Over the next few days, the countryside remained rugged and their speed uneven. Rafe stopped a number of times to dig up edible roots, the wild ancestors of Midwinter vegetables, and to trap small game. The rabbit-horns were smaller here than near Verdanta, but more easily snared.

Coryn sat in front of the fire, knees drawn up against his chest, chin resting on his folded arms. He would rather be curled up in the darkness of the lean-to shelter, trying to ignore the nausea which had grown more intense with the smell of roasting meat. He was shivering again, visibly this time, so Rafe ordered him to warm himself by the fire.

Before his eyes, the flames danced and flickered. At least, they were honest yellow and orange, with only a tinge of blue at the very base. But when he looked away, into the dark of the night, past the little meadow where they'd camped and the thin, poor forest beyond, the world shifted uneasily.

Coryn set his teeth together and forced himself to breathe slowly and evenly. He would get through this night. He must. If only he didn't have to eat any of the brown-crisp roasted rabbit-horn, its fat dripping into the fire to send up puffs of smoke.

Rafe, who had been bending over to check the meat for doneness, suddenly and without straightening up whipped his knife from its sheath. Every line in his body tensed with alertness.

"Come out, and give your names!" Rafe called.

"Put down the knife!" came a voice from the dark beyond the circle of firelight. "You're surrounded and outnumbered."

Rafe, still crouched in a fighting stance, called back, "I hear only one. Who are you? What do you want?"

From another direction came a second voice, and then a third. "'Tis you who should explain yourselves, trespassers!"

"Captain, the boy wears the colors of Verdanta!"

"Leynier!" the second voice roared. "Leynier spies!"

A man stepped into the light, tall and grim-faced, holding a drawn sword. His cloak, thrown back from his shoulders for fighting, had borders stitched with the emblem of Storn of High Kinnally. Coryn rose to his feet, keeping his hands well away from his body. The Storn captain's eyes flickered to Coryn and then back to Rafe.

"You cannot win, old man. You may know how to use that knife, but by Aldones, I'll skewer you before you can touch me."

Rafe shifted his stance. The silence deepened. With a flick of the wrist, a small knife appeared in his other hand. A throwing knife. The captain's eyes widened in understanding. His weapon might outreach Rafe's, but he would never get close enough to use it.

"This stalemate can only end in bloodshed," the captain began. "For the boy's sake—"

"Stop this nonsense at once!" A woman's voice rang out in the night. "Both of you!" An instant later, a small, delicately-made woman with an air of unquestionable authority stepped forward. Firelight reddened her gray cloak and touched unruly auburn curls.

The Storn captain lowered his sword, but did not put it away. Rafe remained as he was.

The woman's eyes snapped, and she looked as if she would stamp one foot and scold them all like naughty children. Instead, she spoke calmly. "This boy and his guide are henceforth under my protection. You will not harm them, nor will you," with a look in Rafe's direction that sent Coryn trembling again, "make any threat toward *my* escort."

"But, Lady—" the Captain protested.

"Is that clear?" She had not raised her voice, yet power rang through her words.

Coryn's knees went powdery. He thought that if he had been holding a knife, he would have dropped it instantly. The Storn man looked about to do just that before he hastily put his sword away. Rafe's weapons disappeared, the long blade back into its sheath, the throwing knife to wherever it had come from.

As the woman moved closer to Coryn, he saw that she was not young. Silver frosted the coppery curls and a filigree of delicate lines bracketed eyes and lips. A half-smile danced around the corners of her mouth.

"Come with me, *chiyu*. We have much to discuss."

She turned and plunged into the darkness. Coryn followed, his feet unable to do anything else. A few steps beyond the circle of firelight, a ball of white light burst into being over her outstretched hand.

Sorceress!

She turned to smile at him. "Hardly. It isn't magic, what we of the Towers do, as you will soon learn."

"Who *are* you?" Coryn blurted out, feeling stupid.

"Bronwyn of Tramontana, *leronis* of the Third Circle."

"Tramontana! That's where I'm going!"

Lady Bronwyn paused, the ball of light flickering over her features. "And who are you, who are destined for the Tower?"

Coryn hesitated. The Storn armsmen already realized he was from Verdanta. If they knew he was Lord Beltran's son, even a third son who would not inherit, they might hold him for ransom or worse.

"Listen to me," the lady said sharply. "I don't care if you're from Verdanta or Valeron or the far side of the Wall Around the World, for that matter. You managed to reach me with your unaided mind. Have you any idea what that means, to be able to do that at your age? Do you think we would let such *laran* talent run wild? Or didn't you realize what you had done?"

For a moment, he was back in the stony shelter with rain pelting and rocks pummeling the hillside. Blue flames licked at him once more. The smells of blood and fear filled the darkness.

"You don't sound anything like—like the voice I heard."

The ball of light over Lady Bronwyn's hand shrank to a pinpoint. "Why, what do you mean?" she said, her voice echoing as if from a distance.

"Bells," he whispered, reaching vainly for the memory, for something to hold on to. "Silvery bells."

Silvery—silvery—sil—ver—ry . . .

The world slid sideways and went white. Coryn's jaw clamped shut, the muscles of his back and legs locked in spasm. Breath hissed between his teeth, then stopped. Pain lanced up his calves, his thighs, his arms. Fire exploded from his solar plexus. He fought for another breath.

Dimly, Coryn felt his body topple. Shadowy hands reached out to catch him, to cushion his fall. Under his back, the ground felt prickly and cold. He heard a woman's voice, jangled bells, crying out commands.

"No, don't restrain him. Get my pack from camp—hurry!"

Footsteps receded, then approached. A hand, soft and warm, brushed his forehead, laced fingers with his. A familiar voice whispered through his thoughts.

Let me guide you through this. Threshold sickness can be frightening. But you are not alone, I am here to help you . . . yes, that's right, breathe softly. I'm right here . . .

"Who's *he?*" came a new voice, like a sulky child's.

"Hush, now." Lady Bronwyn spoke again. "One of you men, take her back."

"I don't want to go back! You can't order me around!"

"Quiet!"

Coryn's heart skipped a beat. The next moment, he could hear nothing at all. His muscles, which had begun to soften at Bronwyn's mental touch, locked tight. Arms and legs jerked under the sudden force of the contractions. His spine arched, throwing back his head. For what seemed an eternity, he could neither hear nor see.

Coryn became sensible of his body once more, his limbs thick and sluggish as clay. His chest heaved, drawing breath into his lungs. The harsh white light of the witch-fire, for he had no other term for it, softened with yellow torchlight.

"No, it's not over," Lady Bronwyn's voice seemed to come from afar. She bent over him. He felt her breath sweet on his face. Something smooth and cold pressed against his lower lip. "Drink this. Quickly, before the next round."

"Whu—"

"*Kirian.* It will help the seizures."

Kirian! *Rumail's vile potion!*

"N—nuh—" Coryn threw his head from side to side.

"Hold still!" For an awful moment, Coryn's struggles halted, as if he were suddenly encased in ice. Hands, men's rough, strong hands, pinned his body to the ground. In his bones, he knew this had happened before—

From the corner of his blurred vision, Coryn caught sight of Rafe's face, grim with concern. It wavered, shifting form to another man's, now gray and terrifying.

A scream tore from Coryn's throat.

"Drink!"

Coryn lay helpless to resist as the neck of a glass vial passed between his teeth. Cool lemony fluid filled his mouth. His traitorous throat swallowed once, twice. Tears sprang to his eyes. He wanted to cough it up, but it was too late. Warmth spread through his stomach, outward to his limbs, melting tight muscles, easing his breath.

Coryn's arms and legs began to shake, little tremors laced with pain. Any moment, he feared, they would build into another bone-wrenching spasm, but after a minute they subsided. As the quivering left him, he sank into the earth in relief, deep and deeper . . .

6

Huge and low on the horizon, the Bloody Sun cast slanting crimson rays over the walls of Castle Ambervale. Men stood at attention at the gates and along the battlements. Tents, picket lines, and food storage bins sprawled across the broad fields to the east, where once summer trading fairs were held. A squadron of spearmen drilled under the shouted orders of an officer, while other men walked sweating horses dry, cleaned weapons, and raked the ground smooth for tomorrow's armed practice. Smoke arose from the cooking pits. To the south, a village, still bustling with activity, hugged the river bank. A breeze brought the aroma of bread newly baked for the evening meal.

Rumail of Neskaya nudged his horse forward, though the weary animal needed no encouragement with home in sight. A shouted hail went up at his approach. At the threshold of the castle, two guards stepped to his side, greeting him with that deference born of fear to which he was long since accustomed. As he rode through sally port, between the newly reinforced gates, he glanced up at the twin banners of Ambervale and Linn, noticing the bright stitching, the freshly oiled hinges, evidence everywhere of discipline and readiness. With Verdanta secured bloodlessly by marriage, Damian could turn his attention to Acosta, maybe even the outlying provinces of Aldaran. And from that mountain stronghold, the hill kingdoms leading to the lowlands, Valeron and the Hastur lands. Yes, his brother would be pleased with his news.

In the courtyard, a gaggle of maidservants wearing white caps and aprons chattered as they swung their buckets to the well. Other servants carried baskets of green-and-gold summer marrows and baskets of steaming round-loaves and meat buns to the kitchen.

Rumail's lower back twinged as he swung down from the saddle and handed the reins to an impeccably-liveried servant. Years of service in the Towers had sapped his physical vitality, yet he would gladly pay that cost a thousand times over. Let ordinary men think him a sorcerer, for their superstitious terror was far better treatment than he'd received as an impoverished bastard. Even the respect accorded him as his brother's representative, voice of the King, paled by comparison to the heady sense of power born of his own abilities.

The *coridom* of Ambervale Castle welcomed Rumail with a deep bow, escorting him to his quarters himself, rather than delegating this task to an underling. Having bathed, shaved, and dined on roasted barnfowl with brambleberry compote and soft white bread, Rumail presented himself to his brother.

Damian Deslucido, King of Ambervale and now Linn and tomorrow who knew what besides, sat in his high carved chair on a raised dais, talking easily with his *coridom* and a pair of men Rumail did not recognize, but guessed must be lesser nobles, possibly from Linn by the cut of their vests and the embossed leather trim of their boots. Empty scabbards hung from their belts.

"Your Majesty," one of them said as Rumail approached, "the levies are too much. We have not enough men to bring in the harvest as it is. We still have not refilled our granaries from your— from the war."

"We will speak more of this later. Once true peace is achieved, full bellies will surely follow." Damian dismissed the man with a gesture. As the *coridom* escorted the two men from the presence chamber, Damian stepped down and embraced his brother.

Rumail was struck, as many times before, by how compelling and yet how uncomplicated Damian was. Not handsome, he radiated something deeper, something which drew men to him and fired them with his visions. *Charisma* or *glamour* came close to describing it, but neither were accurate, for then Rumail would have been able to defend against it with his *laran*. No, this was something different, so that whenever he came

into his brother's presence, all resentment at his lesser status melted away
as he gave himself willingly to Damian's cause.

And what a cause it was. Their father, the unlamented King Rakhal,
had left Ambervale half in ruins, the people starving on lands overfarmed
to pay for his gambling, his women, and his search for the Elixir of Eternal Life. Neighboring Linn had already annexed miles of the most productive lands between them.

Now Linn knelt at Damian's feet, as farmers worked their land without the threat of *clingfire* or any of the other deviltry which stalked the
war-torn Hundred Kingdoms. All flourished in Damian's golden sun.
Only a few malcontents grumbled at the armed vigilance necessary to
maintain this peace.

"So, brother, what news from Verdanta? Was the old man reasonable?" Damian put one arm around Rumail's shoulders, not being bound
by the etiquette which restricted casual physical contact among telepaths,
and started down the hallway toward the private quarters.

"Verdanta will be yours on your own terms," Rumail replied, his
words inflected with the honorifics due his lord. "And you were right—"

Rumail broke off as young Belisar came running to meet them, boots
clattering on the stone floor between the strips of precious Ardcarran
carpet. With his face flushed and his golden hair askew, Belisar looked
younger than his sixteen years. His eyes shone bright and blue as starstones, sure to melt the heart of any maid, although Rumail never considered himself much of a judge of such things. His own liaisons at Neskaya
and at Dalereuth, where he had trained, had been short-lived and unsatisfying. It was no one's fault, for like many telepaths, he found physical
intimacy disappointing without a deeper sympathy, and no woman had
ever stirred him in that way.

"What is she like? Is she pretty?" Then, remembering his responsibilities as eldest son and heir, Belisar drew himself up. He bowed to Rumail,
the precise inclination for one older and respected, but inferior in rank.

"Greetings, Uncle. How went your mission?"

"Everyone assumed the best candidate would be the oldest daughter," Rumail said as they proceeded down the corridor. "But Beltran was
obliging enough to sire three of them so that we might continue our other
objectives. The youngest one has latent potential of the qualities we are
searching for in her progeny. I scanned her right down to the genetic
level, despite her considerable resistance. In the end, I believe, she will

follow her father's wishes. She stood obediently enough for the handfasting. The older daughter, a conventionally boring twit of a girl, will see to it that she's schooled as befits a Queen."

"Schooled? How—how old *is* she?" Belisar asked, struggling not to frown.

"Eight or nine, I think."

Belisar looked horrified. "She's still a baby!"

"So, boy!" Laughing heartily, Damian clapped Belisar between the shoulder blades. "You'll have to wait to bed your bride."

"Father—"

"Oh, but it's only your bride you must wait for!" Damian said. "She'll expect a husband this much older to be experienced, won't she?"

"Father!"

"Leave the boy his dignity," Rumail said. In the Towers, a boy Belisar's age would have had several lovers, although not when actively working in a circle. Both the sexual bonding and the periods of celibacy due to intense *laran* work were considered natural and treated with respect, never this coarse teasing.

"There is more news," Rumail went on.

They reached the private quarters of the royal family. "Come, let's go within," Damian said. "You, too, Belisar. Since you're to marry for a political alliance, you must learn statecraft."

Once inside, Damian dismissed the young page and ordered the guards a distance from the door, so they could speak without being overheard.

Unlike the throne chamber, Damian's sitting room was richly appointed with rugs and tapestries of gemstone hues, cushioned chairs, and footstools. The fireplace mantel, sea marble shipped all the way from Temora, glowed like living pearl in the light of the tiny summer fire. On the low table of ancient wood, so polished with age as to look black, a bowl of blown glass held freshly shelled nuts and candied sugarplums.

Damian lounged in the largest of the chairs and reached for a handful of nuts. Belisar also sat, but on the edge of his seat.

"I went to Verdanta for a marriage contract, as you know, but there I found an even greater treasure. One of the boys has extraordinary *laran,* only now developing. I convinced the father to let me test him, using the excuse of threshold sickness, which indeed he has, and severely enough to indicate the magnitude of his awakening talent. While I was testing him, while his mind was open to mine . . . do you remember our discussion of . . . *other uses* of the family Gift?"

Damian sat up. Nuts fell unheeded to the carpet in the moment of silence that followed. His eyes flickered to his son's face, to the questions there.

"You have not told him, then?" Rumail asked. They had agreed the boy must not be kept in ignorance. But Damian had his own ideas of the proper timing.

"But I shall." Damian turned to his son. "What your uncle means is the very special type of *laran* which only we Deslucidos possess. Some of us, anyway. I have only a trace of it, and Rumail by far the greater portion. The gods certainly made up for our unequal births."

At Damian's laughter, Belisar smiled politely. Rumail, who was years beyond allowing himself to react to such casual barbs, noticed how the boy's eyes remained alert, probing.

Belisar said, with unexpected formality, "You have told me, Uncle, that my own *laran* is recessive, that my sons may have the use of theirs, but not me. And everyone knows you are a powerful *laranzu*. The Deslucido family gift is . . ." he hesitated, ". . . something different from that. Am I to know in what way and how it can serve the cause of unifying Darkover?"

"Ordinary *laran* is useful within its limits," Damian said temperately. "Good for making *clingfire* to wage wars or healing the wounds those wars inevitably produce. The minds of weak, ordinary men can be made to see things which live only in their nightmares. Or their nightmares can be coaxed into sweeter dreams. But never before in the history of the world have we been able to *free* men's minds from misinformation and prejudice."

"Free them? How?"

Rumail stirred, uneasy. Damian tended to get carried away with his own idealistic speeches, forgetting that power needed no justification except itself. Men did not need to understand in order to believe. In fact, talk too often delayed the actions necessary for the common good. It was time to take control of the conversation. "You have seen truthspell?"

Belisar had been present at the surrender of Linn, when a *leronis*, Linn's own, was brought to invoke the blue light which glowed steadily on the face of each speaker only in the presence of truth. In its aura, the Lord of Linn and his vassals swore fealty to Ambervale, and King Damian in his turn promised they would never be forced to wage war against their kin in Acosta. There was no surer bond than an oath made under truthspell.

"Yes," Belisar said slowly, "it is the reason one man can trust another's sworn word and the only sure way of ascertaining the facts in a dispute. Otherwise, a man could hold hidden loyalties, secretly change allegiances, say one thing and mean another."

"What if . . ." Rumail said, "what if a vassal truly *believed* whatever served his lord, believed it so fervently that not even truthspell could tell the difference? What if a king need not be bound by other men's literal truths, but only the necessities of a higher calling?"

Belisar's eyes widened as he glanced from father to uncle and back again. Damian watched his heir work through Rumail's puzzle. "You have found some way to defeat truthspell?"

"Not defeat it," Rumail said, "for truth is hardly an enemy to be defeated. We expand the definition to include a *greater* truth, a *deeper* loyalty. This is the special Deslucido Gift."

"And I, do I have this ability also?" The boy frowned, clearly searching his memory for a time when he had lied over some childish prank and not been found out.

"No, son," Damian said. "And neither do I. You and I are like a lock, useless in itself, but Rumail there, he holds the key. He can reach into our minds and release that gift. And he has done so to me upon a number of occasions. The effect is specific and limited in time."

"You . . . *lied* under truthspell?"

Anger flashed across Damian's eyes, but he continued patiently, taking no insult. "You must understand that the result is not falsehood, not in the sense most men believe it, any more than truth is the mere sterile recitation of facts. Consider this: Is it a truly good thing to reveal a truth which will break apart a kingdom or send a decent man to his death?"

Belisar looked to Rumail. Blood drained from his face, leaving only the reflected color of the summer fire washing over ashen cheeks. "But if men cannot believe what is spoken in truthspell, what will they believe? Will not all treaties be at risk if this is ever known?"

Damian raised one eyebrow. "Then we must make certain that no foolish rumors are ever spread. Gossip can destroy the noblest cause and ordinary men are easily led astray by their own fears. They require the guidance of their betters."

Belisar nodded. The normal color quickly returned to his face; he recovered fast. The lad was sharp, Rumail thought, if a trace arrogant.

"Sometimes," Rumail added, "it is necessary to lance a wound in order for it to heal cleanly, or, to use gardening terms, to cut out the rotten growth and plant anew."

"I understand why you waited until now to tell me," Belisar told Damian. "And I will never betray your trust. The gods have truly blessed us with this gift. We can remake the face of Darkover! Of course, we must follow different laws than other people, for we serve a more noble cause. But what are the *other uses* Uncle Rumail referred to?"

"Rumail and I have studied the special gifts which run in our family," Damian went on. "We have often discussed whether this same technique—the strengthening of belief in a man's mind so that it becomes, for all purposes, literal truth—might not be applied in some other way."

Rumail had often wished this were possible, but other than his immediate family—Damian and now his son—the only one he'd come across who possessed the necessary susceptibility was the Leynier boy.

When Belisar looked puzzled, Rumail said, "Think of it as a window to this Leynier boy's mind, to the very core of his *laran*. He will take training in a Tower, as he should. I have seen to that. With his talent, he should go far, perhaps even become a Keeper."

Rumail could not keep a trace of bitterness from his voice, for that had been his own aspiration, had those fools at Neskaya been able to see his worth. But there was no profit in pursuing such thoughts. One of the unspoken purposes of this journey was to let the last fracas die down, some silliness about him having "unduly influenced" a young student. It was all ridiculous. No one argued he had done anything except for the boy's benefit, yet he'd been censured for his methods, simple and direct though they were. If a Keeper had done the same thing, his actions would have been praised. In a few months, they would realize how badly they needed him in the higher-level matrix circles and would welcome him back. Next time, he'd be more discreet.

He guided his thoughts back to the present and went on, "When the time is right, when we most need such an ally, I have but to open the window in young Leynier's mind and speak our truth. He must listen."

"Must?" Belisar raised one eyebrow.

"Must. As to the voice of his own conscience or the whispers of his beloved. He will listen and he will obey because he will believe with all his heart and might. We will have a Keeper, perhaps the most powerful on Darkover, as our most loyal ally." He paused, letting the words sink in. "No matter which Tower he serves in, no matter what the allegiance there."

Damian closed his eyes, as if deeply considering. A smile spread slowly across his face. "Brother, you are right! You have brought us a far greater treasure than a single petty kingdom! Belisar, what do you think of your uncle's genius?"

Belisar grinned. "I think it would be jolly fun to have a pet Keeper to do our bidding!"

"Never say that!" Rumail stormed. "Never even think it! A Keeper can channel unimaginably powerful forces and direct them at his will. Do you think *clingfire* raining from the skies or rootblight withering a forest are the worst horrors of war? Why do you think the Aldarans are so feared, up there on their mountain?"

"Be at ease," Damian cut in. "This is no child's toy or dalliance, but neither is the vision of a future we are all sworn to. We must have the power to bring our dreams into reality for the welfare of all peoples. Rest assured, we will use it wisely.

"Come," Damian said, rising, "let us hear some music to soothe away the night. Tomorrow will be a new day, one we face armed better than ever, thanks to your fine work."

7

Coryn awoke from dreams of swaying, jolting, rocking, and more jolting. Alertness came slowly as he drifted in and out of uneasy sleep. Finally, insistent pangs from stomach and bladder forced him toward consciousness.

He lay in a bed, not his bed, not his room, with no idea of where he was or how he had gotten here. The weakness in his body when he tried to sit up reminded him unpleasantly of that morning after *Dom* Rumail had examined him for *laran*. This room was unfamiliar, far smaller than his own and curtained by panels of open-weave white linex.

The other furnishings included a backless stool, a small chest at the foot of the bed, an empty bookcase in the headboard . . . and a chamber pot in the far corner. He staggered toward it on unsteady legs. A few minutes later, he made it back to bed, where he lay, breathing hard and sweating.

A gentle tap sounded from beyond the white curtain. He lay still, covers pulled up to his chin, waiting for his heart to stop hammering. He didn't have the strength to get back to his feet and the last thing he wanted was to be lying here helplessly while some stranger approached his bed. Perhaps whoever it was had made a mistake and would go away. The tap came again.

After a long moment he heard—no, he *sensed* footsteps, quick and light, receding down the corridor outside. Coryn drifted back to sleep.

And sprang awake as a door swung open. The curtain was pulled aside to reveal an older man in a long, loosely belted white robe and a girl about his own age carrying a tray of covered dishes.

"I'm Gareth, monitor of the Second Circle." The man sounded kindly enough, though he did not offer to shake hands. "And your serving maid here is your fellow student, Liane. Now then, young Coryn. Are you hungry enough for breakfast?"

Coryn's stomach rumbled at the smell of the food—some kind of honeyed fruit, he thought, and fresh-baked bread touched with cardamom. He thought wryly that this scene was becoming all too familiar.

"No, please don't sit up. This will be brief." The man sat on the bed beside him, but did not touch him. Instead, he ran his hands over Coryn's body, following the contours but never touching. Above his closed eyes, lines of concentration furrowed his brow. His hair was clipped even with the back of his skull as no *Comyn* lord or warrior would wear it. He shook his head slightly.

"Eat now, as much as you can, and you can join the others later today or tomorrow." With those words, Gareth rose and departed, leaving the girl standing awkwardly, still holding the tray.

As she looked around for a place to set it down, Coryn, propping himself up on one elbow, got a good look at her. Straw-pale hair tinged with red hung in neat braids to her waist. Thick, colorless eyelashes fringed eyes of startling green. Freckles dusted her cheeks. She wore a simple robe of spring-green wool, belted with a sash of the same fabric around her slender waist. When she smiled, her eyes crinkled at the corners.

"Here," Coryn said, moving to make room on the bed. She set the tray down and sat behind it, tucking her legs under her. He lifted the domed covers to discover a small feast—honey-stewed fruit, as he had suspected, sliced bread, white and yellow cheeses, turnovers with some kind of spiced meat filling, a flagon of water and one of apple cider.

"I can't eat all this!" He made a face. "Do you want some?"

"I'm always hungry. Auster—he's one of my teachers—says it's because I'm growing so fast. The food here is really good. Lots of meat pastries and no bean porridge for breakfast!" Her chatter reminded him of Kristlin.

Coryn spread a thick slice of nutbread with soft yellow cheese and ate it with a mug of the cider. At his urging, the girl took one of the turnovers. She ate quickly and neatly, leaving no crumbs.

"You're being awfully nice to me," she said, "considering how mean I was to you."

Coryn swallowed a mouthful of the honeyed fruit and blinked at her. "I'm sorry, I don't remember having met you before. I've been—ill, I guess."

"*I'll* say you've been sick. Threshold sick. Auster says he's never seen such a bad case, not in anyone who lived. Oh!" One hand flew to her mouth. "That wasn't very nice to say, was it? I'm always saying whatever pops into my mind, whether I mean it or not. I mean, you really were very sick, you had convulsions and everything. You nearly scared the wits out of me. I'm glad you're not going to die, 'cause then I'd feel awful. Marisela—she's the housemistress—says I must learn tact and something else, I'm not sure what."

Now the girl sounded so exactly like Kristlin that Coryn burst out laughing. "I'm sorry, too," he managed to say. "But I truly don't remember who you are. Should I?"

Bright color shot across the girl's cheeks. She looked down at her hands, fingers laced together. "Yes, the night you—we—Lady Bronwyn was escorting me here, and our guards found your camp." She met his gaze, her green eyes somber. "You were sick, and you wouldn't hold still when Lady Bronwyn tried to help you. I'm afraid I behaved very badly."

The voice, the petulant child's voice in the darkness. "Oh. I didn't exactly—I mean, I had other things on my mind."

A smile flashed across her face, quickly disappearing. "You're nice, do you know that? But I had no right to be so rude just because you're a Leynier and were on our lands. Alain—the guards captain—thought you and your man were spies. You can never tell with Verdanta folk."

"Liane—Liane *Storn?*"

"Yes, but we're not supposed to use our family names here. Every day since we arrived, I've been given a lecture on how none of that matters, only ourselves—'our *laran,* our character, our discipline, our work'. On and on like that." She wrinkled her nose so that the freckles stood out. "Doesn't sound like much fun, does it? But the lessons are interesting. You'll see when you can get up."

"Liane *Storn?*" he repeated, feeling muddle-headed. This girl was one of that pack of brigands who refused to help during the fire, not even to let Petro through to Tramontana! He thought of the days of desperate, bone-breaking labor, the choking smoke, the loss of so many nut trees, the hunger in winters to come. How could they have just sat back and let the fire burn? What kind of monsters were they?

"No, just plain Liane—"

"Storn?" And yet, she didn't look like a monster, even if she was too stuck up for her own good. . .

"We're not supposed to brag about our families," she replied tartly, getting to her feet. "And if you don't stop harping on this name nonsense, I won't come back and visit you tomorrow!" She picked up the tray and, with a toss of her flaxen-red braids, headed for the door.

"Don't!" Coryn exploded. "I never want to see a single one of the whole *cralmac-brained,* self-serving Storn Nest again!"

She whirled, cheeks flushing at the insult. "You! You nobody out of nowhere! You were nothing more than a half-drowned rat when we rescued you! How dare you say that about my family!"

"Get out!"

Liane jerked the curtain aside and slammed the door behind her. Her quick, light footsteps receded and Coryn was left alone, feeling more miserable than ever.

◆

Coryn stayed in bed for another day, growing increasingly bored and restless. Meals were brought by Marisela, a cheerful motherly woman who kept smoothing the covers and tucking them around him. Gareth came to monitor him every morning and evening.

"*Laran* is carried through the body in special channels," Gareth explained. "But these channels also carry sexual energy. In some people, *laran* is awakened at adolescence, when such feelings begin to stir, so the channels are particularly vulnerable to overload. That's one of the causes of threshold sickness. With care and training, this need not be a continuing problem. You will learn to monitor yourself, to learn what is safe for you to do."

"You mean I did something to cause this?" Coryn asked, shuddering.

"Not at all," Gareth shook his head. "Except possibly to grow up. You . . . you seem to be past the worst of it now."

The monitor rose as a figure in flowing red robes entered the room.

Although the movements were quiet and spare, the room seemed to vibrate with a sense of presence. For an instant, Coryn didn't know if this was a man or a woman, for the face was beardless, the jaw delicate. A faint tracery of lines covered pale skin. Moonlight-colored hair spilled over slender shoulders.

"Gareth, please," the newcomer said, gesturing to the monitor to sit again, then smiled at Coryn. "I am Kieran, Keeper of the Third Circle here at Tramontana, and your kinsman."

This must be the Aillard cousin Lord Leynier had spoken of. At the sound of the voice, Coryn decided it must be a man, possibly one of those sandal-wearers who had never participated in any manly activity. Coryn had himself come in for a bit of teasing from the stable hands when it was known he was to go to a Tower. But there was nothing weak in the fiery eyes sweeping over him, nothing effeminate in the sure way those slim six-fingered hands gestured.

"Forgive me, young Coryn, for not welcoming you earlier. It was not from lack of concern for you, for Gareth assured me you were recovering well and he is our most skillful monitor."

Coryn felt he ought to say something. Despite Kieran Aillard's small physical stature, his energy filled the room. His faintly distracted air, as if part of his mind were on other, greater matters, only added to his aura of power.

"M—my father sends you greetings," Coryn stammered, "and thanks for your help during the fire."

"So your man Rafael said. We have not yet come to the point, we here at Tramontana, when we can do nothing more useful than to create weapons for other men's wars. Now, young Coryn, may I examine your *laran* channels, as Gareth has done?"

Coryn gave his assent, wondering a little that a personage as important as a Keeper must ask his permission. Perhaps this was how things were done in a Tower. He lay back on the bed, closed his eyes and composed himself. When Gareth monitored him, Coryn had not felt anything, except perhaps a faint warmth from the other man's hands. Now something airy as a feather whispered over his skin, cool and not at all unpleasant. It warmed, sinking ever deeper until it became a part of him.

Soft, gray-blue light filled him as if he were made of glass. His body relaxed, and his mind began to drift. Dimly, he became aware of a lightless blot deep within his body. When he tried to focus on it, panic rose. He turned away quickly, fleeing to the soothing warmth.

From afar, he heard Kieran say in a soft voice, "Yes, I see what you mean, Gareth. I don't think even an Alton could force his way past that barricade. It doesn't seem to be linked to any of the essential channels. Perhaps as he learns to master his talent and to trust us, he will be able to lower his guard. . . ."

I'm not doing it on purpose, Coryn thought.

I know, lad. Had Kieran spoken aloud, or only inside Coryn's head? *Rest for a moment now, and then come back to us.*

A few minutes later, Coryn sat upright once more, to hear Kieran say, "Gareth, is it your opinion this boy is recovered enough to join the other novices in their lessons tomorrow?"

"Yes, I think he's more than ready," Gareth said with an easy smile. "In fact, I think he's going to start tearing the infirmary apart if we try to keep him any longer."

With a sweep of red robes, Kieran left the room. Coryn stared after him. "So that's Grandmama's cousin. He doesn't look that old."

"Oh, he is close to a hundred years now," Gareth said. "Not all the Aillards are so long-lived, but it's said there is a strong strain of *chieri* blood in that family. Knowing Kieran, I can well believe it."

"And he has six fingers!"

"And he is *emmasca*, but what of any of it?" Now Gareth sounded angry. "When we enter the Tower, we leave behind rank and family, as well as petty prejudices. This is the one place where we are judged by what we make of our own lives, not by the number of our toes or the color of our hair or what lies our fathers told. Or if we have six fathers or none at all! Our bodies are as the gods have made us, but what is in our hearts, that is who we truly are!"

Gareth finished with gentler words, encouraging Coryn to sleep well because lessons would begin the next morning. Thoroughly awake, Coryn lay back, thinking about what the monitor had said and wondering about the new world he had entered.

✦

The next morning, Coryn said good-bye to Rafe, who had waited until he could witness Coryn's recovery with his own eyes before returning to

Verdanta. The Keepers supplied Rafe with a sound riding horse and trail food enough to take him on the circuitous trip. "There should be no more storms like the last one," Mikhail-Esteban, a matrix mechanic who had good weather-sense, said with a hint of disapproval. Rafe gave Coryn a gruff, silent hug and left with his usual lack of words.

Coryn went down to the dining hall, where the other young people had gathered for breakfast. There were six novices at Tramontana at this time, three close to his own age and three older, one of whom was shortly to leave for Hali, to work as a monitor there before leaving the Towers for an arranged marriage. Coryn's two age-mates were Liane and a tall, dark-eyed boy named Aran MacAran.

Liane glared at Coryn when he sat down, then tossed her head and pretended to be interested in the conversation on her other side, something about layering energon rings along a crystalline lattice. Coryn had no idea what they were talking about.

"Is it true," Aran asked shyly, "that you were caught without shelter by the Aldaran storm? And that you had to kill your horses and climb inside their bodies to stay warm?"

Coryn stared at the other boy, mouth open. "Well, yes, there was a storm, but—"

"But they'd never have made it if *we* hadn't come along and rescued them!" Liane snapped her head around.

"We were doing just fine, minding our own business, when *you* came along and picked a fight! Almost got us killed. Some help!"

"Picked a fight? *We* weren't the ones trespassing—spying—"

"That will be quite enough." The quiet voice came from the other end of the table. Coryn recognized it instantly as Kieran's. He flushed. What was he thinking, to let Liane goad him into such behavior and on his first real morning at Tramontana? He was not surprised when Kieran, in a voice just as calmly authoritative, commanded him for a private word after breakfast. Liane's smirk quickly disappeared when she in turn was ordered to see Bronwyn.

Coryn got up from the table, his breakfast untouched. Aran touched him gently on the back of the wrist, a gesture Coryn now understood was common among telepaths.

"I never believed the story about the horses," Aran said. "But it did sound as if something exciting had happened. Maybe you can tell me later. I'm sorry if I got you into trouble."

"It wasn't you, it was that—that—" Coryn managed to stop himself before he said anything else he'd regret.

✦

A short time later, he stood before Kieran in the Keeper's small, stone-walled sitting room. Despite the morning's chill, no fire warmed the fieldstone hearth. Kieran sat at ease in his simple chair, his six-fingered hands quiet in his lap. The austerity of the scene, as much as the temperature, set Coryn shivering.

"It won't happen again," Coryn began.

"Perhaps, instead of making promises you have no idea if you can keep, you might explain to me why Liane irritates you so. Is it merely the feud between your two families?"

Need there be more? Coryn wondered, but did not say so aloud. Under Kieran's gentle prodding, he stumbled through the story of the fire, the storm, the rescue. He realized how unfair he was being. Liane wasn't to blame for her father's decisions and she *had* tried hard to be friendly that first time in the infirmary.

"Yet there is more that troubles you, young Coryn. Liane is a spirited young woman, perhaps a bit unmannerly, but without malice."

Coryn thought suddenly that if Liane had not reminded him so much of Kristlin, he might not have felt such a sense of—was it betrayal?

"Listen to me," Kieran said, leaning forward, his ageless features alight with intensity. "Out there in the world, a man's family name counts more than the quality of his character. Women—and men, too—are judged and sold for nothing more than their bloodlines or the alliances they can bring."

Coryn shivered, thinking of Kristlin's marriage, of Tessa's impassioned words, *I will not be* barragana . . .

"But here in the Tower, while we are in service, we leave all that behind. It is who you are, what you make of your life, your honor and dedication, not your rank or clan connections that determine your future. You were born gifted with *laran*. All that grants you is the chance to know yourself and your fellows in ways you never dreamed possible. You can speak across miles, you can delve into the bowels of the earth for precious minerals, you can penetrate the very fabric of the world. None of this comes easily or without a price. And none of it will come unless you can leave the petty squabbles of the world behind."

Kieran's voice shifted, so resonant that tears sprang to Coryn's eyes and he suddenly understood the passion with which Gareth had spoken of his Keeper.

"You are no longer Coryn Leynier of Verdanta and Liane is not Liane Storn of High Kinnally. You are Coryn and she is Liane. Nothing more. Someday, if you both have the talent and dedication to earn your places here, you may well hold each other's lives in your hands. There is no room for a childish quarrel which is none of your affair. Do you understand me?"

Coryn, swallowing dryly, nodded. He vowed in his heart to take Liane as she was, chattering and all. In that assent, he passed some invisible barrier, some unspoken test, although he had only the roughest idea of what it meant to him. He only knew that he wanted what the Tower offered more than he'd ever wanted anything before.

A moment later, doubt curled like greasy smoke through his thoughts. Kieran spoke of a singleness of purpose, of leaving the outer world and all its concerns behind. But Rumail Deslucido served two masters, King as well as Tower. . . .

"Something troubles you?"

Coryn frowned, searching for words. "*Dom* Rumail, who tested me—" He found it suddenly difficult to breathe.

You will say nothing of this. Nothing.

"—he—he came to Verdanta—not as *laranzu*—but as his brother's— King Damian's—agent—" Coryn broke off, gasping for air.

Kieran nodded gravely. "Yes, some of us are not entirely free of family allegiances, would that it were so. And there is always the fear that we may be pulled to different sides in an outside conflict, though the Hasturs at least have promised never to set kin against kin in Tower warfare." The old *emmasca* paused. "As for that one . . ." The colorless eyes flickered, missing nothing. "He is not your concern. Go now and join the others."

Oddly reassured, Coryn made his way to the big, sunlit room on the south side of the Tower where Gareth instructed the novices in elementary monitoring. They sat in pairs on the ubiquitous low benches around a cot, where one of the older boys lay. Gareth stopped to repeat his explanation of the proper distance of the hand from the body to "feel" the energon channels.

Liane came in a few minutes later, eyes red and puffy as if she had been crying. Coryn decided that however awkward his interview with Kieran had been, hers with Bronwyn must have been worse. He went up to her after the session, wanting to say something but not knowing what. He didn't want to prolong the quarrel, but half of it had been his doing. At least half.

Just as Coryn caught up to Liane, Aran joined both of them, eyes dancing with adventure. "We're to have an hour outdoors after lunch. Anyone interested in getting out of here? Can we take your horse, Liane?"

"Oh!" Her color heightened, but not in embarrassment. "Yes! Can we all three go?"

"You mean go out riding?" Coryn asked. He'd no idea that Tower life could be so normal. In the hours of his recuperation, he'd thought of his lost Dancer.

"Of course!" Aran said. "Once Tramontana kept no mounts, before the days of King Allart Hastur. Now there are always a couple of horses in the Tower stables. We're permitted to use these for our own exercise." He winked at Coryn. "They're always telling us we need to keep strong to do all this matrix work."

An image sprang to Coryn's mind, the three of them laughing as they galloped across the hills, the wind singing in his ears, the sweet warm joy of the horse beneath him flooding up so that he was one with the beast, with the hawk overhead like a speck against the sun, and the singing grass. Green and gold and blue shimmered around him, inside him—

In that instant, too, he knew this was what *Aran* felt, the excitement rising in his new friend's mind.

As they moved down the corridor, Liane caught one foot on an uneven stone and stumbled. Coryn reached to steady her. Her hand brushed his, a fleeting touch. He turned to her with eyes newly opened by the momentary rapport with Aran. It was as if he saw her for the very first time, not just an infuriating child, but a young woman—the woman she would grow to be—proud and loyal. He *sensed* the struggle within her, mirror to his own, the stories she'd grown up with about Leynier greed and treachery, the rages of her father, her love for family, the big brother who'd died in a Leynier cattle raid, all of this pitted against the boy who stood before her. He saw himself reflected in her mind, neither demon nor coward nor spy, not any more than she was.

Kieran was right. The Tower is the one place we can leave behind all this hatred and start anew.

He held out his hand and, with a timid smile now brightening into an outright grin, she took it.

8

Four years later, the three friends rode together through the hills surrounding Tramontana. The bounty of a morning's hawking, a brace of forest grouse for the Midsummer Festival feast, hung from their saddles. The men also had baskets filled with mountain daisies, skyflowers, and even a stalk or two of creamy white bellisma, to be arranged into gift packets for the women of the Tower. Neither had kinswomen to honor according to Midsummer tradition, as Hastur Lord of Light had honored Blessed Cassilda with fruit and flowers. Yet Coryn thought with anticipation of the expression on Liane's face at the river-opals he had found for her, the sort of gift he would have presented Kristlin with.

Now Coryn and Liane rode easily together as brother and sister, watching Aran ride ahead, body moving fluidly with the horse's swinging stride. On this morning, Coryn had lent Aran his fine Armida black, a gift from his father last winter. It was the same horse Petro had ridden on his ill-fated mission to Storn during that terrible fire.

Aran, still lanky and possessed of such dark-lashed eyes as to make most maidens envious, rode with his hands on his thighs, reins loose on the horse's neck. The black arched her neck and broke into a canter, feet lifted high and tail bannered in the wind.

Coryn laughed. "She wants to run!"

"What have you been feeding her, dragon bones?" Aran called back. The horse, released from invisible reins, lengthened her stride. Aran lifted his gloved hand and the *verrin* hawk, which had been hovering at the limit of sight, circled down to meet him. Like many of his clan, Aran had the Gift, the *donas*, of rapport with animals.

Coryn slowed his own mount, closing his eyes to more easily follow the meld of animal, bird, and man. One hand crept to the starstone on its silver chain around his neck. Even insulated in heavy silk, it pulsed with energy as he focused his mind on his friend's.

Wind streamed through his mane, lifted his wings, swept joyful tears from his eyes. Power surged through him, as if he could run or fly or ride forever. Of all the gifts of Aran's friendship, this was the most precious.

Liane drew her horse even with Coryn's, her ladyhawk hooded on her wrist. The years had straightened her nose and faded her freckles, leaving her handsome but not pretty. Yet when Coryn glanced at her, he saw the spirit behind her green eyes, the courage she brought to everything she did. She'd become a skilled monitor and, as Kieran had predicted, had guarded Coryn's well-being on more than one occasion in the matrix circles.

"It isn't fair!" she said, following the black horse with her eyes. "I can follow the course of a single blood cell through a man's body, but try as I might, I can't go with him like this." She meant Aran's oneness with horse and hawk. Although she could monitor and manipulate energon flows in a human body, she was far less talented in empathy, the ability to sense another's emotions, and she had only the minimal telepathy to work in a circle.

"Ah, well," she sighed. In the closeness of the Tower, it was impossible to keep her feelings for Aran secret, or the fact that he had only brotherly affection for her. They had been lovers for one brief night, at Year's End when all normal barriers in the Tower community lifted. What for Liane had been an ecstatic awakening was to Aran only part of the shared sacramental rite of the festival.

Coryn, sensitized by his rapport with Aran, felt the pang of Liane's longing. If she had been Kristlin, he would have felt duty bound to speak to Aran. But he knew that if he took any action, Liane would be furious and humiliated. She was a trained monitor, a *leronis*. As she had so emphatically informed Coryn on more than one occasion, he was not the guardian of her conscience. Furthermore, her own Keeper had determined that as long as she kept the channels which carried her sexual energy cleared, the situation was no danger to either her or to Aran. If she could not be trusted to take such basic care of her own body, then how could she be responsible for the life and health of her fellow workers?

It was a good thing, Coryn mused, that such independence in women was fostered only in the Towers, or the men of Darkover might well find their orders questioned at every turn.

Coryn's horse pulled at the bit, eager to return to stable and oats. "All right, then," he said aloud, letting the beast ease into a jog. He tilted his head back to scan the skies for his hawk, called to it. There it was, jesses trailing from its feet, lazily enjoying the afternoon thermals. Coryn called again, signaling the hawk to return.

With a shriek to curdle a banshee's blood, the bird folded its wings and plummeted toward the earth.

Coryn's heart leaped to his throat. *Open your wings!* he thought desperately. *Now, before it's too late!* The body of the bird filled his vision, falling even faster now, looming larger and larger.

NO!

"Coryn, what is it?" Liane cried out, piercing his terror. "What's wrong?"

"The hawk—" He blinked, and the sky was suddenly empty, the hawk beating its wings as it settled on his outstretched arm. Talons gripped his glove. Bright hooded eyes regarded him calmly.

"The *hawk* is fine," Liane said pointedly. "What's happened? What do you sense?"

"I don't—I don't know." Even Kieran could not probe Coryn's formless, murky nightmares, often no more than a sense of dread and the compulsion that he must not talk of them.

"If you don't know, we must find out," Liane said with her usual practicality, as she turned her horse's head back toward the Tower. "If it's that brother of mine, I'll flay him alive! I swear he has no more sense than a cow drunk on fermented apples!"

Her oldest brother, having come to his majority, had produced not one but two daughters. It was a shame, Coryn had commented, that his own father would not hear of marrying Eddard's son to one of them. An alliance by marriage would put an end to the long bickering. However, with Kristlin handfasted to Belisar Deslucido, there was no reason for Lord Leynier to look elsewhere for alliances.

They pushed the horses as quickly as was safe down the hillside, through the narrow wooded pass and then across the gentle slopes leading to Tramontana Tower. Gray stone walls glimmered in the noon sun, for they had been out hawking all morning, dallying to enjoy the day. They halted in the stable area.

Aran stood talking with the falconer. He broke off, face taut with concern. Before he could speak, Coryn turned to the falconer, who was already taking charge of the birds, settling Liane's ladyhawk on an outside perch.

"Is—has there been any news?" Coryn asked.

"All's quiet here." The man dipped his head and disappeared into the darkness of the mews with the hawk Coryn had flown.

Coryn fumbled with the laces of his hawking glove. His fingers trembled, knotting the ties until Aran reached over and deftly sorted the tangle.

"*Bredu.*" Aran stepped closer, his dark-lashed eyes troubled, and touched his fingertips to the back of Coryn's free hand. "What is it?"

After the joyous melding earlier that morning, Coryn was still lightly in rapport with his friend. "I saw . . . I felt something terrible had happened. I haven't felt this way since . . . well, since before I came here."

I saw the hawk falling, just like I saw the fire.

He closed his eyes, willing himself *not* to see the pale blue flames racing from his hands, up his arms, toward his heart. A gasp told him that Aran, joined by that featherweight physical contact, had caught that older vision. Without thinking, Coryn jerked his hand away, then wished he hadn't. This was his friend, his sworn brother, not some stranger.

Anticipation of the upcoming festivities hung in the air like incense. Laughter rang out from the novice's teaching chamber and song from the kitchen. Two of Liane's closest friends, also monitors but working in different circles, urged her to join them in decorating the central hall. She looked to Coryn, her brow faintly furrowed.

"No, go on," he said, forcing a smile. "And thank you for your concern."

"Oh, *you!*" Very much like his youngest sister, Liane stuck her lower lip out at him and flounced off with her friends.

"Come, then," Coryn said to Aran in a lighter tone. "Let us gladden the cook's heart with these grouse and then gladden the hearts of our sisters with Midsummer gifts."

With the training of Tower discipline, Aran turned away. He might not believe Coryn's easy words, but he had the sense to keep his own thoughts silent, and for this, Coryn was grateful.

✦

Midsummer morning dawned clear and unusually warm. For once, there had been no rain. Coryn yawned as he came down from his chamber. The turning of the seasons marked the end of his rotation on the relays, always more active at night when nontelepaths were sleeping, and he'd been looking forward to the extra sleep. He'd crawled out of bed early enough to leave flower baskets for Liane and Bettina, and also one for Bronwyn, but the rest of the night had been restless, his dreams uneasy.

His spirits lifted as he entered the central hall. The younger women had bedecked the central hall with garlands. He noticed Liane's fanciful touch with the new-made candles and thought of Margarida decorating the hall at Verdanta. As the early sun slanted in through the clear glass windows, the warming beeswax released a faint, honeyed scent.

Already the breakfast feasting had begun and would go on for some time, being breakfast and midday meal in one. Baskets of honey cakes, spicebread, braided egg bread, and iced buns jammed the table surface, crowded by platters of cold beef sliced wafer-thin and laced with mustard sauce, cheeses blended with herbs, dried fruit paste molded into rings like mountain peaks and then dusted with ground nut "snow," mounds of pale butter, bowls of clotted cream. The ale, heated with spicebark curls or chilled and flavored with brambleberries, flowed freely, for no one was expected to do any work today.

At the head table, Kieran sat with the other two Keepers, Brownyn, and the senior technicians. They were keeping discreetly to themselves and would retire early that evening to allow the younger folk freedom to enjoy the festivities.

Coryn slipped into his usual place between Aran and Marcos, a solid but uninspired older matrix mechanic, whose striated facial scars and lowland accent betrayed a troubled past. He was always scolding the younger men for one thing or another—gossiping, playing practical jokes, lack of seriousness. Aran teased him about having no sense of humor until Marcos left him alone.

Liane, at another of the tables with her friends, gestured merrily as she told a story of Durraman's fabled donkey. In this version, the beast had wandered in a snowstorm and been taken inside a travel shelter by a short-sighted monk who, drunk on Midwinter wine, mistook it for St. Valentine. The antics of the aged beast, bedecked with holiday clothing and plied with nut cakes, sent up flurries of girlish laughter.

One of the novices joked that this weather was likely to produce a Ghost Wind, and someone else said that on Midsummer, they needed no help in enjoying themselves.

"Aran, have you heard?" Cathal, another of the mechanics, a lanky young man distantly related to the Aldarans and with the fiery red hair to prove it, called from the table behind. "The latest scandal at Neskaya?"

"Gossip serves no one." Scowling, Marcos shook his head. "Especially gossip heard on the relays at Midsummer—"

"Don't be such a stuffy-pockets!" Aran said, shoving the ale pitcher at the older man. "Tell us, Cathal!"

Coryn raised one eyebrow at his friend's frank impudence. The ale had been flowing freely, true, and Aran had never had much head for it.

"One of their senior *laranzu'in*, bastard brother to the King of Ambervale, you know the one?"

Rumail! Coryn's spine tightened.

"Yes, wasn't there a big stink when they passed him over for Keeper training two years back?" Aran said.

"They caught him with a trap-matrix, an *unmonitored* one." Even slurred by the ale, Cathal's voice betrayed his disgust.

Coryn shook his head, wishing he hadn't had even those few mouthfuls of ale. He'd been drilled in illegal matrices like every other student at Tramontana, how to recognize them and handle them safely until a circle working under strict controls could destroy them. A trap-matrix could also have legitimate uses, such as the Veil at Hali, which permitted only those of true *Comyn* blood to pass within.

"What they said . . ." Cathal lowered his voice dramatically, "was that he'd made one designed to key into a specific person, one which would freeze all movement . . . even the beating of a man's heart."

"Oh, come on," Aran scoffed. "Something that focused can't be kept hidden for long. One of the big Towers—Hali or Arilinn—would surely pick it up on their screens. What kind of idiot would try get away with it?"

"Well, maybe he didn't plan on keeping it at the Tower. Maybe he made it for his brother. It's said that King Damian has ambitions beyond his own borders."

By now, the novices at the adjacent table had stopped their own conversation and listened intently. Liane paused, her words trailing off.

"That's right," one of Cathal's young friends said. "Why go to all the trouble of making *clingfire* when you could just slip one of those—those things—into your enemy's castle? In the confusion, you could just march in—"

Outcry rippled around the table.

"What's he saying?"

"An Aldaran assassin?"

"Neskaya's making assassin weapons?"

"That's ridiculous!"

Cathal held up his hands. "I'm just saying what I heard—"

"And what you heard is too much wagging of thoughtless tongues," Marcos snapped. "Do you see how easily a man's reputation can be damaged with just a few words? While we have been sitting here, from one heartbeat to the next, this *laranzu*, whoever he is, has gone from a blameless stranger to a demon intent on using his *laran* skills to murder some innocent."

"We don't even know there *was* a trap-matrix," one of the younger men pointed out.

"And even if it were," Marcos continued doggedly, "what if it were not even this man who made it, but some other?"

"What, are you defending him?" Cathal said.

Coryn drew in his breath at the audacity of the remark. True, Marcos had not progressed very high in his skills, but he was the eldest scated at the table. Coryn could excuse Aran's earlier taunt, delivered in playful good humor, but Cathal had been deliberately provocative.

"Cathal—" he began.

"I do not know this *nedestro* Deslucido," Marcos interrupted, "nor have I formed any opinion regarding his guilt or innocence. But I do not base my judgments on the idle chatter of children drunk on holiday ale."

One of the girls at Liane's table gasped.

"How dare you say that about me?" Cathal, flushing deeply, pushed his bench back from the table. The legs scraped on the stone floor. His hands clenched into fists.

"Stop, both of you!" Coryn cried. "Listen to yourselves! Look at what this is doing to us!"

Across the room, Kieran rose to his feet with hardly a whisper of his long Keeper's robes. Within moments, the entire room fell silent.

Kieran's clear voice, quiet though it was, rang like a bell through the hall. "Enough of rumors! Rumail, *nedestro* brother to Damian Deslucido, has indeed been dismissed from Neskaya Tower."

Coryn's heart skipped a beat. Kieran was always very particular about his terms. *Dismissed*, he'd said, and not *asked to leave*.

"But—" Cathal's young friend blurted out, "but what *happened?* Is the story about the trap-matrix true?"

"It is not seemly to dwell upon another's misfortune," Kieran said, as sternly as Coryn had ever heard him. "Rumail has been judged by his own Keeper, and appropriate remedies taken. Which of you claims to have knowledge into this matter that Neskaya does not? Which of you now proposes to take over as the Keeper of his conscience?"

Cathal, who was still standing, hung his head. Coryn caught a gleam of wetness in the other boy's shadowed face. "The rumors are my responsibility, Kieran. I was the one who heard the story over the relays last night. Instead of keeping it to myself or bringing it privately to you, I—" He flushed an even deeper red, struggling to continue.

"There is no need to say more," Kieran said. "There will simply be no further discussion of this."

Cathal sank to his bench. After an awkward moment, Aran reached over from his seat at the adjoining table and tapped him lightly on the back. The psychic atmosphere softened under the gesture of spontaneous generosity. One of the girls at Liane's table started another story of Durraman's donkey.

A heady sense of relief rose within Coryn. Rumail was gone from Neskaya, gone from the Towers! Under such a circumstance—being dismissed outright—no other Tower would accept him. Coryn need never worry that one or the other of them might be transferred to the same Tower. He felt as giddy as if he'd drunk an entire pitcher of spiced ale. The Tower was truly his home and he was free at last.

9

As summer wore on, the routine of work and study asserted itself. The flurry over Rumail of Neskaya died down, to be replaced by talk of Bettina's upcoming departure and marriage. An escort from her father's estate arrived on the first frosty morning of the autumn. Bundled in a cloak of shimmering white lambswool trimmed with gold-thread lace, her hair dressed with moonstones and garnets, she sat on her white pony like an overdressed doll instead of a skilled *leronis*.

"Next time, I suppose it will be me," Liane sighed, tucking her feet under her and cupping her hands around a mug of steaming *jaco*. She and Coryn had settled in a cushioned window seat overlooking the road to the Tower. They'd been working all night, he on the relays and she charging *laran* batteries, and had sat up to watch the dawn. At Coryn's shocked expression, she added, "You didn't think I could stay here forever, did you?"

"Actually, that's exactly what I thought."

She sank back, just out of reach. "And I wouldn't want to be anywhere else. *Dom* Kieran . . . and Lady Bronwyn . . . and Aran, and you—"

"Don't get sentimental on me now!"

Liane stuck her lower lip out at him, reminding him once more of Kristlin. She was, after all, a gently reared young woman of good family and marriageable age, capable of bringing her family a powerful alliance. Even as Kristlin was.

Liane's voice dropped to a whisper. "I wish there were some magic to capture this morning forever." Her gaze went again to the road, where the last dust from Bettina's cortege hung like a gossamer veil. The little muscles around her eyes tensed, as if she could peer into her own future.

Back at Verdanta, it would someday be Kristlin's time to leave home, encrusted with jewels that were gifts from her bridegroom and his family, perhaps accompanied by her nurse Ruella, if the old woman could still ride that far. It would be good to have someone from her childhood, someone who loved her for herself only, and also someone whom she'd still listen to once she was Queen.

Queen! Coryn shook his head. He hadn't been home in two years, but she'd still been a child in pigtails and boy's breeches then. She'd be thirteen now. . . .

He suddenly became aware of Liane's intent gaze. Aran or Lady Bronwyn or even Cathal could have followed his thoughts, but Liane's talents ran elsewhere. "Yes?" she said, tilting her head quizzically. "You haven't heard a word I've said for the past five minutes!"

"I—I was thinking of my youngest sister. Kristlin, the one you remind me of."

"The one who's promised to Prince Belisar Deslucido, you mean," she pointed out.

"Are you—are you promised to someone?" he asked awkwardly, for such things were rarely spoken of.

"Why, would you ask for my hand to spare me a stranger's bed?" The slightest edge of bitterness touched her voice. More than once in their years together, he had reached out to her and she'd gladly responded, but it had been no more than comfort and a night's pleasure shared between friends. Connected by their *laran* sensitivity, they were easy and honest with one another, with no pretense of ever having been in love.

"You know what my brother would say to that," she went on, "you being the landless third son of a neighbor he cannot say anything good about. No, my dear brother-of-the-heart, your place in life is here, as is your true talent. And mine—"

"Yours is here also. You are a talented monitor, or do you think Kieran was flattering you?" Only this last winter, Kieran had granted

Liane the responsibilities of a fully qualified monitor in his circle. She was one of the youngest within recent memory to qualify.

"Please." Liane blinked back tears and turned away, chin lifted.

Coryn instantly regretted his thoughtlessness. She *wanted* to stay, to do the work she loved. He was free to follow his vocation here, to make his own life on his own terms within the Tower, an unexpected benefit of being an extra son unlikely to inherit anything but his father's name. But Liane, no matter how many older sisters she might have, could still bring her family a powerful son-in-law.

Closing his eyes, he felt her pain as a shivering of tiny knives over his skin. He reached out to her with his *laran*. Whereas Bronwyn had always seemed to him to be a chiming of silvery bells and Kieran a rocky tor brushed with snow, Liane appeared as thick, sun-warmed silk. She was a natural monitor, for no matter how absorbed he was in the work in relay or matrix circle, no matter how far from his chilled, stiff body he had gone, she could steady his heart or warm his belly without the slightest hint of intrusion. And all this glorious talent, her quick mind, her independent spirit, all this would be thrown away to breed sons for some fat lord who'd probably already buried three wives.

Coryn pushed away the thought and focused instead on the image of spider silk blown by a breeze. He saw the fabric pulled one way, wrung into wrinkles in another. His hand stroked the silk, smoothing the creases.

With a barely audible sigh, Liane welcomed his mental touch. Under his caress, the crinkles gradually eased into unbroken billows, gently swelling in the warm, rain-scented air. The color shifted from dull gray to blue, darkening to violet along the edges.

Encouraged, Coryn went deeper. Through the outlines of her body, he saw streams of light, channels which carried her *laran* energies. Most were gold-white with health, but there, near the region of her heart, strands crossed and darkened to orange, almost red. To his relief, these were not the centers which carried sexual energy, for as a monitor she knew too well the dangers of letting those stagnate. Whatever her feelings for Aran, she had accepted that they would never be returned. Aran loved her according to his nature, no more. Now she was simply heartsick at the idea of leaving Tramontana.

As gently as he'd smoothed the silk, he untangled the orange-red energy streams, teasing one after the other free until each shone with a pale-yellow glow. After he finished, he rested before withdrawing to his own body. In this place, linked by a *laran* bond far more intimate than any sexual union, they knew and trusted one another without hesitation.

He opened his eyes to see Liane looking at him with a curious expression. "Thank you," she said. "That was well done." She got up, covering a yawn with one hand. "You could be a Keeper, you know." She headed off toward her quarters, leaving him too startled to reply.

◆

Night lay like a shawl of ebony velvet over Tramontana Tower and the surrounding peaks. The last light of pearly Mormallor had long since faded, leaving only the faint milky band of stars to break the blackness, for this was one of the few seasons when none of Darkover's four moons shone. At the center of the largest laboratory, huge matrix screens glowed, touching the face of each worker with an eerie blue radiance like that of truthspell. Before them, stoppered glass vessels held powders and simmering fluids, the raw materials for the night's work, and empty containers awaited the final product.

Coryn felt the energy pulsing from the screens, dozens of individual starstones held in a crystalline lattice and linked in such a way to guide and amplify the *laran* of the circle. He closed his eyes to better focus on the task at hand. From time to time, he felt Kieran's sure cool direction or the touch of Gareth, who was monitor this night, Liane being temporarily unable to work because of her woman's cycles.

Power surged from his depths and into the circle, to be blended with that of the other workers, shaped and focused by the Keeper. It was early yet in the evening, and Coryn's energy was high. He felt fit and rested, almost exhilarated.

Their task tonight was one he could give himself over to without reservation—the refining of fire-fighting chemicals. During the last few months, the circle had mined some of the elements from deep within the earth, carried mote by mote through *laran* to the surface, a tedious and exhausting job. Other elements came by conventional transport from the caves not far from Tramontana. Now, with the raw materials at hand, the most difficult part of the work began. It was not as dangerous as making *clingfire,* where the particles must be refined by distilling under intense heat and the glass vessels could explode, scattering bits of the corrosive material, but accidents could still happen.

Under Kieran's command, the circle worked to refine each bit of material to its purest state. The separation process was demanding and more so, the need to keep each type of particle separate and shielded from air and moisture. The glass vessels were not enough; the process required a continuous stream of *laran* power for the protective layers. The materials must be held apart until ready for the delicate process that combined them.

Coryn floated in the unity of the circle, reveling in the swirls and ripples of the mental energy which joined them. Sometimes he felt it as a spiral whirlpool, lifting them ever higher, other times a ring dance or even a choir with each voice blending to a glorious harmony. On one side sat Kieran, deftly weaving them together, on the other, Aran. Across the circle, Bronwyn sang like silvery bells. He had rarely felt so open, so safe, not since his boyhood.

Coryn, bring the fields closer. Kieran spoke within his mind. *Carefully . . .*

This was Keeper's work, and Coryn knew it. He also knew that Kieran would not have given him this responsibility if he were not ready for it. He had come to accept that sometimes Kieran knew him better than he knew himself, and within the circle, his trust in his Keeper was absolute.

With his mind, he reached for the spheres containing the refined materials, two pulsing, hugely swollen orbs and two smaller ones.

Carefully . . .

The larger spheres were easier to handle, but the danger came from the volatile matter in the smaller ones. Coryn concentrated harder. He dimly felt Bronwyn's flicker of approval, Aran's surge of pride. Gareth eased a tight muscle in his upper back and the next breath came more freely.

Now take one particle from here . . . and here . . . and join them thus. As if placing his physical hands over Coryn's, Kieran guided him through the next step. Together they formed a miniature separation field around each mote. Drawing on the *laran* of the circle, Coryn mentally moved the particles into an empty glass vessel.

Yes! The particles, drawn by their complementary affinity, leaped toward one another as soon as Coryn released the protective fields. Dark red and orange, white and muddy brown flared into a ball of yellow-white, then cooled to tiny wrinkled seeds the gray of ashes.

Elation surged through Coryn. For an instant, he pictured this very kernel which he had created dusting the air above a blazing forest. Perhaps even one on Verdanta lands. The familiar mountain slopes appeared in his memory, smoke and leaping embers, Eddard's soot-grimed face and his father's, little Kristlin in boy's breeches—

Coryn. Kieran's mental voice broke through the reverie. Coryn gathered his concentration to return to the task at hand—

And between one heartbeat and the next, he was drowning, suffocating, fighting for breath. His chest heaved, laboring to draw air into sodden lungs. The wheeze and rattle of congested breathing passages filled his ears. Fire raced through his veins.

Dimly he felt hands clutching at sweat-soaked sheets, a cool cloth laid upon his forehead, voices shouting a name he could not understand.

". . . the girl . . . fever too high . . . old man taken sick . . ."

Kristlin! Father!

He struggled to sit up. Images smeared into a blur of delirium, then faded to gray. He was falling, falling . . .

CORYN!

His own name reverberated through his mind, Kieran's stony thunder echoed by Aran's cry of alarm and the jangle of silvery bells from Bronwyn. About him, the circle was breaking up, their unity shattered.

Coryn's physical eyes lit upon the stoppered vessels containing the separated particles for the fire retardant chemicals. They glowed with the backlash of psychic energy. His had been the responsibility to hold the elements separate and inert within their *laran* generated fields. Now one rocked as if on the brink of explosion. He leaped from his bench and lunged for it.

Coryn's fingers curled around a smooth-sided inferno. He smelled singed flesh and for a nightmare moment, saw blue flames leaping from his hands up his arms. Reflexively, he dropped the vessel. It smashed on the stone floor. His body arched and spasmed, half in physical agony, half in mental. Someone caught him under the armpits and gently lowered him to the ground. He blinked, looking up into Aran's eyes, dark with concern.

"Aldones!" Gareth cried. "What happened?" Swiftly, he ran his hands scant inches over Coryn's body, monitoring him.

Lung fever . . . Gareth's thoughts ran in Coryn's mind. *How can that be? Only a moment ago, he was healthy and strong . . .*

"It was not him." Kieran rose from where he and Bronwyn had knelt together over the spilled chemicals, stabilizing them until they could be contained once more.

He bent over Coryn in silent question.

"Something—I don't know," Coryn stammered. Yet he did know.

Shivers began deep within his body, rippling outward. His teeth chattered, and he could not control his hands. He held them aloft, gazing at the reddened flesh as if it were not his.

✦

Long after the others had gone to their beds and the sky lightened in the east, Kieran sat with Coryn. Gareth had salved and bandaged Coryn's hands, saying he thought the burns would heal without scarring. Fortunately, no one else was injured, although two of the workers needed additional rest.

Coryn picked at the wrappings on his hands. "I was criminally careless," he said, miserable with guilt and fear. "I let my concentration lapse while I thought of nothing but my own glory. You entrusted me with a crucial task, and I failed you. I failed the entire circle. Someone else could have been badly hurt—"

Kieran silenced him with a gesture. "You are not the first to indulge in a little self-congratulation and then suffer the consequences. If we could all do everything perfectly the first time, there would be no need for training. But you will learn from this accident, far better than if I warned you with mere words."

For a long while, Coryn dared not speak of his vision. Something terrible had happened at home, of that he was sure. When he had been open to the circle, his natural barriers had lowered. In that wash of exultation, his thoughts had gone to his family, to his childhood dreams. Kristlin, with her undisciplined *laran*, had swept through his mind like a firestorm. For a moment, he had *been* his dearest sister, delirious with fever, struggling for each breath.

I was thinking of home, of Father and Kristlin, of bringing the fire-fighting chemicals to them as I'd dreamed I once would. And suddenly—I was in another place, another body . . . a dying body. Kristlin's body.

"My sister—my father—Dark Avarra, have mercy on us all!"

At Kieran's suggestion, Coryn now took out his starstone and focused on it, striving to mind-touch Kristlin once more, or his father, or even his other siblings. Sweat beaded his forehead and his fingers cramped, but he could not sense Kristlin's life force. Petro, Margarida, even Tessa, he knew they still lived. Eddard, he was not sure, for the answering surge of sadness and terror when he thought of his eldest brother was too strong to penetrate. As for his father, he felt only an emptiness.

Kieran, too, was unable to contact anyone at Verdanta. No one there was trained in the use of their starstones. "Even I cannot reach so far with my mind," he said, "for though I have ties of blood to your family, I do not know these people. You have a far deeper bond, especially with your sister."

But Rumail reached Neskaya when he sent for help during the fire.

"Rumail is a powerful telepath," Kieran answered aloud. "And he had trained many years together with the folk at Neskaya. This is no failure on your part."

Though Kieran's words brought little comfort, his presence did. Coryn had always envisioned Kieran's energy signature as a rocky tor. Now as the hours passed until dawn, the old Keeper's inner stillness seeped into Coryn, steadying him.

"We will send word through the relays," Kieran said as he prepared to leave Coryn's chamber for his own. "Perhaps someone at Neskaya has word of your family."

"I must go home. I must be sure," Coryn said, struggling to sit up. The room blurred sickeningly. As he coughed, racking pain lanced through his chest.

Kieran brushed his fingertips against Coryn's face. To Coryn, the touch burned like frozen fire. He shivered.

You are in no condition to go anywhere. Your energy body was in reso-nance with your sister's and it has affected your physical lungs. This is a very dangerous state. Gareth, and Liane when she is able, will monitor you until your channels are clear.

Coryn heard a faroff wailing, like a banshee on the heights, like the wind through a deserted castle, a blizzard across the barren heights, and recognized it as his own grief.

The hawk fell from the sky, he thought numbly. *Was it an omen?*

◆

A tenday later, Coryn woke from sleep, ravenously hungry. Gareth counted this a good sign, for his body needed food to repair and rebalance the disruption to his energy channels. The outward injuries, the burns on his hands, had healed to the slightest tinge of red, quickly fading.

He went down to the kitchen, where Gareth and Marisela, the house-mistress, sat over bowls of stewed rabbit-horn. Steam, fragrant with the aroma of wild mushrooms and rosemary, arose from the huge pot, and five loaves of seed-encrusted bread sat cooling on racks. The last few slices from the sixth loaf, along with some soft *chervine* cheese, sat on a platter. Coryn helped himself and sat down with them, glad for their easy company. He remembered sitting around the chopping table back in Verdanta, munching on nut crullers or leftover meat pies with Petro and Margarida.

No, it was dangerous to think of home. Of home and what might— what *had*—happened there. The urge to go running home had returned along with his health, but Kieran had forbidden it outright.

Not until we know for certain what has happened.

So Coryn reined in his thoughts, calmed his breathing, and tried to concentrate on the present moment. He waited for the news which must come

The kitchen at Tramontana was set out from the body of the Tower itself, to vent the huge ovens and let in natural light through the banks of windows along the far wall. One of the early Keepers, a gourmand, had bribed the best cook in the kingdom to join the Tower staff by building it just for her. Whatever the truth of the tale, the sunlit room stayed cheerful on all but the gloomiest winter days. It occupied one full corner of the ground floor, with its own doors leading outside to the courtyard and down into the cellars filled with casks of wine, huge waxed wheels of cheese, barrels of nuts, apples and cabbages, enormous bins of flour and smaller ones of seeds and dried salted fish.

Because of the location of the kitchen, Coryn heard hoofbeats approaching on the road.

One-eyed Rafe.

Coryn stiffened, and the composure he had fought for vanished. His hands unconsciously gripped the edge of the table so hard one knuckle popped.

"A rider this late?" Marisela said. "He will want his dinner."

"He's ridden that poor horse pretty hard, by the sound of it," Gareth said. He took his bowl to the huge scoured-stone sink where a panful of dishes already sat soaking, and ducked out the side door.

Coryn downed the last of his *jaco* as Marisela bustled about, preparing a hot meal for the poor traveler. It was all he could do to regain a tattered semblance of calm. Following the exercises he'd been drilled in since his first year at Tramontana, he breathed deeply, slowly, smoothing the tension in his muscles and focusing his thoughts.

Aran stood waiting in the kitchen doorway. With his empathic sensitivity, Aran knew something more had happened. His silent presence spoke more than any words. Coryn touched the back of Aran's wrist with his fingertips.

Bredu, *I am glad you're here. I—*

One of the novices rushed up. The lad's hair stood out about his flushed face.

"There's news from Verdanta! A rider! Kieran wants you—"

Although Coryn had waited long days for those very words, icy fingers now froze his spine, reaching for his heart. *So, it has come.*

You are not alone, my brother. For an instant, Aran enveloped him in soothing warmth.

Moments later, Coryn, with Aran and the novice only a step behind, knocked at the door to Kieran's private quarters. At a word from within, he lifted the latch and entered. The scene reminded him for an instant of that very first interview: the stark simplicity of the room, the chill which he now understood was not from any forced austerity but from indifference to temperature. Kieran sat in that very same chair, gesturing him forward. The Keeper seemed not to have aged at all since that day, except for a trace more thinness in the shoulders.

"I am sorry to see you, Coryn, under such circumstances," Kieran said formally, "but pleased that you have a friend to stand beside you. Huy," to the boy, "you may leave us now, but do not say a word of this. Remember what we agreed, that this is Coryn's business and not yours."

With a nod, the youngster clattered back down the stairs.

Coryn let the door close behind him to see One-eyed Rafe standing in the shadows behind the door. As the old mercenary stepped forward, the light fell across his face. He looked as if he'd aged a century, all his iron strength gone to rust. His clothes were dark with travel filth.

Kieran's colorless eyes rested on Coryn's, reflecting only kindness there. "News has finally come from Verdanta."

Coryn searched Rafe's face, the deep seams lining the mouth, the rheumy eye. With the discipline of his years of Tower training, he waited for the words he knew would come.

"An epidemic of lungrot swept all the area around Verdanta," Kieran said. "Your father—and your sister—and many others—"

"Merciful Avarra!" Aran whispered.

The hawk . . . the hawk fell from the sky.

"Even a man in his full strength can be felled by lungrot," Kieran said, his voice shaded with bone-deep weariness. "Many died before the thing had run its course. No household was spared, from the poorest farmstead to the castle itself. Half the smallholder families are gone. And of those who survived, many have such scarring on their lungs as will shorten their lives."

Coryn lowered himself to the nearest bench. Not only Kristlin and his father, but men and boys who had labored beside him on the fire-lines and feasted together at Midsummer, gone! He felt Aran's light touch on his shoulder, the pressure of fingertip on muscle, a pulse of strength, *I am here . . .*

Lungrot . . . Unlike natural diseases, this horror was *laran*-made. Tramontana had never done so, and Coryn had heard Kieran speak out against weapons which respected no boundaries and killed so many innocents. Bronwyn, who had seen her home razed under firebombings from *laran*-powered aircars, had raged, "We should make warfare even more dreadful, then, so dreadful that no lord dares to strike at another for fear of what might be unleashed on his own lands!"

"I am so sorry," Aran murmured. "Your father—"

In those few words, Coryn caught the echoes of pain long past, of losses set to rest but not forgotten. Never forgotten. Aran's father and grandfather had died in a rockslide when he was seven or eight, old enough to remember them but young enough to need the guidance of a loving parent. His mother, bereft and embittered, had turned inward on her own grief, leaving Aran and his brothers to find their own way through the tempestuous, lonely years that followed. All this he had whispered to Coryn as they sat up, sleepless and a bit drunk, on Midsummer Festival night of their second year.

"It was Kristlin who died, a day afterward," Coryn said in a hollow voice.

Nodding, Rafe covered his face with one raw-scraped hand to hide his tears.

Coryn had not seen Kristlin for two years. It had been Midsummer Festival the last time he'd been home. He had thought there would always be another Midsummer, and then a wedding . . .

"And Petro? Tessa? Margarida? Ruella my old nurse? The *coridom?* Old Timas?"

Rafe pressed his lips together, silently gathering his composure. "Petro and the other *damiselas,* they live, although how well they do, I canna say. Ruella—Timas—I don't know these names, but few of the old people made it. The fevers hit them hardest, them and the wee ones. I—I was riding the border with High Kinnally and was late returning," he added, as if in explanation or perhaps a plea for absolution.

Coryn found himself getting to his feet, Aran's hand falling away. "I will prepare to return home for the funerals."

Kieran said, "There can be no funerals for those who die of lungrot. The bodies must be burned and the ashes laced with salt to prevent further contagion."

"I don't care." Coryn's vision blurred. "This is my family—I must go home."

Rafe lifted his head. "Your brother Eddard, he that's Lord Leynier now, he bade me tell you that he and his one son still live. He says—he says—" he inflected the word to mean *commands*, "—not to come, not when there's still danger from the lungrot."

"Not come—just as if they were strangers and their lives meant nothing to me?" Coryn heard his own voice rise in pitch, his ragged breathing. "What am I supposed to do, pretend nothing has happened? Gods, man, does my brother think I'm so unfeeling or that Tower work has stripped me of all courage?"

We almost lost you to threshold sickness, Kieran said, mind to mind. *I will not risk you again to some accursed plague.*

"If anything happens to your brothers, you will be the next Lord of Verdanta," Aran pleaded. "You must stay here, where you are safe.

"When this thing has run its course, someone must be left to stand against High Kinnally," Rafe added, iron ringing in his voice.

"Kinnally . . ." *Liane's family!* "Has the plague reached Storn?"

"Who knows?" Rafe looked as if he wanted to spit, but dared not, here in a Keeper's private chambers. "We sent no word to them nor they to us. For all we know, they set it on us! Or so Lord Eddard says."

"There has been nothing from Neskaya," Kieran commented mildly, meaning no news along the relays or any hint of who might be responsible.

Coryn thought again of returning home, but he had nothing to offer the desperate survivors, not even money to purchase food against next winter's hunger. He could not just sit here idly at Tramontana. Yet there was nothing he could do to bring back Lord Beltran or Kristlin or to change the course of the plague.

An idea struck him, something he could do, even so far away. Not for this crisis, but for others still to come.

"With your permission," he said, nodding to Kieran and then turning back to Rafe, "I will send a messenger-bird home with this good man and say to my brother that he has but to release it in the event of a forest fire, and I will send chemicals which I have myself made."

"That is a good offer," Kieran said. "Now, young Aran, take this man down to the kitchen for some hot food and make sure his beast is well stabled. They both deserve rest."

Coryn lingered in the Keeper's chambers after the others had gone. His thoughts jumbled one on top of the other, things he wished he had said or had left unsaid. Now that the news was sure, pain pierced his body like a fire-tipped arrow, only to recede into numbness.

"It is a grave loss," Kieran said. "And such things can take a long time to mourn, even when we anticipate their coming. I think we do not so much forget as we reach a new balance." Something in his tone told Coryn that he spoke from his own experience. "You need not join us in the circle for a time."

"I—I would like to work. I think it would help take my mind off—all the things I keep thinking."

"Sometimes it does happen that way. When you are ready, you must first have Gareth monitor you to make sure you are fit for the work. Grief can cloud our judgment of many things, not the least our own clarity."

That made sense, even in Coryn's dazed state. He went back to his chamber, where he lay curled on top of the covers for what seemed like hours, until Liane slipped in. She lay down behind him, curving her body around his, her arms around him, and held him until silent tears came and went and he finally slept.

10

"So the old man and the girl are both dead." Damian Desludico stood with his brother on the balcony outside his private quarters as the great Bloody Sun lowered on the horizon. Autumn was fast turning into winter, and ice edged the wind even in Ambervale's sheltered valleys. He had been idle for too long, playing the benevolent king, and the inactivity rankled.

Rumail drew his cloak around him and made no reply. It was too bad, Damian reflected, that his brother had been caught before he completed the *laran* device which was to have protected the girl. Damian hadn't planned on releasing the lungrot so soon, but Old Lord Leynier would have seized upon Rumail's expulsion from Neskaya as yet another excuse to delay. Damian had to act decisively. Nor was it Rumail's fault that the lungrot, purchased at great expense and with many bribes of secrecy from an unregulated Tower near Temora, had gotten out of control. But the end result was the same—Verdanta in shambles, ripe for the taking.

Originally, the plan had been a sound one. With the father and brothers dead from the lungrot or else so weakened as to be incapable of fielding an effective defense, the Ambervale forces would have swept through Verdanta like a heated knife through butter. The girl's age or wishes would have mattered nothing. There would have been an end to temporizing, to placating the brat and her doting sire. Backed by the legitimacy of marriage, Verdanta would have been theirs now, not in another four or five years, as that unreasonable Lord Leynier kept insisting.

As a boy, Damian had once ridden his father's favorite mount, a huge yellow unruly brute of a stallion, just to see how far and how fast he could go. The horse raced through fields shimmering with new-sprouted wheat and barley, hooves throwing up great clods of earth. Even now, Damian remembered the wind singing in his ears and the coarse mane whipping across his face. Up into the hills they ran, as if possessed.

There seemed to be no end to the horse's strength. Each fallen log, each ditch, each rockpile or stream seemed only to add to the animal's frenzy. Foam splattered the front of Damian's shirt. They burst through a copse along the crest of a hill and stood poised for a moment over a long, boulder-strewn slope. Damian tightened his grip on the reins. His legs trembled with exhilaration. The hill was too steep for safety, the rocky footing too uncertain.

But the stallion ducked its massive head and seized the bit. It leaped from the ridge and plunged downhill as if all the demons of Zandru's nine hells were lashing at its tail. The horse seemed to suspend itself in the air for a sickening moment, so steep was the hillside. Then it landed with a bone-cracking jolt. Damian was almost unseated. The pommel of the saddle dug into his stomach as he lurched forward over the sweating, arched neck. The horse slid, scrambled, heaved itself onward. Metal shoes sparked against rock.

All Damian could do was hang on. The reins were useless, for nothing could have slowed that mad, careening downhill course. He had not even time enough to pray. With his fingers laced in the horse's mane and blood hammering through his skull, the hot raw power of the beast flowed into his own body.

An eerie peace had settled on him, one he remembered and thirsted for to this very day. His body had shifted in perfect balance with the horse's. Without thought, he adjusted to each landing, each stumble, each soaring leap. He no longer thought of falling, of dying, or even of reaching the bottom—only of the wild joy of the moment. Never before and rarely since had he felt so intensely alive, every fiber of his being throbbing with exhilaration.

That was the trick of it, in war and in love as well as riding a maddened horse, to meet each obstacle as it came. To be rooted in the present moment, not the unchangeable past or the uncertain future. If his plans for a bloodless conquest of Verdanta went awry, then he would find some other way. Verdanta was the key to the surrounding stretch of Hellers and the gateway to Acosta, Acosta which he must have safe before the accursed Hasturs settled their death grip on all the lands around it.

But war took planning, the careful assessment of strengths and liabilities. Rumail, now, represented both.

As if on cue, several figures entered the room adjacent to the balcony on which he and Rumail now stood.

"Ah, here are my son and my senior general," Damian said, keeping his voice light. "Let us see what inspiration they can bring to our present situation."

They drew up chairs around the table of polished golden-pine fitted with racks of rolled maps and shelves of account books. A servant set down goblets of watered wine and as silently disappeared.

"What's the assessment of Verdanta?" Damian asked the chief of his generals, a man once so fair as to arouse speculation he was Dry Towner by birth. Years and weather and uncounted battles had grizzled his hair and seamed his face like bleached leather. His men called him The Yellow Wolf. Damian, pleased with the idea of a wolf at his service, did nothing to stop them.

"Confusion continues," The Yellow Wolf answered. "The contagion has burned itself out, yet there is little order restored. My scouts were able to ride within sight of the castle without challenge. They saw crops rotting in the fields, trees bending under unpicked fruit, cattle untended in their pens. Hunger will surely follow the loss of the harvest. This Eddard Leynier might become a competent ruler in time, for he appears to be well liked and to have training in organizing fire-lines if nothing else. Only someone with a true genius for leadership—" a flicker of those pale eyes in Damian's direction, "—as well as Aldones' own luck could bring the people together under these conditions."

"If we marched on Verdanta, we could still take it with minimal losses." Belisar said. "We must strike first before they can mount a defense."

Damian looked on his son and heir with pride. The boy might be impulsive, but he had a good mind when he chose to use it. The years had brought some measure of insight even as they pared away his boyhood softness. The lungrot plague might not have gone the way they'd planned, but with a little of that luck The Yellow Wolf swore by, even better opportunities might come their way. Belisar, with his quick mind and hard-edged masculine beauty, would have been wasted on that insipid little country girl. Now he was free to make a far more advantageous match elsewhere.

"It's not the taking of Verdanta itself which poses risks, Your Highness," the Yellow Wolf explained without a hint of condescension. He pointed to the unfurled map. "It's the possibility that their neighbors, the Storns of High Kinnally, might seize this opening for themselves."

Rumail, who had spoken little that evening, stirred. "There is scant love lost between those two families. As you remember, when I visited Verdanta to assess the daughters for *laran*, High Kinnally had refused their aid in a forest fire, even denying them passage through to Tramontana. Their quarrel, like so many of these petty mountain feuds, goes back farther than living men can remember, with each new generation renewing the animosity. I have not heard of any mending of that breach, or of any desire for peace on either part." He looked disgusted. "Given access to it, they'd be pelting one another with *clingfire* and worse at the slightest excuse."

"Meanwhile, men die and their families starve for a cause no one remembers," Damian said. "It will be so much better for everyone once they are joined under a single King. No more incessant vendettas, no more needless famines."

"Shall we then stand back and let High Kinnally fall upon Verdanta, so that they spend themselves upon each other and fall the more readily to our greater strength?" Belisar put in, eager to return to the subject.

Damian shook away the recurrent vision of a glorious united Darkover and leaned back in his chair. "An interesting idea. Tell me what's wrong with it."

"Sire?"

"Every plan, no matter how apt or well-planned, has its own pitfalls," Damian said. "Since you have so readily proposed this one, you may now point out for us all the things that could go amiss. As an exercise, if you will."

"Well—" Belisar swallowed hard. "We could end up with two enemies instead of one. High Kinnally and Verdanta might settle their differences and join together against us as a common opponent."

Damian nodded. Belisar might be a bit overly dramatic, but he could think on his feet. In fact, he seemed to do so better than when he'd prepared what to say.

"And—" the boy went on, "—and Verdanta could fall too fast. Then High Kinnally would have all their own resources and Verdanta's. We'd face a united enemy, one already primed for battle. Fighting on their own territory. Oh, I said that before."

"Our forces could also be spread too thin," Damian pointed out, "over strange country—mountainous country—which both of them know intimately and are better trained and equipped for fighting in than our forces are. We'd have long supply lines and disadvantage of terrain."

"Yet in every crisis there is opportunity," The Yellow Wolf said. "We had not planned on having to take High Kinnally, at least not at this time. It's too remote to govern well." *Too far from Acosta*, he meant. "We'd face the same problems in holding Verdanta, that we cannot afford to weaken our own armies by leaving an occupying force great enough to put down incessant uprisings. We could hold family hostages against the current lord's fealty or perhaps we could leave one of the lords—Leynier or Storn—in place to govern both lands."

"Oh," Damian permitted himself a dark laugh, "they'd *love* that."

"They'd direct their anger at each other, not rebellion against us," the general returned.

Damian bent over the table, studying the map as he thought aloud. "Verdanta we must have, one way or the other. We cannot hold it without making sure of High Kinnally. Whether by alliance or conquest, then, we must deal with the Storns as well." He looked up. "I want three plans drawn up: one, we deal first with High Kinnally and then go on to Verdanta; two, we strike Verdanta first and hope for an easy victory, whether Kinnally backs down or we must wrestle them into submission also; and three, we follow my son's suggestion and let the two of them have at each other, so that we face only the weakened victor. I especially want to see fallback plans, should each of these schemes go wrong."

When the meeting broke up, both Belisar and Rumail remained behind.

Damian sighed and drained his goblet in a single draught. The faintly acid taste of the watered wine lingered on his tongue, leaving him hungry for stronger stuff. Belisar was still at the map, tracing the borders of Verdanta with a thoughtful expression.

"They *will* fall to us, both of them," Damian said. "The only question is the details. You are not fretting over the loss of your promised bride?"

"No, why should I?" Belisar shrugged. "I never knew her except as an indifferently rendered portrait. She looked much like any other girl-child still playing with her dolls. I have always known I must marry for the good of Ambervale, but I had hoped for a more suitable wife. If Verdanta can be ours without my having to bed a spoiled brat, I am just as happy. I have heard that one of the Storn daughters is of marriageable age—"

"Such an alliance now is not only unnecessary, but beneath you," Damian cut him off. "No longer need we bargain with these mountain peasants. Acosta is the key, and it is there you will find your bride. I had not planned on being able to move against them so soon, but recent events—" he meant Rumail's departure from Neskaya and the premature release of the lungrot, "—have changed the timing. Once Verdanta is peacefully ours, I will seize whatever gifts the gods present me with."

Belisar looked puzzled. "But the heir to Acosta is male, and newly married. To a Hastur daughter, I believe."

"You are well informed," Damian said. "What you may not realize is that because of her higher rank, *she* will inherit upon his death. She cannot rule, of course. Outside of those dim-witted sandal-wearers at Aillard, no woman can. But her next husband will."

A slow smile spread across Belisar's face. "So instead of a reluctant child, you present me with a young—*experienced*—widow. Is she beautiful as well?"

"She's probably a hellcat, like all the Hastur women," Rumail said with a curled lip. "But she'll bear you *laran*-gifted sons. Of that you may be certain."

"A dozen at least!" Belisar laughed, throwing back his head.

"Away with you, then!" Damian said to his son, laughing also. "Sit with my officers and see what you can learn from their planning. Your uncle and I have other things to discuss."

In the silence that followed Belisar's departure, Damian studied his half brother. Rumail's mood showed in every deep-etched line of his face, in the hunch of his shoulders and his very stillness. Except for his comment about the Hastur girl, he'd seemed to pay scant attention to the discussion. If Rumail were to be of any use to him at all, he couldn't go on like this, fretting and sulking. Eventually, given enough time, Rumail would come to see his expulsion from the Tower as a blessing. He was far superior to those sandal-wearers and their esoteric mysteries. But with the schedule for conquest accelerated, Damian could not afford to wait.

"Regardless of which plan we adopt, intelligence will be necessary," Damian said. He used the inflection to mean *spying.* "A team of sentry-birds, able to fly over the enemy's encampment or supply lines, would give us a valuable edge. Such information might save many soldiers' lives."

"You know I cannot link with a sentry-bird," Rumail said. "It is not a matter of training, a skill which anyone with *laran* can learn. One must have a certain empathic resonance with the birds, which I have not."

"Ever since you got home, it has been *I cannot do this* and *I cannot do that!*" Damian snapped. "Have you suddenly become a cripple? Do you have no powers of your own, or do you exist merely as an appendage of your precious Tower?"

Rumail flushed under the goading. "I am as I have always been, Keeper in all but name! But I cannot work in isolation. Cut off from a circle, matrix screens, monitors, and technicians to support me—"

"And why must that be?" Damian pounced on the opening.

"You know as well as I do! All those fools at Neskaya cared about was their prissy, headblind traditions! Rules and more rules, with no room for vision or creativity! I opened new vistas for them—and they forced me out. Ingrates, after all I'd done for them! They closed their eyes to my discoveries, rejected my innovations, refused to listen. If it hadn't been done by their grandfathers, they weren't interested!"

He wasn't seeing it. Not yet. Damian went on, "And are *all* the telepaths on Darkover confined within these Towers?"

"Of course not. There are *leroni* who work alone, in noble households or with their lords on campaign. There are even those with untrained *laran* who work as horse-handlers or country midwives, little knowing what they truly do. That Nest down near Temora will sell lungrot spores or anything else to whoever meets their price. But once I . . ." Rumail's voice trailed off as understanding dawned. "Are you proposing, dear brother, that I assemble and train my own circle?"

"Who live and work by your laws, not some Tower's? Why not?"

"I would have to search out those of the proper temperament." Now a spark lit the darkness of Rumail's eyes. "Yes, there are others of like mind . . . but not enough to make a circle capable of doing anything beyond charging a few glow-lights. I would have to train my own . . . that boy from Verdanta, for instance, so talented—"

"How long before you have a circle capable of, for instance, *cling-fire?*"

"Oh!" Rumail pursed his lips. "If they'd had early training with a matrix, such as a household *leronis* might give, if they were the right age . . . perhaps five years to come to strength. That is, if I can enlist a fully-trained matrix technician and a mechanic or two."

"I have a war to fight, and I have not the luxury of time," Damian said regretfully. "I cannot wait for years while you train a bunch of youngsters."

"You offer me my own Tower and as quickly snatch it away." Rumail's expression verged on a snarl. "What kind of game are you playing with me? I am a Tower-trained *laranzu*, not some vassal you can break promises to whenever it pleases you. Do you think *I* would not know it if you tried to lie to me? If you were not my brother and my liege—"

Damian held up a hand. "You will have your Tower and you will accomplish great things, of this I am certain. The only question is when. I need the weapons and the power which only a working circle can give me." He shook his head again. "I cannot wait."

Rumail drew himself up with dignity. "As always, I and my abilities are at the service of your great cause."

Although his words were spoken graciously, Damian caught the hint of another meaning, as if for that moment, Rumail gave his allegiance to some other, even greater vision. But that was nonsense! Rumail had no political ambitions or experience in leading armies. He'd never expressed the slightest interest in ruling a kingdom.

"Meanwhile, I must use whatever resources are at hand," Damian said, shaking off the moment. "Temora would be happy to lease me air-cars and even make *clingfire*, but at an exorbitant price, and with no guarantee that the next time I have need, they will be willing."

Rumail turned away, a thoughtful expression flickering across his features. "But that may not be necessary. It might be possible to gain lordship over an established Tower.'

"I—I don't follow you," Damian said, blinking in surprise.

"I speak of allegiances and those ancient traditions the Towers are so fond of. Neskaya was in Ridenow hands for centuries before the Peace of Allart Hastur. Now they look to Hastur, although they are so far distant, they've never been asked for war matériel. But Tramontana . . . Tramontana's legal obligations have long been unclear, or so I understand. Long ago, they were said to answer to Aldaran. And in the days of the Keeper Ian-Mikhail, they had strong ties to Storn."

"Storn of Storn or Storn of High Kinnally?" This could be an unexpected difficulty, if Tramontana were to enter the battle in defense of the latter.

"I'm not sure, for that was long ago and the records may no longer exist. But we—I mean Ambervale and Linn—may have an equal claim. Certainly we can keep Tramontana out of any present conflict, but perhaps we can also compel their fealty later. The difficult part will be persuading Tramontana that it owes *any* loyalty. Kieran Aillard, oldest of the Keepers there, is notorious for his advocacy of Tower neutrality." Rumail gave a derisive snort.

"Which can work both for and against us," Damian said. After a few moments of reflection, he had formed a plan. A search would be made at Ambervale Castle and at Linn for any record of past lordship of Tramontana Tower. At the same time, he gave permission to Rumail to contact any disaffected Tower workers he knew and make discreet inquiries of any likely youngsters. For the long run, it would be better to have an Ambervale Tower, workers specially trained and devoted to the Deslucido line. Some benefit might eventually come of it.

For today, Damian accepted with a sigh, he would continue to pay the renegade group at Temora. His treasury was still low, drained by the fees for the lungrot and aircars, on top of the ongoing expense of maintaining an army. Perhaps, though, treachery would prove as powerful a weapon as *clingfire.*

11

Word arrived at Tramontana one bleakly overcast morning that Verdanta Castle had fallen to King Damian Deslucido. The messenger, a half-grown boy from one of the outlying small farms and son of one of Old Timas' cousins, clattered up to the gates on a lathered, exhausted pony, barely able to babble out the news. The takeover, hardly enough to be called a battle, had been short and almost bloodless. Eddard still lived, although a prisoner in his own castle, with his wife and surviving infant son held as hostages. The boy did not know what had happened to Petro or Margarida, although there had been a hasty wedding, presumably Tessa's, to one of the Deslucido officers. One-eyed Rafe, the *coridom*, and several others had died defending the gates.

When Kieran banned him from doing any matrix work, Coryn paced his narrow room by the hour, muttering curses at Deslucido Oathbreaker, who could shift from eager ally to usurper in such a short time. All he could think of was racing back home. He knew how useless and foolhardy that would be. It would not bring back either his father or sister, nor could he free Verdanta singlehandedly. All he would accomplish would be to get himself killed or, worse yet, imprisoned along with Eddard in his own home. He couldn't hold Eddard's surrender against him; Eddard was probably doing the best he could for his people. Weakened by lungrot, his forces disorganized, what else could he do? Verdanta had no chance against a trained, healthy army.

Liane and Aran did their best to calm him. He would have none of their soothing, reasonable words. He could not sit still. Images flamed behind his eyes

—*Margarida and Petro, crouching in the farthest root cellar, digging their way out with their bare fingers, holding hands as they raced across the moonless night for the safety of the forest*

—*Rafe slashing at a man in Ambervale livery with his long knife, then another, then facing six at a time, his one eye red with madness*

—*Tessa biting down hard on her rumpled pillow to stifle her sobs every night.*

When he spoke of these things, Aran tried to comfort him, saying they sprang from his natural feelings, the shock of the news.

"Leave him," Coryn heard Liane saying to Aran, outside in the corridor. "There are some things each of us must do alone."

Late one night, Coryn stood at his unshuttered window. Three of Darkover's four moons were scattered like jewels across the cloudless sky. The night air smelled of snow. He drew it into his lungs, welcoming the shiver which rippled through his muscles, and tried not to think of how much Kristlin had loved those moons.

The faint scuff of boots on the stone floor behind him reached his ears. So finely tuned were his senses, he felt the whisper of air as the door closed, the warmth of another human body.

"Aran," he said and turned around. Moonlight silvered his friend's face, accenting the dark hair, the eyes like pools of midnight. The stark beauty of that face sent another shiver through him. "You need not have come. Liane said, rightly, that I must face this alone."

Coryn felt Aran's feather-light touch on the wrist. "I can almost see what you're seeing—images of people I don't know, of scenes neither of us could have seen." Aran's empathy, naturally strong with horse and hawk but honed by hours of minds joined in a matrix circle, now laid him open to Coryn's raw emotion. "At first, I thought they must come from your own pain, the way so many dreams do. But these are not dreams. I can feel the difference."

"I don't know if they are real or not," Coryn answered. "They could just as well be products of my own mind. I suffered hallucinations during threshold sickness. Those were just as vivid."

"They are real . . . here." Cool fingers curled around his, lifted his hand to Aran's breast. Through the thin linex shirt, Coryn felt a fluttering, light and quick. "Sometimes the heart speaks in pictures," Aran said, "things we have no words for."

Coryn's breath caught like a sob in his throat. He bent his head, buried his face against Aran's shoulder. Strong arms enfolded him.

"Bredu." The word meant *brother* . . . but also *beloved.*

Warm breath whispered through the fine hairs on Coryn's neck. In that instant of intimacy, standing so close that the same body warmth enfolded them both, Coryn felt Aran's lips tremble against his hair. Part of Coryn wanted desperately to open himself to that uncomplicated love. Beyond the fumbling experiments considered normal for all boys of a certain age, Coryn felt no particular attraction to other men. But neither did he feel any revulsion. Aran loved him according to his nature, loved him for who and what he was, and Aran was a good and decent man.

Yet now, something within Coryn clamped down in an icy knot. For an awful moment, he could not move, could scarcely breathe. He had not felt this loss of control, this paralysis, since his arrival at the Tower and his attempts to describe what Rumail had done to him.

In the silence that followed, Aran drew back, dropping all physical touch. The set of his shoulders showed clearly that he knew something was wrong. And Aran, being who he was, would assume it was his unintended overture.

Oh, my friend, my sworn brother, what is wrong is not you! Coryn opened his mouth to speak, but his throat had frozen. The place deep within his belly, the old wound he could barely remember, the wound without a scar, throbbed.

"I'm sorry," Aran said in a thick voice. "I didn't intend for this to happen—I would never—"

Miserable and mute, Coryn watched Aran stumble from the room. He lowered himself to the bed, wondering if he would ever be able to repair the hurt he had caused. The pale, multihued moonlight shone through his window. He found no solace in its terrible, stark beauty.

✦

A second message arrived shortly afterward, this one from High Kinnally. The forces of King Damian had not stopped with the easy conquest of Verdanta but had marched on. Kinnally Castle was under siege and could not hold out for long. The Storns in their desperation appealed to Tramontana for aid. Tramontana's fealty by law and custom was unclear, one reason Kieran had long advocated a neutral stance. Originally, some believed, the Tower had been allied to Aldaran. At various other times, it had served Storn, Ambervale, or another small kingdom bound to Acosta but long since absorbed into neighboring lands.

Liane, her reddened eyes set in a face as set and pale as ice, urged Coryn to add his voice to hers.

"We have no standing army, any more than you did, Coryn," she said. "No matter how bravely our guards fight, they are no match for Ambervale. I've known these men from before I could walk. They will hold out as long as they can. We must act quickly, before it is too late."

"We?" Coryn, stirred out of his misery, asked, "What must we do?"

"Tramontana must give us *clingfire* and the means to deliver it. Rain it down on the tyrant! Destroy his armies and scatter their ashes to the winds! Free both our lands! Once we have lifted the siege, we obliterate the vermin's nest itself."

Clingfire was indeed a potent weapon, and it was High Kinnally's only chance. A few men, flying overhead in gliders or shooting arrows tipped with the deadly stuff, might well destroy a small army.

Coryn shook his head. "Ambervale now occupies Verdanta. For all I know, Verdanta men march with their armies. Would you have me turn against my own?"

"No! I would have you destroy the outsider! Or have you so quickly given up any thought of saving your people?"

"I hardly think it would be *saving* my people to drop unquenchable fire down on them." Coryn thought of that terrible forest fire so many years ago, of how his father had battled to protect everyone under his care, from closest family to poorest smallholder. He had never witnessed *clingfire* in battle, though he had seen what a small slip in concentration making the stuff could do. Each droplet of *clingfire* adhered to whatever it touched. It would go on burning, through metal as well as flesh and bone, as long as there was anything left to be consumed. A trained matrix worker, especially one armed with a fire-talisman, might contain a stray bit here and there, but not a coordinated onslaught.

In a flash, he saw himself swooping over Verdanta, hands filled with fragile glass spheres. Each glowed like a malevolent ember. Eddard's face, pale and furrowed, lifted to see him, eyes straining wide in disbelief.

The vessels slipped from his fingers, bursting into corrosive fire. Tessa ran screaming, her unbound hair a curtain of flame down her back. A slender skeleton staggered through the familiar courtyard, bony arms smoking, and fell into a heap which continued to glow and smolder.

I cannot do it! I cannot betray the people I love!

"What," he cried, his voice shaking, "should I firebomb my own brother in Verdanta Castle, attack my home and my people? What kind of monster would do that?"

"*You* may think it better to live under an invader's yoke," Liane shot back, "but I do not! If it were *my* brother torn from his wife and baby—as well he may be if we do not act quickly—I would stop at nothing to free them! Even death would be better than such a life. And if I were held captive there, I would say to you, I would beg you, *Send the* clingfire! *Burn the castle to the ground beneath my feet! Better a quick death than a lifetime of slavery!*"

Liane went on with scarcely a pause for breath. "Have you heard of the Sisterhood of the Sword? Each one carries a dagger around her neck, so that she may never fall alive into the hands of the enemy. Can a mere woman have such determination—such courage—such *honor,* and you have them not?"

"Liane, that's not fair! My honor has nothing to do with it! Our enemy is Damian Deslucido, not each other. I want him gone just as much as you do. But I will not sacrifice the lives of my family and all those who owe us loyal service. I love my country! Besides, I can no more save your homeland than you could save mine. The fate of High Kinnally hardly rides on my decision."

"No," she said in a voice gone suddenly grim. "But Kieran listens to you. And his word rules here at Tramontana. If he says, 'Send *clingfire* to High Kinnally,' then *clingfire* will be sent."

I once thought to go back to Verdanta in a glider, carrying the fire-fighting chemicals I had created myself. Now the thought of returning home in the glider of his dreams, bearing the living hell of *clingfire*, brought only soul-deep sickness.

Yet, in her overly dramatic way, Liane had the right of it. Damian Oathbreaker, for so he would always be in Coryn's thoughts, must be stopped. Already, a handful of smaller, weaker kingdoms lay under his rule, adding their resources to his. With each new conquest, his power grew. Coryn, like any mountain-bred boy, knew that the longer a forest fire burned unchecked, the higher the cost of putting it out. The inferno that was Deslucido must be put out before it grew beyond any man's control.

In the end, Coryn went with Liane to plead her case with Kieran, determined to temper her argument and persuade her to reason. He prayed with all his heart that some other way might be found to deal with Deslucido. Surely Kieran with his experience and wisdom would see a less horrendous path. At least, Liane's desperate grief might be restrained until she could see reason, even as his own pain had been. This much he could do for her without betraying his own people.

Once more they met in his chambers and stood beside the fireless hearth. After listening to Liane's petition with a grave expression, Kieran flatly refused to supply her with *clingfire*. It was, he said, too dangerous for any Tower to meddle in local politics of which it knew nothing.

"Local politics!" Liane flamed, for once losing her usual deference in the Keeper's presence. "My family and my home are at stake! Even Coryn, whose land has long held a feud with us, agrees we must take action! What do you propose we do, think nice peaceful thoughts at them?"

Kieran shifted in his chair. His mind was tightly shielded, but Coryn read his distress in that small movement.

"If you will not command your circle to make the *clingfire*," she went on, begging now, "then let me gather one. Coryn will help me—and Aran, if I ask him—and some of the others. We can do it on our own time, the Tower need not be officially involved—"

How can I? Yet how can I refuse her? Aldones, Lord of Light, show me a way!

"And who will act as your Keeper, binding such a circle together?" Kieran's pale brows pulled together and his voice grew a shade quieter, more deadly.

"More importantly, who in the outside world will believe the Tower had nothing to do with it? You would endanger everyone working on the project—under criminally careless conditions, I might add—and you would put the entire Tower at risk of retaliation. The reason, the *only* reason," he repeated the phrase for emphasis, "for a Tower to make such weapons is at the lawful order of the lord to whom it owes fealty. We do not make policy, nor do we decide the fate of kingdoms."

"You sit up here on your mountain while people suffer and die and you could prevent it!" Liane cried, wiping away a splash of tears. Coryn put out a hand to steady her, but she brushed him off.

"What do you think the world would be like, if we in the Towers allowed ourselves to be drawn into every petty quarrel?" Kieran said. "What if we had supplied High Kinnally with *clingfire* years ago? Oh, yes, your people asked us. As did yours, Coryn. They used the same desperate words you do now. If it is not one good cause, it is another. Then you would have used it on one another with the same fervor you would drop it on this King Damian."

Coryn's heart skipped a beat, as he realized where Kieran's argument was going. Verdanta and High Kinnally, each armed with an inferno, with all the simmering years of hatred and nothing to restrain them. Forest fire would be as nothing compared to the destruction *clingfire* would have brought. Might still bring.

"If you had," Liane went on stubbornly, "then we would not be in this position now! We could have defended ourselves. Ambervale would never have dared—"

"Ah, but what if we had supplied both High Kinnally *and* Verdanta?" Kieran repeated. "As both of you had asked when the feud first began?"

Liane's eyes widened. "No . . . No, we would not—"

"We would both be ashes many times over," Coryn said as gently as he could. "Kieran's right. Listen to him, *breda*. Ambervale and its king must be stopped, yes, but not this way."

"What—" Struggling visibly for control, she turned in his arms. "What else can stand against them? And while High Kinnally falls under this invader, what should I do?"

What I did when Verdanta was taken. Accept. Heal. You helped me then. Let me help you now.

"You are a *leronis,*" Kieran said in a voice so colorless it hardly sounded human. "You must use the discipline you have been taught. Gareth will monitor you to safeguard your health, so that you may return to work as soon as you can."

Coryn took Liane's slender hand in his, drew her toward the door. She came passively, her fire quenched. Outside the door, in the stillness of the corridor, she drew a shuddering breath. He reached for her, to draw her close.

She whirled and slapped him full across one cheek, hard enough to snap his head around. *"That's* for not standing up for me! I thought I could count on you. How could you give up so easily?"

"Kieran was right," Coryn said, his face burning.

"You idiot, you worship the ground he walks on! If he said the sky was green and there was only one moon, you would agree with him! What does he know of family, of honor?"

"He is Keeper at Tramontana. He answers only to his own conscience. Listen to me, Liane. I would give anything to have my father alive again—" *and Kristlin!* "—and Verdanta free. Anything! But Kieran is right. Can you imagine what would have happened if *Ambervale* had been armed with *clingfire?"*

"Tell that to King Damian! If we are not able to defend ourselves, what is there to stop *him* from using those weapons anyway?" she snapped.

"Liane—" He held out his hands.

"I really thought Kieran would listen!" she cried, brushing him aside. "What a fool I was!"

"Fool, no. Just blinded by what you wanted to hear, the false hope of a quick victory."

She spun around and strode away, leaving Coryn standing there. This time, he made no attempt to go after her. Verdanta was gone, his family dead or scattered; then Aran, who had been like a brother to him; now Liane. He had never felt so desolate in his life.

12

Coryn, after several sessions with Gareth monitoring and clearing his *laran* channels, returned to work. The intense concentration allowed him to leave his grief behind for a time. The Tower, with Kieran at its heart, seemed to him as solid as the rock upon which it stood. If it would not move as he, in his anger, wished it to, then neither would it fail him, home and sanctuary in one.

Liane took longer to join the others at communal meals and gatherings by the fireplace, on the lengthening winter nights when one or another might take out a *rryl* and sing a ballad.

As for Aran, Coryn ached every time they passed in the corridor or acknowledged each other with only the most polite words. Though Aran kept his eyes averted, Coryn dreaded the pain he would see there. Surely the other workers, especially Kieran or Bronwyn, felt the coolness between them, but no one commented on it.

What was there to say? What was there to do? If he reached out for his friend, he would only make things worse, intensifying Aran's distress. He drew on the discipline of the Tower and forced his heart to beat more slowly, his breath to come more deeply.

One morning, when the frost lay thick upon the dry curled grasses, more news came to Tramontana Tower. A squadron of armed men halted just outside the gates. They wore the livery of Ambervale, breasts crossed with scarves of the colors of both Verdanta and High Kinnally. Under a white flag of truce, their captain spoke privately with Kieran and the other Keepers.

Coryn, still awake after a night working the relays, sought out Liane. He feared the arrival of the squadron meant High Kinnally had fallen. He did not know what he might offer to comfort her, but he knew he had to try. He found her rushing from Bronwyn's quarters, followed by one of the novices who often ran messages for the Keepers. Her eyes were reddened and swollen, her cheeks pasty. She pushed past him without a word, not even meeting his eyes, and hurried off in the direction of Kieran's chambers. Even though she had shielded her emotions, he caught the edge of barely-contained panic.

Aran was waiting in the central chamber, along with Cathal and a few of the others who were neither asleep nor working the Second Circle.

"Liane's been summoned to the Keepers," Coryn said.

Aran nodded. "It doesn't sound good."

Coryn lowered himself on to a bench beside his friend, his hand a hair's breadth away from Aran's. This was the closest they'd been since that awful night. He struggled to think of the words that would set things right between them.

Deliberately, he laid his hand on Aran's. Under the warm skin with its feathering of fine crisp hairs, he felt clean-edged bone, warm flesh. He half-closed his eyes, letting himself sink deeper into the contact. Aran's mind rose to his with that unmistakable touch, filled with Aran's personality. Coryn saw him as a shaft of sunlight, as a bird dancing on the wind, as a horse running free across moonlight-silvered fields. The images faded, and it was as if Aran spoke to him without words. He knew then why Aran had avoided him these past few weeks. It was not from any offense or injured feelings. Quite the opposite, Aran's love for him ran just as strongly as it had before. In that moment of rapport, their friendship had changed. Aran had *desired* him and, knowing that Coryn could not return that desire, had withdrawn rather than risk their friendship.

"I'm sorry," Coryn said, in a half-whisper.

Aran, turning away and blinking hard, slid his hand out from under Coryn's. "I surprised myself as much as you. I didn't know I felt that way. Maybe I didn't, until that moment. Times like this, they lay us open and raw, running for comfort. And then, once it was done—anything I said would only add to your burden."

"I'm sorry, too," Coryn said. "You caught me by surprise. It isn't— you know I love you. I would trust you with my life. Aran, *bredu,* you didn't offend me. But something inside me—" He felt the muscles of his face tighten, his belly clench. He couldn't go on.

"It's all right," Aran said with a fleeting smile, likea ray of sun break- ing through storm clouds. "Things will get better with time. They always do."

Kieran and the other two Keepers swept down the staircase, along with a handful of senior technicians. One Keeper led the way for the armed Ambervale soldiers, while the other two brought up the rear. Coryn thought that if any of the armed men had stepped even a hair's breadth out of line, he might be blasted as he stood, so grim were the Keepers' expressions. The men seemed to realize this, for their faces were as white and set as stone.

After the soldiers had been escorted outside the gates, Tomas, Keeper of the First Circle, returned to address the group, which had swelled to almost the entire population of the Tower. Gareth stood at the back of the room, still clothed in the thick white wool which he wore while monitoring a working circle.

"We have striven to remain apart from the petty conflicts of the outer world, excepting the lawful commands of those who hold our loyalty," Tomas said. Neither his voice nor his posture gave away anything, so complete was his mastery. "Yet upon occasion, the world intrudes. The home castle of Liane Storn, who has lived and worked as one of us as monitor, is now claimed as fiefdom by King Damian Deslucido. He has sent his men to demand her presence as hostage for proof of her brother's fealty."

A ripple of emotion swept the room. One of the younger women cried out. Aran drew in a sharp breath.

Coryn got to his feet, his hands curled into fists. "You will not give her over? You cannot!"

Tomas turned slowly to lock eyes with Coryn. "Ordinarily, we would not surrender one of our own to any petty lordling who takes it upon himself to issue such commands." Beneath the harmonics of his words rang another message, one everyone in the Tower could clearly hear. *And we have the means to defend ourselves against such rabble.*

Then he drew his breath and Coryn's heart sank. "In this case, the lines of fealty are not clear. This King Damian may indeed have the legal right to make such a demand. We will consider his claims in light of historical precedent and the titles he now possesses. However, Liane herself has consented to go with them."

"What!"

"Why?"

Coryn started to join the protest, but a sudden realization stopped his voice. If Liane stayed, Ambervale might well use the refusal as a reason to retaliate. Even if Tramontana defended itself, it might well be drawn into a larger conflict. This was the only way to remain neutral, if for a short time only.

Tomas held up one hand for silence. The moonstone ring on his middle finger glinted in the light. "For her own reasons, Liane has chosen. Her Keeper has permitted it. There is nothing more to be said. It is a private matter."

Cathal jumped to his feet. "Other men with ambitions won't see it that way! They'll think all they have to do is march up to any Tower they please and make demands!"

The muscles of Coryn's hands ached, and his nails dug crescents into the flesh of his palms.

"Then we must teach them otherwise!" someone else cried.

"For the moment, we will not do any teaching at all," Tomas said. "We will go about our business and let Liane go about hers." With those words, he swept from the room.

Like an arrow loosed from a bowstring, Coryn bolted up the stairs for the women's quarters. Aran followed a pace behind. Liane's door was slightly ajar, revealing her, along with Bronwyn and one of the younger matrix mechanics, a shy girl from the mountainous country near Aldaran, sorting through clothing and folding it into Liane's carved chest.

"Liane!" Coryn cried. "You can't go! You—"

Bronwyn drew herself up to her full height, eyes flashing cold light. Coryn's next words died on his tongue. Liane herself, after a quick expressionless glance which took in first Coryn and then Aran, bent once more to smooth the creases from a delicate linex chemise.

"This is no place for you," Bronwyn said to Coryn, her voice firm but not unkind. She stepped outside the room and closed the door behind her.

"But Liane—"

"If you care for her at all, you will not add to her distress in this manner! Do you think this is easy for her? Do you think she would willingly choose the life of a hostage?"

Coryn shook his head. "She doesn't have to go! Kieran will not surrender her if she refuses, and as her Keeper, he has ultimate authority. She doesn't know what she's doing!"

"She knows *precisely* what she is doing," Bronwyn answered in a voice like the crack of a whip. "And it is not many who would demonstrate her courage or her loyalty. Tomas did not explain the terms of Ambervale's demands, for such are truly not the business of the Tower. But since you are involved as possible heir to Verdanta . . ."

Her eyes flickered to Aran, standing beside Coryn. Coryn shivered, realizing the vulnerability of his own position. With Eddard a prisoner in his own castle and Petro missing, he might well be the next legitimate Lord Leynier. It was a role he had never wanted, scarcely even considered. How long would it be before Deslucido commanded Tramontana to surrender *him?*

Now Coryn drew himself up. If he might be a lord, he could act that way. "Aran is my sworn brother," he used the inflection suggestive of paxman. "Speak before him as before me."

The outer edges of Bronwyn's mouth curled slightly. "Then understand this. Liane is to travel not to Ambervale but to Linn. She may be a prisoner, hostage against her brother's obedience, but she will be treated gently there. Her surrender is the price of her brother continuing to hold High Kinnally as an Ambervale fief. The alternative," she paused briefly, studying him, "is to place High Kinnally under *Verdanta* rule."

Two thoughts burst across Coryn's mind. The first was that King Damian was very sure of his control over Eddard. The second—the threat to the Storns that they submit to their long-held enemy? Once he might have rejoiced, even gloated, at the thought, but his years in the Tower and his friendship with Liane had given him a larger perspective. Now he asked himself what if the situation were reversed, and Verdanta were forced to bow to High Kinnally? It was not to be imagined, not to be borne! So Liane, too, must have felt.

The moment of silence drew on. Bronwyn said in a softer voice, "Do you see why she cannot speak with you? Not even to say farewell?"

"I would have hoped—" Coryn's throat tightened around the words,

choking them. "She and I, all we had together, our work in the circle—
Kieran's dream of putting all that behind us—I thought she loved me."

"She does, as a brother. Which is precisely why the kindest thing is
to leave her with her choice."

Oh, Liane! His heart ached for her.

"And I," Aran spoke up, "may I see her?" Coryn heard the generosity, the compassion behind his words. Aran might not return her love in
kind, but he offered what he could.

Bronwyn's expression betrayed nothing. "Once she has settled things
here, I will ask her. Go now, both of you. Let us do our work."

Aran did see Liane, although he said nothing to Coryn of their conversation. Coryn saw her from a distance, as he watched from one of the
turrets as the Ambervale soldiers escorted her away. He wondered what
might have happened if Tramontana had sent *clingfire* to High Kinnally,
if Liane had not been right all along. Bronwyn said Liane did not blame
him; he wished he could be so generous to himself.

✦

As days melted into weeks, Liane's absence shifted from a raw wound to
one slowly healing. Two pre-adolescent boys from Rockraven, carrot-
haired twins, arrived in a flurry of activity. They were younger than the
usual novices, but because of their twin-bond, their mother, who had had
some Tower experience as a young woman, determined that they needed
early training.

Midwinter Festival came, along with a blizzard that made any sort of
travel impossible. Except for a few rumors along the relays from Neskaya
Tower, nothing more was heard of King Damian or his newly-conquered
lands. Coryn told himself that surely there would be news if something
major—a rebellion or assassination—had happened. Through the long
winter nights, when he was not working, he could not help thinking about
Liane, about Eddard and Tessa, hostages in their own home. He wondered, too, whether Petro and Margarida were even still alive. He felt
sure he would know if they were not, but he could not locate either of
them. Perhaps they had found some way of shielding themselves against
laran search, a wise precaution if Rumail were involved in the occupation.

Work brought blessed relief, and Coryn's skills sharpened even more.
In these days, he found an unexpected confidante in Bronwyn. Of all the
senior workers, she understood the conflicting loyalties of blood and

Tower. She'd never spoken of her own family, or why she remained in a Tower when so many other nobly-born women were called away to marriages after a few years. Rumor had it that she was related to the powerful Hastur clan, that she had used her rank to refuse more than one marriage offer. So it was to Bronwyn that Coryn took the disquieting thoughts which would not go away, no matter how long or deeply he meditated.

Would Ambervale forces soon appear on Tramontana's threshold, demanding his custody to enforce their control over Verdanta?

"I do not want to leave the Tower," he told her as they sat together in her chambers, cradling cups of hot spiced wine while the winds outside the walls wailed like starving banshees. "This is my place. This is the work for which I was born, not ruling some small but charming mountain estate."

"I think you are right," she said slowly. Her mind brushed against his with the sweetness of chiming silvery bells. "We knew when you came to us that you would become a *laranzu* of great power. The Keepers saw how skillfully you handled assembling the screens."

She meant the construction of a sixth-order matrix, which had been a major Tower project all winter. One of the younger women had been careless in calculating her cycles. Under shifting hormone levels, her control had slipped. Coryn had strengthened his own hold on the energon rings, taking over for her and steadying them until Kieran could reconfigure the circle. Months of work had been saved in that single reflexive action. As Kieran had said afterward, Coryn alone could not have saved the screens, but no one else could have done what he did.

"As long as you remain a technician, regarded by the outer world as dispensable, you remain a political threat to King Damian. Should an opening arise, such as your brother's death, you could return to the outside world and claim Verdanta. Or so Damian might think. That he has not sent for you so far and made sure of you, speaks for your brother's good behavior."

Bronwyn paused to stare at the fire before going on in a more pensive tone. "Verdanta is not a land he intends to occupy, I think. To hold, but not to rule. A stepping stone, but to what?" She shook herself, a little gesture like a shiver. "Ah, that hardly matters now. Idle speculation is a habit I've never been able to break. But for you, young Coryn, if you would seal yourself to a Tower, and I think this is indeed where you belong, you must convince even the most ambitious king that you have resigned the outer world."

Coryn shrugged. The only workers who were untouchable by outer concerns were the Keepers themselves. He had never hoped to be trained as one. Tramontana already had three Keepers and could not support a fourth. Although Kieran was old, he was still in full command of his powers. Now Coryn said as much to Bronwyn.

"I am glad to hear you thinking in that way," she said, smiling. "Kieran and I have had this very discussion. You are right, there is no place for another under-Keeper here. However, such is not the case everywhere. We telepaths are not so strong or so many that we can afford to waste even one potential Keeper. And the hard truth is that you would be safer almost anywhere else. You must leave Tramontana."

Leave Tramontana? Coryn's first rush of refusal quickly gave way to logic. Bronwyn was right. As long as he remained here, he and everyone in the Tower were at risk from Deslucido. It was only a matter of time before a demand would be made to turn him over. Kieran might hold the Tower neutral, but as time went by, the situation might change. Tomas' search of the ancient records had turned up positive proof that once Ambervale, as part of a greater Aldaran alliance, had some legitimate claim of sovereignty over the Tower. *If Kieran died—* No, that was not to be thought of!

"I will be sorry to leave you," he said, meeting Brownwyn's warm gaze.

"As we will you, but not so sorry as to lose you under less happy circumstances."

"Yes, that's true enough. If there is a place for me, I will go."

"Then since you are willing, we have already received a request for someone to train as under-Keeper. From Neskaya Tower. They have just lost the best of their candidates in a rock fall."

Neskaya? Coryn blinked, astonished. His first thought was of Rumail, but Rumail was no longer there. Neskaya had dismissed him. And Neskaya was bound historically to Ridenow and now, after Allart Hastur's peace, to Hastur, and so would be free from the Deslucido wars. He would never be asked to choose sides in any dispute that involved Verdanta . . . or High Kinnally. With a sense of relief, he said he would go.

Brownwyn nodded in satisfaction and sipped her wine. After a brief, awkward pause, the conversation resumed but on a lighter tone, of the

sort of everyday things two companionable friends might find to talk
about on a long wintry evening.

✦

The morning of Coryn's leavetaking from Tramontana, although officially
in the spring, started off as blustery as any winter day. Gareth, sitting at
breakfast with Coryn and Aran, joked that the mountains themselves
wanted to keep him behind the Tower's walls.

Coryn rose from the table, Aran a shadow at his side, determined to
be on the road before noon. He had known the rough, unpredictable
weather of the Hellers all his life. Should a little rain now keep him from
his new life? It couldn't be worse than the *laran*-fueled storms which had
overtaken him and Rafe on his way here. Not even a trained matrix
worker was immune to such elemental forces, but his starstone would
give him warning.

Aran helped him check his horse's gear and baggage, then stood
stroking the black mare's nose. She swished her tail, eager to be off.
Coryn, standing on the other side of the horse, closed his eyes and
touched his forehead against the hard-muscled neck. For a moment he
thought of leaving the mare with Aran, if only for the joy the two of them
had shared. But the mare was his last gift from his father, and he couldn't
relinquish her.

"You'll need her where you're going," Aran said quietly.

The mare took a step forward, so that the two men faced each other
over the polished leather saddle. "Aran—" Coryn began. But now, looking directly into his friend's dark eyes, he realized that he truly did not
need to say anything. It was only his physical presence he was taking away.
The two of them had spoken mind to mind, had shared in a different sort
of passion, the joy of Aran's *donas*. Coryn's love for his friend would
remain, even as Aran's would go with him. He found himself smiling as
he slipped his foot into the stirrup and swung on top of the mare's back.

"Ride her well!" Aran called as Coryn clattered down the rocky trail.
Or perhaps the words, distorted by the noise of shod hoof on stone, were
Fare-thee-well.

BOOK 2

13

Taniquel Hastur-Acosta, *comynara* and niece to King Rafael Hastur, second of that name, stood at the balcony of the tallest tower and scanned the horizon to the northwest. It had been raining steadily for a tenday, the soft spring drizzle that brought such intense green to the rich Acosta farmland. The river, frothy gray, wound through the hills, past orchards of flowering plum and cherry trees, and through the vineyards which produced the heady dark wine for which Acosta was famous.

Now she stole a moment from her vigil to close her eyes and lift her bare face to the mist. From the time she was a little girl, fostered here at Acosta along with the boy who would later become her husband, she always found ways to escape the supervision of her nurse or tutors and go running in the rain. Jumping over puddles, or rather *in* them, had been her chief delight. "Wicked child," her nurse had scolded. "Water maiden," her foster father called her.

Sometimes she thought that although she was fond enough of Padrik, he who was now Lord Acosta, she would never have married him if it meant leaving this place.

Sighing, she raked her fingers through her thick, crimpy hair, pulling more blue-black strands free from the butterfly clasp of costly copper filigree.

I look like a hoyden, not a Queen.

Nor, she thought wryly, was she behaving like one. Instead of sitting demurely over her embroidery or chatting with her ladies about the latest handfasting or how many honey cakes her junior lady-in-waiting, Piadora, who was three months along with child, ought to eat, she was up here, standing guard as if she were a trained soldier and not a lady.

This day she could not force herself to sit still. Something had been building for the last few days, an invisible pressure behind her eyes like a headache about to break. She had done her best to ignore it, to argue herself into dismissing it as mere womanish vapors, to dissipate her restlessness in games of chance or dancing lessons, activities deemed proper for a lady of her rank. The one thing she had not done was to speak of it to Padrik. An odd emotion held her back, one she reluctantly identified as shame.

Shame that she had not the *laran* of a Hastur, or at least not enough to be worth training, or so the *leronis* from Thendara Tower had said when she examined Taniquel on her fourteenth birthday. Any talent she might have would have shown itself by then. She might have a little empathy, the Keeper thought, enough to make her a sympathetic listener for her husband. There would be no place in the Tower for her, not that she'd ever wanted to be shut up in one. But . . .

But it was *not* empathy, this pressure in the center of her skull. That much she knew. She began pacing. The nearest guard tried hard to look impassive, all the while watching her with his mouth half open.

What was it?

She muttered beneath her breath to keep from shrieking out the words. That sort of outburst certainly would alarm the guard. Everyone from the castle midwife to the household *leronis* to Padrik himself would come rushing to cosset her, put her to bed, dose her with herb-laced goatsmilk and speculate endlessly over whether she were at last breeding.

Maybe that's it. Maybe this is normal for pregnancy.

She hadn't told Padrik yet, for reasons that she herself did not completely understand. Her woman's cycles had not yet ceased, yet she knew the night, the very hour, she had conceived. It had been the night this rain had begun, a mere tenday ago. She knew, too, that she carried a boy, the son and heir Padrik longed for. Ah well, there would be time enough for rejoicing. And for endless chatter over whether honey cakes or plum syrup gave a mother more milk. With her full breasts, she didn't think she needed any help in that matter.

Lost in thought, Taniquel slowed her steps. A smile rose to her face, softening the tension between her brows. She turned back toward the balcony, facing away from the guard so that he would not see her hand low down on her belly. Beneath the finely woven amber wool, she touched muscle, flat and strong from hours on horseback.

How pleased Padrik would be. She would tell him when he returned tonight. He had taken the day to inspect the border defenses and renew his ties with the outlying vassal lords.

A noise crackled across the sky above the clouds, high and sharp-pitched. For an instant, Taniquel wasn't sure if she'd heard thunder or felt it through her bones. She threw her head back just in time to see an elongated teardrop of some glassy material plummet through the layers of rain-swollen gray.

Taniquel had seen aircars as a child, at Hastur Castle. Her clan was one of those few rich enough to afford the fabulous devices and with telepaths strong enough to pilot them. The craft were powered by *laran* stored in batteries. They required huge expenditures of energy to charge them and highly skilled matrix technicians to guide their flight. As this one dipped, she got a better sense of its size and silhouette. It looked to be one of the smaller models, seating perhaps two passengers. And it was headed straight for the front of the castle, still descending sharply.

The gates!

Without thinking, Taniquel hitched up her skirts and sprinted for the nearest alarm bell. She caught a glimpse of the guard's face, confused and open-mouthed at the sight of her stocking-clad legs.

"Attack!" Screaming, she raced past him, not daring to slow an instant.

She skidded right into the bell, wrapped her hands around the rope, and yanked as hard as she could. After the first impact, the clapper swung of its own weight, faster and louder with each stroke. Her ears stung with the clamor as she pulled again and again. Behind her, men scrambled for the stairs.

Light flashed from the main gates below. Even through the vibration of the bell, Taniquel felt the stones beneath her feet shudder. Though the clapper continued in its momentum, she paused to look down.

Yellow tongues of fire laced the thick gray smoke, obscuring the entrance to the castle. A few soldiers and house servants darted here and there. One horseman was down, his mount knocked from its feet. It struggled up, flailing wildly and rolling over his lower body. One of the servants, a woman, dropped the yoked buckets she had been carrying and rushed to him.

The aircar turned to swoop down again, like a dragon from an ancient ballad returning to its prey. Its outer surface, like a curved mirror, reflected sky and stone, but for an instant, Taniquel caught sight of a figure in the cockpit, bent intently over its mechanism. As the aircar passed, a rain of arrows burst from the castle wall, but if any hit the mark, there was no sign. The smooth side of the aircar parted and out fell a handful of small glittering spheres, each no bigger than a child's ball. They scattered as they fell, as if guided by an unseen hand. Where each one touched earth or castle wall, it exploded in a ball of light and clap of sound.

Clingfire? *By all the gods, did Damian Deslucido, who had menaced their northwest borders for the last two or three years, did he have* clingfire *at his command?*

Taniquel's blood ran like ice. Her body shook and her fingers gripped the unyielding stone of the parapet, tearing nail and skin, but she took no notice. Instead, she fixed her eyes on the conflagration below, struggling to make sense of what she saw. Each detail engraved itself upon her memory.

The second round of bombs spread out in a line, rather than being concentrated at the gates. The first attack must have involved a number of them, a cluster, judging by the amount of smoke.

The aircar circled once more before disappearing back into the clouds. On the muddy ground, the woman was still kneeling over the fallen horseman, but another of the servants and one of the soldiers had taken up her buckets, passing them in a line between the outside well and the wall.

Taniquel saw no more flames. The stone of the walls, although smoke-blackened, had taken no further damage. The bronze-strapped wood, damp from the constant drizzle, would be slow to burn. That they caught fire at all suggested some kind of chemicals in the bombs.

But not *clingfire*, Taniquel thought with an odd sense of relief. Nothing, certainly not ordinary water, would have extinguished those unnatural flames.

Horns sounded to the north. Along the river road galloped a body of mounted soldiers. Taniquel could not make out the exact pattern of their banners, only the black and white of Ambervale. *Deslucido.*

Taniquel judged the size of the attacking force moving so quickly along the rain-soaked road that they must be only lightly armed. She choked back a laugh. Did Deslucido think to take Acosta with so small a force? The castle, even with its lord and his personal guard absent, commanded half again that many. The horsemen would be fighting against the upward sloping hillside as well as the castle defenders. To reach the gates, they would have to pass along a narrow strip of land like a funnel, where Padrik had lately carved deep stake-lined ditches on either side.

The gates below her swung open, and armed Acosta soldiers moved out in ranks. The captains had clearly decided to meet the attackers head on, rather than sit inside at siege and be bombed again.

Perhaps it was just the perspective or some trick in Taniquel's mind that made time elastic, but the approaching cavalry seemed to slow, first to a canter and then a trot. She held her breath, waiting for something she could not name. The Deslucido forces neared the bottom of the final hill. Shouted commands and battle cries ringing with confidence reached her from below. A thrill of victory sang through her.

Deslucido thought to break our will to fight with his firebombs. He didn't count on Evanda's blessed rain.

Then why did the pressure behind her eyes continue to build and build, blurring her vision, sending her stomach into a churning mass?

A second mounted force burst over the horizon. They had been traveling for some time from the way they were strung out along the road. One rider outstripped the others. Even at this distance, Taniquel recognized the huge white horse.

Padrik! She wondered at how quickly he had come, on the very heels of the attack. Perhaps the Deslucido cavalry had been spotted along the road, and some messenger sent to him. *Now Deslucido cannot turn back,* she thought in rising triumph, *and we will crush him at the gates.*

"Your Majesty!" Piadora, the young lady-in-waiting, stumbled down the parapet. Although the day was mild, she clutched a shawl around her head and shoulders, as if the sweet misty rain might somehow injure her. There had been rumors that the child she carried was Padrik's. Should it be a boy, he could be raised as foster brother and paxman to Taniquel's son. She must speak to Padrik about it.

"Blessed Cassilda!" Piadora gasped, "you are safe!"

Taniquel suppressed her annoyance. Of course she was safe. Here in her own castle, with her husband riding to the rescue—how else should she be? But the girl had been weeping and even now wiped damp cheeks with one hand. "You should be indoors with the other women."

"But—but you must not be unattended!" Piadora was practically beside herself in agitation. "And with the castle under siege! The fire! The explosions! I swear, the very stones beneath my feet shook! Oh, my lady! What is to become of us? What will those monsters do next? Some say they are from Shainsa, to take us all back in chains! And still others say they are Aldaran and need human sacrifices for their evil rites!" At this, she threw herself at Taniquel's feet to gather up the hem of her robe. "Oh, save me! Save me!"

Taniquel wanted nothing so much as to scream some sense into the child, but she was a Queen and *comynara*. Gently but firmly, she lifted the girl to her feet and pulled her toward the parapet, where she could watch the scene being played out below.

"Look, *chiya,* we are in no real danger. See how few the attackers are, and see our lord riding to defend us. In only a few minutes, he will catch them. How slow they are, how stupid to not know their error. They approach as if they know nothing of who rides on their heels. Our soldiers will hold them at the gates, where they cannot escape."

"The gates still stand?" Piadora leaned far out, gasping in excitement. She would have been within when the first bombs hit and might well have thought them destroyed.

"Yes, and we will not open them until victory is ours. We *must* not open them." Taniquel frowned at her own words. What an odd thing to say.

We must not open the gates. Must not open the gates.

The words pounded through her brain. Her temples throbbed with each syllable. She covered her eyes with one hand and half-fell against the stone balcony.

"My lady!" There was real alarm in the girl's voice now. "What ails you?"

"I—don't—"

Cries rang out from below, the shouting of a hundred men's voices and more. Some sounded near, below on the threshold, others approaching . . .

Must not open the gates . . .

More horns echoed, closer now. Taniquel jerked her hand from her eyes, blinking in the sudden pain which lanced through her skull. The Ambervale men were within a spear's throw of the gates, the defenders waiting for the signal to join the battle. Padrik and his men raced along the road, only minutes away. Behind them, from every copse, every hedgerow and sheltered orchard alley, Ambervale soldiers came streaming. For an instant, Taniquel saw them as giant insects, swarming from their underground burrows. Then she saw how they had lain hidden, waiting for Padrik and his men to pass.

It was he who would be crushed at the gates, not the first Ambervale force. The cavalry attack had been merely bait to the trap.

As Taniquel watched, horrified, Padrik kept coming. He was as yet unaware that he was racing into an ambush. If only he could win through to the gates, she thought, his men could hold the castle through a siege—

Must not open the gates . . .

—but the castle soldiers would not know that, not with the Ambervale horsemen ready to breach the stronghold. They could not see the immense army descending upon them like a nest of scorpion-ants.

There were so many of them! The clouds broke suddenly over the sloping land and their arms glittered.

Taniquel shook. She must do something, warn Padrik! She glanced at the bell, knowing it would be useless. She could ring and ring until Zandru's coldest hell melted. No one at a lower battlement could see what she saw. Not yet. Not until it was too late.

Do something!

Grab a spear and storm out through the gates? The very idea of touching the massive crossbar sent unnatural terror scintillating along her nerves. Whatever happened, however desperate the situation, she *must not open the gates!*

Then, Taniquel thought furiously, she must fight from within them! The next instant, she had gathered up her skirts once more and was running for the armory. She could not wield a sword with any skill, for although she had played with wooden blades with her Hastur cousins as a child, she had been forbidden to touch one since becoming a woman.

At the entrance to the armory, the smells of oiled steel and leather mingled with the acrid tang of fear-sweat. The gimp-legged sergeant who served as castle armorer was setting out fresh quivers of arrows along the stained trestle boards and lining up spears, shouting orders to a dozen pages at once. His face turned pale and scandalized when he saw her. "My lady! Get within!"

Ignoring him, Taniquel went to the wall racks and took down a bow and wrist guard. The leather wristlet was new and stiff. She held it out to him and extended her left arm.

"*My lady*— Your Majesty! You must not endanger yourself! The King—"

"Oh, dear. Oh, my lady! What are you doing?" Piadora skittered to a halt at the armory door.

"Strap it on me or I will do it myself!" Ignoring the whimpering girl, Taniquel held up the bow, demanding, "Is this the best you have?" and proceeded to rattle off a string of orders.

A moment later, with the wrist guard tightly in place, two arrow cases tucked under her right arm and the bow in her left hand, Taniquel raced back up the battlement stairs. She'd lost the simpering child somewhere, maybe to the nearest water closet. From here, where a small contingent of archers waited, the bulk of the Ambervale forces were only now coming into view. Thank Aldones, the captain of the archers recognized her.

"We must destroy the Ambervale cavalry," she said, knowing this meant targeting the horses as well and hating the idea. The captain nodded.

Taniquel chose her place with the other archers, calculating where her first arrow might create the most confusion. The flag bearer rode a dusty chestnut with a bobbed tail. As she took aim, the black-and-white diamond pattern of the Ambervale pennants shook loose in the breeze. She loosed her arrow and bent to notch another, not pausing to determine whether she'd hit her target. She shot again and again, rapidly emptying her first quiver.

Screams marked where arrows found their targets. The ground below churned with bodies, men and horses, spears, swords, and shields. Now Taniquel held her hand, lest she strike one of her own men. The forces were so entangled, interweaving so quickly that not even the most skillful archer could have picked out only the enemy.

With a blaring of horns, Padrik burst upon the scene. His men caught the Ambervale cavalry from behind. But Deslucido's forces did not scatter. They must be brave men, seasoned men, to turn and fight instead of scattering.

Blessed Evanda, if only we've weakened them enough so that Padrik may win through to the gates before it's too late!

"We must let him in as soon as may be!" She saw immediately in the captain's eyes the same mindless terror in her own.

We must not open the gates!

Her head pounded as if she'd been kicked by one of the warhorses down below. Must not—*why?*

Because it is not real—it is a spell! Because some laranzu *down there wants Padrik trapped outside his own castle!* Caught and held until the army drawing even closer could do its work.

"Ah!" Taniquel cried out as if she'd been pierced by one of her own arrows. She threw down her useless bow and ran for the stairs.

She took them two at a time, reckless. So many precious minutes had already been wasted in the thrall of that *laran* command. If she'd gone at a saner pace, she might have turned back, but as it was, she practically fell over her own feet and kept going. When she thought of *opening the gates*, raw fear surged through her. An iron grip tightened around her heart.

No, I will not open them. I will only see if they are all right. Yes, that was it—to run her hands over their solid bulk, to make sure they would hold, to test the weight and strength of the crossbar. . . .

Taniquel kept saying the words to herself, even as she curled her fingers around the thick, use-polished wood. For an awful instant, the crossbar would not budge and she feared she had not the strength to move it. A moment's doubt and she would be lost. But Padrik's *coridom* had kept the seasoned wood smoothly oiled. It slid the length of her hand, then her arm.

"Your Majesty! What are you doing?" the armorer bellowed at her.

She must not take her eyes from the task, watching the massive bar slide along its tracks. Not opening the gates, no never that, but closing them tight. She must not think of anything except throwing her weight into it, keeping the castle safe. . . .

Rough hands grabbed her, jerked her back. Her concentration shattered. Panic shrilled along her nerves, the sick sharp-tasting fear of the spell. With horrified eyes, she saw the bar now clear away from the center, the gates parting under the weight of the crushing bodies outside. The old armorer shoved past her, placed both hands against the opening gates. For an instant, they held. Then something heavy, a horse's body perhaps, thudded against them and they sprang apart. Scorch marks streaked the outer surfaces where the firebombs had struck.

Released from the narrow spit of land where they had been penned, men and horses spilled into the courtyard. The clash of steel and the screams of the wounded rose above the shouting. Within moments, the courtyard became a churning, muddy bedlam. Foot soldiers mixed with mounted. Ambervale black and white dotted the colors of Acosta. Everyone seemed to be struggling in a different direction.

The armorer, who had leaped aside as the gates swung open, pulled Taniquel toward the stronghold steps. Heart pounding, she searched the chaos below. Just outside the gates, she caught a glimpse of Padrik's immense white horse. She saw then that he was still fighting to win past the first Ambervale rally, was having to push through not only his enemies but his own men, who were still gallantly trying to hold the gates.

"My lady!" The armorer screamed above the din. "You must get within!"

Reluctantly, she saw the sense in his words. She could do nothing here, not even if she were to put on armor and take up a sword, the way she heard some lawless women did. Unable to take her eyes from the battle before her, she allowed herself to be drawn to the open door and into the arms of her waiting women. Their voices fluttered about her like the cooing of anxious doves. The darkness of the castle entrance surrounded her.

Her last sight as the door swung shut was of Padrik's huge white horse rearing above the heads of the fighting men, the red blotch behind its shoulder where a spear struck. She heard the animal's scream, cut off suddenly, and then . . . so slowly she thought her heart would break . . . horse and rider stretched upwards toward the sky and toppled. The battle surged over them just as the doors blocked her sight.

14

For a long minute, Taniquel could not breathe. Her heart froze within her body. The close darkness of the entrance smothered all her senses. As if a veil lifted from her eyes, the moment of shock passed. She lifted her chin. She was *comynara* of the blood of Hastur and Cassilda, as well as Queen of Acosta. She had no time for sentiment or weakness.

She swept through the inner gates, where the household guards stood at attention, and into the central hall. The three senior counselors—once her husband's and now hers—waited, faces grim. None of them had put on their formal robes of office, for they were not men who ordinarily prized the appearance of rank. The eldest had helped tutor her along with Padrik. In the back of her mind, she could almost hear his voice painting the dull facts of history and protocol in vivid colors. Gavriel was his name, *nedestro* son of a minor branch of Elhalyn, come here as a youth in the days of Padrik's father to make his way in the world.

"The gates are breached and my lord fallen in battle," she told the counselors. With an iron will she had not known was hers, she kept her voice steady. "We must prepare to receive the invader."

Gavriel nodded imperceptibly. The slight movement steadied her beyond any words.

"Let us prepare quickly." She motioned to the castle *coridom* stand-ing with his cadre of servants. He stepped forward and bowed to her.

"There will be wounded to attend to," she said. "See that a place is prepared for them. Summon the chief surgeon and have anyone with healing skill made ready. We will need hot water, bandages, salves, and beds."

As he bowed again and turned to give instructions to his people, Taniquel studied the hall. Tapestries covered the stone walls, some of them faded, already ancient when she came here as a child. A few shone with brighter colors, including the scene of Cassilda and Camilla which she and her ladies had finished only last Midwinter. The great carved throne gleamed with polish, although the cushions were a bit threadbare. Not a spot of dust marred the room, for the *coridom* and his housekeep-ers were nothing but efficient. Watery gray light sifted through the high slit windows to blend with the soft yellow of the wall sconces. The im-mense fireplace, stones in shades of gray pieced together in an exquisite mosaic depicting the Acosta eagle, stood dark and cold, for winter had passed and Padrik was not one to waste fuel on ostentation.

Rapidly, Taniquel gave orders for every candle and torch to be lit. She passed over the fireplace, for there would not be time for a proper blaze. "You and you and you—" she pointed to the three ladies who seemed to still have their wits about them. "Come with me." They scram-bled after her as she strode off toward her chambers. Piadora, the preg-nant girl, waited there, face blotched with tears. She opened her mouth but closed it again when she saw Taniquel's expression.

In the dressing chamber, Taniquel went to the huge wardrobe, carved in an ornate style of flowers and swans. She jerked open the doors. The profusion of colors and textures assaulted her senses—the gown of pea-cock silk dripping with silver-edged lace, long tunics stiff with gold-and-purple embroidery or of soft wool the color of the finest Acosta wines, the cloak trimmed with snow-leopard fur, and boxes of headdresses, fans, gloves and slippers. The mingled smells of cedar incense and rosemary filled her head. She pointed to the gold brocade gown.

"That one."

"My lady?" squeaked Verella Castamir, a sweet young willow of a girl from the Venza Hills.

Taniquel's temper came perilously close to the breaking point. What did these idiots think, that she would meet Deslucido—or her victorious husband, if by some miracle he had survived, though by the pangs which split her heart, she had no hope there—with her hair every which way, wearing an old, mud-stained dress?

"Quickly!"

Given something familiar to do, a routine they knew as intimately as the insides of their own boudoirs, the ladies sprang into action. Verella unlaced and eased the amber-colored dress over Taniquel's head, Rosalys unstrapped the wrist guard and wiped away the mud with rose-scented water, while Betteny, the third, readied the laced, boned linex undergown and silken hose. By the time the brocade was settled into place, Piadora had joined in, helping to hook the rows of tiny yellow-diamond buttons. The gown's neckline was higher than was currently fashionable, but it hugged her breasts and hips, flaring out from a waistline which came to a low point in front to give the illusion of greater length of torso. Delicate spider-silk lace touched with gold threads hung from the wide sleeves.

"Colors," Taniquel said, and a moment later, wore two tartan sashes, Acosta and Hastur. The gold of the gown and its unadorned bodice set them off perfectly.

Verella and Betteny stood ready with powder and paint, brushes and combs, crystal bottles of scented oils, matching jeweled hair netting and a necklace of precious copper filigree.

Just as Rosalys held out the velvet-lined box of rings, there came a tap on the door. At Taniquel's command, a young Acosta officer entered. Bright blood soaked the cloth over his right shoulder.

Taniquel brushed aside the box of rings. She had run out of time.

"M–m— Your M–m—" He threw himself to his knees before him, head bowed. His shoulders trembled with weeping.

He's barely a child, she thought, although she was but a few years older. She knew, with deadly certainty, what he was struggling to say. With that fragmentary *laran* which had been deemed not worth training, she knew.

"I saw him fall," she said. Would she be repeating those words all day?

Oh, Padrik!

"He—he is slain, lady. He is—" Another spasm shook the boy's frame. With a visible effort, he gathered himself and looked up at her. Mud and tears streaked his beardless face

"You have come from Captain Branciforte? Then return to him with this command. He is to offer a truce to the Deslucido forces in order to negotiate the terms of surrender. Let the fighting cease, let there be no more bloodshed. I will receive their representatives in the throne room."

The boy scrambled to his feet, bowed deeply, and departed.

"Attend me." In an instant, Taniquel assessed her ladies, holding on to one another, eyes wide, visibly shaking. They had been raised to nothing more challenging than a complicated embroidery stitch or how to decline a second dance with a suitor they found unappealing. If they turned into rabbit-horns in the face of battle, that was hardly their fault.

Taniquel schooled her voice to gentleness. "And whatever happens, remember that you are nobly-born and serve a Queen."

✦

Taniquel entered the throne room through the side door which Padrik had always favored. With a courtly word of welcome, Gavriel offered his arm and escorted her up the dais steps.

The *coridom* had done his work well. The hall blazed to rival the sun on Midsummer Day. Gold and velvet glowed like gemstones, and even the age-faded tapestries shone. A few courtiers, ladies and men too old to fight, stood talking in whispers. As one, they bowed to her, all except the lady sitting on the bench against the far wall, comforting a sobbing page. The two steel-gray wolfhounds that had been Padrik's favorites paced and circled the base of the throne. The bitch growled as Taniquel approached, but the dog ran to her and licked her hand.

Taniquel passed by the smaller chair which had been hers and lowered herself on the throne, for a moment grateful that Padrik scorned the softness of pillows. She needed its unyielding support.

"Stay by me," she said to Gavriel, and he took up his usual post behind Padrik's chair.

More and more of the castle household streamed into the room, each one bowing silently to her, although few approached the throne. Many, she saw, had never appeared in formal court before, had probably known this room only as a place to be polished or dusted. Some bore children in their arms, one a nursing baby.

Gavriel approached with the scepter which had been so rarely used. "The wounded are being tended," he said, and detailed the arrangements.

"Tell the *coridom* he has done well," she told him, with a gesture encompassing the brilliance of the room and the presence of the community.

He bowed again. "Is there anything else we might do for Your Majesty?"

"No, there is nothing to be done. Our fate is in the hands of the gods. Take your place."

Oh, Padrik! came a silent wail at the back of her mind. *You will never know about your son!* She smothered the words into silence, set her jaw, and lifted her chin. Her free hand she kept on the arm of the chair. She would give away nothing, no trace of agitation or grief, before the invader.

She had not long to wait before the clatter of boots and the jingle of spurs and harness sounded in the corridor outside. Adrenaline tinged the air. Men in Deslucido colors, swords drawn, swept into the room. Courtiers cringed before them. A few cried out, while others glanced wild-eyed toward the throne. Though her heart yammered against her ribs, Taniquel sat without moving. As long as she held firm, as long as she herself did not break, neither would her people.

I am comynara *and Hastur. I carry the Acosta heir.* The thought brought desperation as well as strength.

She recognized the Ambervale officers by their dress and carriage, the arrogant way they took up positions to the side of the dais without so much as a nod in her direction. Opposite them stood a figure in a long gray robe, hood shadowing the face.

Laranzu! She knew that she looked now at the source of the compulsion to keep the gates closed. A feeling akin to dread crept over her.

Horns sounded from outside, a brassy five-note challenge which set the stones ringing. The mass of armed men parted. Two men strode down the center of the room, followed closely by an older, grizzled man in a general's uniform. The first man moved with unbridled confidence and ease. The armor beneath his black-and-white cloak was modeled with exquisite simplicity and shone with the patina of much polishing. Not until he had approached did she see the lines of his face, for his movements gave no hint of his age. He might have been sixteen or sixty. This must be Deslucido himself, Taniquel realized with a quickly suppressed move of surprise, come to do his own negotiating instead of leaving it to a lieutenant. He must be very sure of himself.

Her gaze flickered to the younger man, carefully positioned to the side and a half-step behind him. Rarely had she seen a man of such surpassing beauty. Eyes blue as chips of summer sky regarded her levelly, measuring her in a way that sent prickles up the back of her neck. Golden hair glittered as if the room had been created specifically to enhance his brilliance. In her experience, such looks often betokened arrogance and self-centeredness. Although she saw no trace of either in the young man's bearing, she disliked him immediately.

Deslucido took a stance a few feet away and gave a short bow, as a gentleman might accord a lady of lower rank. "There is no need to rise, *vai domna,* as you bid us welcome."

"I have no intention of quitting my seat," she replied stiffly, "and you are hardly *well come* to Acosta." Brave words, she told herself. What did she hope to gain by a pitiful delay? Yet . . . there must be something he wanted, or he would have dragged her from the throne and either cut off her head or thrown her into the apple cellars, which passed at Acosta Castle for a dungeon.

A smile flashed across Deslucido's features as he caught her play of words. Then his mouth hardened. "Your lord husband lies dead, your forces disarmed, your castle occupied by my men. Even if you had some means to resist, you could not rule this land by yourself, a mere woman. Your only option is a graceful surrender."

Taniquel swallowed a barbed retort. The fingers of her free hand dug into the carved arm rest, but she permitted herself no other sign. "What are your conditions, then?"

"My lady, gracious Queen," this time he bowed in earnest, "I have no desire to molest you or your people. Indeed, it is my wish that all within these walls, all within the bounds of Acosta, live in peace and fellowship. I understand this may be difficult for you to accept, with this rabble," a jerk of his chin indicating his own men, the quirk of a smile inviting her to share his joke, "occupying your home. Yet in time, you will come to see that no more harm was done than was absolutely necessary and that the greater good, a secure and lasting peace, merited this small sacrifice."

A secure and lasting peace? Sweet gods, what is the man talking about? Is he mad?

"This is what I intend, that your people will continue to live as they have always done, by their own customs, owing allegiance only to Acosta, but an Acosta now bound by unbreakable ties of alliance to my greater kingdoms of Ambervale and Linn. You yourself shall live here, in the manner to which you are accustomed, attended by your own servants. You may bury your husband with all the rites and honor due him, just as if he had won. Because, in the far larger sense, Acosta has already won."

These last words rang through the hall, met with stares of confusion and surprise.

"What conditions do you demand in return, *vai dom*?" Taniquel repeated with as much politeness as she could summon. "What tribute? Are you saying you have no plan to rule Acosta yourself?"

A smile lightened the seamed features, as brilliant as the sun after a storm. "*I* have no such plan." He paused as a second ripple of astonishment swept the room. Cries and whispered comments buzzed like a dozen honey swarms. Taniquel's heart gave a little jerk despite her suspicions. As quickly, the outcry died down. Every ear turned to what would come next.

"It is my son Belisar who shall be King of Acosta, with you as his Queen."

As if at a distance, she heard the few scattered cheers which went up. Deslucido was offering her an honorable alternative to execution or exile.

No altruistic motives lay behind this proposal, for the situation would be greatly to Deslucido's advantage. As Belisar's bride, her position as Queen and her rank as a Hastur daughter would grant his reign legal and moral legitimacy. The chances of a revolt, even a futile one, would be reduced, for who could claim a loyal rebellion against their true Queen?

You may have conquered Acosta by magic and by trickery, but you have not conquered me! I would as soon slit my own throat right here than give you and your spawn any true right to the throne.

Chill sluiced over her skin as if she'd been doused with a bucket of half-frozen water. The figure in the hooded gray cloak—the *laranzu*—had sensed her reaction and focused on her as if she were a fatted deer. He thrust against her mind, a spear point of ice.

"Oh, yes," the *leronis* who had examined her as a skinny, adolescent girl, had said, "you carry the heritage of powerful *laran*. But your gifts are of no real use to anyone but yourself. You have only a little empathy, which should make you a sympathetic wife and mother, and strong barriers. That is why we bothered to test you, to see if anything lay beyond them."

Strong barriers. For the first time, she prayed the *leronis* had been right.

Get out! Get out! she screamed silently. The next instant, the pressure withdrew, to be replaced by brooding awareness. Sweet Evanda, she would have to guard her very thoughts as well as her actions!

Taniquel realized with a blink that the silence had drawn on overlong, that the entire assembly waited for her reply.

"You must—" she began, then realized she was hardly in a position to demand anything of this smiling conqueror. But some stubborn core would not ask, would not *beg* anything of him. "We will retire now—" She meant to continue, *to consider these terms,* but he cut her off.

"Excellent!" He turned the word into a jubilant shout.

Just as Gavriel stepped forward to assist her in rising, for the seat of the throne was deep and the brocade skirts stiff and full, Deslucido bounded up the step of the dias and offered his own arm. His timing was so perfect that she had no choice but to take it or sprawl unceremoniously back on to the throne.

"I give you into the care of your lovely ladies," Deslucido said with an engaging grin that brought forth blushes and downcast eyes, "so that you need not trouble yourself further with the affairs of state."

Without pausing for her acknowledgment, he settled into the empty throne and gestured to Gavriel, "Attend me, counselor."

Taniquel's muscles went rigid and her face felt as if she had stuck her head into the oven, as she had one time on a dare from Padrik when they were both children.

Gavriel would not look at her; he had no power to help her. Somehow, she found herself at the private side door, her body moving like a wooden puppet. As the door closed behind her, she heard Deslucido's voice ringing out in golden tones, telling her people of the glories that awaited them under his son's reign.

15

Taniquel lowered herself onto the ornately padded stool where she had sat just a short time ago, having her hair looped and plaited, her face touched with paint.

She shivered, although the room was not cold. *Shock,* she thought, *shock and grief.*

Her ladies fluttered around her like billowy summer wind-roses adrift on an icy stream. Their perfumes caught in her throat. She could not think with all this noise and fuss—and she must, she must!

She must give the ladies something else to do. She roused herself to issue commands—to help her from the brocade gown which now seemed more a cage than armor, and into an old skirt and tunic of undyed fawn-colored *chervine* wool, to comb out her hair and plait it simply, to fetch hot *jaco* and lady-pies, to light a small fire.

A short time later, she was able to draw a free breath. Her old, comfortable clothes, her house boots worn to buttery softness, the low tapestried stool which had been Padrik's mother's, and a cup of steaming *jaco* cradled between her icy fingers all helped steady her nerves. She sipped and gazed into the lightly flickering fire, no longer trembling. Here in her own quarters, she no longer sensed she was being watched by the hooded *laranzu.* For the moment, she was safe. But she must go carefully, for every action would be watched.

Verella, noticing Taniquel's mood, offered to play the *rryl.* She sang only passably, so Taniquel took up the instrument herself and cradled it on her lap, trying to remember the chords of Padrik's favorite song. It had been far too long since she had played, and her fingers were stiff as old women on the strings. Slowly the words came to her.

> *"Over the mountains*
> *And over the waves,*
> *Under the fountains,*
> *And over the grave,*
> *Under floods that are deepest,*
> *Over rocks that are steepest—"*

Taniquel broke off, aware of Verella's stare. She'd forgotten it was a love song. Or rather, she thought as she put the *rryl* aside, a song of lost love, of promises that could not be kept.

When that song and the next, a pastoral ballad, some lovelorn nonsense about a shepherd's love for a lady, came to a close, Taniquel bade her ladies withdraw. They would not go far, but at least she had a small measure of solitude. Let them think her the broken, weeping widow. Let them carry that message to Deslucido. It would buy her time to gather allies and resources.

What allies? Gavriel's first loyalty must be to Acosta, his efforts focused on softening the conqueror's grasp. If he could help her, he would, but it would not be soon, not until his own position was secure. She could look for neither advice nor succor there, any more than from her ladies.

Alone, Taniquel crawled on to her bed, nestling between the pillows and comforters. Her eyes ached, although she had not wept. Perhaps she dozed a little; half-formed images like waking dreams flickered across her mind.

Padrik's great white horse pawing the air, slipping into the mass of fighting men . . . bells ringing . . . rain misting over green grass . . . a man's face, copper-bright hair framed in blue fire . . . Belisar reaching for her with that arrogant smile . . . over and over again, the white horse falling . . .

Slowly she went over the facts in her mind, forcing herself to think instead of feel. There would be time enough for mourning once she was free. First, Deslucido now ruled Acosta. She had no power to challenge him. Second, he meant to marry her to his son, to use her as a path to legitimacy. Nothing she could say or do would alter that.

She had never hoped to wed for love. Fortune had been generous once, for her family chose a husband who offered both companionship and kindness. Only a fool would expect that much a second time.

How could she possibly marry this golden prince, son of the father who had murdered her childhood companion and seized her homeland by deception?

And what of her son? Blessed Cassilda, guardian of babes in their mothers' arms, *what of her unborn son?*

She had not missed her woman's cycles, not yet. Desperately she thought if she were forced to marry this Belisar, if she permitted him to bed her and then presented the pregnancy to him as his own . . .

I would as soon couple with a cralmac!

The very idea brought a rush of bile to her mouth. Her muscles shook with revulsion. She could not even seek her own death as an honorable escape, because she carried another, innocent life. No matter what the odds, she must survive.

She calmed herself, digging her nails into the palms of her hands hard enough to leave little blood-dark crescents.

The hushed crumple of a falling log brought her to her present surroundings. The room had grown dark and cool with the setting of the sun. Piadora slipped into the room to light a branched candelabrum. In the soft light, Taniquel saw that she had been weeping.

At least one of us has, she thought with a pang of guilt.

Meanwhile, there was much work to do. There was an old proverb about the wisdom of thrusting a stick into a nest of scorpion-ants. Just so, she must avoid arousing any greater suspicions than already existed.

Taniquel had helped arrange the funeral for Padrik's father, old King Ian-Valdir, five years ago. She at least ought to keep vigil and ride with the body to the family burial area. Acosta was too far from Hali and the *rhu fead* to bring Padrik to lay in an unmarked grave there, as was the custom among the *Comyn*. Besides, there was no chance Deslucido would simply let her ride out of his control and back to her own powerful family. Not if he truly intended her as his son's bride.

Tomorrow, she told herself, there would be a proper ending to Padrik's reign. She would bid farewell to him and stand as witness as his closest friends and advisers shared their memories of him.

And I, what will I say? She prayed to whatever god would listen that something would come.

Meanwhile, there were arrangements which would not make themselves. Taniquel got up, brushed the folds of her tunic into smoothness, gestured to the girl to follow her, and went to the door. It would not move; the latch could not be locked from the outside, but had been jammed in some way.

She stared at the handle as if it had suddenly turned into an iron snake. Trying it again brought only the same result. It would not budge. In a spasm of sudden panic, she pounded on the door itself. "Open up! Open this instant!"

The door swung open. She jumped back, heart racing. Outside stood a young officer, but not one of her own. The face above the black-and-white diamond surcoat bore the marks of little sleep and hard riding.

"Vai domna." When he spoke, she realized he was not as young as she'd thought. The voice was firm, the dark eyes wary but confident. He blocked the opening with his body, turning only to make sure he had room to draw his sword.

"Are you my escort?" she said in the iciest tone she could manage. "I will now go to the chapel to see that my husband's body is resting as is proper." *As your King Damian promised me,* she thought but did not add.

The soldier's expression did not change, not even the tensing of the smallest eye muscles. "Regretfully, His Majesty has not given permission for you to leave these chambers. If you wish, I will send a page with your request."

A page! My request! *So that is to be the way of it.*

But there was nothing to be done except withdraw with whatever grace she could muster and to wait. She was not a helpless prisoner, as Deslucido might think. This part of the castle, the oldest, was riddled with secret passageways which she and Padrik had delighted to explore as children. Some of them had been created accidentally as a result of centuries of repairs and additions, but others were quite deliberate, she thought, ways for the lord to discreetly visit his mistress or spy upon his counselors. Very untrusting souls, those Acosta ancestors. But she must not risk anyone else finding out until the right time—when Deslucido had relaxed in his victory, when her absence might not be noticed immediately, so that she had a decent chance of escape. She would keep the passageways secret until she needed them.

Meanwhile, she would play at submission and find out more about Deslucido's plans.

✦

Half an hour later, Taniquel found herself alone in Padrik's quarters, in the comfortable sitting room where they had passed so many winter hours since he had become King. Verella and Rosalys attended her only so far as the antechamber, where the guard, too, had withdrawn. A table had been set for dining. Candles gleamed on the utensils and copper-chased goblets.

Taniquel strode to the table, thinking to hide an eating knife in her sleeve or boot, but there was none. She had only a moment to spare, for with a clatter of spurs and boots, Damian Deslucido burst into the room. At his heels came a grizzled man in general's attire, two younger officers, and his golden-haired son. Air swirled in little currents in their wake, carrying the mingled smells of leather and rain. Mud from their boots smeared the carpet runner.

"Ah!" Damian rubbed his hands together. "I have such an appetite tonight! Where is dinner? Sweet lady, how gracious of you to join us."

Taniquel hesitated, then gave him an abbreviated curtsy, one she had been taught in Castle Hastur as befitting a noble young girl to an older man of lower rank.

King Damian seemed not to notice the implied slight. He had already turned away, clapping his men on the shoulders and dismissing them. Another uniformed man brought in a tray with bread, cheese, a bowl of winter apples, and a tureen of some kind of herbed soup, the sort of hearty food the kitchen could prepare quickly when there was no time for anything more elaborate. She waited, standing quietly, while Damian and his son took their seats.

"Lady, please sit. This is hardly a formal dinner and the meal comes from your own kitchens. Reynaldo! Where is the chair for the lady?"

"I thank you," Taniquel said, her throat tightening, "but I have come about quite another matter. You promised me I might bury my husband in honor. Yet when I went to see that all was properly done, laying him out in the chapel, I was forbidden to leave my rooms."

"Ah, a minor miscommunication, nothing more." Damian took a

knife from his belt and began slicing the pale, waxy cheese into neat slivers. "I regret any inconvenience, but the establishment of order must take precedence over less urgent matters. Be assured, all will be done as it should."

"Why was I not allowed to leave my rooms?"

"It would not be seemly—or safe—for a gentle lady to wander through the castle at this time," Damian said. "In the aftermath of the battle, blood runs hot. My men are well trained and loyal, but they are, after all, men. For your own safety—"

"I want to see my husband's body." Taniquel's jaw muscles ached with tension as she bit off each word.

"Calm yourself, please," said Damian, carefully putting away his knife. "This is a difficult time for you. You can have no reason to trust us, for you do not know us. But you will, and will see how foolish these present fears are. All things happen in their proper order. Please understand that while no disrespect is intended, for your lord was a most worthy opponent, it is to no one's benefit to turn his burial into a rallying point for malcontents. We must go carefully here. Quietly."

Quietly. What did that mean?

"His own *coridom* and chief counselor," Belisar spoke for the first time, "—what was the old man's name, Father? Gabriel?"

"Gavriel," Taniquel said in a low voice.

"—yes, they have laid him out in the chapel. I myself made sure that candles and incense have been provided. He is well attended." Belisar sipped his soup as if that concluded the matter. "You need not trouble yourself."

"Am I not to be permitted to see him, then?" Taniquel persisted.

"Domna," Damian said with an edge of steel in his voice. "His face was damaged during the battle. We men of action are accustomed to looking upon the unfortunate effects of war, but a lady of breeding and delicate sensibilities must be protected against such sights. Be guided by us in this, rest content in our care. Tomorrow you will walk with the funeral party, as is your right."

"Walk? Would you deny Padrik the traditional rites as well? It is the custom in Acosta to ride—"

"It is *our* custom to walk to the burial site, out of respect for the dead. However, if the distance is too far for you to manage on your own, a litter can be arranged."

"I—" Taniquel reined in her tongue, struggling to think clearly. She had stumbled into some terrible gauntlet, where each blow followed hard and fast upon the one before.

"Once that is done," Damian went on, "we will celebrate both a marriage and a coronation."

"I have not yet consented to the marriage," she reminded him, and knew in an instant how futile protests would be. Her own wishes meant nothing. More than one unwilling bride had been married by proxy, with a lackey speaking the words for her. Or drugged or forcibly held while the *catenas* bracelet was locked upon her wrist.

After Damian's speech in the throne room, all of Acosta would think her lucky to have such a handsome, noble, generous husband. Her only hope was to escape before the ceremony and as yet she had no plan. A botched attempt would be worse than useless, for she would be guarded even more closely, perhaps even chained as the Dry Towners did their women. She would have only one chance.

After once again refusing food, she retired back to her chambers, pleading a long and tiring day. Her words proved more true than she intended, for she was reeling with exhaustion by the time the guard escorted her back to her chambers. Without the ministrations of her ladies, she would have fallen across the wide bed without bothering to take off her clothes.

16

Taniquel never knew who made the arrangements for Padrik's funeral, although she hoped it had been Gavriel or the *coridom,* someone who loved him. Never since the time she had arrived at Acosta Castle as a scrawny, rebellious orphan had she felt so shut out of things. When Padrik's father, old King Ian-Valdir, had died, she had worked from dawn into the evenings, helping with the funeral plans, preparing rooms for senior vassal lords come for the burial, and supervising the kitchens. Now her door stayed locked until after noontime, when two Ambervale officers presented themselves as her escort. She took Rosalys and Verella with her for the long slow walk to the Acosta family plot.

Taniquel had watched dawn come through the high slit windows. Gradually the sky lightened to the color of tears and then to softly opalescent gold. But the day which had begun clear and fair turned overcast by the afternoon. Taniquel's ladies had insisted on a thick cloak and layers of veils, for which she was now grateful. She wore them like armor to hide her face from the curious stares of Deslucido's soldiers.

Neither Damian nor his son accompanied the funeral cortege, and Taniquel, somewhat paradoxically, found in their absence a greater respect and dignity than any token appearance. The stern-looking men in the Ambervale black and white and the silent, gray-shrouded *laranzu* were witness enough. She spotted Gavriel and some of the senior household staff. The older courtiers and ladies could be excused by the hardship of the journey. But of the young lords who had been Padrik's closest companions, his *bredin*, of the officers who had fought under him, she saw none. It was cruel of her to not have taken Piadora, to give the child a focus for her grief.

By the time they reached the hill where, surrounded by immense cragged cedars, the Acosta lords from time out of mind lay in unmarked graves, the sky had turned from white to scudded gray.

The sky itself weeps, she thought, and decided she was being maudlin. Padrik had been good-tempered and dutiful, but he had hardly been a king to sway the heavens to grief at his passing. No, if the threatened rain were a sign of celestial sadness, it must be for the fate of Acosta itself.

At the open gravesite, a white cloth completely covered the body. Taniquel was seized by the impulse to tear the thing aside, to make sure it really was Padrik under there. To make sure he really was dead. In that moment, the battle seemed so distant, the losses so unreal.

One by one, the mourners began to speak. Gavriel, as senior counselor, told a story from Padrik's boyhood, from just before Taniquel had come to Acosta. She remembered thinking that Padrik was not as handsome as her Hastur cousins and that he was more than a bit spoiled, being the only son of an only son. She had deliberately tripped him and blackened his eye, only to be chased three times around the courtyard with a horsewhip. In an attempt at retaliation, she'd filled his bed with frogs, which he thought truly wonderful, and after that they'd gotten along tolerably well.

Her smile faded as one story followed the other, each one about some long-ago incident, some quirk of Padrik's humor, some generous gift. Nowhere was there mention of his kingship, of his death. People mourned in different ways, but even when the old King had died, unheroically in his bed, there had been some recognition of what he had been. Padrik had not been a great king, not yet, but he had tried his best. He had outgrown his boyhood bullying and taken on a man's duty. In another time, the land would have prospered under his rule. Was there no one here willing to say so? Was he to be remembered only for a few charming pranks?

In Acosta tradition, women stayed silent at burials. But Taniquel was Hastur, of higher rank, and Hastur women *did* speak. In a pause, she stepped forward and swept back the veils, baring her face. Drops stung her cheeks.

"I saw him fall." Her voice sounded reedy to her own ears. "He came racing back from the border when we were under attack, little knowing he rode into a trap. He died at the gates, defending us, a true king to the last."

"Vai domna!" Rosalys whispered desperately.

Taniquel paused, taking in the hunched shoulders, the lowered heads, the furtive glances toward the Ambervale soldiers. Not one man would meet her eyes, not even Gavriel. Their fear shivered through her. Not just of what might happen if they were seen to be in agreement with her, but for her own safety.

She had spoken as she always had, saying what she felt to be right, owing nothing except to her own conscience. In all her life, as pampered Hastur daughter, as noble fosterling, as adored young Queen, she had seen others suffer the consequences of imprudent speech. Until now, she had not given a thought to what might happen to her.

I must appear reconciled to my fate, a little irrational with grief perhaps, but not rebellious. . . .

"Perhaps," she stammered, "it is better to remember him in happier times."

It was raining full downpour by the time the funeral cortege returned to the castle. Taniquel tried to walk closer to Gavriel, to exchange a word or two with him, but he slid away from her with a courtier's consummate skill. The rebuff stung until she realized that her actions would only put him at risk. His future, his very life depended upon the favor of the new king. He could not afford to be seen speaking privately with her, even if she had not made such a provocative speech. She must be more tired and more muddled with grief than she realized, to even attempt it.

Taniquel was stumbling in earnest as she made her way up the stairs to her tower room. She was locked in once again, an armed guard at her door. Docilely, she allowed her ladies to strip her soaked garments and coax her into a bath. The scent of rose petals and dried citron peel sprinkled on the steaming water, once a source of sensual delight, now sickened her.

That night, she sat up into the small hours, watching the flames cast dancing shadows on the back of the fireplace. Rain lashed fitfully against the thick glass windows.

Word came the next day from Damian that he had set the date for the wedding and coronation within the tenday. He desired her to join him for dinner. Taniquel snapped at the officer messenger that she was still in mourning and would not see him.

✦

That evening, Taniquel plucked at her *rryl* as she mentally reviewed her situation. She could not hope for sanctuary at any of the smaller neighbors. Verdanta had already fallen to Deslucido, and the others stood no greater chance. Her only hope was to make for Thendara and her Hastur relatives. The journey would be long and difficult, especially at first, when she dared not stop to hunt or buy food. She would have to stockpile trail supplies, take a bow from the armory and a good horse—

She looked up from the *rryl* on her lap at the sound of a man's laughing voice in the outer hall. She laid the instrument on the low, tapestried footstool. Verella, who had been accompanying her on guitar, got to her feet.

"Ah, there you are." Belisar stood in the doorway, a smile hovering over his lips.

"What are you doing here?"

"I have come to escort you to dinner, and make sure that this time you are properly dressed." His eyes flickered from her face, now flushing despite her best efforts, slowly downward, pausing over breasts and hips. "No old rags this time."

He turned, dismissing her ladies with a few words. Before she could protest, she was alone with him, her bedroom only a short distance away. Clearly, he meant her to understand that while she might be locked in her room, he could enter where and when it pleased him.

"You needn't be afraid of me," he said. His words were pleasant, his voice medium in pitch and inflected to mean that he had plenty of women falling over themselves for his attention.

"I do not fear you, *Va'Altezu*," she said, knowing it was not quite the truth. Until that moment, she had feared him only so far as he was his father's son.

"Highness?" He moved toward her in a fluid stride. "Is that how you address your promised husband? The customs of Acosta must be strange indeed. Come," he held out his arms, "give us a kiss."

Deftly, she stepped to put the stool with the *rryl* between them.

"Oh, so it's like that? You want to play games? Good! I like a woman with spirit."

"I will not be pawed like some barmaid! Remember who I am, and that I have just lost my husband!"

He circled around the chair and placed both hands on its back, grinning more broadly now. "Your pretty little maid wasn't so shy. What was her name? Betheny, Britteny, something like that. Oh, yes, she was most welcoming." He ran his fingers through his golden hair, and she saw it was slightly damp as if he had just come from the bath. And bed.

Taniquel's hands tightened into fists as her face flamed in earnest. She managed to think instead of physically striking him. Why would he tell her this? Was taking her lady-in-waiting for an afternoon tumble an unsubtle reminder of his power, something designed to humiliate her? Did he intend to keep the girl as *barragana* under her own roof?

"You have no decency!"

"Oh, I have a great deal of decency. Like the *cristoforos,* I take no woman unwilling. We must understand each other."

She shook her head. "You mean that *I* must understand *you.* That *you* intend to do whatever you please, whether *I* agree or not."

"Just the opposite. What happens depends entirely on you." He moved toward her, hands low, voice soothing as for a young and restive horse. "I have no desire to frighten you. Look at you, trembling like a leaf. I would have you tremble for quite a different, infinitely more pleasurable reason. I'm a simple man, easy to win over. A word here, a caress there, and you'll have my heart at your feet. You're a very beautiful woman, did you know that? I shall bring you looking glasses of silver polished like the face of Mormallor, so you can see the light of your face. How ravishing you are, with your cheeks all red like that!"

Taniquel swayed on her feet, half-lulled by his rhythmic words. She shifted to keep the stool and chair between them, only slower now, so that he gained on her.

"No, don't move away," he murmured. "I won't hurt you. I only want to touch your cheeks, to feel your hair. It's like a cloud of unspun silk. I've never seen anything like it. You have nothing to fear from me. Nothing will happen unless you want it to. And believe me, my lovely, that when you beg me to touch you, when you welcome me with the passion I know is within you, I will have no desire to look elsewhere."

Taniquel flinched as if he had slapped her. He was suggesting—this arrogant lecher—that she beg him to touch her, that *she* make love to *him*! *Hell itself will melt before I lie with you!*

"I have not consented to this marriage," she said stiffly.

"Why do you make things so difficult for yourself? We will be married, and I would far rather have you as an eager bride. Was your first marriage such a burden? Are you a secret lover of women? If so, I will show you the pleasures to be found in the arms of a real man. Oh, yes, I look forward very much to showing you that. And every word out of your mouth only tells me how very much you need it."

Taniquel gasped, but managed to keep silent. He was *enjoying* her resistance! She lowered her eyes, trying her best for the appearance of confused modesty. Perhaps if she seemed to be persuaded . . . "Please, it has all been so sudden. I need a little more time."

"I am no barbarian, as you will see. I grant you until our wedding night. I will even leave you now, so that your ladies may properly dress you. Something that suits your coloring, I think."

With those words, he left her. Taniquel stood for a moment, chest heaving as if she'd run the length of the castle and back again.

I have to get out of here. I have to get out of here now. But if she did not appear at dinner, the hunt would be up within the hour. She could not get far enough to escape them. Somehow, she must find a way to keep Belisar at bay and that accursed *laranzu* out of her thoughts until her chance came.

Minutes later, Verella, Betteny, Piadora, and a coarse-faced girl she didn't recognize, swept into the room. Betteny giggled a great deal, and Piadora looked as if she'd been crying again. The new girl jumped whenever spoken to and could only stare in confusion at the contents of the wardrobe.

"No, not that," Taniquel said when Betteny held out the gown of peacock-hued silk. The color turned her skin into creamy porcelain and heightened the brilliance of her eyes. The last thing she wanted was to appear healthy, lively, or beautiful. She pointed to a stiffly embroidered tunic of dull orange, a gift from the old King, who had no color sense. She'd worn it exactly once and had kept it only in his memory, for the orange made her look, as Padrik had put it, "half cousin to a fungus, kept out of the light in damp dark places."

"That one."

Piadora wrinkled her nose. "The embroidery is very beautiful. See how skillfully the threads of gold are worked into the starburst design, but . . ."

"But it's something your grandmother would wear!" Betteny giggled, smoothing her own softly draped bodice across her generously curved breasts. "It won't show anything of your figure!"

Taniquel sighed inwardly. "It is both costly and dignified. Entirely suitable to honor the new King." *And you can have both of them together if you want them!*

◆

The last few days had seen the sitting room transformed. A huge, age-worn carpet replaced the runners which had showed the pale stone Padrik loved. Taniquel didn't recognize the furniture; it must have come from one of the rooms in the old, disused wing. As before, a table, this one even more richly set, had been laid out for three.

King Damian, no longer in soldier's gear but a robe of midnight-blue velvet trimmed with patterned black-and-white marlet fur, sat in the huge chair before the fire. Belisar stood leaning on the mantlepiece, a goblet in one hand. His eyes gleamed in the firelight. The *laranzu* glided in from one of the smaller rooms to stand behind them.

Taniquel tried not to look at the gray-robed figure, though she felt his attention upon her. The pressure of his mind on hers was slight, but relentless.

I must appear confused with grief and the suddenness of events, but not unwilling.

Damian greeted her without rising. With an effort, she kept her features composed. She bowed deeply, then allowed Belisar to seat her at the table.

As if they had been waiting in the corridor for his signal, a quartet of servants rushed into the room, setting out covered dishes, trenchers of fine white bread, and two bottles of wine still powdery with dust from the cellars. As they seated themselves and the servants removed the covers, Taniquel recognized the artistry of her cooks. A joint of spring lamb, crusted with herbs and tiny garlands of garlic cloves, nestled among piles of honey-glazed root vegetables. Tiny roasted fowl spread wings whose feathers had been replaced by layers of wafer-thin redroot slices. One of the servants opened the wine, an older vintage that always smelled to Taniquel like sunshine mixed with ripe plums and smoke.

At the table, Damian lifted his goblet, swirling the wine to intensify the aroma, and sniffed deeply. Taniquel watched, a bit surprised that an outlander should know how to approach the proper tasting of wine. The savory smell of the meats and the pungency of the herbs sent her senses whirling.

He sipped, his expression one of inner concentration, and swallowed. Then he smiled with such evident pleasure that she thought he might have conquered Acosta simply for its wines. Few areas on Darkover grew suitable grapes, and fruit wines tended to be too sweet for Taniquel's taste, but cold-tolerant vines flourished in the Acosta valleys and brought forth drier, more complex flavors.

The officer filled her goblet and then Belisar's.

"To the future of Acosta," Damian said. "To its new King and its beautiful Queen, who in three days' time will join as one to bring prosperity as rich as this wine."

"And to the sons who will rule after us," Belisar added. He drank his wine in a gulp, not pausing to savor it.

Sons! Taniquel lowered her eyes, bending over her goblet to hide her startlement. Surely he couldn't know, not yet! No, he meant the sons *he* would sire upon her.

"Sir," she said, once she had collected herself, "let us not hurry things. A royal courtship must be conducted with dignity. I am but newly a widow."

Damian began carving a slab from the haunch of lamb. Dark juices oozed from the slash, dark as living blood. He placed a sliver on her plate, the inside still faintly pink.

"Please, drink. Eat something." Belisar lifted her goblet and held it out to her. "Or are you still being stubborn?"

She took the goblet. The smell, so evocative of happier times, blended with the savory smell of the roasted meat, the pungency of the herbs, the aroma of the freshly baked bread. A pulse beat sent little lightnings of pain through her temples. How easy it would be to take a sip— she could taste it already on her tongue, slipping down her throat like ruby heat.

Never had she felt so terribly, so dangerously alone. She glanced from one face to the other—father and son, mirrored in their happy certainty—and there, in the corner, shrouded against the light, the unmoving figure in gray. She could not see the man's face, but with that fragmentary *laran*, she felt him probing her in earnest—

Instead of the ice of their first contact, fire now bloomed behind her eyes, lancing through her skull. Her vision swam. His mind pressed against hers, searching for a way past her barriers.

He must not find out about my son! I must think of something else— anything else!

With an expression she hoped looked like resignation, Taniquel began to eat. Taking one slow mouthful after another, she tried to concentrate only on the taste of the food. It wasn't hard. The crust of the bread broke between her teeth. She tasted its soft yeasty interior. Savory meat juices swirled over her tongue. A tiny piece of gristle crunched. She focused on each sensation, as if building a wall of placid gluttony. Slowly, the fiery pressure receded, leaving a deep ache in her temples.

"What did I tell you?" Damian said to his son. "She is not only beautiful but reasonable. A fitting bride, and one you will not have to wait for until she grows up to be truly yours."

Damian and his son smiled and went on with the conversation, small pleasantries about the food, the wine, the rain, something about one of their horses. Taniquel murmured empty comments when it seemed expected of her. Watching them from under lowered lashes, she saw the shift in their expressions. For now, they clearly believed they had won her cooperation.

The headache eased a bit by the time she fled back to her quarters, but did not dissipate. She dismissed her ladies, barred the door behind them, and went to the chest where her old, everyday clothes were stored. Her hands shook and her stomach roiled with tension and wine, but she could not afford to rest. Not yet.

She did not know how completely she had been able to fool the *laranzu*. But she knew with bone-chilling certainty that she could not continue to do so much longer. She had run out of time. To delay the inevitable search, she must make them think she was still within the castle. This meant taking nothing whose absence would be noted.

There! Crumpled in a corner was the amber-colored wool she had worn the day of the battle. Dark stains ran along the hemline. It was cut loose to a dropped waistline, with a skirt that was full enough to move easily in, which was why she had worn it. She pulled it on and rolled up the tunic and underdress of undyed *chervine* wool, along with extra underthings and heavy socks. Quickly she assembled the rest, a small purse of silver coins from the last market fair, a couple of old, bent copper hair ornaments, the cloak she had worn at the funeral. Dressed in the stained, rumpled amber wool, covered with an equally stained cloak, her hair tucked in an old kerchief, she looked more like a servant girl in her mistress' cast-offs than a young Queen.

One more thing. Her lips curved as she took the gown of peacock-colored silk and stuffed it between the flower box and the balcony wall. It was raining again, harder this time, turning the silk into a dark, sodden mess. Betteny would immediately notice its disappearance and conclude Taniquel was wearing it.

Slipping behind the headboard of the canopied bed, she pressed the stumpy brick which unlocked the narrow door. Beyond lay the warren of passageways where she and Padrik had played at brigands and spies, once or twice eavesdropping on their elders, slipping out of the room when a stern tutor was on his way. Perhaps every generation of Acosta children had used them, she didn't know. Now she would never know what her son might make of them.

The passageway was chill and shadowed, but dry. She had already decided not to take a candle, lest the light, gleaming through one of the many peepholes and crannies, attract the eyes of some watchful Amber-vale guard. Her fingers, lightly skimming the familiar walls, were guide enough.

Voices filtered through from the main corridor, growing louder as the speakers approached. The accents were those of Ambervale soldiers. Taniquel froze, her heart racing. She strained to catch the conversation, something about extra requisitions of food from the village below.

"Peasants are the same everywhere," one said. "They always complain they have nothing left, when you know they're hoarding sacks of grain in the usual places."

"Aye, that's the truth," the other laughed, his voice already receding in the distance. ". . . teach them a lesson . . . like those *ombredin* in Verdanta . . . remember that time . . ."

Slowly Taniquel let her breath out. She tightened her grip on her bundle and went on. The *slither-hush-slither* of soft boots over stone rang in her ears. The passageway narrowed and twisted so that sometimes she was forced to turn sideways. As a child she had not minded the closeness of the space, but now the walls closed in upon her, compressing the very air. Twice she brushed away cobwebs from her face and hair, and once a many-legged creature which scurried along her hand. She was glad she couldn't see what it was.

She hurried down three floors, along twisting narrow stairs and a ladder which creaked maddeningly under her weight, to emerge into a corridor by the pantries. Fortunately, the area was mostly deserted at this hour, since the cooks and their helpers had already finished the last of the scouring and gone to bed. They would rise well before dawn to get the day's baking started. She took a quarter-round of cheese still in its sealant wax, a double handful of honeyed dried peaches, and what was left of a loaf of brown bread, all wrapped up in a dish towel that looked as if it had escaped last month's laundry.

Durraman's own luck was with her, for the outer kitchen door was unlocked and unguarded. No one challenged her as she crossed the courtyard, head lowered against the rain.

The Ambervale forces had set up tents in the open space, with all the attendant equipment and stench. One of the gates stood open, with more encamped men and picket lines beyond. Sentries looked outward, clearly still awake and alert.

Taniquel tiptoed through the gate, hugging the wall, trying to look as inconspicuous as possible.

"Hey, you! Girl!" one of the guards called out. "Get back inside!"

What would a woman of the village do? Keep going, make a break for it? Obediently creep back, hoping for a better time? Taniquel had no idea.

"Let her be," said one of the others. "Can't you see how scared she is? She's just a little village tart who got caught inside when the fightin' started. Goin' back to her own people, most likely. Why else would she be out in this muck?"

"Or maybe she's out to have some fun," the first said, laughing coarsely. "Come here, girl."

"*Vai dom* . . . please . . ." Taniquel pulled the folds of her hood tighter around her face as she shrank away.

"Give us a kiss." Hands like huge steel paws tightened on her shoulders and pulled her close. Before she could draw breath, the sentry planted his lips on hers. His clipped beard prickled her face, his skin cold and damp with rain. He pushed his tongue between her slack lips. For a long moment, Taniquel hung in his grip, unable to move. She felt a curious nothing, neither pleasure nor, surprisingly, any sense of revulsion. The man's breath was sweet enough, nor had he been drinking. She simply waited until it was over.

He released her so suddenly she staggered backward. "No juice there. I'd as soon kiss a frozen prune." The others laughed. He spun her around and pushed her stumbling toward the village. "Go on home to mama, girl. Come on back when you're ready for a real man."

Taniquel scurried away, half-unbelieving of her good luck. It wasn't until she was well past the camp that she wiped the wetness from her mouth.

◆

Mud dampened Taniquel's boots by the time she reached the village. Droplets beaded on her wool cloak and hood. The rain had let up slightly, the clouds thinning so that two of the four moons shone with diffuse, multi-hued light. She kept to the outskirts, heading for one cottage which stood, with its paddocks of sheep and ponies, isolated from the rest. Like the others, it was silent and dark except for the faint glow of a banked fire.

Three brindled hounds bounded from the yard at her approach. One, the younger bitch who did not know her, yipped once and then subsided. The oldest dog thrust his muzzle into her hand, searching for remembered treats. She stroked their ears and scratched the itchy places at the base of their tails, whispering that she had no food for them.

It was an easy enough matter to catch the old horse with a handful of oats. The beast came to her readily, as if it also remembered her from happier days, and rubbed its bony head against her shoulder. Padrik had left it here at pasturage, the sedate half-cart horse which had been his first mount after he'd outgrown ponies.

Taniquel grasped a handful of forelock and led the horse to the shed where the gear was stored. Moonlight shone through the opened door, gleaming on the lovingly polished saddle which had been Padrik's. As much by feel as by sight, she put it on the horse along with the second bridle, then tied on her bundles.

Behind the almost-empty grain bin, she found sacks which she identified by smell as barley and more oats. These were seed stock for the second planting or in case the first should fail, as sometimes happened with late ice-storms. She hesitated, one hand on the smallest barley sack. The food from the kitchen would not last long and she had no bow for hunting. If Deslucido's men had found the store, they would have thought nothing of taking it all.

That was no excuse. They might not find it. They might not find all of it.

Sighing, she tucked the sack back into its hiding place.

A muffled sound made her jump. She was not alone in the shed.

17

Lamplight struck Taniquel's eyes, fell on the seamed features of the cottager. She searched her memory for a name. Ruyven. Painfully aware of how it all must appear—her own disheveled dress, the saddled horse, the uncovered cache of seed grain, she got to her feet.

"Lass." The single word held a paragraph of questions.

"You have not seen me!" she cried. She dug out the small purse and placed it beside the oat bin. "I never left this here. You have no idea where the horse wandered off to."

He crossed the space between them, lifted out a sack of barley and one of oats, laid them with deliberate care on the dirt floor. "That old horse, always sticking his fool nose into the feed." The next moment, he was gone.

Taniquel, wasting no time, gathered up the sacks of grain and tied one on either side to the saddle. She swung up on the horse, tucked her skirts around her legs, and spread her cloak over her precious bundles.

The old horse moved off with a spring in its step. Perhaps it remembered other moonlit rides, years ago.

They would look for her on the road, if they looked for her at all. Taniquel did not know how good their trackers were, to pick out the prints of a single unshod farmhorse amid the churned-up muck of many.

She cut across the pastures and then the orchards, heading for higher, rocky ground. When the last moon set, leaving the sloping hills in darkness, she kept going, trusting to the horse's instinct and the stars. The old beast had lost its first bloom of energy by then, but she could not let it rest, not yet.

✦

Taniquel awoke with a start, half-slumped over the pommel. The first gray tinge of dawn showed nothing familiar; she must have passed the outermost orchards. The horse trudged on, head lowered, ears flopping. It had apparently found its stride, an easy amble broken only by the occasional dip of the head to gather up another mouthful of spring grass. Around her stretched eroded hills strewn with boulders, fit only for goat pastures. Stunted ashleaf trees huddled together, their leaves still softly gray. From afar, a fox barked. Something stirred in the heathery brush—a lone *chervine*, wild by the way it shook its antlers and bounded off. There was no sign of human habitation.

She pulled the horse to a halt, kicked free of the stirrups, and with some difficulty slid to the ground. The stirrup leathers had rubbed the inside of her knees, her hips ached, her face and hands felt half-frozen, and her nose dripped. She slipped the bit from the horse's mouth, leaving it to graze in earnest, and took out the bread and a portion of cheese.

Settling herself on a stony outcrop, Taniquel considered her situation. She had no way to kindle a fire, even if she found dry wood. Although her cloak was still damp, it was wool and would hold her body heat. Worst, she had only the vaguest idea where she was. She had meant to cut across country and join with the main road that led in one direction to Neskaya and the other to the lowlands and Thendara.

Well and enough, she told herself, sniffing and fighting back tears of weariness, *you've gotten away from Belisar. Almost anything would be better than marrying him.*

Using the position of the new-risen sun for her marker, she headed out in the approximate direction of the road. As the sun climbed above the horizon, frost melted on the grasses and rose in waves of mist. She urged the horse into a trot along a smoother stretch of road. She saw no other living thing except for an occasional hawk.

Late in the day, Taniquel stopped again along an eroded cliff face to water the horse at the waterfall which came tumbling over the rock face and into a pool. She debated staying where she was for the night, for the water and the brief shelter of the overhang. The air quivered with the promise of cold. She had, after all, seen no sign of pursuit. That meant nothing. How did she know they would not be waiting for her at the road—no, they would not have traveled that far with no sign of her passage. She was too tired to think clearly, and if she expected the old horse to carry her all the way to Thendara, she had better let it rest. While she made up her mind, she unsaddled the beast, hobbled it, and poured out a measure of grain on the saddle blanket. Her stomach roiled at the idea of eating.

Taniquel wrapped herself in her cloak, her back against the rock face. What an idiot she'd been, to take off with so little forethought. No way to make fire, no weapons, only a little food. But what else could she have done?

It would be all right; she would find the road and on it would be a travel shelter, with wood and tinder and dry blankets, maybe some food. And then, Thendara and her uncle's castle. A blaze in the enormous marble fireplace in the central hall. Hot spiced wine, meat pastries, spice cakes. A down comforter with a heating brick at her feet, no, two comforters, and a mound of pillows. . . .

Within a few minutes, her body felt soft and heavy. Her thoughts drifted, slower and sleepier with each passing breath.

✦

A tenday later, Taniquel found a road. She had long since finished her own food and the last of the horse's grain, soaked overnight in a rain-filled rocky cup and chewed slowly. Fernheads and dry, over-wintered wild lady-apples had furnished several meager dinners, although she dared not spare the time to gather the more nutritious nuts. The road wasn't much, a slender thread of beaten-down earth cleared of stones, winding through the steepening hills. She went dizzy with relief.

The horse, which had grown visibly gaunt during the journey, stepped on to the road with a heaving sigh. It walked gingerly, head bobbing with the rhythm of its stride, one ear cocked back toward her. No wonder it was footsore, with the rocky terrain of the past few days. She patted its neck and urged it from that leisurely amble into a more animated walk.

The road ran east and west, not north and south as she expected. It might be one of the many uncharted trails which ran all through these hills. She made the best decision of which direction to take, telling herself that eventually it must join the main road to Thendara. It looked like it had enough usage so there would be travel shelters, stocked with fire-wood and trail food, at regular intervals.

The weather had been unseasonably clear since that first night, so much so that she had thought once or twice of the dangers of a Ghost Wind. At midmorning, however, the air temperature dropped and dark-bellied clouds rose beyond the far line of hills.

Snow weather. Shivering, she pulled the cloak around her shoulders and prayed the travel shelter was not too far.

✦

Taniquel pulled the horse to a stop, wind lashing her hair to icy threads. Her cloak was already crusted with tiny pellets of ice and half-frozen rain. White and gray masked her vision. Only the horse's instinct had held them to the road. Moving stiffly, she slid to the ground and slipped the reins over its head. Frozen breath edged the curved nostrils. She tried to speak encouragingly, but her throat closed around the words. When the horse walked on, she followed gratefully, keeping to the shelter of its body.

As she went on, Taniquel began to feel less cold. The pain in her feet and fingers subsided. A curious languor suffused her, all sense of urgency gone. She must not stop, she knew this, although it made less and less sense to go on. There was no hurry, and she was tired. Surely she could sit down—the snow was not so cold—

Taniquel knew what the numbness in her hands and feet meant. The longer she struggled on, the more powerful would become the longing to rest, to lie down, to never get up again. For the sake of her unborn son, she must not let that happen.

She could not go on like this, in the lashing storm, unable to see more than a few feet of trail in front of her. The gray-white of the sky was already darkening with the coming night.

Taniquel stumbled on a rock and caught herself on the stirrup, lean-ing into the horse. Shelter—she must find shelter. She'd heard of men wrapping themselves in blankets against the bodies of their horses, but she did not know how to make the horse lie down. A cliff face with an overhang, even a tree—something to cut the wind and give some measure of dryness—

She peered through the driving sleet, but could make out no details of the landscape. To search, she must leave the trail. What if she could not find it again? At least, it held some hope of reaching a safer place.

Blessed Cassilda, help me!

Taniquel repeated the words like a silent chant. *Help me . . . Help me . . .* Each syllable formed a step and then another. Time lost all meaning in the sameness of the icy snow and wind, moving each foot in turn.

Gradually, the last light seeped from the blowing whiteness. The horse stopped, bringing her up short. Without forward momentum, her legs gave way under her. The stirrup slid from between her numb fingers. She found herself sprawled in a graceless jumble with no idea how she got there.

Knees first. Get up on your knees.

Her legs would not move. For an awful moment, she thought she had broken one of them, but it was simply that she lacked the strength.

Then I must find it somehow.

With an effort, she rocked forward, taking her weight on her hands. The icy crust of the snow slashed her skin, drawing blood, although she felt no pain. Taking a deep breath that shivered all through her chest, she brought one foot forward. She was able to brace herself on that knee, push off the ground, and reach up for the stirrup. The horse, miraculous beast, stood firm as she pulled herself up to stand panting.

She clucked to the horse, indicating it should walk on. For an awful moment, it just stood there, recalcitrant beast, with head lowered and tail clamped to its rump. Then with another of those heaving sighs, it ambled forward.

How long she went on like that, Taniquel could never tell. Often it seemed that the horse was dragging her forward. Once or twice, she jerked awake, suddenly aware that time had gone by without her knowing it. Was it possible to sleep while walking? She didn't know.

At last, the horse came to a halt. She released the stirrup and continued a few paces. The wind had died down and the sleet ended, so that only an occasional dusting of snow fell. The air felt warmer, although she could not trust that. The horse had led her along the lowest part of a series of jagged hills, following a dry riverbed. On this side, a long featureless slope lay buried under snow and ice. Ten feet or so below her, a stream churned and bubbled.

Worse yet, there was not the slightest trace of a trail.

Taniquel had no idea how long ago she'd left it. With the sky a uniform overcast, she could not have told east from west from Zandru's coldest hell. At least she could make out the hills on the far side. Some distance upstream, the smooth contours fractured into jagged shapes, mounds and fingers of stone which promised some sort of shelter if she could get across the stream.

She gathered up the reins and led the horse, now clearly reluctant, down to the water. It was deeper and wider than she'd first thought. A well-trained horse, given enough room to make a balanced jump, might clear it, but not this horse and not on this ice-slick bank. Perhaps farther upstream . . .

Taniquel had to pick her way around piles of deadfall wood to follow the stream. It seemed to take forever to advance only a short distance. But as she went on, the opposite hill looked even more promising. In the gathering dusk, the face of one promontory looked as if it well might have a cave, or at least a deep crevice.

The rocky bank forced her away from the stream and the horse balked at stepping over a fallen tree. Briefly, she considered crawling under the trunk and curling up there for the night, but the ground was soaked by a rivulet. The horse at last yielded to her coaxing and stepped, one high-raised foot at a time, over the barrier.

By the time she got the horse down to the stream again, the shadows had melted into gloom. If she did not get across here, it would soon be too dark. She picked the stretch of water which seemed the least turbulent, the shallowest.

It took her two tries to haul herself on the horse's back. The saddle leather felt icy against her legs. The horse lowered its head to smell the water, then hunched its back. When she nudged it with her heels, she felt the muscles of its body tense in refusal.

"No! Not now!" she wailed, and then took hold of herself as well as the reins. "You idiot horse! Don't you dare!" she yelled, then clapped her heels against its ribs.

The horse flinched sideways, then set itself again.

"Get yourself over there, you walking banshee-fodder! Or I swear, you'll regret it!" She gave it another kick, this time as hard as she could muster.

The horse grunted, took a step forward, then threw its head up and shuffled backward.

Screaming curses, Taniquel reached forward and cuffed the horse on the side of its raised head, by its ear. The horse went *whuff!* in surprise and turned away from the blow. She tightened the rein on that side, pulling its head to its shoulder, and gave the horse another kick. Startled, the beast jumped, turning tightly around itself. She kept cursing, kept kicking it.

Five or six tiny circles later, Taniquel released the rein and pointed the horse straight at the stream. Without hesitation, it stepped into the water. She felt unhappiness through every fiber of its old, tired body, for horses resist stepping where they cannot see. The horse staggered, as if the footing beneath had slipped, and as quickly regained its balance. The water rose foaming to its knees.

Without warning, the horse went down, dumping Taniquel into the icy water. The shock of the cold stopped her breath. The current rolled her over and over. Everywhere she saw roiling dark. She flailed with her arms, searching for the surface. Her feet found something hard and she kicked out. Slipped on river-weed. Kicked again. The toes of one foot caught, wedged in between two rocks.

The water pounded against her, dragged her down. Frozen fire seared her lungs. The muscles of her thighs screamed in agony.

Her head burst through to the air.

Gasping, sputtering, Taniquel fought her way to standing. The currents surged around her hips. Beside her, the horse flailed and heaved itself to standing. She lost her footing and went down again.

This time, she had a better idea of what to expect. She didn't try to stand, but crouched with her head and shoulders just above the surface, moving her arms as if swimming.

The horse began to move off, toward the far shore. She hurled herself at it. As she leaped, her feet went out from under her. The current slammed into her body. Against all hope, she reached out as far as she could. Her hands curled around the horse's tail. She knotted her fingers through the coarse hairs. The horse took no notice of her, but kept going.

Once on the rocky bank, she tried to let go, but found her fingers stiffened and bound by the tail hairs. "Whoa! Whoa, there!" Thanks to whatever god was in charge of horse brains that day, the beast stopped after dragging her only a few feet.

Somehow, she got her fingers loose from the horse's tail. Half-frozen water drenched every bit of clothing, from her cloak to her boots. Shivers seized her, wave after wave of them, shaking the marrow of her bones and rattling her teeth.

If I die out here, my son dies with me.

She had to find shelter very soon, had to get going while she still had the strength. She tried to pick up the reins, but her hands were shaking too badly to hold them.

Moving as quickly as she dared, given the falling dusk and the uncertain rocky footing, Taniquel headed for the nearest of the outcroppings. The horse shook itself vigorously and trailed after her.

The rocky mound was farther than it had first appeared or perhaps she was moving more slowly. It receded before her, like a fevered dream. Taniquel trudged on, head lowered, shoulders drawn up against the cold. Her hair dripped on to her face, but she didn't bother to wipe away the droplets. Several times she slipped and came down hard on her knees, then laboriously clambered up and kept going. Even her thoughts turned numb. Once, she glanced up and caught a sliver of orange light. But when she looked again, a few minutes later, it was gone, a will-o'-the-wisp born of her own desperation.

More than once, she felt herself at the very end of her strength. Her shivers had begun to subside, and dimly she realized that meant exhaustion. Grimly, she kept climbing, kept hauling herself up every time she fell. She no longer knew or cared if the horse still followed her.

Then came the moment when, shadowed against the darkened hillside, the mound of rock loomed larger than ever. Its corners took on a squared appearance. Taniquel had no energy to spare for hope. She lowered her head and kept on going.

But as she came on to the smoother, more level approach, she saw that it was a building, and that what had seemed to be a hump to one side was a shed. From it came the nicker of a horse. Her own mount pushed past her, ears pricked.

She made out the rough shape of a door and windows, with streaks of yellow-orange light peeking through the closed shutters.

A dream. It must be a dream.

Warmth. Life.

She placed both hands, quivering now with emotion as well as cold, on the wooden door latch. The door swung open. Heat and light bathed her face. She stepped up on the rough-hewn threshold, hardly daring to believe her eyes.

Like the shelters on Acosta land, this one was a single-roomed stone structure lined with storage bins and beds—wooden frames with some kind of pallet, probably straw. One had been made up with blankets. A fire, small but merry, danced in the fireplace. A black-iron pot sent forth the smell of stewed meat and herbs. A metal trail bowl and spoon had been laid out on the hearth.

I am either dead or dreaming.

Taniquel unclasped her cloak, leaving it in a sodden heap just inside the door, and rushed to the fireplace. She knelt, holding out her hands. Her fingers burned and tingled. The heat felt wonderful on her face.

With the spoon, she ladled out a portion of stew and began to eat. The meat, some kind of jerky which had been soaked and then simmered, was still tough. She didn't bother chewing, just gulped down the chunks. The hot liquid filled her stomach, warming her from within.

She would lay her clothes out on the hearth to dry, keeping them well away from any stray spark. The blankets would make a warm wrapping. She could rest here for a day or two, for surely there would be more food, as well as fodder for the horse. . . .

With a click of the latch, the door swung open and then caught on the rumpled cloak. Taniquel swung around to see a figure in a hooded riding length cape standing framed in the doorway. For a terrifying instant, she thought the ghostly *laranzu* from Ambervale had followed her. But the cape was forest green, not gray.

The man pushed back his hood as he stepped forward. Taniquel's first impression was of gray eyes filled with light, a halo of unruly copper-bright hair, an expression of deep concern.

"Praise Aldones, you're safe," he said. "I thought I'd never find you."

Sweet heavens, he thinks I'm someone else.

The thought slipped away as the room went sideways, vision dimmed, and her legs gave way beneath her.

18

Coryn rushed forward and caught the woman in his arms before she hit the floor. Even soaking wet, she was surprisingly light, as if all her substance had blazed forth in her eyes, leaving nothing but a delicate shell. As he laid her on the bed, he looked into her face. The firelight touched but did not mask the porcelain translucency of her skin, the masses of midnight-black hair, the sweep of the lashes over deep circles like bruises.

She had called to him in his sleep for two nights now, her voice a song that went beyond pain, beyond longing, beyond courage. He had heard her sobbing in his dreams with a poignancy and power that shook him to the core. And now he held her in his arms, a girl not yet out of her teens.

He shook himself back to practical reality. Her fingers and face were half-frozen. Whispering that he meant her no harm, he gently pulled off her boots and sodden socks with holes worn in the heels. The dress was more difficult, but he knew from his early training as a monitor that she must be dry to be warm. Her skin felt icy. He dried her with the extra shirt from his pack, soft thick *chervine*-kid wool, and wrapped her in the blankets, laying his own cape over them.

She had not awakened by the time he'd seen to her horse and finished his dinner. Her skin felt no warmer and her breathing was quick and shallow. If she had been any of the Tower women, he would not have hesitated to do what must come next. But she was a stranger, not used to the closeness of Tower living. Moreover, she was clearly well-born, and just as clearly hunted and desperate. He had seen the look of terror in her eyes. He pulled off his own clothes and slipped between the blankets next to her. If she survived the night, he told himself, she could berate him all she liked.

The cold of her body sent Coryn's heart pounding and caught his breath in his throat. He settled in behind her, fitting his legs behind hers as he wrapped her in his arms. She smelled of snow and wet wool and some sweet herb. Lessons in body control came back to him, how to deepen his breathing, to generate more heat. The *cristoforos* developed techniques of staying warm through the terrible winters at Nevarsin, and the workers at Tramontana, where it also got very cold, had adopted some of them for use during long nights of work with little movement. He visualized the core of his body as a furnace with the flames leaping ever higher. Within minutes, the warmth from his own body enveloped both of them. The woman's muscles softened, she gave a little sigh, and sank into a deeper sleep.

✦

Coryn woke just before dawn, as had been his habit on the trail. Outside, his horse stamped restlessly in the shed. The woman still slept, snoring lightly. Her hair had dried into an ebony tangle. He slipped out from under the blankets and into his own clothes. After adding more wood to the banked coals, he attended to the horses. In the gray light, he saw that the greedy beasts had made short work of last night's feed. He left them placidly munching on breakfast. The girl's horse was in poor shape, so he gave it a double portion of grain and covered it with his own mount's blanket.

The rising sun showed more storm clouds from the north, enough to keep both of them pinned here for days. He filled a bucket with snow for meltwater and went back to the shelter.

"Stop right there!" The woman sat up, blankets clutched to her chest and eyes blazing. "What happened to my clothes?"

Coryn put the bucket down and pointed to the hearth, where he'd spread them out to dry. "They're still damp. You'll be better off as you are."

"I have more, tied to my saddle."

He shook his head and took a step toward his own pack.

"Don't move!" Her voice lashed out, imperious enough to stop him in his tracks. She ran her fingers through tendrils of still-damp hair. "They must have been washed away in the river . . . How did I get here . . . like this?"

"Damisela—"

She glared at him.

"Damisela, if I meant you harm, you would not be alive to scold me now. Your clothes were drenched and you half-dead from cold. I'd been out in the storm searching for you—"

"Why? Who sent you?"

"Let's begin again. I am Coryn of Tramontana, matrix technician of the Third Circle and on my way to train as under-Keeper at Neskaya. And you?"

"Tani—just Tani."

Coryn sat on the edge of the bed, although she shifted away from him. "You have nothing to fear from me, Just Tani. I knew you were out there because you called to me—" he gestured to his forehead, "—here. Surely you know of such things among the *laran* workers of the Towers."

She nodded, an oddly pensive expression flickering over her features. "I'm afraid I've been . . . ungracious. You were already here, at the shelter. I stumbled in, ate your soup, you put me in your own bed, and I'm treating you no better than an outlaw." She gave him a half-smile like a flash of sun on the first spring morning. He thought he'd never seen anything so beautiful.

"I—" For some reason, his voice wouldn't work right. "I'll make breakfast."

Tani sat quietly while Coryn stoked the fire, melted the snow in the little iron pot and brought the water to a boil. Then he added the mixture of rolled grain, ground nuts, and chopped dried fruit sweetened from his precious store of honey, the staple breakfast at the Towers. She swayed, struggling to stay upright as she accepted a bowl. He talked of the horses, of the weather, inconsequential things.

"You are . . . very kind," she said, laying aside her half-eaten breakfast and slumping back amid the covers. Within moments, she slipped into a drowse.

When Coryn returned to check on her a short while later, she still slept, now coughing fitfully. His heart sank when he saw how fragile she looked, the delicate bones showing beneath the fine-grained skin, the hectic flush of color, the huge dark shadows around her eyes.

"Tani." He touched the back of his hand to one cheek. Her skin burned. "Tani!" She murmured and rolled away from him. Nor did her delirium lighten when he lay damp compresses across her forehead.

Coryn stood for a long moment, irresolute. Kieran and his Tower teachers had emphasized over and over again that he must never intrude into another person's energy body without their consent. He found the very idea repugnant. Yet to monitor her, to descend into the cell-deep level to fight the lung fever, he must do just that. Or let her die.

He knelt beside the cot and took one of her hands in his. How frail the bones felt, the skin so thin and soft. A lady's hand, that not even days of neglect on the trail could disguise. Farther up on the wrist was a mostly-healed sore, just where an archer's leather guard would rub. A lady, indeed. A warrior queen. He held the hand to his face, the slender fingers cupping his cheek. All he had to do was turn his head slightly to kiss the palm.

Awake. Awake.

Bruise-dark lids fluttered open. For a moment, she stared at him . . . pupils dilated . . . lips moved soundlessly. Then the startled look faded.

"Cor— Coryn? I'm so cold."

He lay her hand on the blanket and patted it. "You have a lung fever. From exposure, most certainly. Listen to me, Tani. In the Tower, I first trained as a monitor, learning to use my mind to heal. I can help you fight off the fever. May I do so?"

"Your . . . mind. Oh, *laran.*" Her gaze slipped, and he thought she had drifted back into sleep. A spasm of coughing shook her and he saw how weak she was. "I had that done once, when I was a child." There was an odd inflection to her words. Had something . . . *happened* to her?

"I will examine your body, not pry into any secret thoughts," he hastened to say. "It will not hurt. In fact, it would help if you slept."

"You have brought me nothing but good," she murmured. "In every way, you have been a blessing. . . ."

Silence lengthened, until he realized that she slept once more.

A blessing . . . That was all the consent he would get.

He composed himself and went to work, first skimming the outer energy levels of her body, then sinking deeper into the structure of tissues. Tramontana had its share of injuries from cold, so he recognized the frostbite damage in her feet. It was a simple matter to stabilize dam-aged cell membranes, to increase the flow of blood to bring in added nutrients and carry away the waste of dead cells. She might lose a toenail or two as well as some skin, but these would heal with time. At this level, he also found bruises and a cracked rib, all of which would resolve on their own.

Still deeper, he followed the stream of air through her parted lips, down the breathing passages to the airy sacs of her lungs. Fluid choked the lower lobes, where the channels glowed red darkening to brown. The defenses of her body, weakened by hunger and exposure, responded only sluggishly. He searched for any sign of spore or poison, such as those responsible for lungrot, and to his relief found none. It was a natural illness, one which rarely struck a healthy young adult. Could she have some other, underlying disease?

Calming his own thoughts, Coryn sank even deeper. He checked the channels carrying life force through the glands in her throat, her heart, her liver and spleen . . . kidneys . . . womb.

She was with child, he realized with surprise. Only a few weeks, but there it was, that soft golden glow.

Who would send a pregnant woman out in weather like this? What would drive her to risk it?

Pregnant . . . alone . . . and very desperate . . .

And brave. And heartrendingly beautiful. If he had not been half in love with her already, her plight alone would have brought him to it.

Gently, gradually, he began shifting the fluid in her lungs, reabsorbing it through the membranes which lined the air sacs. Here and there, he found minute pockets of infection, blots of darkness which her body's weakened defenses could not resist. Into them, he sent pulses of energy, which he visualized as white light. Some dissolved immediately in bursts of rainbow colors, others more slowly. As her lungs began to clear, he sensed the warmth of rising oxygen levels, a pastel iridescence like the inside of a pearl shell. The glowing light drew him, and he paused on his way back to the surface. Music surrounded him, filled him, the rippling arpeggios of harp and woman singing together without words. Without meaning to, against all his intentions, he had brushed against her mind.

For a moment out of time, he saw her, the form of a woman bathed in shimmering radiance. Hair like spun black glass floated like an aureole around her face. Her eyes were open, her mouth laughing. She stretched out her arms to him and then in a flicker was gone.

Coryn returned to his own body, stiff from prolonged motionlessness. The fire had died down, leaving the shelter chilly. Outside, winds battered the shuttered windows with renewed force. He stretched, suddenly aware of the energy drain which accompanied *laran* work. He had thought Marisela overly protective when she insisted on packing extra supplies of concentrated food. Now, shaking with hunger, he gratefully brought out the bars of honeyed nuts.

Tani slept all the rest of the day, while the storm blustered and swept the hills with another few feet of snow. Coryn tended her, tended the horses, and rested to replenish his own energy reserves. He thought a little of what might happen if they were storm-bound for long. His food stores would stretch for himself, but not for two people, even eked out with what had been left in the shelter.

None of this seemed terribly important. He had only to glance in her direction to see the slow, easy rise of her chest, the profile of her face, the contours of shoulder and hip under the blankets. Once she rolled over and stretched one arm above her head in artless grace. In a few hours, in a few days, the storm would break, she would be strong enough to travel, and he would never see her again.

✦

The sun rose with Tani on the third morning, bright and clear. When Coryn returned from feeding the horses, he found her dressed, her hair plaited neatly in a single long braid, and in the process of burning the porridge. Laughing, he took the spoon from her hand and added more water.

"I'm afraid I'm not much of a cook," she said.

"Neither am I, but it's necessary if you're traveling," he said. The bottom of the pot would take a bit of soaking, that was all.

When the porridge was ready, he divided it and added the last of his honey. She sat cross-legged on the cot, cradling her bowl in her hands. After a time of eating in silence, she cleared her throat.

"Coryn, I'm grateful for all the help you've given me." Now she sounded hesitant, about to say she had no way to repay him.

"My Keeper believes we have an obligation to use our *laran* in service to others. I'm glad that I had the skills to heal the fever." It struck him that in an odd way, he was evening the score for Kristlin's death.

"I—I have to keep moving," she said.

"Because whoever's looking for you might find you?"

Her eyes widened, then shifted as she realized how many ways she must have given herself away. "There is no safety here, and none for you if they catch me with you. My only hope is to reach Thendara. But I'm afraid I've lost my bearings."

"Thendara! Oh," seeing her look of dismay. "Yes, you have. This road leads to Neskaya Tower. Would—would that not be safe enough?"

Her lips tightened, but she shook her head. "If it were only myself— No, I have kin in Thendara who must be told, who—I must reach."

Some ways back, Coryn had passed a crossroads with a slender path, little more than a goat trail, which joined the main road to Thendara. It would take Tani perhaps two days in clear weather to get there, if she did not get lost again. Of course, he could go with her and then continue on down toward the lowlands . . . and the perfection of the meeting would dribble away, an hour or a day at time, in useless longing.

He described the road to Thendara and its distance, adding, "I could go with you—"

"No," she said with a firmness that spoke of years of command, "although I thank you once again. Please—you would be putting yourself in needless danger. I would not see your kindness repaid by harm. Even knowing my destination . . . Well, all Zandru's smiths can't put that chick back into its egg. But I can read a map, if you can draw one."

He had maps, wrapped carefully in oiled silk against the damp, although nothing to copy them to. She bent over them, spread out on the hearth, her lips moving as she studied the landscape contours. "Ah yes, this is where I went wrong . . ." Murmuring, she traced a path with one finger.

"There are trading villages here and here," he said, pointing. "I can give you food enough to reach there and a little money to pay for lodging." He grinned wryly. "It isn't much."

"I have no way to repay you. What little I had, the river took."

"I'm not asking for anything in return."

"What do you want?" Her eyes searched his.

The firelight burnished her features, turning her into a woman of gold and ebony. All he had to do was lean forward and kiss her.

He lowered his gaze. "To have you safe and well."

"We none of us can be sure of safety in these dreadful times."

He thought of little Kristlin, dead by *laran*-spawned lungrot in her father's own house. "No, that's true enough."

Coryn packed up the food and insisted she take his second set of knitted cap, scarf, and mittens, though the mittens were too big for her. To these he added a sleeveless woolen jacket. When she protested, he said, quite truthfully, that he could wear only one at a time. He was no longer the boy who set off for Tramontana with packs bulging with extra comforts.

Once all the preparations were complete, Tani settled herself in the saddle and gathered up the reins. The air had already begun to warm in the rising sun, promising a fair day. The old horse looked rested, no longer limping as he brought it out to be saddled. Coryn stood beside the stirrup, looking up at Tani, remembering how Kristlin had looked up at him the day he'd ridden away to Tramontana.

Tani's brows drew together and for a moment, her eyes took on that slightly distracted expression. She looked as if she were about to say something.

No, he decided. *Let it end here.* He would carry her memory like his mother's handkerchief, folded close to his heart.

"*Adelandeyo,*" he said, stepping back to slap her horse on the rump. *Go with the gods.* Then he turned and went back into the shelter to gather up his own gear.

✦

Coryn came over the last hill and caught his first view of Neskaya Tower, rising beyond the ancient yet thriving city of the same name. It was late in the day and the gathering dusk cast an opalescent sheen over the vast, open sky. His heart rose up and caught in his throat at the sight. He wondered if he were dreaming the turrets of pale translucent blue stone that glowed softly like moonlight in the distance.

The city of Neskaya was by far the largest collection of human habitations he'd ever seen. As he rode through it, he marveled at the different styles of architecture, stone and brick as well as timber, so much precious glass, the bright colors of plaids and painted signs, the blended strains of music, street sellers' cries, chatter, and animals.

His horse, tired and footsore, picked up the pace as it scented hay and a dry stall ahead. The details of the Tower became clear as he approached, the grace of its lines, the superb *laran* workmanship of the fitting of the stones, the arched entrance, the windows set to catch winter sun.

The front doors, ashleaf wood polished to a high golden gloss, had been thrown open and a group of adolescent children were playing a game with sticks and balls in the courtyard. A man in plain warm clothing, tunic over trousers tucked mountain-style into laced boots, came forward to greet Coryn.

"Ah, we've been looking for you these past three days," the man said, after introducing himself as a mechanic. He had a broad, open face, seamed with laugh lines around his eyes and mouth, and rust-red hair worn in a dozen slender braids past his shoulders. He did not ask the reason for the delay, only expressed his relief at Coryn's safe arrival.

Others came to welcome him, including the Keeper under whom he was to train. After dinner, Bernardo Alton invited Coryn for cups of *jaco* flavored with sweet spicebark. Unlike Kieran, whose inner stillness imbued his austere quarters, Bernardo was always in action, his rooms reflecting a richness of interests. Brightly colored sketches of mountains and eagles, candles sculpted into the form of trees, a chest of beautifully carved black wood with rows of tiny drawers in a style Coryn had never seen before, a contraption of leather and metal springs and a bale of unspun wool in shades of orange, caught Coryn's eye. Like the room itself, Bernardo sizzled with energy and invention; thin and whip-strong, he was rarely at rest.

"I am sorry to welcome you with sad news, but last night we received a message from Tramontana along the relays," Bernardo said. "Kieran has died after a bout of fever."

Coryn lowered his eyes, bracing for a lash of pain. None came, as if the Keeper's last gift had been a peaceful heart. He remembered the gray light in Kieran's eyes as they parted, how tired and frail the old man had looked.

He knew that as soon as he left us, Tramontana would be forced to meet Ambervale's demands and I would be at risk. He hung on until I was safely free.

"I thank you for telling me," Coryn said formally.

"He will be sorely missed among us. He was a great Keeper."

"And a good friend."

"And a friend," Bernardo nodded. "If you wish, you may speak with Tramontana in the relays tonight."

"Again, I thank you."

For a long moment, the two sat in silence, broken only by the soft hush of embers falling and the tapping of Bernardo's fingers on the arm of his chair, a complicated mathematical pattern.

There will be time enough to mourn, Coryn thought, remembering Kieran's patient compassion after the death of his father and sister. Kieran's parting gift had been his freedom and this new life.

Bernardo said in a lighter tone, "When we sent word to Tramontana, asking if they had anyone suitable for training as an under-Keeper, Kieran told us that you are not afraid to take the initiative and try something new."

"Is there some particular project you have in mind?" Coryn asked, rousing to the question.

Bernardo laughed, which seemed to be his usual response to questions, from the few short hours Coryn had known him. "Not yet, anyway. However, I'd like your view of an idea I've been working on, a way to make *clingfire* more stable, less explosive. If we succeed, we'll need to devise a separate detonator device . . ."

He went on, but Coryn's thoughts remained on the subject of *clingfire*. It seemed that even Neskaya was making the stuff. There was, he reflected with a bitterness that surprised him, no place on Darkover safe from the ravages of war. Maybe Bronwyn was right when she said that the only way to security was to make the cost of aggression too high.

19

Thendara at last.

Taniquel peered over the top of the farmer's cart in which she'd ridden those last painful miles, in exchange or perhaps in pity for the horse who clearly could go no farther. With her cloak hanging loose about her shoulders against the mildness of the morning, she perched between heaped sacks of spring rye, bushel baskets of cherries and early carrots, mesh bags of potatoes and redroots. The cart turned a corner, and she craned her neck for a better look at the city of her birth.

From a distance, the city resembled a sprawling marketplace at the foot of an immense cluster of fortifications and towers. It assailed her senses: the size and depth of the walls; the rows and rows of noble houses; the stables and warehouses; the clattering of armed cavalry; the shouts of tradesmen; the chants of the *cristoforos* wending their way along the streets; the smells of dust and cabbage and refuse.

The cart lurched over the unpaved roads, jostling against wagons of hay, droves of sheep, and an immense dray of rough-cut lumber pulled laboriously by two dun horses with feet the size of dinner plates. The farmer hauled his team of *chervines* to a halt and held out his arms to help Taniquel get down. "Yon's the gate to the inner city, *d'msela*. I must be off to sell me wares."

He had already made himself late for the market opening by taking her on and tempering his speed for her comfort. Taniquel slipped to the ground, fishing in the folds of her makeshift sash for the last of the copper hair clasps. She was almost ashamed to offer it to him, so battered and poor-looking, although a richer thing than he could ever afford to buy.

The farmer lowered his head and refused at first to take it, saying he needed no payment—meaning he would not wring the last belongings from someone in such pitiful need. But she pressed it into his callused palm, saying it was not for him, but a dowry for his daughter, the bright-eyed child she'd seen peeking out from the woven door hanging.

Easing the empty saddlebags across one shoulder, she approached the gates to the inner city. Two City Guards in smart uniforms, sheathed swords in plain view, barred her way. The older bore the bright red hair of his caste, probably a cadet son of one of the great houses, on a tour with the Guards to fulfill his civic duty.

Expressionlessly, with a flick of the eyes, the Guards assessed and as quickly dismissed her. She must look like an outlaw's doxy or worse, disheveled, filthy, and travel-worn. But she lifted her head, with all the pride of a *comynara,* and asked admittance.

"What business have you in the city?" Red-hair asked, omitting any more polite form of address.

She gave him a short bow of the head, one suitable for an indispensable but recalcitrant servant. "I bear an urgent message for King Rafael Hastur, second of that name. Pray escort me to him without delay."

The younger Guard snorted in derision. "Give us the message, then."

"It is for his ears, not yours," Taniquel said. "He will not thank for you delaying me."

"Now see, Missy, we can't let just any riffraff go wandering about the streets," the older one said. "Anyone can claim what you're claiming and lie or worse, be up to no good. How can we be sure His Majesty knows you from a sack of redroots?"

Taniquel suppressed the impulse to strike the guard with the empty saddlebag across his grinning, mocking face. "You can only believe— from my speech and bearing—that I am not as I appear. I have been long on the road and under difficult circumstances. Pray take me to someone who *can* make a decision, if you cannot."

"Get on your way!" the older Guard said, gesturing. "Ply your stories down in the lower market. A few pretty speeches may get you a bed for the night, if that's what you're after, or a hot meal. Aldones knows you could use it."

"I will not be dismissed in this way!" Taniquel stamped one foot, wincing as her sore heel came down on a cobblestone. "I demand to see my uncle, Rafael Hastur!"

The Guards exchanged glances, grinning once more. "Oh, so it's her uncle now, is he? You could be charged in the *cortes* with spreading lies like that. Better stick to your own kind." The younger Guard took her elbow.

"How dare you!" Taniquel whipped her arm away. "If you had the intellect of a pea-hen, you would instantly recognize I am no—no—" She could not bring herself to say the word *prostitute.* "Men of discernment are not blinded by fine clothes or feathers, nor deceived by their absence!"

The younger Guard reached for her again, with the plain intent of handling her far less gently this time.

"I am Taniquel Elinor Hastur-Acosta, daughter of Jerana, sister to King Rafael!"

The young man dropped his hand as if burned. His face paled as he clearly considered for the first time that she might be speaking the truth and what would be his fate for mauling her.

"Damisela," the older Guard said, "let us try the truth of your words. Come with us."

With some measure of courtesy, the older Guard escorted her through the teeming streets and byways to the servants' entrance of the castle, where they were greeted by a lower assistant *coridom*, a rather officious man of middle age. He offered her *jaco* and brown bread and asked the Guard if she had kin within the city.

"She claims to be the King's daughter," the Guard said, raising one eyebrow to underscore his disbelief. Rafael Hastur had sired only sons, as everyone in Thendara knew.

"Niece," she said, only to be further ignored. She decided that any further mention of her uncle would get her summarily thrown out. At least she was inside the castle, which was progress.

"I simply don't understand why you bothered to bring her here when I must attend to so many more pressing matters than to listen to the tales of unkempt young women," said the assistant *coridom*. "I am a person of importance. I have schedules, protocol meetings, arrangements to make!"

With some persuasion, Taniquel convinced him that her present condition was due to exposure and travel, but not that she had any legitimate business inside the castle. He decided she was some servant's child, given to dreams of grandeur as a result of her mother's romantic stories.

"Please," she said, "let me speak with someone who can vouch for me."

Gerolamo, her uncle's paxman and chief councillor, would surely remember her, but when she brought up his name, the assistant *coridom* scowled and turned impatient. Running out of time, she racked her memory for some horse-handler or cook's assistant who might remember her from girlhood. Each name was rejected as unknown or with the comment, "Oh, Old Elfrida, she passed on three winters back," or "What could a slip of a thing like you want with him?" and finally, "You've taken up enough of my day. Off with you!"

Weariness mixed with the taste of poorly roasted *jaco* and the trembling in her limbs. She had not escaped from Belisar's bed and come across all these miles, past Deslucido's soldiers, through flood and snowstorm, to be dismissed by a headblind fool!

"Zandru's scorpions take the lot of you!" she snarled, near the very end of her temper. "Is there not a single person in the whole castle who can see past appearances?"

The Guard, the red-haired one, flinched at her words, as if struck by an invisible blast. He hurried from the room after ordering that she be kept there. Taniquel was too tired to protest. She sipped the last of her *jaco* and wondered if she had the strength to try a dash through the kitchen and up the back stairs. The assistant *coridom* summoned a pair of chef's aides, the kind of burly young men capable of turning the huge castle spits, to watch her. Then he went about his own business. Scullery maids with pans of soapy water or baskets of vegetables passed in and out, along with a page, who stared at her round-eyed before hurrying on his errand, and a number of others Taniquel took little notice of.

After waiting what seemed like hours, Taniquel found herself in the presence of the slightly built woman whose once brilliant red hair had now faded to gray. She blinked, recognizing the *leronis* who had tested her for *laran* so many years ago. Lady Caitlin Elhalyn-Syrtis would have looked elegant in rags, but was formidable in a rich blue tabard over a flowing spider silk underdress of the same color, setting off the brilliance of the starstone which nestled at the base of her throat. The servants backed away respectfully, and the assistant *coridom*, who had come bustling back in, turned pale and silent at her glance.

"This is indeed the niece of the King." The *leronis* did not need to study Taniquel to recognize her. A swift, feather-light mental touch quickly gave rise to an exclamation. "My dear child, whatever has happened?"

"Acosta has fallen to Damian of Ambervale," Taniquel replied. Although it was rude of her, she simply did not have the energy to rise to her feet. "King Padrik has been slain and the castle taken. I alone escaped."

"Send word to the King at once!"

The assistant *coridom* jumped into action and vanished down a hallway.

The *leronis'* eyes flickered to Taniquel's belly, flattened by weeks of semistarvation on the trail. "Sweet Evanda, we must lose no time! I must monitor you properly."

Taniquel drew breath to answer and then burst into tears, the very last thing she wanted to do. The *leronis* issued a string of orders and very shortly, Taniquel found herself ushered into a suite of luxuriously appointed rooms, suitable for the most highly ranked visitors.

Lady Caitlin did not wait for Taniquel to undress or wash, but insisted on examining her right away. Taniquel, stretched out on a sheet spread over the enormous bed, winced at the psychic sensation of sand scraping over skin. By contrast, Coryn's mental touch had been so smooth and gentle as to border on pleasure. She could not remember ever feeling so safe and so real, as if he saw all through her with those light-filled eyes and accepted whatever he found.

Now she gritted her teeth and tried to breathe slowly.

"Your child is alive and well, unharmed," Lady Caitlin commented. "And your body is in surprisingly good shape. You have had some *laran* healing—"

"Yes," Taniquel said, struggling to prop herself up on her elbows. "I spent some days at a travel shelter along the Neskaya road. My fellow traveler was a *laranzu*." Under Lady Caitlin's sharp glance, she added, "Coryn, his name was."

"Coryn of Tramontana? Oh, yes. When I do my rotations at Hali, I sometimes encounter him over the relays. I wonder what he was doing on the road to Neskaya."

"Something about training as an under-Keeper."

"Oh, great fortune for them to have gotten him! Now, you must bathe, but not in water too hot, and then sleep as long as you like. I will have proper food brought up, and you must send for me if you suffer any stomach sickness."

The next thing she knew, a bevy of maids appeared to free Taniquel from her filthy dress and help her into a tub of pleasantly warm water. The mingled scents of bath herbs and rosewater eased the ache from her lungs, even as the seductive warmth melted her weary muscles.

She stretched, examining her skin. Scratches and bruises covered her arms and legs, even the sides of her body. Her toes itched where new skin had formed under the frost-dead layer.

A huge soft sponge, lathered with fine-milled soap, hung from her limp hand. Now that she was safe, the last of the willpower which had driven her these past few days evaporated along with the wisps of steam. Her hair, a tangle of knots and burrs, trailed in the water. In a little while, a maid or three would be along to help her wash and comb it. For now, though, it was good to rest against the smooth wooden slats of the tub, her head resting on a rolled towel. To close her eyes and drift for a moment . . . to dream . . .

Coryn's face floated in front of her closed eyes. Her lips curled in a smile. Which was the dream—the hours of numbing cold, the present luxury of warm, sweet-smelling water, or the memory of those light-filled eyes, those strong arms around her, the feel of his skin against hers. . . .

She startled awake as the maids came back in, clucking at the state of her hair, and in short order she was lathered, shampooed, rinsed, dried, combed, rubbed with soothing ointments, bandaged, swathed in a downy-soft night dress, and tucked into a feather bed under several layers of comforters. Her final thoughts were that her long ordeal was at last over.

✦

She slept for two days, waking only to gulp down citrus-flavored water from the pitcher at her bedside. On the third morning, nausea drove her from her bed and the maids came fluttering in to find her crouched over the chamber pot, retching. She waved away both their offers of help and any sort of breakfast. A few hours later, she felt steady enough in her stomach to dress and be presented to the King.

King Rafael Hastur II met her in the suite of rooms reserved for family. Although he had set aside the formal tokens of his kingship, his belted robe, purple brocade trimmed with royal ermine, set off his figure, still graceful as a dancer even at his age, that charismatic beauty which graced so many of the Hastur men. He bent to give her a kinsman's embrace. The hairs of his neatly clipped beard, silver-frosted rust, prickled her cheeks. Although average in height, he seemed smaller than she remembered him as a child.

"Dear niece, it grieves me to welcome you back under such circumstances. I hoped you would have a long and happy life in your new home. Now Caitlin says you bring news of Acosta's defeat."

"Oh, Uncle!" she cried as he guided her to a padded chair. "Acosta has fallen to that son-of-a-Dry-Towns-bandit, Damian Deslucido!" She took a breath, gathered herself under control, and began her story.

Rafael retired to his own, much more massive chair, and looked pensive as she told of the attack and battle at the gates, the trap and the spells cast by Deslucido's *laranzu*. Here he broke in, making her go over each detail of the aircar bombings. In response to his probing questions, Taniquel searched her memory for each detail, the shape and number of the airships, their markings, the color of the flames.

"At first, I feared they had dropped *clingfire* on us," she said, shivering at the memory. "But the flames quickly smoldered like normal ones, given how damp the wood was."

Rafael's dark brows drew together. "If Deslucido meant to rule Acosta, not destroy it, then he would not want to damage the castle if he could help it. And the compulsion—you say that everyone was affected by a terror of opening the gates?"

"You see, the gates had to stay closed to trap Padrik." Taniquel stumbled through her explanation. "If only I'd acted sooner, he might have won through." She heard the bitterness in her own words.

The King shook his head. "You must not take such a burden of guilt upon yourself. You have done more than your part in bringing us this news. I must convene the council."

For a moment, he looked distracted, and Taniquel recalled that, as Hastur of Hastur, he had long headed the effort to restrain the use of the more fearsome *laran* weapons. His concern went beyond the fate of his niece's small realm.

"Deslucido has been annexing weaker kingdoms for some years now," he went on, "but we had thought he preferred peaceful means. We'd had word of an honorable marriage offer in some cases, in another, the absence of a legitimate heir claimant to the throne."

"That is hardly the case here!" Taniquel said with some vehemence. "Uncle, I carry the *di catenas* son of Padrik, lawful King of Acosta. Damian Deslucido may have seized control of Acosta Castle, but he cannot rightfully claim the throne as his. You must declare my son king, with me as regent, and restore the true line of Acosta!"

"Tani," he said, sighing and shaking his head, "the headstrong girl we knew has matured into an equally headstrong queen."

"There is no time to be lost! For all we know, Belisar Deslucido will be crowned King as we speak! Even without me as his Queen, the longer we allow him to continue without challenge, the stronger his claim will grow."

"Calm yourself, child." He spoke in such a tone, with that quiet Hastur *command*, that even if he had not been King, she would have fallen silent. She reminded herself that he had not come lately to his own throne, and had held it against more than a handful of challengers.

"I am listening, Uncle."

"Firstly, I bid you well come to Thendara and to my court. You will always find a safe home with us." *And you need not behave like an unmannered child with a pack of Ya-men yammering on your track.*

She dipped her head. "I thank you, Uncle."

"We must have your needs attended to, and either the castle midwives or Lady Caitlin to make sure both you and your unborn child recover full health. And after that, I suppose all your aunts and cousins will want to make much of you, even those who remember you as a small, obstreperous child, one they were more than happy to pawn off on poor Lady Acosta."

Taniquel caught the twinkle in his eye and smiled despite herself. "I will try to do my best to bring honor upon my foster parents. Lady Acosta did manage to teach me a few manners, even if my arrival in Thendara did not give me ample opportunity to display them."

A flickering smile played over the corners of King Rafael's mouth. "You did well enough. As for the political situation, there is no immediate action which is both appropriate and prudent. The Hellers are a tinder-box ready to go up in flames."

"Then now is the time to stop Deslucido, before his strength has grown," Taniquel said, too tired to back off although she already knew the answer.

"Now," he repeated with regal deliberation, "is the time to go slowly and thoughtfully. And most especially to not go seeking out a battle which might not otherwise be thrust upon us."

"It will," she said, lowering her eyes to her lap, where her fingers had curled into fists. "On Deslucido's terms or on ours, it will."

"The world goes as it will, my dear, and not as you or I would have it—or, in this case, create it out of our own fears. You have survived a difficult trial and you have borne yourself with pride. Now rest, and let wiser heads take on the world's burdens."

Taniquel knew when she had been dismissed. She rose, curtsied as a nobly bred lady to an equal, and withdrew.

20

Spring melted into a hot, sticky summer such as came only in the low-lands. Under the watchful eye of Lady Caitlin and her royal aunts, Taniquel recovered her strength. Good food and a healthy pregnancy smoothed away the drawn look from her face and rounded her breasts and belly. She dutifully swallowed the herbal concoctions, ate the special foods urged on her by the midwives, and took the gentle exercise prescribed for her. But that was where her meekness ended.

Taniquel had attended the first meeting of Rafael's council by his formal invitation, as a witness rather than a participant. He wanted her first-hand testimony of the use of *laran* in the conquest of Acosta. But soon, she took her own place, debating the issues as freely as any of the men.

The council included other branches of the powerful Hastur family, Hastur of Carcosa and Hastur of Elhalyn, as well as several collaterals. Taniquel didn't know them, although the mark of kinship was plain on their features. Some followed Rafael's lead in considering the spread of weapons like *clingfire* to be of paramount concern, while others regarded the use of *laran* mental coercion, such as the compulsion spell at the Acosta gates, a more serious threat.

"A gross abuse of *laran*," was the opinion of Lewis Hastur, one of the Carcosa representatives, as they met at their regular session.

Taniquel's chair, smaller and plainer than the others, was set diago-
nally back from her uncle's around a circular table. On the other side of
Rafael, his paxman and chief councillor, Gerolamo, stood with watchful
eyes and his usual impassive expression. Maps and an opened journal, as
well as a pitcher of watered wine and one of plain water covered the
polished wood. The mullioned windows were thrown open against the
heat of the late summer afternoon, admitting honey-thick air.

"And yet it is not unknown in warfare," Rafael said. "*Laran* workers
have long used similar methods to instill fear by tapping into each man's
private nightmares, for example, or giving water the illusion of fresh-
spilled blood. Our highest priority must be halting the development of
new weapons."

"None of this justifies the present use of such compulsion spells,"
Lewis responded.

"But it *can* be resisted," Taniquel said. They turned to look at her.
"In the battle for *our* castle . . ." She gently emphasized the word to
remind them that she was Queen of Acosta as well as *comynara*. Despite
her subordinate placement about the table, she formally outranked all of
them except Rafael. ". . . In that battle, I myself was able to overcome
the compulsion. So defense is possible."

"That's true," Darren-Mikhail, *nedestro* nephew to the reigning Elhalyn lord and youngest of the council, nodded. "But only if the defending
lord has his own stable of trained *laranzu'in*. Ordinary soldiers . . ." He
shrugged.

"Which brings us to the latest news," Rafael said. "We have received
word across the relays at Hali last night that Tramontana Tower has ac-
ceded to Deslucido's sovereignty."

"What!"

"Yes, the situation is now quite different than when we met last
spring. Previously, we were concerned only with Deslucido's occasional
minor use of *laran*."

"The compulsion spell and the use of aircars in battle is hardly
minor," Lewis snapped.

"Deslucido did not use *clingfire* in the attack, although he clearly
could have delivered it from his aircars," Rafael said patiently. "Whether
because he would not use *clingfire* or he could not, we may never know.
Our relays in Hali tell us that Tramontana has now begun making *clingfire*
and other weapons for him. There are rumors—unsubstantiated at pres-

ent—of his past use of lungrot, bought from a renegade circle. All the smaller neighboring kingdoms are in a panic over his recent expansions. He may be angling to eventually bring the battle home to us here at Hastur. Or he may be content with what he has. Whichever, he is now to be reckoned with in the overall balance of powers. Will he use the weapons at his disposal with restraint? We have no way of knowing."

Listening, Taniquel thought, *Rafael will not provoke Deslucido into outright conflict. He should have struck before Deslucido gained access to* clingfire.

The time would come when Rafael Hastur would have no choice, when Deslucido must be stopped. Taniquel felt certain of it.

After a long discussion of which Towers were making *laran* weapons and where they might be used, particularly the stockpiling of bonewater dust in Valeron, the council adjourned for the day. More meetings were planned later in the tenday, as well as evening festivities. Taniquel thought wryly that no matter how dire the cause for bringing Hastur cousins together, they could not pass up the chance for a rousing good party.

◆

Flushed from dancing, Taniquel made her way to the double doors thrown open to the mild summer evening. The veranda outside gave way to gardens, their leaves silvered by the mingled light of mauve Idriel, blue-green Kyrrdis, and pearly Mormallor. Tonight, three of Darkover's four moons formed a rough triangle in the sky.

Behind her, the musicians had shifted to a lively *secain*. It was just as well she'd chosen this time to slip away. Her aunts would be watching the men whirl and leap in the wild mountain dance and would not notice her absence.

Beyond the gardens, she rested her gaze on the lights of Thendara and wondered how many other families were celebrating on this night. At least she was not so far advanced in her pregnancy, her belly yet a small bulge in the skirts of her gowns, that she could not enjoy an evening of the more sedate dances.

Sighing, she leaned on the balcony railing. A soft, cool breeze ruffled her hair which had pulled loose in tendrils about her face. Her thoughts wandered toward Neskaya Tower.

Was Coryn even now gazing up at those moons? Was he thinking of her?

Ridiculous idea! He was far away, studying to become a Keeper. In all probability, he'd forgotten the few days they'd spent together.

"Vai domna?"

Taniquel dipped her head in greeting as Darren-Mikhail Elhalyn approached. "It's a beautiful evening, isn't it?"

"Yes, I've always loved this season. My tutors used to say that there were more conjunctions of the moons at Midsummer than at any other time."

"Oh, really?" she said lightly, for want of any more intelligent comment.

She regarded him more closely, noticing the awkwardness of his stance, as if he didn't quite know what to do with his hands and elbows. "I'm afraid that if you've come to ask me to dance, you must wait for a bit. Whether it's the night or my—right now, I'm too warm for dancing."

"Actually, I was hoping for a quiet word alone with you."

Taniquel startled. Darren had hardly spoken two words to her at the council meetings. "Whatever about?"

"Please, can we not sit down?" He took her arm and guided her toward a low stone bench in the shadows beyond the light streaming from the ballroom.

Taniquel allowed herself to be escorted to the bench. She told herself she had no reason to be uneasy. He was her cousin, after all, and there were plenty of people just inside the room. As soon as the *secain* ended, her aunts would doubtless come looking for her.

She settled herself on the bench, facing half toward him, and arranged her full skirts. He lowered himself awkwardly. Instead of releasing her, he grasped her hand.

"Please, cousin," she said, deftly extracting herself. "If there is something you would say to me, you must speak frankly. We may not be well acquainted, but our families are, and I remember you from when we were children here together."

"I would not speak of us as children, but as man and woman," he blurted out. "Taniquel—if I may be so bold to use your name—surely you must have noticed the effect you have on me? You are so beautiful—"

Zandru's frozen teats!

"Darren," she said as firmly as she could, "the moonlight is very beautiful, but please refrain from anything which will embarrass either of us tomorrow morning. Even if we were not kin, I am a married woman, and with child."

He moved closer to her in the shadows and his voice took on a new, disturbing resonance. "We are not so closely related that we cannot marry, and you are a widow."

"But—"

"A widow bearing a child who will need a father's name."

"Need a father's name?" Taniquel said, stung. "What are you saying?"

"Why, what should be obvious to anyone who can count the passage of moons and knows when Acosta was taken. You were pledged to the Deslucido heir, were you not? And you lived in the castle with him for at least a tenday."

"He never—I never—"

Thoughts raced through her mind. Darren was right. By now, everyone knew she was to have wedded Belisar and it was not uncommon for such marriages to be secured by a premature bedding. In the custom of the mountains, that in itself would have constituted a marriage—the sharing of a bed, a meal, a hearth. Who would believe that was not the case?

Who will believe my son is not Belisar's bastard?

"I will swear under truthspell this child is Padrik's son and heir," she said.

"Sweet lady, I am not your enemy. Indeed, I lay my heart at your feet and offer you an honorable way to restore your reputation. Let me give your son a name and a place in the world. Marry me."

Taniquel stiffened involuntarily, drawing away. "My son already has a name—his father's. And he has a place in the world—the throne of Acosta. I—" she paused, realizing how ungracious she sounded. Darren was not Belisar, and she could hear in his voice that he truly cared for her, or whatever glamorous image he had concocted of her. He might be *nedestro*, but he had been acknowledged and granted a place in Elhalyn.

"I appreciate what you are offering, Darren. Truly I do. You will make some woman a fine husband and I hope she cherishes you as you deserve. But I am not free to marry to please myself—" *Would that I were!* "—I am called to a greater duty, to free Acosta and see my son placed on the throne there."

Silence answered her, broken only by the sound of Darren's harsh breathing. Finally, he said. "You are all that is good and noble in our caste, *domna*. But you take on too much for any mere woman. What will you do, raise an army to march on Deslucido? What man will follow you? No, you will only fail and risk your son's future as well as yours. I beg you not to make this terrible mistake."

"Let it be, Darren. I do not know if I will succeed, only that I must try. I have come this far with the blessing of the gods. I must trust they will grant me the means to do their bidding."

She rose to her feet, skirts rustling. "Would you be so kind as to escort me back to my kinswomen?"

"As you wish, cousin. Perhaps after a little reflection or reasoned discussion with those older and wiser, you will see that my offer is in your own best interest."

Taniquel heard the disappointment in his voice and sent a silent prayer that it would soon pass. He held out his arm and she placed her fingertips along it. He had not asked her to dance, and she was glad of it. Meanwhile, she had a few choice words for her uncle who, she suspected, had encouraged Darren's suit.

Taniquel entered the brightly lit room, surging with the energy of the dancers and the bubbling conversation of those standing on the periphery. She hesitated, reconsidering. It would do no good to approach her uncle here or to demand that he take immediate action to ensure her son's claim to the throne of Acosta, much as she might like to do so. Rafael had already made clear his commitment to caution and neutrality.

No, she would have to go slowly, build her case point by point. Once she would have given no thought to consequences or strategy, but she had learned much, including patience, since Damian Deslucido's army came riding over the green fields of Acosta.

She seated herself beside her favorite aunt, an elderly lady who was already dozing off from the late hour and a second cup of wine punch. Presently, her uncle walked up to her, moving stiffly. He had not danced at all this evening and clearly his knee pained him. Bowing, he asked how she was enjoying the ball.

Taniquel caught the subtle shading of his words and realized that he meant her interview with Darren. So Darren had spoken first to her uncle. How like men, she thought with an instant of temper.

"It has been a pleasant evening," she said, smiling innocently. "But I grow tired from all the dancing. I will retire now." Taniquel held out her hand for him to help her to her feet.

As she headed for the door which would take her toward the private quarters of the castle, she thought briefly of asking for a word with him the next morning, but discarded the idea. He would think it had to do with Darren. A marriage there would conveniently remove her as a problem, along with her son as exiled heir to Acosta and all the political entanglements they brought.

But I will not quietly disappear into Elhalyn or anywhere else. I intend to remain a problem, a very vocal one, right here where all the world can see me.

✦

Taniquel waited for a tenday more, until the council had adjourned and Darren was safely gone. Since then, she had had little to do, beyond the embroidery and music which occupied the time of the other royal ladies. After the stimulation of the council meetings, she found these diversions tedious at best. Restlessness gnawed at her. Every day that passed allowed Deslucido to tighten his hold on Acosta and here she was, doing nothing.

Now Taniquel paused at the intersection of a corridor leading to the small reception room where the council had met and where her uncle heard private petitions. Perhaps Deslucido thought her dead, perished in the unseasonable storms. Unless someone had seen her at the ball and brought word, he might not know she survived. Her brows drew together as she considered the possibility, and how she might use it to her advantage.

Men's voices reached her from the public areas of the castle, not the usual quiet rumble but raised, clearly agitated. Her curiosity aroused, Taniquel headed in that direction. There they were, a knot of guards and men in short cloaks and boots suitable for riding, of clearly good quality. Immediately, she recognized the accents of Acosta. She hurried, moving as briskly as her long dress allowed. Once she would simply have picked up her skirts and run.

"You must leave now," a guard insisted.

"Not without seeing the King!" "He must hear us!" "At least give him a message—let him decide!"

"Take your troubles elsewhere."

Taniquel slowed her step to a more regal pace as she approached the men. A guard, recognizing her, bowed. They had not drawn their weapons, she noticed.

The strangers broke off their argument. One of them, a man of middle age whose cloak was thrown back to reveal a tunic bearing an eagle emblem to indicate his fealty to the Acosta throne, opened his mouth in surprise.

"*Vai domna!* Queen Taniquel!" Rushing forward, he fell to his knees at her feet. After a stunned instant, the others did the same. There were four in all, one of whom seemed to be a paxman, from the way he stood behind another. This close, their once-fine clothing showed the wear of hard usage and harder travel.

"Now, see here—" the senior of the guards began, for they knew her only as the niece of King Rafael. Taniquel held out a hand to prevent their interference.

"We thought you dead!" the Acosta noble cried.

"Dead at Deslucido's treacherous hands!" said another.

She reached out her hands, gently raising the men to their feet. "As you can see, I am alive and well. But what has brought you to Thendara, my lords? Come, this is no place to welcome you, standing here in the middle of a hallway." She turned to the nearest guard. "Does my uncle hold audience in the council chamber at this hour?"

"*Vai domna,*" the guard said, looking plainly unhappy.

Clearly, Rafael had refused to see these men. He would not give even the appearance of partiality to their cause, she thought angrily.

"Come with me!" She turned and, with the Acosta lords at her heels and the guards a pace behind, headed for her own quarters. The guards exchanged shocked looks as they realized her destination. Right now, she was too angry to care about her modesty or reputation. These men were hers now that Padrik was dead, hers to command and defend. If her uncle would not give them the courtesy of a private hearing, that was the least she could do.

Her sitting room, although spacious and filled with late morning light, had been furnished as a lady's retreat. Taniquel seated herself in her favorite chair. The lords, after surreptitious glances at the dainty furniture, remained standing. The effect, she realized with a secret smile, was very much as if she were holding court.

The eldest of the Acosta lords, Esteban of Greenhills, presented their case. After Acosta Castle had been so quickly taken, Ambervale forces had descended upon each vassal in rapid succession.

"It was the first we knew of the invasion," Esteban said. "What choice had we, with no time to gather our fighting men or contact our neighbors? And with his aircars overhead . . ."

Taniquel nodded. They feared *clingfire* more than they feared conquest. The mere threat of such a terrible weapon was perhaps its greatest power.

Esteban had bowed his head, as if pleading for forgiveness for a weakness that was none of his fault. "We had no idea any of the royal family survived. Later we heard rumors that Deslucido's heir, he who now wears the crown of Acosta, had married—" He broke off at her involuntary expression of horror.

Quickly she said, "You did not come to Thendara to seek *me* out. What is your mission then?"

"We came to beg Hastur's protection, to offer him our fealty," said Esteban.

"To be ruled by Hastur instead of Acosta . . ." she murmured confused. They must be desperate indeed. She remembered Deslucido's speeches about the welfare of all Acosta, how the people would profit from his rulership. Esteban and the others did not look like hothead rebels who would march to war for an abstract idea. They were practical, hard-working men, she saw that in their weather-seamed faces and callused hands, the unselfconscious way they wore their once-fine clothes. "Please go on."

"Deslucido, he promised us fairness, that we'd all be part of a greater kingdom. Not that we had any power to negotiate terms—Javier of Terrelind put up a fight, and he and his two sons were killed. And then his tax collectors arrived."

The faces of the other lords hardened. Esteban went on, "We used to tithe ten or sometimes fifteen parts to the hundred of our harvest to Acosta. Deslucido wants *half*."

"Aye, and any lord who so much as breathes a protest finds his son or daughter or wife seized to guarantee his loyalty," the second lord put in.

"Your Majesty—" Esteban held out his hands, his expression questioning whether she understood what Deslucido's demands meant. The lands of Acosta produced a bounty in rich years, but not every season. Half the harvest might feed the people at famine levels, with nothing left to store for the truly lean years. She remembered, and not too long ago, when she and Padrik had gone hungry after the royal granaries were emptied. Three poor harvests had followed a year of floods and killing frosts. It was the way of the world and she had been taught her duty was to share in the hardship of her people.

Her hands had clenched into fists in her lap, crumpling the fine silk of her gown. What did he intend to do with all that food? The answer came to her mind almost as quickly.

Feed his armies.

Acosta was a stepping stone, not an end in itself. Deslucido needed its farmlands productive, its fighting power intact. For his own use. Next would come conscriptions of fighting men and horses, seizures of wagons, arrows and swords and the precious metal to make more of them.

So, before starvation stripped their lands and harsh penalties weakened them past the point of effective action, these men had come to place their case before the Hastur King, only to find he would not even hear them.

Deslucido will bring war to Hastur lands. The only question is how long we will wait while he gathers power.

She rose, smoothing her gown around the rounded contour of her belly. "Hastur is not yet a party to these wars, but you have done better than you guessed by coming to me. I bear the son of Padrik Acosta, true heir to the throne."

She paused, caught by the sudden flare of light in their eyes. Their hope and awe swept through her, amplified by her empathic *laran.*

A son . . . a true Acosta son! . . . We are saved, all is not lost. . . .

And darker, like an underground river, *We will have our kingdom back. She will lead us to freedom!*

Taniquel paused, her throat momentarily closing around the words. She stiffened, lifting her head to the demands of the moment. "Return to Acosta with this news and with my promise. My son and I will return . . ."

. . . will return . . . The words tolled through every fiber of her being.

For this I was born comynara. *This is my destiny.*

Esteban's face drained of color as he knelt once more before her. She had rarely seen such naked devotion. In that moment, he would have died for her.

"Will you accept my oath?" he asked her.

She had never done so before. It was Padrik who ruled as liege to the vassal lords, as his father had before him. She'd been daughter, wife, and now mother, never thought to be more.

I am Acosta's hope, and I bear her future. If my people are to have any chance of freedom, I must be a true Queen to them.

She had already given them her oath. All that remained was to accept theirs in return, to complete the balance, question and response, power and responsibility, birth and death.

The ritual phrases rose unbidden to her tongue. Her hands enclosed Esteban's in the ancient gesture of loyalty received and given in return.

After they left, she remained in the chair while the sun moved slowly overhead. She had given away her life, without quite understanding why, only that it was the will of the gods and that she had no choice. She did not know if she ever had.

21

Taniquel rose reluctantly from sleep, as if she were drifting through molten honey. In the months since Julian Regis was born, her dreams had been increasingly vivid, but rarely so pleasurable. After fragments of the usual familiar bits of day thoughts, she'd found herself on a smooth gray plain under a featureless sky. The sense of utter, unchanging stillness might have smothered her if she had not as quickly been caught up in a forest of gauzy scarves, growing like exotic plants from the tile-smooth floor and waving in invisible breezes. Their colors reminded her of her gowns back at Acosta, red and bronze and shimmering peacock. As she moved among them, letting the finely-woven fabric slip between her fingers, she caught the mingled scents of cedar gum, incense, and rose petals. Music reached her, the faroff ripples of a harp, then deeper—a hunting horn. Soon the reds gave way to blues, often as pale as ice. She seemed at times to be wading through cool blue flames. They parted as she passed.

An open space appeared before her, circled round with flickering blue lights. In the center stood a man, naked except for the fire. Even though he faced away, she would have known him anywhere. Her heart leaped.

He turned with that smile which she remembered a thousand times. Blue flames lapped at him, and yet his bare flesh bore no burn or blister.

"Through water, you came to me," he said, although his lips did not move. The words echoed in her mind. "Through fire, I will come to you."

Taniquel reached out her arms to him, but he was gone. She was alone in her huge bed in Hastur Castle. Only the faintest dawn light glimmered outside the east-facing windows.

Slipping from her bed, she padded barefoot to the cradle only a few feet away. Her son slept on in perfect serenity. Now four months old, he was quickly losing the shapelessness of the newborn. His cheeks, smooth as damask rose, curved gently into lips which moved softly as if nursing. A cap of curls, dark like hers, covered his scalp.

Looking down at him, her heart grew steady and her breath softened. A smile touched her lips. She had struggled through the icy wilderness, the frozen river, and more for his sake, never thinking what he might give her in return.

From the moment of his birth, he had been an unfailing source of the most remarkable feelings, a bubbling of golden warmth from the depths of her heart, a certainty, a peace. She'd had no idea such happiness existed until she'd held him in her arms. Yet how fragile a baby's life could be and how uncertain his future. She shivered at the thought of anything happening to him.

By the time Taniquel had finished dressing, quietly so as not to arouse the attention of her maids, Julian had woken. She nursed him, sitting in the big padded chair by the fireplace. Just as she was finishing and tucking the folds of her loosely gathered gown into place, the nurse bustled in, full of exclamations that she should have been summoned at once, that it was not seemly for Her Majesty to tend the baby all by herself, and similar nonsense which Taniquel had heard a dozen times too many.

"Never mind!" Taniquel said with an edge of sharpness to her voice. Reluctantly, she handed the baby to the nurse. "I'll be in my uncle's chambers. If you would be so good as to change his clouts, you may bring him to me there."

She found Rafael finishing his breakfast and poring over the day's agendas. He brightened as she entered and kissed him on the cheek, inviting her to eat with him.

Taniquel helped herself to generous portions of the breakfast laid out on the sideboard, sausages, pastries stuffed with spiced fruit, and boiled eggs. Having finished, she resisted the urge to pace and instead seated herself beside the small spring fire.

He regarded her, eyes bright under bushy brows. "I see that you are restless this morning, *chiya*, but what would you do?" His hand swept across the neat lines of secretary's script. "There's nothing more exciting here than an embassy come from Isoldir to discuss fishing rights and river tariffs."

She pressed her lips together. In a glance, she'd recognized the Elhalyn crest on one of the documents. Darren-Mikhail again. He'd written once before, formally asking for her hand in marriage. Undoubtedly, as she'd told her uncle, he fully believed he was saving her from a future as a disgraced and homeless widow. Rafael's response was that since she had matured with motherhood, a man did not need to take pity on her in order to desire her in marriage. To which she replied, with some tartness, that if the man were that entranced with fertility, he might woo a she-*oudrakhi* in her place. As Taniquel, Queen of Acosta, she had obligations beyond the entirely unnecessary attentions of a husband.

It became a game between them, that whenever she would remind him of her determination to regain Acosta for her son, he would reciprocate with a reference to Darren's offer of marriage.

After a knock on the inner door, one of Rafael's personal pages entered and bowed deeply. "Your Majesty, the Councillor requests your presence. There is a—" the child stumbled over the unfamiliar word as he struggled to repeat exactly what he had been told, "—a deputation arrived at the castle."

"Indeed?" Rafael, clearly in a good humor from the morning's light banter, raised one bushy eyebrow. "What sort of deputation?"

"Men. On horses. With banners." The child grinned. "I saw them riding up."

Taniquel's throat went suddenly dry. "What color were the banners?"

"White and black."

Her eyes locked with her uncle's. *If you will not deal with Deslucido for my son's sake, then you must for your own.* She kept silent. If she pursued the matter too aggressively, he grew resistant and ill-tempered. With a degree of self-control she'd never had to practice as a pampered young queen, she refrained from bringing it up again.

Rafael's expression remained tranquil as he said, "Ask Gerolamo if he would be so kind as to inform these messengers I will receive them. Have them standing ready."

After the page departed, Taniquel burst out, "Uncle! You will not—"

"I agreed to receive them, but I did not say *when*. If you would *be* Queen rather than playing at it, you must learn that all things happen in their proper time, whether it be an assault on Ambervale Castle or the protocol for receiving uninvited guests."

She caught the wry note in his voice. "And so, the audience will be at your pleasure and not necessarily theirs."

"Naturally. There is nothing so deflating to a man's self-importance as to arrive in the morning with pennants flying and colors bright, and not be able to speak his speech until just before dinnertime, knowing that by then no one will be able to concentrate on his words. A grumbling stomach can be an excellent ally."

"Then I will attend to my own affairs," she said, rising, "rather than drive both of us to distraction. These emissaries may spend the day in idleness and worry, but I have better things to do."

"Ah," he sighed, "that is exactly what your mother would have said. You look much as she did at your age, have I told you that?"

Even as she smiled and kissed him on the cheek before departing, Taniquel thought, *One way or another, no matter how this business with Deslucido falls out, I must leave Thendara eventually. I can never go back to being a child in my uncle's castle.*

✦

In the great hall, Taniquel waited in her usual place to the side of her uncle's throne. Her chair, although small, had armrests and now she was grateful to have something solid to wrap her hands around. Beyond the dais, the hall was already abustle with preparations for the evening meal, servants arranging trestle tables, replacing *laran*-charged glows, laying down fresh rushes, carrying pitchers of watered wine and ale, baskets of bread, bowls of fresh cherries and redfruit. A maid stooped to pick up the nubbin of gnawed bone left by the pair of spaniels which were Rafael's companions, and sent them yipping and frolicking, as if it were a game.

At the *coridom's* announcement, the men from Ambervale approached. They had come unarmed, with scabbards empty. Taniquel recognized the officer from the occupation of Acosta, although she did not know his name. He and the others bowed to Rafael with proper deference given a host king.

The officer, although not a trained Voice capable of the exact replication of the words he was entrusted with, including the vocal tone and inflection of the original speaker, nevertheless recited his messages well. After the usual courtly greetings, he phrased an elaborately polite demand for Taniquel's surrender. He reiterated the peaceful transition of power at Acosta, the many courtesies extended to the young Queen, the offer of honorable marriage, the lamentations and grief when she had been thought lost in an unseasonable storm, the bridegroom so anxiously and ardently expecting her return. He did an excellent job implying that she had freely consented to marry, that she and Belisar were in fact already husband and wife by the old mountain traditions, lacking only the formality of the *di catenas* ceremony to make their union incontestable, and that to prevent her return constituted nothing less than interfering with the most solemn and private family matters.

Taniquel could not see her uncle's expression as he listened. *He knows I did not consent,* she thought. *He knows this is a lie.* Yet it was the sort of lie so easily given. Deslucido's agents would of course portray him in the most flattering tones, a just and generous king, a devoted father-in-law, and she a mere woman, fickle and capricious, giving her promise one moment and running away the next, a woman who did not even know the father of her son, if Darren's report of the rumors were true. In the end, it would come to Belisar's word against hers that they had not shared a bed as well as a meal and a hearth.

The discussion then shifted to territorial issues, with nothing resolved. So smooth was the transition, that an implied message lay in its very ease. The two missions were inextricably linked. Deslucido had laid claim to the Hastur lands bordering Acosta, a thinly inhabited hilly area called Drycreek. Taniquel thought that the time to answer this threat was before Deslucido had time to solidify his hold on Acosta, but she said nothing. The time for preemptive action had passed, despite her urging. All the smiths in Zandru's forge couldn't put that banshee chick back into its egg. And now Deslucido knew she lived, knew where she was, and intended to use her as a bargaining point.

The messenger did not, of course, explicitly say that Deslucido would withdraw his claims to the Drycreek borderlands if his son's marriage were successfully consummated, but his meaning was clear.

The audience went on long enough for Taniquel to wonder at the stamina and persistence of all parties involved. Nothing was concluded except an agreement to continue the discussions.

Taniquel had no doubts that Deslucido would launch an armed assault without hesitation. If it were necessary for the welfare of the Hastur kingdom, she might well be offered as the price of peace. She must not expect otherwise.

They may ask, but I will not agree. I cannot.

Not just for Julian's sake or for Acosta's, but for her own. She was no longer the dutiful child who left her uncle's house for an arranged marriage. She had become something more, the Queen who accepted the fealty oaths from men twice her age, the woman who stood alone against Belisar and the Deslucido *laranzu,* who fought her way through ice and storm and *laran* spells. Before Ambervale marched on Acosta, she had no idea she was capable of any of this.

What am I now? And what will I become?

Shuddering, she wished for a small portion of the unearthly calm she had seen in Lady Caitlin's eyes. At least, decorum required her to sit still, to show nothing of her inner turmoil. Gradually, heartbeat by beat, her anxiety quieted, to be replaced with a new resolve.

✦

As the days piled one on the other, Taniquel grew heartily wearied of the long hours of sitting, listening to very little of substance and a great deal implied in language so indirect and flowery as to be infuriating. More than once, she was tempted to excuse herself to play with Julian, or walk in the gardens, or practice her archery or ride out beyond the city walls, attended by a horseboy or two. If this is what it meant to rule a kingdom, to sit for hours and fence with words, then she must learn it.

The morning after the first audience, Rafael had invited Taniquel to talk strategy over breakfast in his sun-filled sitting room and this soon became their habit. Today, more informal than before, she cradled Julian in her arms. He'd fallen asleep nursing and the thin shawl she used for modesty still draped her breast.

"If there is any hope of avoiding outright warfare and a return to the Ages of Chaos," Rafael said, "we must find it."

The baby must have felt the sudden leap in tension in her body, for he whimpered and stirred. She patted him, rearranging the folds of her bodice and folding the shawl.

"No matter what you give him, Deslucido will not be satisfied," she said. "He is only testing you for weakness."

Gray-frosted brows lifted minutely. "Never fear, I am not in the least considering giving him what he wants. I think this problem is part of a larger, one small feint on the chessboard. It isn't clear what his game is, but this," he jabbed the armrest of his chair with one blunt finger, "is only an opening gambit, a carefully calculated move." Seeing her puzzled expression, he went on. "Charming as you are, my dear niece, you are not worth a war. Why should Deslucido go to such trouble to secure but one of a half-dozen kingdoms? Why not marry his son to an eligible daughter of Linn or Verdanta or Hawksflight?"

"Acosta is richer than any of those," she pointed out.

He shook his head. "In the taste of its fine wines, perhaps, but not overall. And he does not need you to hold what he already has."

"With me at Belisar's side, he needs only a minimal occupation force . . . and it is true, what Hawksflight lacks in vineyards, it offers in copper ore and *chervine* wool." She tapped her fingertips together, thinking, remembering the Acosta lords, how they had looked at her as their savior. How she had pledged herself to them. She forced her thoughts back to the problem at hand. "But Hawksflight and Verdanta and High Kinnally are all rugged hills and forest, terrain which is difficult to hold."

"Or to cross."

"I don't understand, uncle."

He smiled encouragement. "You have a keen mind, even if you have not been trained to use it. These tiny mountain kingdoms have no strategic importance except as gateways to one another. And they lead to—? Where, Tani?"

She envisioned a map, the funnel-shaped location of Deslucido's conquests, and shivered in the sudden sensation of cold.

To Hastur.

"At first, I thought it might be necessary for me to go," she said, lowering her eyes. "But now—" She met his gaze, unflinching. "It is not only for my own sake, for my son's and the whole of Acosta that I refuse. Deslucido must be stopped and driven back to his own territory. Do you remember the deputation of Acosta lords who arrived just after the Hastur Council meeting last summer? They had come to beg your protection against Deslucido's rule. He promised peace and fairness, but delivered only tyranny. Javier of Terrelind, who was as loyal a subject as any one could wish, was executed out of hand, along with his two sons. They were desperate, these men."

Rafael's expression shifted to questioning. "And as their Queen, how did you answer them?"

"How must I, in all honor? When Padrik placed the *catenas* on my wrist, I promised myself to the land as well as the man. My son is the only rightful King of Acosta, and I have pledged my life to restore him. If I cannot rule as a woman, am I no less a daughter of the Lord of Light? Does my duty compel me any less than a man's? Was I not born for this, bred for it, raised for it?"

"You were, indeed, but not many men could match your courage." After a moment, he said in a thoughtful voice, "You did not mention this to me."

"What, and begin the argument we had already been over a dozen times?" she flared. "I myself had answered them. What cause was there to make you responsible for my freely given oath?"

"I have wronged you, niece. I thought you spoke only from vengefulness, that with a lusty new husband, you would give up your wild schemes of reconquest and be content. It would have been foolhardy to risk a single Hastur soldier in such a personal cause. But now the stakes have shifted."

Taniquel flushed with pleasure at his apology. Then she remembered the trap at the Acosta gates. "Deslucido will not give up easily. I have seen this man in action and I fear to underestimate him. If it is war with Hastur he wants, he will bring it here, right to your doorstep, no matter how you wish to avoid it."

"We shall see," Rafael replied. "I am not as easy an opponent as those he has met before."

A delicate tracing of ice laced the back of Taniquel's neck. She remembered her dream from the morning of the messengers' arrival. Coryn, standing surrounded in blue flames.

"Through water, you came to me," he had said. *"Through fire, I will come to you."*

She had no reason to think she might ever see him again. But one thing was sure. The fire would come.

22

Twilight shrouded Ambervale Castle in a pearly aura and then gave way to ever-deepening shadow. Servants darted across the courtyard from the kitchen, bearing steaming platters, baskets of round loaves, soup tureens, and pitchers of hot mulled wine. Torchlight and the bustle of the evening's meal filled the central hall.

Rumail paused at the bottom of the steps leading to a little-used wing of the castle and took two practiced breaths to still his rising excitement. The others were waiting for him, above. His first circle. *His* circle. For this he had dreamed and trained all his life.

The training room was small, its stone walls unadorned and rough-cut, following the general contours of the surrounding turret. Rumail found it a fit setting for his own Tower, austere and honest. He'd had it prepared, floor and walls scrubbed, every cobweb swept away, furnished simply but comfortably.

The two teenagers he had found on his search and the one trained *leronis,* a monitor who'd been dismissed from Arilinn some years back on some pretext or another, sat on padded benches around a bank of fine beeswax candles. Other candles in freestanding candelabra, placed at precise distances, gently illuminated the room. They provided enough light to see, but not enough to distract.

Rumail greeted them all and took his place on the last empty bench, facing Ginevra, the monitor. Together they would form the anchor points for the circle. Rumail suppressed a frown, for she refused to wear the gray robes he selected for them as emblem of their uniqueness, outward tokens of the things which would set them apart from all other Towers.

Ginevra's white robe shone in the muted light. Now, she nodded to him—challenged him. He refused to be provoked. It was, after all, her prerogative to wear the robes of her rank, but if she saw herself as only a monitor, that's all she would be. He hoped—no, he needed—her to be much more.

Rumail lowered his eyes to sharpen his own concentration. He had instructed his students to prepare themselves with breathing and muscle-relaxation exercises, and then to focus on the candle flames. Since the beginning of their training, he had used a candle flame as a focal point, so that ought to make the evening's task easier.

When he dropped into a state of deeper awareness, reaching out to each of them with his *laran*, he was pleased with what he found. Each sat in a balanced way, spinal muscles relaxed, eyes unmoving on the candles, comfortable with Ginevra's light contact. After achieving rapport with them individually, he would be ready to link them into a single unity, one which he could mold and direct as he wished.

He would be a Keeper at last.

The girl, a sullen creature he'd found in a brothel using her talents to convince each customer she was a virgin, swayed gently with the flickering of the candles. With a start, Rumail realized there was no movement of air in the room; she was manipulating the fire by adding energy to the air above it.

Darna, no. You must focus on the light, not play with it. He mind-spoke her gently, for he did not want to discourage her. Such a talent could be valuable later. First she must learn discipline and fundamental techniques. She could not hear him clearly, not yet, but she felt his mental nudge.

I'm bored. How long are we going to sit here?

Nor was she aware how easily he could pick up her thoughts. She had not yet learned to trust him as her Keeper, she barely knew what a Keeper was. And how should she, who'd led a life in which people saw her only as a thing to be used? He intensified the rapport, felt her tighten in resistance. She was sixteen, older than most Tower novices, and she had lived alone and in fear since the awakening of her talent. Any contact from outside, he knew, would be painful, but not unbearably so. He was no Alton to smash her defenses, forcing rapport.

That will hold her attention.

Then, still retaining his mental grasp of the girl, he turned his attention to the boy. Kyril's attention had also wandered, but not from boredom. The boy was simply undisciplined, had never tried to do anything more complicated than carve a piece of meat for his dinner. He was some *Comyn* lord's by-blow, raised in a comfortable but ignorant cloth-merchant's shop in Temora. Aldones only knew who his father was or why he'd ignored such an obviously gifted son. Maybe he'd never thought to ask or even known he'd fathered a child.

Rumail himself had never gone cold or hungry; his *laran* had been identified and trained. He had everything a *nedestro* could expect—a place in the world, training for his gift, a brother's love. When he'd seen the boy, something had stirred in him, so that he could not have turned away even if he'd wanted to.

Kyril. As with the girl, he kept his touch light, soothing. *Concentrate. Use the light to gather yourself. See only the point of brilliance, nothing else.*

Not the itch on your backside, nor the curve of Darna's rump, he thought to himself.

The boy squirmed on his bench, but his mind, a blur of colors, grew clearer. Rumail envisioned his own *laran* as a net, settling softly over the luminous colored globe of Kyril's mind and Darna's sharp-edged crystal-line facets. Slowly, he gathered up the strands.

Easy, easy . . . There is nothing to fear. He knew this next part wouldn't be easy. Normally, by the time novices joined in a circle, they'd had years of Tower discipline. They'd studied matrix theory and the fundamentals of monitoring, they knew what their own *laran* talents were and the basics of their use. Even the youngest had extensive training in controlling their own breathing, body temperature, and muscular tension. But Rumail had to accelerate the process for these two. Ever since the lungrot plague, everything seemed to be happening ahead of schedule.

Well, Rumail thought, he'd done the best he could in this short a time. For all he knew, the traditional, lengthy methods of Tower training were unnecessary. If anyone could find a simple, direct way of creating a working unit, he knew he could. Once joined in a circle, he'd be able to directly manipulate the minds of his workers and eliminate the mental rubble that usually took years to clear away.

As Rumail began to draw them closer, Darna stiffened. Her mind recoiled, and she gasped audibly. Rumail felt her response in both mind and body. He sent out a wave of reassurance.

Trust me. No harm will befall you.

In response, she pulled back harder. He sensed her pain increase as the muscles in her shoulders and belly tightened. She caught her breath and held it. Ginevra moved in, easing the girl's muscles, shifting her posture, and smoothing her breathing. Panic flared as Darna realized that she was no longer in control of her body. Ginevra held her fast.

Rumail had rarely seen a monitor take such agressive action, but he himself had only the basic level of skills. He could serve as a monitor, just as any other technician of his rank—*Keeper*, he reminded himself, but he was no expert.

Darna no longer offered any physical resistance, but her mind was as turbulent as before. Rumail had to admire Ginevra's deftness. But why did she ignore the girl's pain level? It was no matter, for once included in the unity of the circle, it would abate along with her psychic friction.

Kyril . . . The boy's mind opened to Rumail almost lazily. He had some natural barriers, but they were haphazard and easily diverted. By far, the greater problem would be that the boy himself would be unable to sustain his part of the contact. *Kyril, you must concentrate. You must hold on.*

Oh . . . all right. The thought came slurred, like a yawn.

Satisfied, Rumail deepened his rapport with the minds of his circle. Ginevra—practiced, easily flowed with him, observed the other two, and held the girl immobile. The girl's mind darted this way and that like a hunted animal. Rumail bore down on her, caught her. For a moment, she continued to twist in his mental grasp. Then, with a flicker of mixed pain and despair, she surrendered.

Yes!

The boy, the last—whatever focus he'd achieved was already shredding into bits of daydreams, memories, body sensations.

Hold! Rumail commanded, and in the next instant, he had them all. The unity poised, currents shifting uneasily, pulling his energy in three different directions at once.

He hesitated, unsure of how to proceed. Although he'd intended this first rapport to be an initiation, a cleansing ritual, he hadn't anticipated how fragile, how unstable a circle might be. Gathering up the minds of the members had always seemed so easy when Bernardo of Neskaya did it. There was nothing for it but to go ahead. Between the two of them, he and Ginevra had more than enough strength to control the youngsters. First, though, he needed to move them all on to a more ethereal astral plane. He signaled Ginevra to support him as he shifted the circle to the Overworld. She fed him energy and tightened her hold on the girl.

In his mind, Rumail visualized the chill gray place that lay beyond material existence. It had terrified him the first time his own Keeper had taken him there, although he knew the many safeguards in place. Its vastness, its utter lack of features had engulfed him as if he were no more than an insect. But he had learned to build structures there, using only his own thoughts, to sculpt and shape mind-stuff beyond anything material.

He saw himself lifting the circle, straining with very little movement. The girl felt like a leaden weight, the boy a sack of jelly. He would have to leap, to blast through their inertia with raw power—

Darna shrieked as if doused with liquid fire. Her agony reverberated on both physical and psychic planes.

The circle shattered. Gasping, Rumail jerked back to his own body. His eyes snapped open. Darna bent over, arms wrapped around her ample breasts, screaming over and over, scarcely pausing to draw breath. The boy lolled back, propped on one arm, blinking in confusion. Ginevra gave a little shiver, collecting herself, and glided over to the girl. She put her hands on the girl's shoulders, but did not attempt to raise her.

Rumail tried to get to his feet, but his knees had turned to powder and gave way beneath him. He fell heavily back on the padded bench.

What—what happened? He did not know if he spoke the words aloud, or merely thought them. What was wrong with him? He was *Keeper*, by all of Zandru's frozen hells, and he ought to know!

"Some kind of backlash," Ginevra murmured. She sounded drunk, or in a half-trance. "I've never seen it before. . . ."

Summoning the rags of his strength, Rumail hauled himself upright and stumbled the two strides to Darna's bench. She was still hunched over, face covered by shadow and the fall of loose red-black hair. Her screams continued, raw now as if torn from a bloody throat.

Then he saw Ginevra's expression. She'd knelt before the girl, eyes half-closed, whites glinting, lips curved and partly opened. In pleasure, he realized.

In pleasure so intense, it bordered on sexual ecstacy.

Rumail shuddered, his stomach seething. Acid filled his mouth and cold sweat broke out on his forehead.

She—she was *feeding* on the girl's pain.

Rumail grabbed Ginevra and pulled her backward, not caring whether she fell. He took Darna's face in both his hands and lifted it to the light. Her face and hands were streaked with crimson, where mental energy had burned along the channels, searing the smaller nodes beneath the skin. He could only guess at the internal damage. But her eyes . . .

They were no longer soft brown-green set off by sweetly curving lashes. Nothing of the structure of lid or eyeball remained. Both sockets, from brow to cheekbone, were lightless, charred black.

"*Ginevra!*" he roared, whirling on her. "This is your doing, isn't it?"

The monitor picked herself up from where she had stumbled, brushing the folds of her white robes. She met his gaze with her own, insolent glare. "And if it is? What are you going to do about it? *You* are the Keeper here. Don't you know the first thing about being a Keeper is that you are solely responsible for whatever happens in the circle?"

She pushed past him toward the door. In shock, he made no move to hinder her.

Darna's cries died rapidly into whimpers. She seemed to crumple in on herself as she fell sideways and then slipped to the floor. Stiffly, he bent over her. Before he could touch her, her muscles jerked in spasm and then loosened. She lay very, very still.

The boy stretched and yawned, his jaw popping audibly. "Is it dinnertime yet?"

Rumail lowered himself to Darna's bench and buried his face in his hands. Never in all his years, not even when he stood before the Keeper at Neskaya for the pronouncement of his dismissal, had he ever felt such utter failure. Tonight's experiment had been doomed from the start.

And these were the best I could find! It's hopeless! Hopeless!

His shoulders sagged. He realized he was in shock, or he would surely have wept, and done so without shame.

Only men laugh, only men weep, only men dance. The old proverb whispered through his mind.

Bitter laughter burst from him. What more could he do, except to get up and dance?

As quickly, the black mood lifted. What did he expect, with such raw materials—two flawed teenagers, already too old for proper novice training and damaged by their short lives—and a perverted, sadistic monitor? The failure had nothing to do with him. No one, not even Aldones himself, could have turned them into a decent circle.

But there was already a fully trained, functional Tower out there . . . Tramontana. It had not yet fully acknowledged its fealty to Ambervale, and it might not. Even after death, Kieran's influence was powerful. If not Tramontana, then some other Tower. Perhaps even Neskaya would bend to his will.

He would be Keeper some day. He must. It was his destiny, the means by which he would shape the future of Darkover, even as Damian dreamed.

◆

Some tendays later, after the ambassadors returning from their mission to Hastur had made their report and bowed themselves out of the King's private quarters at Ambervale Castle, Damian Deslucido turned to his brother with an exultant grin.

"That old fox, Rafael! Because he sees the trap, he thinks he can avoid putting his foot into it. But we have him now. He *must* deal with us."

Rumail stood uneasily and watched his brother begin pacing, as he so often did when feeling expansive. "Consider the situation," Damian went on, gesturing as he thought aloud. "We have put forth our claims based on right and custom. And no man may say we do not have sufficient cause. Now is the time to strike, and strike decisively!"

Damian paused, eyes blazing with inner vision. What Rumail had once seen as the certainty of a true mission now turned to brassy, empty blustering.

Rumail frowned. *I must find a way to slow him down, before he rushes us into disaster.*

Their original plan had called for consolidation of resources, including Tramontana Tower, before taking on the might of Hastur. Prospects had not looked good until the *emmasca* from Aillard, that bastion of neutrality, had died, presumably of extreme old age. Even then, the Tower resisted the legitimate claims of fealty as unclear and conflicting. Tomas, Keeper of the First Circle and now by seniority and personality the leader of the Tower, might be a distant Ardais cousin, but he was the fourth son of a third son, coming from a small holding with few defenses. With only a little effort, Damian was able to bring Tomas' mother and only sister to Linn, where he could keep them under watch along with the Storn girl. It had not taken much further suggestion to enlist the Keeper's cooperation.

The original timetable had begun to disintegrate with the lungrot plague at Verdanta. Despite their victory at Tramontana, Rumail's attempt at forming his own circle had ended in disaster, one of his students dead and the other little more than a drooling idiot unable to accept the discipline of a circle. The memory still had the power to shake him.

There was no point in moaning, *If only we had waited, we could have controlled the plague, if only I had taken the time. . . .* Rumail was pragmatic enough to know that the only problem which mattered was the one they were facing. And right now, that was his brother's unbridled confidence.

Rumail picked his words carefully. "Is this a war you could win? Have we grown that strong?"

"We are as we have always been, ready to act when the right opportunity opens itself. Daring must prevail when in the service of right."

"Yet Hastur is a family with many branches, rich in resources and arms. Need you stand alone against them?"

"A powerful ally, one pledged to the defense of another, can be a great asset," Damian said, although without conviction. In the past, Damian had never sought allies in the established Domains, either by treaty or marriage. He conquered, he did not compromise. His was not the sort of personality which easily accepted a subordinate role. And after the defeat of the Ridenow of Serrais some two hundred years ago, no other clan would consider challenging Hastur.

"That is not exactly what I have in mind," Rumail said. "Rafael Hastur is formidable, but his might is nothing compared to the combined strength of all the great houses of Darkover. What if we need not resort to force of arms? What if we could appeal to a court of his peers to judge the issue?"

"A court?" Damian said. "You think Rafael Hastur, who knows no law but his own, would meekly submit himself to an outside judgment? He would listen and smile and do exactly what he pleased." But the idea clearly intrigued Damian. "And who would these peers be?"

"The *Comyn* Council itself. It has not been particularly active in recent years, but it once had great authority throughout the Domains. No heir could take up his father's place without their inspection and approval, nor any marriage of consequence take place. These are, after all, matters of *laran* lineage."

"Bah! The Council has no real power today. Hastur will never abide a verdict that went against him."

Mentally, Rumail waved his brother's objections aside. True, King Rafael II had no particular strength of *laran* and only a few seasons at Hali Tower as part of a royal education, but too many of that accursed family were Gifted. The breeding programs of the last few centuries had produced strange, wild talents, including the Deslucido Gift for evading truthspell. Other talents ran throughout the great houses, particularly strong in Hastur.

Rumail could have sworn the Hastur girl had been the one to break free from his compulsion spell at the gates of Acosta, although later, when he had probed her on several occasions, her mind had either churned with the expected emotions of a new widow or else been as blank as a cow's. The way she focused on her food, she'd likely be as fat as Durraman in a few years. She had some *laran,* that was clear, but not enough to be worth training. Belisar still wanted her, Aldones only knew why, probably because she'd refused him. He would keep her pregnant until she died in childbed or was so worn out as to pose no further threat.

But Hastur was *Comyn* and made a grand show of his support for the Council. He even had his own group of counselors, whose primary goal, so far as Rumail could tell, was to advocate elimination of the most effective *laran* weapons. Hastur had considerable military might, but his influence over the other Domains and even the branches of his own family, depended upon his reputation and his leadership. Having sworn himself to the Council, he dared not back down.

"Think of it, brother," Rumail said. "Instead of spilling more blood to establish our rights, we take our case before the Council. Hastur has publically declared his loyalty to them. He will agree to their judgment or reveal himself as a consummate hypocrite. With a little help from me, Belisar can swear under truthspell that the Hastur girl agreed to the marriage. The Council will order her returned to us. Then Hastur must either comply—which he will not—or risk standing alone against us. Then you will be justified before all the world in taking what is rightfully yours."

Damian's eyes widened. Slowly he smiled. "How right you are, brother. The girl herself means nothing to me, only a means to separating Hastur from his allies. And in the time we gain by this wonderful ploy, men and matériel, and most of all, those *laran* weapons that will ensure our victory will be ours."

Rumail settled into a padded chair and folded his hands across the belly which had grown broader and fuller in the year since Neskaya.

This is your time, brother, Rumail thought with an unexpected feeling of contentment, *and I will have mine. Not a couple of spoiled, untrained children and a renegade sadist, but a true Circle of Power.*

For the time would come when diplomacy and maneuvering failed, when ordinary weapons became useless. Stockpiles of *clingfire* would be exhausted. Then the true might of one Tower would be pitted against another. Peace would eventually come, but a far more glorious peace than any Damian could imagine. As long as ordinary men ruled, commanding the Towers this way and that, there could be no lasting ceasefire. Damian's objective, a united and harmonious Darkover, was a true one. Limited as he was by his own lack of *laran,* he could see no farther than military solutions.

The day will come when the true rulers of Darkover will take our own. We will speak mind to mind, understanding each other in perfect clarity. No man will be able to deceive another.

23

For the last three days of the journey to the Hidden City near Arilinn, where the *Comyn* Council held its gathering, dry lightning ran jagged across the summer sky. Taniquel's skin prickled with restless, pent-up energy. Even Lady Caitlin, who rode with King Rafael's entourage as *leronis* and chaperone, slept badly, ate little, and began sentences which trailed off distractedly.

Taniquel's appetite had fallen off as her milk dried up, but even now her empty breasts ached, and at night she found herself reaching for Julian. More than once, she had buried her face in a pillow to keep from crying out. No one had forced her to leave him behind with a wet nurse. She, more than anyone, knew how dangerous it was to bring him anywhere near Deslucido's reach. When she had first heard of the summons to *Comyn* Council, she had burst into her uncle's chambers, where he sat over a light summer dinner.

Her uncle had fixed her with the same blend of mildness and tolerance as he once used after the worst of her childhood pranks. "We would be obliged to attend in any event," he pointed out, "or send some suitably important representative. I am, after all, Hastur of Hastur." He bent to his chilled cherry soup.

There would be other legitimate Council business, though Taniquel was not sure what that might be. In all her years in Thendara and then Acosta, she'd had nothing to do with the Council, being neither an heir nor possessed of any *laran* worthy of their attention. Their seasonal gatherings came and went without any special awareness on her part.

"This may be our best hope for a peaceful resolution," Rafael said. "Deslucido may think he can use the Council for his own purposes, but in the end it is *they* who will rule *him*. Just as the wild dog creeps to the campfire, thinking only of warmth and a full belly, so Deslucido cannot enter into the world of the *Comyn* without bending to their will."

You do not know Deslucido. Taniquel lowered her eyes and kept still.

Once she would have looked upon an entry into the Council meetings as an adventure, but now, as the towers of Arilinn and the Hidden City drew ever closer, her head ached with the relentless pressure she recognized from the day Acosta was attacked. As a warning, it was useless, for she already knew that danger, and, most likely, treachery lay ahead.

As she rode along, having stubbornly refused to share the carriage with Lady Caitlin, she dropped the reins on her horse's neck and pressed both hands to her temples, massaging the tight muscles. One of the guards must have seen her, for a few minutes afterward, a halt was signaled and she was summoned to her uncle. He asked if she were unwell and she realized how easy it would be to delay their arrival for a few hours' respite. But she shook her head and said she would rest once they were settled within the city. She accepted a little wine and quickly regretted it, for it lingered, sour and uneasy, on her tongue.

She had always known how much grander Thendara was than Acosta, for it was the largest city on all Darkover and everything there, from the special *cahuenga* dialect, to its two Towers, set it apart. Acosta, which had once been all her heart's desire, seemed shabby by comparison. Arilinn, though smaller, was no less magnificent.

Two mountains lay beyond the city and framed it like a precious gem, multihued and faceted, glittering in the shadow of the Tower of the same name, which was by far the tallest building. Even as a small child, Taniquel had heard stories of its mysterious Veil and guards in crimson and gold. Now she had no heart for viewing either.

Between the twin peaks, within an easy ride from Arilinn itself, lay the Hidden City, visible only as a swathe of blue-tinted whiteness, its very contours obscured by a permanent cloudlike mist. It was here the *Comyn*

Council would meet, behind gates set with a matrix lock which only a Keeper could open. Her uncle had explained to her that over the centuries, since before the Ages of Chaos, it had been used as a place of refuge by the *Comyn*.

Refuge. And perhaps also justice. She lifted her head, straightened her shoulders, and mounted up. *But for whom?*

✦

Shortly after their arrival, the Keeper of Arilinn led them to the gates of the Hidden City. Taniquel followed her uncle, his paxman Gerolamo, and Lady Caitlin into the low-lying cloud cover. Only a mixture of pride and training kept her face impassive, her hands quiet.

Fog closed around them and for a moment, she could see no farther than the length of her arm. Energy currents swirled around her, turning her skin at once hot and cold. The sounds of footsteps echoed, ghostly in the mist.

Then, as if a sudden breeze had sprung up, the mists parted and they faced a stone wall pierced here and there with mullioned windows which glowed dimly blue by a single pair of gates. There was no visible latch or lock, yet Taniquel knew, with that half-developed *laran* sense, that she could push with all her might and not budge them by the thickness of a silken thread. She might as well try to shift the twin peaks.

The Keeper, a stocky man with hair once red but now the color of bleached straw, drew out a starstone from the folds of his red robes. It shimmered with its own inner light. His brows creased with concentration as he bent over it, lips moving soundlessly. Taniquel's headache, which had subsided into a vague discomfort, now throbbed through her entire skull. The pain eased as the gates swung open.

Taniquel caught a glimpse of a garden courtyard, a well hung with yellow-flowering ivy, cobbled lanes between buildings which might have been dormitories or warehouses, all leading to a central hall. A pair of *cralmacs* scurried by, covered baskets in their tiny furred hands, and Taniquel remembered that no human servants were permitted within the walls.

Their quarters were modest in size, furnished plainly, but fresh and clean. There was a bedroom for Rafael with a smaller adjacent room for Gerolamo, as well as a chamber for the two women, separated by a small sitting room whose sole ornament was a vase of fresh daisies. A pitcher of water and a basket of fruit had been set out on the table beside a window looking out onto the garden. The Keeper arranged for *cralmacs* to bring them anything they needed before leaving them.

That night, Rafael attended the opening meeting, with Gerolamo a silent shadow. Taniquel might have gone as a visitor, but he cautioned her it would be better for her case if none of the Council members had formed any previous opinion of her. Some, such as the irascible head of the Altons of Lake Posada, were traditional enough to consider the presence of any woman, even the matrilineal Aillards, as incompatible with serious business.

Lady Caitlin used some *laran* technique on the oil lamp, causing it to glow brilliantly enough to sew by, and then sat with her work, stitching the flat-felled seams of a man's shirt. The cloth was fine Dry Towns linex but bore no embroidery. It was, despite its quality, an everyday shirt.

Taniquel sat for a time, watching the needle flash in the light as it dipped in and out of the fabric. It was lovely to be still, soothed by the steady rhythm. Since Julian's birth, she had scarcely had two empty minutes in a row. "I never thought to see you making something so—so practical."

"Why?" Caitlin looked up, amusement twinkling in her eyes. "Because I am too highly born to be of any use?"

"No, because you are a *leronis*. You do important work in a Tower."

"Why so I do, but not every waking hour. Minds as well as bodies need to rest. I have always found sewing to be restful. And no matter what else we do, we still need warm, comfortable clothes, and someone has to make them."

"You could have a sewing-woman do that." Taniquel had never voluntarily sewed anything, certainly not her own clothing.

Caitlin nodded, returning to her work. "And then I would not have the pleasure of creating something beautiful for someone I care about. This," she held the shirt up, "will give years of good service if I am careful with my stitches."

Taniquel leaned forward, interested. "Is it for your father or brother?"

"It is for a dear friend at Hali." Caitlin inflected the word to delicately convey a deeper intimacy.

Taniquel found herself blushing. Did the prim and upright Caitlin have a lover? She had heard that Tower workers did not observe the usual rules of propriety.

The image of Coryn, standing naked in the blue flames, reaching out for her with such tenderness, flashed behind her eyes.

"Oh, my dear," Caitlin said, laying down her work with a smile. "You never told me you were in love."

"I never—" Taniquel's words skidded to a halt. She had not mentioned Coryn except briefly upon her arrival in Thendara, to explain the healing of her frostbite. "Did you read my thoughts?"

"You fairly blasted me with the image of your young man—the one from Tramontana, was it not?"

Taniquel blushed a shade deeper. "But he is to be Keeper at Neskaya, just as I am to be Queen and Regent of Acosta, if it is the will of the gods."

Caitlin brushed her fingertips across the back of Taniquel's wrist in a gesture that reminded her poignantly of Coryn. "I cannot read the future, so you may indeed be right. But this much I do know," and now Taniquel heard the ring of experience in the older woman's voice, "that a life which has been touched by love, no matter how fleeting, is infinitely better than a life without it."

✦

Taniquel went with her uncle and his paxman, chaperoned by Lady Caitlin, to the meeting room the next morning. As they crossed the courtyard, the sun warmed her and the fragrance from the clusters of tiny pink blossoms of the trellised vines washed over her, but she could not respond to the beauty of the day. When she had asked Rafael what happened the night before, he refused to say more than,

"Tomorrow, when you testify, answer only what you are asked and no more. Above all, do not challenge Deslucido. All you will gain is certain defeat."

They passed through an outer foyer, where in colder seasons, outdoor cloaks and mud-coated boots could be removed and hung on the pegs and racks, frost-stiffened fingers warmed around goblets of steaming *jaco*, and pleasantries exchanged. Now the room was only a well-proportioned, if slightly empty-feeling space. A bowl of yellow rosalys had been set on the side table, their scent so delicate as to be barely a hint.

Taniquel had hardly a moment to glance around at the inner chamber before taking her seat beside her uncle, with Lady Caitlin behind them. Her first impression remained, the curved walls terraced upward so that each person could see the faces of all the others. Clearly, it had been designed for far more than the dozen and a half who now sat, watching her with calm, serious faces. She had expected only men except for herself and her chaperone, but there was a scattering of women. She looked at them curiously and felt the faint brush of presence as they glanced back.

Damian Deslucido, on the opposite side of the oval table, met her eyes and in them she thought she read the certainty of victory. The Keeper who had opened the city to them sat a little apart, as witness perhaps, but not an equal participant. She could not tell who was presiding until an elderly man in a clan tartan she did not recognize lifted one hand for silence. Age had bleached his skin like parchment and whitened his hair past any trace of its original color.

The Keeper now rose, his crimson robes falling in narrow folds about his spare frame. He took out his starstone, which flared briefly at the touch of his bare fingers. Eyelids half lowered and lips moved in soundless concentration. The assembly waited and Taniquel waited with them, unconsciously holding her breath.

"In the light of the fire of this jewel, let the truth lighten this room and all which proceeds within."

The starstone brightened again, softer and yet stronger. Azure radiance suffused the face of the Keeper and radiated outward until it filled the room. Inanimate objects—the table spread with pitchers and goblets of pewter-dull metal—quickly darkened back to their natural colors. But on each face it remained, as if emanating from within, with no two the exact shade and brightness. Some turned deeper blue, others whiter, but all shimmered with an inner luminescence. Taniquel thought it must be the *laran* shining out from each person. She felt the cool, sweet touch of the light and knew that, no matter what Lady Caitlin had said so many years ago when she was tested, that she belonged here.

As *comynara*. As Queen of Acosta.

"My lords, you may proceed," the Keeper said. "If any dare knowingly speak a falsehood, the light of truth will vanish from his—or her," with a flicker of a glance in Taniquel's direction, "face."

After a few formal comments, the old man in the tartan introduced the morning's discussion. In the opening session, Damian Deslucido,

King of Ambervale and Linn, had appealed to the *Comyn* Council for the return of his son's promised bride, whose marriage would heal the scars of Acosta's turmoil, promote peaceful alliances, and ensure prosperity. The old man spoke in such neutral tones that Taniquel had no idea if he believed any of what he said, only that this was how Deslucido had presented his case.

Now the old man looked at Rafael and, in exactly the same monotone, went on to describe how the aforementioned bride, one Taniquel Hastur-Acosta, had fled from a forced remarriage to the man who had so recently slain her beloved husband and conquered her kingdom, that she had naturally sought the protection of her own family, who loved her, and had no intention of leaving.

Taniquel wished she were a telepath, that she might read the thoughts of the assembled *Comyn*, or at least enough of an empath to catch their emotions. All she could sense was her own battering fear. Who would they believe? Who did they *want* to believe?

"Let us hear from the woman herself," said a younger man in the Ridenow colors of green and gold. A century and more ago, Allart Hastur had brought the long feud between Hastur and Ridenow to an end, so that Serrais and Thendara might well be considered allies.

"Taniquel Hastur-Acosta," the old man said.

She lifted her chin, so that everyone could see she had no fear. *"Vai dom."*

"What have you to say? Is this marriage, this alliance of peace, welcome to you?"

Answer only what you are asked.

"It is most definitely not, my lords." She looked directly at Deslucido, eyes steady. "I never consented to it." As she spoke, Taniquel felt the unwavering light shine forth from her face.

She felt rather than heard the ripple of reaction around the room. Triumph sparked within her. She had faced Deslucido and been borne out by truthspell itself. Who would dare question her now?

"Do you now wish to remain in the household of your uncle, Rafael Hastur?" another of the *Comyn* asked.

I wish to rule Acosta as is my right, to preserve and hold it for my son.

She did not say the words aloud, only in her heart. She said, "I do."

"More to the point," the bushy-bearded lord in Alton colors said, not to her but to the assembly, "will she do as she is bid? Will she honor our decision and the commands of her King? Or will we have another round of this running about the countryside, following her own whims, thinking only of herself, heedless of the consequences?" By his tone, he indicated she ought to be married off at once to someone manly enough to keep her from causing any more trouble.

Stung, Taniquel bit back a reply. Was he trying to goad her, to test her, or was he simply thoughtlessly rude?

Truthspell blazed from Rafael's face as he said with perfect politeness, "I am this woman's kinsman, *vai domyn,* and I am responsible for her behavior. If you have anything more to say on that subject, Alton, you had best say it to me."

"N–no—not at this time."

"Are there any further questions?" the old lord said. "Then we will hear the response."

For a long moment, Damian Deslucido looked down at his hands, spread palms down before him on the table. The fingers were wide and strong, callused from swordplay, the back of one hand crossed by an old scar. He wore no rings, although whitened, shiny skin at the base of several fingers betrayed their absence. These were the hands, Taniquel thought, of a man other fighting men would respect.

He lifted his head so that all could see the shimmering blue light on his face. "My lords, what can I answer except the truth? War is war, a thing women cannot understand. I do not deny that I defeated Padrik Acosta on the field of battle and now rule his kingdom. When words failed to resolve our differences, steel triumphed and that was an end to it. We men know this is the way of things, and so did the men of Acosta. They knew, as do we all, that after such a quick, decisive victory, bloodshed ends and the new order prevails. Once the castle was secure, every courtesy was extended to the late King's widow. Attended by her own ladies, she remained in the security of her own quarters with all the familiar comforts. What cause had she to complain of that?"

Around the table, heads nodded. The old man said to Taniquel, "Were you mistreated—molested, starved, humiliated, thrown into a dungeon?"

"I was— No, none of these things happened." *But that is not what happened.*

"She was offered an honorable marriage to my son," Deslucido went on, his voice becoming ever more silken with confidence, "who, as I have told you, is my sole heir. She would have been Queen not just of Acosta but of all the lands of Greater Ambervale." With the briefest gesture of one hand, he managed to convey the vastness of his conquests.

Taniquel flushed as Old Alton snorted his disapproval. She saw in the faces of the *Comyn* that they all thought her a weak-minded fool for turning down such wealth and power.

She shook herself a little, realizing she had missed a beat of Deslucido's speech.

". . . gave due consideration to the sensibilities of a woman who is young, inexperienced, and newly a widow. Despite the urgency of a smooth and complete transition of power, my son was willing to be patient. She was given leave to sit vigil in the chapel at her husband's body and to see him properly buried, before her answer was required."

War, as Deslucido had said, was war, Taniquel thought miserably. No pouting or ranting could bring back Padrik or undo what had been done. As a woman, she was expected to accept what had happened and to make the best future she could.

"The very night she disappeared, she dined with my son and me. She toasted the future of Acosta with us. She gave every indication that the match was acceptable to her. What were we to think when no trace of her could be found the following morning? We feared for her safety, we searched everywhere. Why should a bride who had appeared so content leave the comfort and safety of her own home, unless something terrible had happened to her? But we found no body, no trace of assassin or kidnapper."

No, it was not like that. It was not like that at all. Taniquel remembered the hours of terror and exhaustion on the trail, never daring to rest for long lest they find her.

"Now I discover she is safe when we thought her dead or worse, she has been so all along, and," Damian raised his hands in a gesture of incomprehension of such capriciousness, "it does not please her to go back. Perhaps life at Acosta has paled beside the entertainments of a big city like Thendara. Perhaps she has found some other suitor, one more biddable to her whims. Who can tell?

"Should she come to her senses and decide to return to her home, we will accept her gladly and on the same terms as before. A proper marriage *di catenas,* to be Queen of Acosta and consort to the heir to Greater Ambervale, the security of everything she had known. However," and here Deslucido's golden voice darkened to brass, "we are not Dry Towns barbarians, to impose our will on a woman who is truly unwilling, if she has just cause. Those who are weak of will or simply misled can be guided and the ignorant given instruction."

He shook his head. "I leave it to your wisdom, my lords, to decide which is the case with Taniquel Acosta. I ask for nothing which is not fair and right. If you feel she has good reason to break her implied assent, then simple justice demands the payment of a dowry in recompense."

The border lands!

So it had come to this, even as she had feared. Taniquel rose to leave the room as she was commanded. A *cralmac* servant escorted her and Lady Caitlin back to the apartment. The touch of the slender furred fingers on her own brought no comfort, for the creature had no speech. Thoughts jumbled together in her mind, all the things she would have said, *should* have said.

The *cralmac* left them at the door. Taniquel had not realized how tense she was, her muscles tight as the strings of a *rryl*. Something gnawed at the back of her mind, something which was not right.

Caitlin reached out with a feather touch, her fingertips under Taniquel's arm as she led her into the sitting room and to a chair. "My dear, you are shaking like a leaf."

Taniquel accepted a cup of cool herbal tisane, although she was not thirsty. Caitlin had blended mint and honeyleaf along with something astringent.

"It is no use," Taniquel said. "We should never have come. The Council will surely demand that the King either return me or surrender the Drycreek lands. Deslucido—damn him to Zandru's coldest hell!—has won."

24

"You do not know the verdict of the Council yet," Caitlin cautioned Taniquel.

"If they meant to dismiss his case, why not do so at once? Why take so long? Unless—unless he has already gotten what he wanted, to be accepted as one of the *Comyn*, to be counted as a member of the Council. No," Taniquel went on, answering herself, "it's got to be more than that. He's a proud man, but not in that way. It isn't rank and recognition he wants, but power."

"Now you are sounding just like your uncle," Caitlin said with a smile.

"I mean to take back Acosta to hold it for Julian," Taniquel replied. "I could do worse than learn the ways of the great lords from my uncle."

Caitlin settled back in her own chair and reached for her sewing. "It is a pity women cannot rule, for some—like you—have the mind for it, just as others have a talent for cooking or baking bread or matrix work, as I have. For all I know, there are women with a talent for swordplay. Even if you had *laran*, you would have been wasted in a Tower—

"What is it, child?" she exclaimed as Taniquel leaped to her feet and began pacing.

"Oh! I do not know! Yes, I am upset because the Council sided with

Deslucido. There is something more—something that man said—wrong, wrong! I wish I could remember what it was. Ah, what is the use?"

Taniquel sat down again, picked up the cup, set it on the table once more. Her body refused to be still, her arms and legs in constant motion. She wanted to jump, to scream, to throw something.

"*Everything* Deslucido said was wrong!" Taniquel exclaimed. "And yet his words were true, they must have been. I saw the truthlight on his face—and it never vanished."

Serenely, Caitlin inclined her head over her stitching. "Truthspell is the trust that makes the Council possible."

"And what good is the Council?" Taniquel's temper flared. "Where were they when Deslucido used aircars and smokebombs to trap Padrik at his own gates?"

"The Council," Caitlin replied, lowering her work to her lap and gazing at Taniquel with darkened, serious eyes, "is the one place on Darkover where warring kingdoms may work together for their mutual benefit. Where issues of *laran* can be openly aired and knowledge exchanged. Without such communication, the breeding programs might have gone unchecked, with horrors beyond even the lethal recessives and energon mutations we know about."

Taniquel brushed aside the comment. No one in these times forced marriages between brother and sister, father and daughter, in a mis-guided attempt to strengthen rare *laran*. What had this to do with bring-ing Deslucido to justice?

"Perhaps," Caitlin continued, as if thinking aloud, "some day the Council will evolve into a body capable of resolving differences without fighting. Rafael shares that hope, which is why we are here."

Taniquel realized then that while Rafael would never give in to Des-lucido's demands, he would consider himself bound by the united will of the Council. It was the price of using that same Council to stand against Deslucido, to eventually contain and subdue him.

"It is one thing for ordinary men to bash each other with swords because they have neither the wit nor the patience to control themselves," Caitlin went on. "It is quite another when the Towers devote themselves to mindless destruction. Do you think *laran* is but a toy, useful only for detecting lies and sending messages quickly?"

Taniquel flushed. "I have seen aircars swooping down from the sky on my home! I am not ignorant of *clingfire*."

"But have you ever seen what it can *do?* The burning that never stops, that eats everything in its path?"

"Even before we came here, we knew that Deslucido had commanded the workers at Tramontana to begin making *clingfire,*" Taniquel said.

And his word cannot be trusted, she thought. She felt it, rather than knowing exactly why. The sense of wrongness about Deslucido's testimony sizzled along her nerves. Perhaps it was seeing him again in the flesh, listening to his words. No, more than that: something . . . something had happened.

Sweet Evanda and all the Blessed Ones.

The vigil for Padrik.

"Zandru's coldest curse upon him!" Taniquel whispered.

Deslucido lied under truthspell.

No, it wasn't possible. Yet it had happened. He had, almost in passing, said a thing which was the very opposite of what had happened. It was such an insignificant detail, it hardly mattered—so small he need not have guarded his speech, and yet he said it. The pale blue light had not faltered on his face.

She had thought him devious, unscrupulous, willing to use trickery and to twist his words to accomplish his aims, but no more so than any other ambitious lordling. The ruse at the Acosta gates, the swift assumption of power, forcing her to marry his son in order to ensure legitimacy—these things, while unpleasant, were actions an ordinary man might take during war.

He lied under truthspell.

Her uncle was making a terrible mistake in thinking to contain Deslucido, to include him in the *Comyn* Council, to use their combined influence to restrain his use of *laran* weapons. If Deslucido had devised some trick of *laran* that rendered him immune to truthspell, he could promise them anything and then do exactly what he liked.

Taniquel's knees turned to water. She caught herself on the arm of her chair. Her skin turned icy, as if she had fallen into the river again.

"What is wrong?" Caitlin cried, clearly alarmed. She rushed to Taniquel's side. "What has happened? Are you unwell?"

Taniquel opened her mouth to reply when footsteps sounded outside the door and Rafael Hastur entered. Although the morning was mild, a chill breeze swirled in before him. His eyes were clouded, stormy, his mouth set. Gerolamo closed the door behind them.

Taniquel wished she had no *laran* at all, because she already knew what had passed in the Council. She followed him with her eyes as he went to the side table and poured a goblet of wine, not pausing to add water. He downed it in gulps, the only sound in the still room.

The air trembled about her, laden with a sense of deadly purpose. She had, without knowing, taken a step from which she could never draw back. That it might mean her death, and that of her son, and uncounted men she would never know, meant nothing. She wanted to run weeping from the room, to lose herself in the winter-gray hills and that lonely travel shelter. Those memories, like dreams of other impossible things, must remain secret, locked away. As Queen, as *comynara*, as a woman of integrity, she must speak the truth, no matter what the cost.

If only she did not know what she knew . . . but she did, and so had no choice but to speak.

"Uncle," she said with as much dignity as she could summon, "there is something I must tell you before you speak of the Council's decision."

His look shifted, as if he braced himself against some last, desperate argument.

"Damian Deslucido has found a way to lie under truthspell."

There it was. Simple, unadorned. Deadly.

She saw shock sweep across Rafael's face. Behind him, Gerolamo gasped.

"Don't talk nonsense, child," Caitlin cried. Her usually pale cheeks flushed.

Scowling, Rafael took a step toward Taniquel. For an instant, she feared he might strike her, he looked so angry. Through clenched teeth, he said, "Such things are not to be joked about."

He thought she was hurling ridiculous accusations in order to avoid being sent back to Acosta.

"Surely she does not realize what she is saying," Caitlin said. Quickly regaining her composure, she turned back to Taniquel and began explaining, as if to a small child. "Men may say misleading things under truthspell, depending upon how the question is phrased. But it is impossible to tell a deliberate falsehood."

Certainty, colder than ice and harder than steel, settled over Taniquel. "I know what I heard. He said a thing which was not true. He knew it was not true. And the light shone on his face."

"You must have been mistaken—" Caitlin protested, her voice faltering.

"I know what I know. I heard what I heard."

"What thing?" Rafael's voice rumbled, gravelly with emotion.

"He said—he said I was given leave to sit vigil for Padrik. Uncle, I will swear by Aldones and Evanda and any god you name, that I was locked in my chambers and forbidden to do so."

"Perhaps this was done by Deslucido's subordinates," Rafael said. "He might well have believed you free to do so. Then he would not have been lying, if he himself was deceived."

Taniquel shook her head. "I went to him, to demand an explanation when he had previously assured me that I might perform all the proper rites for Padrik. He brushed me off with a flimsy excuse, and then flatly refused to honor his word. It was by his own orders that I was confined."

"Clearly, he did not want you in plain sight, grieving over your slain husband, at a time when he sought to establish control over the castle," Caitlin said.

Taniquel did not give a rotten fig for Deslucido's motivations. "He explicitly forbade me. And then, today, he swore I had been free." She shuddered. "No wonder something felt wrong."

Caitlin glanced wild-eyed at Rafael, her former confidence in shreds. No wonder, Taniquel thought with a sudden flash of compassion. Caitlin's work, her entire world, was based on surety and knowledge of *laran.* If truthspell, the cornerstone of that certainty, were breakable—and by such a blackguard as Deslucido!—what could be trusted?

Rafael must have been thinking the same thing. His face congested with blood. His breath hissed between his teeth. With a visible effort, he walked to the farthest chair and sat down.

Caitlin calmed herself with visible difficulty. "Yet it is your word against his. For such a grievous charge, there must be incontrovertible proof."

"I believe her," Rafael said.

But Caitlin would not be moved. "This is no private matter. It . . . were this to be known, or even suspected . . ."

"I need no instruction in what would happen then," Rafael said.

"Everything we have worked for in bringing the Ages of Chaos to an end will be for naught. No man will trust another's word—"

"Or the truth of *laran*, the very fabric which binds our world together—" Caitlin said.

"I will swear by anything you wish," said Taniquel, lifting her head. "Under truthspell." Though the idea sent shivers of terror through her, she looked to Caitlin. "Or a direct examination of my mind."

"Child, you do not know what you are offering."

"I do. We must be sure." Taniquel met her uncle's eyes. "*You* must be sure."

Because he knows that if I am right, he cannot compromise. He must destroy Deslucido and any trace of what he has done, even if it means standing alone against the Council.

Rafael nodded to Caitlin.

"There is a risk—" the *leronis* said.

"There is *always* a risk," Taniquel cried. "But there is far greater danger if we do not act."

"Very well." Caitlin gave a little sigh as she reached for the starstone which she wore in a silk-lined locket around her neck. "Come into the sleeping chamber with me."

◆

Afterward, Taniquel remembered very little of what had passed. She was never sure if her mind suppressed the memories or if Caitlin had gently softened them so as to spare her lingering pain.

She had lain on the bed, focusing on her breathing at Caitlin's direction. Pressure built in her head, reminding her of the morning of the Acosta invasion, only deeper and unrelenting, shaped and aimed at the very center of her thoughts. She found herself once more in Padrik's quarters, only she now saw the once-familiar contours of the sitting room through a gauzy veil that muted some colors and intensified others. As before, Deslucido sat at the table, hands moving over the food laid out there. Blue-and-crimson lights played over his face and his eyes, when they flickered in her direction, burned like yellow fire.

"You promised . . ." Taniquel heard her own voice, muffled and distant. ". . . went to see . . . in the chapel . . . confined to my rooms."

". . . minor miscommunication." Damian's voice, too, shivered with that ghostly resonance. With each phrase, his words gained in strength and clarity, as if coming nearer. ". . . regret any inconvenience . . ."

"Why was I not allowed to leave my rooms?"

"It would not be seemly—or safe . . . For your own safety . . . it is to no one's benefit to turn his burial into a rallying point for malcontents."

"Am I not to be permitted to see him, then?" Taniquel's voice wailed, a mourner's cry.

"A lady . . . must be protected against such sights. Be guided by us in this, rest content . . .

"Rest content . . . Content . . ." The final word echoed through her as the images shredded. The sense of pressure intensified into outright pain.

Truth? Truth? pounded relentlessly through her temples. A spear point of fire probed deeper. At one point, she might have screamed, she could not be sure. Later, she slept.

✦

In her best gown and with her hair dressed by Caitlin as befitted a Queen, Taniquel appeared once again before the *Comyn* Council. There was no need for her to speak, only to stand by her uncle's side.

Never before had he looked so grim, as if he were granite made flesh. His expression had shifted from the tightness of facing an unpleasant task to a stony determination. Below that, she sensed anger and something more.

Fear.

Not of the Council, although his disappointment in all that he had hoped for ran through him like a vein of poison. Fear—of Deslucido and his ability to defy truthspell, fear of shattering the fragile bonds of trust which stood between the many lands of Darkover and true chaos.

Fear that he had already delayed until too late.

He held himself with a dignity and power she had only glimpsed in him before. He was *Comyn,* subordinate to no man, and he was Hastur, Son of Hastur who was Son of Aldones, Lord of Light.

His solemnity reflected in the assembled company, for as he spoke, calmly stating his position, there were no outbursts, no visible reactions. Taniquel sensed rather than heard the isolated points of disapproval, of agreement, of incredulity. She dared to glance in Deslucido's direction, to see his face darken, jaw rigid, the hard light of fury in his eyes when he looked at her.

With the *Comyn* Council as his witnesses, Rafael Hastur publically declared Acosta a Hastur protectorate, with Julian Regis Hastur-Acosta its lawful ruler, and Taniquel Hastur-Acosta as his Regent until he attained his majority.

When Rafael finished, the old man who was head of the Council rose to speak. "Think carefully on what you are doing, Hastur. If you mean to carry through these actions, you will place yourself in direct defiance of our orders."

"You know as well as any man how strongly I support the Council," Rafael replied. "I believe in our united purpose and always I have worked for negotiation and compromise. My past actions speak for themselves. But in this matter, my duty and my conscience are to a greater good. I cannot and will not bow to an unjust decision."

"Unjust! What do you mean by that, Hastur?" rumbled Old Alton. "If you have charges to make, out with them! Don't diddle around with bullying games!"

Calmly, Rafael turned to face the older man. "I will not see this Council used for *any* man's private purposes." With the slight emphasis, he indicated, *Including mine.* "I believe this is now a private affair between Damian Deslucido, myself, and Taniquel, Queen Regent of Acosta."

"So you have named her," Damian Deslucido said in a voice taut with suppressed anger. "But words cannot make her anything other than an obstinate girl-child who would leave a whole countryside in smoking ruins rather than submit to proper authority. When you lend your name to her cause, Hastur, you do her grave injury."

"It is not *I* who have done her injury," Rafael replied temperately. "And as you all can see, she is no child but *comynara* in her own right."

"She is a woman!" one of the lords grumbled. "Who has no voice here."

"Husband or kinsman must speak for her, although I don't much care which," another said.

The Aillard lady, who had until now remained silent, stirred. "My lords, if you are saying that *no woman* may speak in this Council, you had best reconsider your words."

The second speaker, whose lands bordered the powerful Aillard Domain, closed his mouth.

"What say you, *vai domna?*" the old chief asked Taniquel. "Will you join in this Hastur rebellion against the Council?"

"Deslucido invaded my country," she replied, "seized the castle by trickery, slaughtered its rightful king, and attempted to force me into an unwelcome marriage with his son. But the rightful King of Acosta, the *di catenas* son of Padrik, son and true heir of Ian-Valdir, lives. For his sake, I will not give up my claim, not for a hundred Council verdicts. The gods have seen fit to bless me with the support of my kinsman."

"So be it!" Damian slapped his palm flat on the table and sprang to his feet. "You will regret those proud words, lady. On the battlefield, in chains. Acosta is mine by the will of the gods. Never will I permit you or your *kinsman,*" he spat out the word, "to diminish the glorious kingdom I have built with my own two hands." He bowed to the assembly. "*Vai domyn,* I thank you for your support. But I have no choice but to enforce it myself." With a jangle of spurs, he strode from the room.

After a moment of silence, Rafael said, "I ask the Council to take no further action in this matter."

The old lord shook his head. "It is already out of our hands. I do not know if we, in our attempt at a peaceful resolution, have only made the situation worse. *Adelandayo,* Rafael Hastur. Go with the gods, and may their wisdom guide you."

BOOK 3

25

Winter was no time for warfare, Coryn reflected, even if Neskaya Tower were not snowbound like Tramontana at this season. And yet war had come.

He drew back from the casement into the warmth of the room. Even from inside, the translucent stone of Neskaya Tower caught the light of the slanting late afternoon winter sun. He remembered the first glimpse he had of the Tower, rising above the city of Neskaya like a pillar of glimmering sky-tinted ice, and how his heart had risen in delight.

Within, Neskaya Tower was organized somewhat differently from Tramontana. Without Kieran to exert such a dominant influence, decisions and power were spread more broadly over the Keepers and senior technicians. This was, Coryn suspected, in part due to the personalities of the last few generations of Keepers. Bernardo Alton was no exception in his willingness to listen to other ideas, and his innate respect for the people he regarded as his colleagues, not his subordinates.

"A Keeper's work is like any other," he had told Coryn when they first began to work together. *Work together* was Bernardo's phrase. "More glamorous to the public, perhaps, and certainly more demanding at times, but of no greater value. A Keeper without a circle is merely another technician. Never forget that the instrument with which you create your music is your circle, not yourself."

The second reason for the more democratic flavor of Neskaya Tower became apparent only after Coryn had been there some months, through the fall harvest and the beginning of winter. Unlike Tramontana, which had seemed a world unto itself, Neskaya owed clear obligations to its lawful lords, the Hasturs. For centuries it had been in Ridenow hands, until the peace forged by Allart Hastur between those two Domains. Bernardo once referred to Neskaya's present allegiances as having been forged by a peace treaty.

Neskaya had been asked, no, *commanded*, to make *clingfire* for the Hastur lords. Until now, Bernardo's experiments with a safer, more stable form had been the only active work with the corrosive stuff, and only the Keeper and a few of the more senior technicians were involved. Once, Bernardo had told Coryn, there was not a Tower from one end of settled Darkover to the other which was not making *clingfire*. Once, he said, it was used as readily as arrows in warfare. But in recent times, the Domains lords had often held their hands, relying on plain steel instead.

"Oh, *laran* still has a vital role in warfare and it always will," Bernardo said. "How else can generals communicate quickly with one another, or spy out the land with their sentry-birds, if not with our help?"

Now Coryn was to learn the creation and use of *clingfire*. He began by separating out minute particles of the flammable stuff and bringing it, bit by bit, to the surface. Once refined, the elements had to be kept separate in fields generated by great artificial matrix screens, or they would ignite. It was very much like the process of refining chemicals for fire fighting, only with far more disastrous results if an accident were to occur. Before long, he, and every other Tower worker who made *clingfire*, bore scars from momentary lapses in concentration.

From those few accidents, Coryn tried to imagine what it would be like to have the deadly liquid fire dropping on him from aircars or shot over castle walls on the tips of arrows. He wondered what it would be like to pilot an aircar, to look down on the lands and fortifications of an enemy, to see them burst into unquenchable flame. The Hastur lord had not yet asked for the *clingfire* to be delivered, only made ready. Coryn found himself grateful for the respite.

The light drained from the sky with the suddenness of winter. Dark settled over Neskaya's walls, softening the shadows into velvet. Only

Kyrrdis swung through the blackness overhead, and the Tower's walls gave off a faint blue shimmer in its light.

Coryn robed himself warmly for the night's work. Neskaya was not nearly as cold as Tramontana, but the long motionless hours left everyone stiff. Constructing the huge artificial matrix screens for Bernardo's experimental *clingfire* required even more concentration than other *laran* work. He could not afford the distraction of aching fingers or shivering muscles.

He came down the staircase from the living quarters, on his way past the kitchen for a hot drink before joining his circle.

"Coryn! There you are!" Amalie called to him. Slender and almost androgynous, she trotted toward him, pushing back an unruly cloud of pale-straw hair. "Come up to the relay room. You're wanted."

He raised one eyebrow in question, a gesture he'd half-unconsciously adopted from his new friend Cormac, the matrix technician who'd first welcomed him and then dubbed him *the other Cor of Neskaya.* Coryn, in retaliation, had dubbed the older man *Mac* and the nickname stuck.

Like everyone else in the Tower, Coryn took his turn at the *laran* relays, sending and receiving messages from other Towers. He could not think what difficulty could not be as capably dealt with by Mac or even Amalie herself. "What's going on?"

She gestured for him to follow her up the stairs. At Neskaya, the chamber housing the relay screens was set apart in its own tower to isolate communications from the stray mental energies generated by other projects. Chill radiated from the walls, for this section was part of the original Tower, old beyond imagining, constructed of fine-grained granite rather than the translucent blue stone of the central Tower. Amalie, swathed in the thick soft robe of a monitor, hugged her arms to her body as she climbed.

"It is a personal message," she said once they were well out of hearing of the lower common room.

Coryn could not imagine who would send to him in particular, unless it were bad news, another death at Tramontana perhaps. Lady Bronwyn—

No, surely he would have known. Their minds had been too closely linked for him not to sense her death.

They came to a halt outside the relay chamber. White light from the glows mingled with the blue radiance of the screens to cast eerie shadows across the girl's face. He thought he saw the glimmer of tears in her eyes, or perhaps it was the white flash of fear. .

At Neskaya, the relay screens sat on low tables, so that the workers did not need to crouch, but could sit on padded benches. A small coal brazier, its smoke contained by a heat-permeable *laran* shield, filled the room with gentle warmth.

Amalie went to the bench covered by a rumpled shawl. Coryn recognized it as her favorite, thick *chervine* wool knitted in a ferny design with threads of green and brown. He picked it up and draped it over her shoulders. With a fingertip gesture, she motioned for him to sit.

Coryn did so, bringing his mind to focus on the screen before him. It was active, the lattices tuned to Amalie's clear, almost geometric thought pattern. Subtly, he shifted them to his own and felt himself rise into the moony radiance. He always thought of contact along the relays as swimming through a sea of light. Ripples of brilliance and shadow passed over him. Elongating himself like a sea creature, he plunged through cross currents of shivery cold, moving ever deeper. Music vibrated through him, the deep-throated resonant calls of mythic beasts. Light faded, colors muting to blues and purples, finally to inky shadows. Vision dimmed as he dropped into rapport.

Coryn, are you there? Words touched him like the brush of a falcon's wings. The sea fell away, and Coryn floated in a crystalline sky, surrounded by the mental presence of his friend.

Aran.

A rush of warmth and pleasure answered him. For a long moment, he savored the sense of loving union, of acceptance. A loneliness he had not known was there lifted from him. All was right, perfect, complete.

I have missed you more than I knew, he thought.

And I, you. A pause, an awkward pulling away into separateness. *Lady Bronwyn is well, and sends her love. She asked leave to return to her family, but was refused.*

Coryn startled. *What is it? What is going on? Why would she wish to leave?*

She asked surety that she would not be forced to make war against her kin. She is of Hastur blood.

Coryn had not known that. Bronwyn had so clearly been highly born, she of the silvery bells. She had never referred to her rank.

Wage war?

This will be our last relay to Neskaya. Sadness weighed every syllable. *We are to cease contact, least we betray some secret. . . .*

The clear skies darkened and Coryn struggled to keep the connection. Neskaya was making *clingfire* for the Hastur lord, but he had not thought of its target. Since coming here, he had thought little of the politics of the outer world beyond distaste at their intrusion.

Without saying so, Aran had made his meaning clear. Tramontana and Neskaya were to join in the conflicts between their respective lords.

◆

"Yes, that is always a possibility," Bernardo said in answer to Coryn's question about friends or even kinsmen finding themselves on opposing sides in a conflict, once Towers became involved. "It has happened in the past and will again."

"But surely it is not right, especially when the quarrel is none of our making," Coryn said, sitting forward on the chair in the Keeper's study. He'd had to move a stack of diagrams for a new scheme of interlocking matrix screens, a stuffed owl, and three crumb-laden platters in order to make room to sit down.

"The world goes as it will, not as you or I would have it." Although Bernardo's voice was neutral, fear and sadness resonated behind his words.

Coryn was struck by how thin Bernardo looked, as if life's struggles had pared him to the very bone. Coryn then remembered Bernardo was an Alton, and not immune to divided loyalties. As far as he knew, there was peace between Hastur and Alton, but in these uncertain times, that might not always be true.

"If we are to serve Hastur in this campaign against Deslucido," Coryn said slowly, "then we might be ordered to drop *clingfire* on any of the lands which he holds."

Verdanta going up in flames, Tessa screaming as her body burned like a torch, stone walls tumbling. . . .

And Coryn himself in an aircar, looking down on the scene, wishing with all his heart it was he himself down there, burning, dying in agony, instead of his loved ones.

Bernardo reached out to brush Coryn's wrist with a featherlight touch of the fingers. It was meant as reassurance, but both of them knew that even though Bernardo might try, he could not lighten Coryn's duties.

Coryn still had a few years to complete his Keeper's training, but there was no doubt that he would; his abilities and talent for the work had shown themselves clearly. He would be Keeper of Neskaya after Bernardo; his would be the responsibility.

"There must be a way to remain neutral, to do all the constructive, peaceful work we may do and yet stay apart from the conflict," Coryn said.

"Are we wise enough, then, to decide what quarrels we will join and which we will pass by?" Bernardo asked. "It is said that power clouds judgment. And with such power as we wield, can we be trusted to use it wisely? Or is it better to leave such decisions to those trained to it, just as we are trained to the use of our *laran*?"

"You speak in questions, as if we can not know the answers," Coryn said. He had heard these questions, or those very like them, too many times already. It was no use asking Bernardo to refuse to make *clingfire* for this brewing war, or to ignore a command from the Hastur lord, no matter how hateful. But perhaps, if their case were to be put directly to the King . . .

Bernardo listened gravely as Coryn outlined his idea. "Hastur can call upon Hali Tower," Coryn said, "which surely is closer to hand and has fewer conflicts of loyalty than we do. Let us use our talents to heal instead of harm, make chemicals to fight fires instead of ignite them, promote peace through communication and the solid trust of truthspell."

"I cannot say whether the Hastur King will agree," Bernardo said.

"But we must try!" Coryn sat even farther forward on his chair, so that he perched on its very edge. "Let me go, let me speak to him, plead our case."

"Oh, you make an eloquent spokesman, indeed," said Bernardo, his familiar smile flashing like summer lightning across his features. "And I think you are right. Asked respectfully, and whatever answer accepted in good grace—"

"Of course!"

"Then as soon as the snows have passed and it is safe to travel, you may go to Thendara and put your ideas before King Rafael."

✦

Coryn found himself again on the road, this time in the company of a traders' caravan and two younger landless sons of minor lords on their way to Thendara to serve in the Cadet Guards. Coryn, listening to their bravado chattering, wondered if he had ever been so young. Had the world gone in another direction, his father might have had to make a similar provision for his future, although he doubted that would have included a cadet's commission.

More than ever before, he appreciated his place in a Tower. Here he had honorable work which used his talents to the fullest, as well as companions he respected and who valued him. Perhaps, he thought in a moment of expansive gratitude, Rumail had not served him ill after all.

Coryn presented his packet of introductory papers to the Hastur Castle sergeant, was courteously greeted, shown to guest quarters rather than barracks, and given an appointment for the following morning. He had arrived too late to visit Hali and meet the workers whose minds he had touched over the relays, or to see the mystical cloud-filled Lake or the holy place called *rhu fead*.

Instead, he went down into the city. Somewhat to his surprise, people moved out of his way, murmuring respectfully and occasionally bowing as he passed. A few children pointed to his red hair before their mothers hurried them away. The deference amused and troubled him, but each place had its own ways and he felt only uncomfortable, not in any danger.

Energy sizzled through the Thendara streets in a brilliance of colors—banners, trade booths, tartan skirts and cloaks, the emblemed livery of servants, even the headdresses of the carriage horses. Music skirled from streetcorner musicians to mingle with the cries of fruit peddlers. Everything seemed to be for sale at one place or another and Coryn had no doubt that if he asked discreetly in the right neighborhood, he would find illicit Dry Towns drugs as readily available as apples or boot-knives.

He suspected that with the right contacts, too, a message could be sent to Verdanta, to let Eddard and Tessa know he was alive and well. However, he had only a few coins to his name, not nearly enough to pay for such a service, even if he could find someone both trustworthy and brave enough to venture it.

The afternoon sun bathed the narrow streets in a reddish light as it sank over the horizon. Although it was summer, the temperature in the shadows fell rapidly. Coryn drew the hood of his lightweight cloak over his head, covering his hair. Within a few blocks, people no longer avoided him. After the careful distances of the Tower, the jostling felt oddly intrusive.

A half-grown street urchin tried to pick his purse. Coryn caught the small hand as it reached out. The boy froze, rigid. Button-black eyes

glared out from beneath a mop of hair so filthy and matted, its true color
could be only guessed. The wrist bones were small, fragile. Coryn caught
a flash of emotion—anger, fear . . . hunger.

"I'm new in town and looking for a guide," he said in a conversa-
tional tone. "Do you know anyone who'd like to earn a few *reis*?"

"If ye'r lookin' fer a guide, I'm it," the urchin chirped. "Ten *reis*, all
in advance. Anywhere yer want to go."

Coryn released the boy with a smile. "Two, for the evening. An inn
with decent food and some information."

"Throw supper in?"

"Done!"

The boy led him through twisted alleys, down a street or two, deliberately circling so that a confused stranger might be willing to pay double
for finding his way again. Coryn had always had a good sense of direction,
and his time at Neskaya had given him a sense of familiarity with city
landscapes. He would have no trouble finding his way back to the castle,
although he was not about to let the boy know. The adventure of the
moment was too appealing.

A couple of men in patched leather-plate armor watched from a doorway as they approached. One took a step into the darkening street, hand
on a well-worn sword hilt. Coryn picked up a flicker of half-formed *laran*
from one of them and sent back soothing, inoffensive harmlessness.

"Now then, lad," he said to the urchin, "you wouldn't be leading me
into a den of thieves, would you?"

"Oh, no, sire! It's just everyone's jumpy these days. Looks to be war
comin' on."

"War?" Coryn tried to sound unenlightened. "What war?"

"I couldn't say, not me, no."

Coryn halted, gesturing as if to turn back. "Then maybe I should ask
someone more grown up. Perhaps our friends back there?"

The boy grabbed his hands and pulled him further down the street.
"No way messin' with *them.* Let's get indoors."

Within minutes, they entered an inn which from the outside resembled a bordello that had long since seen better times. They found a
cracked wooden table in one corner. Coryn settled himself against the
wall facing the door, sipping a tankard of ale whose acrid taste belied a
dubious ancestry, while the street urchin dug into his second trencher of
stew. From this vantage point, he could hear snatches of passing conver-

sation from the street beyond. He was not telepath enough to pick up any thoughts, even if his years of training in Tower ethics would permit it.

Below the expected anxiety, he *sensed* deeper emotions. There was no resentment at the Hastur King for having brought the city and all its lands to the brink of a war which had not yet been declared. He remembered how the people in the street shrank away from his red hair, the mother scurrying her child out of his path, the whispers.

Laranzu . . . *wizard.*

Fear?

"So," said the boy, wiping his gravy-smeared lips on a tattered sleeve edge, "what d'yer want to know?"

"I've been traveling for a long while, out of touch. Who dares to make war on Hastur?"

"Oh, it's him that's stirrin' up the pot, not that the other one don't deserve it. Seems the King's taken it into mind to put a baby to rule over some place Old Oathbreaker claims as his, or maybe it's the other way around for all the difference it makes. No wonder Smarky don't go for it! You tell me! A baby king! What would he do, play daddles with his crown?" The boy whooped at his own wit.

"There would be a regent," Coryn said mildly.

"How's some more stew?"

Coryn had grown restless listening to the urchin's speech. He had come on a fool's errand, unlikely to yield anything of real value. A boy king and a regent, claims supported and disputed, these were the machinations of lordly powers, as like as not pretext for something else. He shifted in his chair, debating a third round of stew for the child, who certainly looked hungry enough to devour it.

Two men had paused outside the inn, just out of his line of vision, so that he could not see the details of their faces or clothing, only the shadowy outlines.

". . . attack on the borderlands . . ." one was saying in heavily accented tones. "Half the fields gone up in smoke . . . some kind of witchery . . . fires kept burning and burning . . ."

Clingfire? Coryn sat straighter, focusing.

"I say, strike back hard," came another man's voice. "Make the filthy *ombredin* pay. Land's ours, that's what I say. Take it all back and more."

"Aye, a clean fight is one thing, but when those accursed Towers get involved—" Fear edged with hatred resonated in the man's voice.

"Rafael Hastur's a just king—"

"Where was he and all his fine men when Maire's village was burned to ashes and there weren't nothing left to bury? By Zandru's bloody bones, some day there'll be a reckoning. Some day—"

"But not tonight and not here in the open. What do you say we get a drink?" One shadow moved to fill the doorway.

The other man, the one who'd spoken first and whose Maire had lost her village and perhaps her life, held back. "No, I've had enough tonight . . ." The man's voice muffled. ". . . nothing for me here . . . Maybe . . . enough Ambervale blood, her shade will let me rest . . ."

"What, enlist in Hastur's army?"

The answer was indistinguishable, even though Coryn strained to catch it.

". . . take you home . . ."

The street urchin had fallen silent, eyes glued on Coryn. The calculating stare had returned. Coryn got up and tossed the boy another small coin. "Here. Finish your dinner. I can find my own way back."

He was careful to draw his cloak hood down around his head as he left the inn.

26

The next morning, Coryn washed, combed his shoulder-length hair, dressed in a gray robe edged with red bands to denote his status as under-Keeper, and presented himself for his interview with King Rafael Hastur II. He was greeted courteously by an older man who did not name his position but carried himself with quiet authority, perhaps a *coridom* or paxman.

"Please follow me," the man said, and led the way past the entrance to the great hall. Guards in Hastur colors, impeccable in their appearance and alertness, stood spaced along the corridor. *This must be the private royal wing,* Coryn thought. The walls were of a stone so fine it resembled marble, interspersed in decorative fashion with pale blue, translucent panels. The effect was one of depth and spaciousness, although the passageway was not exceptionally wide.

At the end of the corridor, Coryn was ushered into what looked like a council chamber, with six chairs drawn up around an oval table. A bowl of snowdrops perched on a lacy round beside half a dozen blown-glass goblets and a pitcher glistening with condensation. No fire burned in the grate, although Coryn judged that even a small blaze would make the room cozy in the worst weather. The mullioned windows had been thrown open and sunlight streamed through to glitter on dancing motes like a golden bridge to the sky. The entire effect was one of richness, order, and serenity.

From the far end of the room, in a corner beside the fireplace, a woman arose from her chair and came toward him. She smiled in greeting, although she did not hold out her hand. Gray frosted her dark red hair, coiled low on her neck. She wore a tabard and underdress of midnight blue. A starstone of unusual brilliance sat in the cleft between her collarbones. Coryn prepared himself to bow to her, although he had not known that King Rafael had a Queen.

"Coryn of Tramontana and now of Neskaya, on behalf of my brothers and sisters at Hali, I bring you greetings." Her words, although formal, came with such an ease and elegance that his hesitation vanished instantly. Her mind touched his briefly, almost playfully.

"Caitlin of Hali!" He would know her *laran* signature anywhere. "I did not realize you were part of the royal household."

"Yes, I have been Rafael's family *leronis* for many years, besides serving at Hali," she said. Now that they were closer, he saw the tracery of lines around her eyes and mouth that betrayed her age. "I was to return yesterday, but Rafael asked me to stay a little longer. I am so happy to meet you in person."

The door swung open and a man of middle age and height, slender yet in no way frail, entered. He wore riding leathers and smelled of the outdoors. The room seemed to vibrate with his energy as he crossed to Caitlin, gave her a kiss on one cheek, and turned to Coryn.

"So this is our young Keeper-to-be? Bernardo has great faith in you, and I have great faith in *him*!"

"Your Maj—" Coryn began what he hoped was a properly respectful bow, after having stared like a farm boy at his King's entrance.

"None of that now!" Rafael forestalled any further awkwardness by clapping Coryn on one shoulder and steering him into one of the chairs at the table. Caitlin took the adjacent seat, hands folded neatly on her lap. Within moments, a convoy of servants carried in pitchers of *jaco*, trays of meat pastries still steaming from the oven, fruits in honey syrup spiced with cinnabark and nutmeg, boiled eggs, and a casserole of mushrooms simmered in white wine and herbs.

Coryn had not realized how hungry he was, or how good food could taste. The cooking at both Tramontana and Neskaya had been simple fare designed to meet the strenuous energy needs of *laran* work. This food was its own enjoyment. He feasted as if he'd been up working the relays for three nights running.

While they ate, Caitlin asked polite questions about the various people at Neskaya and Coryn replied with equally polite questions about the news from Hali. Very little of note had happened at either Tower since he'd been on the trail and out of touch.

"Last night, we sent word to Neskaya that you'd arrived safely," she commented.

"My thanks." Coryn glanced at King Rafael, who had been finishing his mushrooms and *jaco*.

The King turned his chair so that it faced half away from the table and toward Coryn's. "Welcome as you are to Thendara and delighted as we are to see you, what brings you all this distance? What was so important it could not have been sent along the relays and passed through Hali?"

Before Coryn could reply, a knock sounded from the back of the room and a small door swung open, evidently a private entrance. A woman slipped through and hurried toward them. Coryn, turning, caught a swirl of russet skirts softly gathered beneath a tapered bodice, and a cloud of ebony hair and flashing green eyes.

"Oh! Forgive the intrusion, Uncle. I didn't realize—" the woman began.

Coryn scrambled to his feet, almost tripping over the legs of his chair. *"Tani?"*

She turned an astonished gaze to him, her mouth forming a rosebud of surprise that sent his heart racing. Good health had burnished her skin to peach-cream, set off perfectly by the scooped neckline of her gown. Her movements sparkled with vitality. As if to greet her, a sudden breeze had filled the room from the opened windows, cool and fresh with the scents of spring growth.

"Coryn! However did you find me?" She smiled, sweet and radiant, and came toward him, hands outstretched. Her fingers slipped between his, warm and strong for all their slenderness.

"Tani—" he stammered, "I had no idea you were here—"

She laughed, tilting her head back ever so slightly but creating the effect of joyous abandon.

"So this is *your* Coryn," Lady Caitlin said, as if that explained everything, just before all three of them, plus the paxman who had escorted him there, began talking at once.

King Rafael summoned wine, but Coryn dared not drink. His head was spinning enough, thoughts tumbling together. He had known Tani's desperation, her fearful flight, but he'd had no idea of her station in life. Seeing her here now, she seemed a jewel set in a royal diadem.

Sitting with Tani and King Rafael in this elegant, sunlit room, he felt even farther from her than he had in the months before. Until that moment, he had not realized how he cherished the memory of their brief hours together, the silken touch of her skin against his, the smell of her hair, the brilliance of her eyes, the moment when she turned to him in utter trust. As *laranzu* and under-Keeper of Neskaya, he reminded himself, he was no man's inferior. Now he saw the unbreachable gulf between their worlds.

Before Tani had properly begun her story, the paxman bent to murmur in Rafael's ear. "Gerolamo reminds me of my own schedule," Rafael said. "You young people can carry on very nicely without me. Gero, arrange a banquet tonight in this young man's honor, as thanks for his services to my niece."

"Your Majesty, please, it's hardly necessary—" Coryn began.

"Nonsense!" Rafael called over his shoulder as he left the room.

Tani smiled fondly as the door closed after him. "You've given him an occasion to celebrate, which puts him doubly in your debt." She rose without any of the skirt-fluffing Coryn associated with ladies and fine gowns. "There's no need for us to stay indoors on such a fine morning. Let's walk in the gardens. Caitlin, would you be so kind as to ask the nurse to bring Julian to us there?"

Without waiting for an answer, Tani walked briskly from the room, striding almost as fast as a man even in her long skirts.

"I am like my uncle in this," she said as she led the way through a series of corridors and down a narrow stone stairwell. She turned to flash a smile at him. "We're both happier in the fresh air, doing things. You must forgive his brusqueness. It's *cortes* season." Her tone implied that King Rafael would be sitting long, tedious hours in judgment on the cases brought before him. An occasion for celebration would indeed be a gift.

The garden was small and immaculately kept, the gravel of the walkways gleaming like marble pebbles. New green sprouted from the carefully pruned cherry trees, rose trellises, and sculptured borders. A pair of birds nesting in the ancient oak at the center chirped a warning at their approach but did not fly away. Around a corner, Coryn caught a glimpse of topiary in the form of a dragon.

Tani talked of inconsequentials, how unexpected his appearance was and the fine weather of the morning, until a nurse approached, leading a sturdy toddler with dark hair and glowing cheeks. Shrieking with delight, the boy ran to Tani and she caught him in her arms.

"Your son," Coryn said.

"Yes, I—" She broke off and set the boy on his feet, then lowered herself beside him on the bench. He promptly crawled into her lap.

"I was pregnant with Julian when I escaped. Without you—" Now she lifted her eyes to meet his and when she continued, her voice brimmed with emotion he could not put a name to. "Without you, neither of us would have survived the journey. I owe you my son's life as well as my own."

He sat immobile from the Tower-trained habit of avoiding direct physical contact. "You called the King uncle. Who exactly *are* you?"

"My name is Taniquel Elinor Hastur-Acosta," she answered. "King Rafael is my mother's brother. I was orphaned at an early age and fostered here in Thendara and then at Acosta."

As she spun out the story of her childhood and marriage, it seemed to Coryn that the spirited girl grew into a determined, resourceful young woman before his eyes. He could well believe she had braved such a terrible journey alone.

When she spoke of the assault on Castle Acosta, the toddler in her arms grew restless, as if sensing her anguish. One of the servants brought out a ball and a hoop and stick.

"Come on!" Laughing, she tossed the ball in the air for her son to run after. Coryn felt a pang, remembering such games with Kristlin, but Taniquel's joy infected him and he soon joined in with a will.

After the child grew tired and was taken away by his nurse, it was time for the midday meal. Taniquel excused herself, saying she had other duties.

That evening, as Rafael had proposed, a feast was held in the great hall, with music and singing. If it was quickly organized, it was no less joyous. Rich food and wine filled each table. After the meal, the entertainment began. Acrobats leaped and tumbled, and climbed on each other in feats of balance. A small troupe of professional dancers executed an elaborate and extremely athletic version of a mountain dance. A minstrel had composed a ballad about Taniquel's journey to freedom, although Coryn thought he'd taken great liberties with the landscape as well as his own part. He had not, as the song suggested, appeared to the fugitive Queen as an angel surrounded by blue light. Nor had Taniquel borne any marks of physical torture; her outward injuries had been from exposure, not assault. Coryn glanced at Taniquel. Her eyes glittered and a fevered color rose to her cheeks. Invisible wounds often ran far deeper than those which could be bandaged.

Toward the end, the song turned invective rather than narrative, building to a call to arms against the tyrants who had usurped the place of Acosta's rightful King.

✦

King Rafael was busy with the *cortes* for the next tenday and Coryn found himself much in the role of a courtier of the household, welcome but his business considered of no particular urgency. It was not until a number of days later that he heard the rest of Taniquel's story as they walked together, once more in the garden. Her voice never wavered as she told of aircars bombing the gates and the use of mind-compelling *laran*. An undercurrent ran through her words and he sensed there was much she did not say aloud. Perhaps she could not. She sat there on the bench, with the sun lighting rainbows in the ebony cloud of her hair, her head held so proudly, her hands momentarily still. Her eyes clouded as if she were looking within, at what she could see only in memory, and he thought he had never seen such quiet grace, such courage.

"We have a common enemy," he said during one of those silences which arose, when feeling took the place of words. "Damian Deslucido, he whom you call Oathbreaker."

"How did you come to cross his path?"

"Rather ask how he brought sorrow to me and mine," Coryn said ruefully. "Before he rode on Acosta, he conquered several small mountain kingdoms, Verdanta among them. That was my home."

"Yes, I have heard of it," she said, brows drawing together and mouth tightening. "Verdanta, one of the Storn realms, and Hawksflight. He was maneuvering his position to strike at Acosta."

"His son Belisar was to have married my youngest sister in a peaceful alliance," Coryn said. "But she died, as did my father, and Deslucido took what he wanted by force. Another of my sisters and my second oldest brother disappeared and I do not know where they are."

"Perhaps they perished with the rest."

Coryn shook his head. "I would know, just as I know Eddard and Tessa still live. They are hidden from me, which is probably for the best, for if I cannot find them, neither can Damian's *laranzu* brother. But whether they have found their way to freedom or outlawry or languish in some dungeon, that I do not know."

Taniquel reached out and touched the back of his hand with her fingertips. "We are all of us in the hands of the gods." Then she added, with a bitter laugh, "You know, for one so handsome and full of himself, not to mention heir to a great kingdom, Belisar seems to have unusually bad luck in finding a bride. I almost feel sorry for him. Now his father has fomented a border squabble with my uncle, although I do not for a moment believe it is me he wants."

"The more fool he," Coryn murmured.

"No," she continued, getting to her feet as if she had not heard, "his ambitions have grown so grandiose as to encompass half the Hundred Kingdoms and more. We will have great need of your skills in the times to come, you and your comrades at Neskaya."

Coryn did not want to set himself against Taniquel, but he could not let her continue in the assumption he was there to offer help. "That is what I have come to Thendara to speak with your uncle about," he said slowly, "to ask him not to involve us in any argument with another Tower."

Taniquel continued pacing, gesturing, not looking at him. "In warfare, against such an enemy, one cannot afford the loss of such a valued weapon."

"But to set Tower against Tower—"

"Or soldier against soldier, what difference is there?" She whirled to face him. "Each of us is duty bound in one way or another. No one is exempt. It feels so odd saying these things to you, for usually it is men explaining the ways of war to women."

"You do not understand. Each of us has kin or close friends at the other Towers. In the relays, we speak to each other, mind to mind, far closer than any words." He saw from the shift in her expression that his words had struck some chord within her. "I was trained at Tramontana. I would not make war on the people I love."

"I am sorry," she said in a low voice. "but it cannot be helped."

"Surely there must be another way. Negotiations. Treaties—"

"We tried that in the *Comyn* Council and he set them against us." Now she sounded angry, her hands jabbing the air, eyes flashing. "Do you know what they are calling our stand against his aggression? The Hastur Rebellion, as if *we* were the ones who had started all the trouble. I do not much care how history regards our cause, but I would not see our own people—or our allies—turned against us through misunderstanding."

"Then why bring the Towers into it at all? Why not fight your own accursed wars?" he asked, hearing emotions strident in his voice. He reined them in, for they did not belong here in this garden, spoken to the lovely young Queen before him, but to the Hastur lord, the only one who had the power to act. "I, too, am sorry. I spoke out of turn. You are not the one responsible for these decisions."

She flushed, a wave of anger and something more. "Let us not quarrel," she said, her voice shaking. "Coryn, I never thought to see you again. This short time the two of us have together is a gift. I would not let our common enemy come between us."

She put her hand out and grasped his in a gesture of impulsive warmth. Her touch burned along the nerves of his arm. Through the physical contact, he caught the edge of her mind, half thought, half emotional memory. An instant of utter revulsion, the dizzying moment when her world and everything she believed in turned inside-out, the cold-iron taste of desperation driving her through the storm, a vision of her uncle's face, gray with horror. And in the heart of it, like a spider lying in wait for its prey, Deslucido.

She must hate him very much.

Deslucido, for all his greed and ambition, was only an ordinary man.

Rumail . . . But Rumail was outcast from the Towers. Rumail could do no more harm.

And yet . . . Blue flames leaped hungrily behind Coryn's eyes, part memory, part mirror to the fear he sensed in Taniquel.

In his mind he saw her, turning toward him, eyes filled with light, hair a corona of spun black glass framing her face. She lifted her arms toward him even as the flames rose higher, an incandescent barrier.

Through water you have come to me, he thought. *Through fire I must come to you.*

Then the moment of clear vision passed, and together they sat in the miniature walled world of the garden. She still held his hand, her body curving toward his. Rosy color, as clear as a summer's dawn, tinted her skin. They were so close, he could feel her breath, could taste the faintly spicy scent she wore, could see the faint pulsation at her throat.

With his free hand, Coryn cupped Taniquel's cheek. She closed her eyes. He realized as his fingers brushed her face that she had some measure of empathy. Untrained, instinctive, it swept all through her senses. She felt not only his touch, the warmth and texture of his hand on hers, the smell of his sun-warmed skin, all the things her body experienced, and she also felt his emotions.

Without thought, he brushed her lips with his, or perhaps it was she who moved to meet him. A feeling he had never known, a tenderness so exquisite it bordered on pain, unfolded in him. Her heart opened to him, a mirror to his own.

Never in all his years of Tower work had he experienced a joining so complete, so uncomplicated, without reservation or condition. She held nothing back, matching his passion at the exact instant it arose in him. Time lost all meaning.

The rustle of a leaf, the snap of a twig brought him back to the day. Coryn opened his eyes to see a tiny bird take wing. The fingers of one hand were still entwined with hers, while the other lay gently along the side of her face.

Dark lashes fluttered open to reveal eyes filled with luminous tears. He had never seen anything so beautiful as those eyes. In some other world, in some other life, he thought, he could drown himself in them forever.

Taniquel blinked, sniffed, pulled away. He straightened up. The muscles of his lower back twinged from leaning forward too long.

"I . . ." Her voice failed her.

Coryn thought that if she reached out to him, he would not be able to refuse her and they would both be lost, all duty forsaken. Instead, she lifted her hands to her hair and drew out a copper pin, gracefully curved and topped with a filigree set with tiny sparkling stones. Around it twined several delicate ribbons of the same russet silk as her gown, ending in tiny knotted rosettes. She held it out to him.

His fingers closed around the pin, still warm. Several long black hairs had been caught in it.

In remembrance of this gift of time . . . Her mind brushed against his.

As Coryn slipped the pin into the inner pocket of his robe, he touched age-worn fabric. Since the day he left Verdanta Castle for Tramontana, there had not been an hour when his mother's handkerchief had left him. Now he drew out the folded square of embroidery. Without a word, he pressed it into her hand. There was no need to explain, to tell her what it meant to him. She already held his heart, as he did hers. Their bond went beyond words.

For a long moment, an eternity of heartbeats, a single breath, neither moved.

"Lady Taniquel! *Vai domna!*" A woman's voice called from a distance. The nurse.

She stirred, and the moment shattered. He sat immobile as she gathered up her skirts and headed back toward the castle.

27

Clouds, layered so thin and fine that the sky itself seemed white, cast a filmy veil over the rising Bloody Sun. Morning mist burned off from the open fields of Drycreek, although the surrounding heights remained shrouded in white. As the night's chill lifted, the mingled scents of grasses, summer field flowers, and warm earth drifted on the gentle breeze. A hawk hovered overhead while mice scurried for their burrows. In the distance, a family of deer bounded for the safety of the wooded slopes.

Belisar Deslucido sat on his massive red-gold stallion on the knoll which was the highest point of the valley and waited for the battle to unfold below him. As the horse shifted under him, he yawned and rubbed the dregs of wine from his eyes.

The Ambervale forces had arrived late the night before, with barely enough time to slaughter and roast the bullocks seized from the little trading village on the river. They'd been delayed by the guerrilla forces which had lately come down from the Verdanta Mountains, stinging and harrying like a nest of scorpion-ants. Unlike the poisonous insects, they posed no serious threat, certainly not to disciplined troops, but they had delayed his passage.

In preparation for the campaign, Damian Deslucido had moved his headquarters to Acosta and from there, launched the assault. Belisar should have been much deeper into Hastur lands when this battle occurred, so that even a stalemate would win him miles of borderland. His general, The Yellow Wolf, insisted that it was better to meet the Hastur forces here in the foothills rather than on the rolling plains where their greater numbers and easy supply lines would work to their advantage.

Now The Wolf had ridden down to his army, advancing the left wing, holding men behind the center in reserve. The natural contours of the land gave them partial cover, although they were not yet in the best position. Day and the enemy had come upon them too soon.

A few changes in plans and times were mere details, dependent on chance circumstance. Victory must be his in the end because his cause was just. Over the last few years, the goal of unifying Darkover had taken on a life and momentum of its own, like some raw elemental force.

Belisar felt restless, but perhaps it was only his resentment at being up here, at a safe distance, instead of leading his own men as he had wished.

"With power comes responsibility," Damian had told him. "A king cannot risk his life like any ordinary soldier."

"I am not yet king," Belisar had said.

"And if you are killed in battle, you never will be!" After that, there was nothing more to be said.

Rumail, in the hooded gray cloak which had now become his customary garment, sat on his mule a little apart from Belisar, head bent to speak privately with the two *laranzu'in* from Tramontana. He'd been fussing over something all morning.

From the fingers of low-lying fog, the Hastur men approached in units, both mounted and on foot. A rider broke away from the foremost troops, white banner held aloft. Ambervale men intercepted him and, after some discussion, escorted him to the hill. Belisar watched them approach, amused.

A parley? What was there to parley about, except to delay the day's work?

The messenger, an earnest young officer, did not dismount but lowered the white standard in greeting. His mount blew froth from its nostrils and shook its head.

"In the name of Rafael Alar Julian Hastur, King and second of that name, I command you to cease this unlawful incursion of armed forces

on our lands and depart forthwith to your own country." The youthful
voice rang out unwavering, a singer's voice.

Belisar said, "And if I do not? If it pleases me to occupy these lands?"

The officer wet his lips. "Then by strength of arms, His Majesty will
enforce the sovereignty of his territory."

"And we will have a battle? Good!" At the messenger's startled response, Belisar threw his head back and laughed. "Gods, boy, what do
you think this is about? Does your high and mighty Majesty think we
came all this way for polite conversation?"

Belisar then sent the signal for The Yellow Wolf to advance to the
point of maximum advantage. He added the order to take the young
messenger prisoner. "Burn the white flag. Make sure they can see it down
below. *That* will be their answer."

The boy, to his credit, had enough presence of mind not to make a
fool out of himself with useless protest.

Belisar's horse pranced in place, scenting the rising adrenaline. For
what seemed like hours but were actually only minutes, the Ambervale
forces crept forward.

The Hastur men held their position. Belisar could almost hear their
banners flapping in the wind and the horses whinnying, harnesses jangling. He smelled their rank, intoxicating sweat. Part of him wished he
was down there with them, a battle cry swelling in his throat, the reins
held fast between his fingers, his mount quivering with eagerness.

Below, a wordless yell pierced the shuddering tension. Belisar did not
care which side it came from. It was time; the battle demanded its own
birth. Both forces rushed forward like arrows released from bows too
long held taut. Within moments, dust churned by the charging cavalry
rose in billows. War cries and neighing pierced the clamor. The red-gold
stallion snorted and pranced beneath him, pulling at the bit.

Through breaks in the billowed dust, he caught sight of the fighting,
colors and banners. Spear points glittered in the sun. One horse ran rider-
less and another reared so high it toppled backward.

Seen from this vantage, the battle moved with agonizing slowness,
although Belisar knew the action on the ground was frenzied. Swords
slashing, spears thrusting, horses rearing, death always an instant away, a
flash at the edge of vision, that instinct that made a man turn and miss a
blow by the breadth of a hair. The music of steel against steel. The mingled taste of dust and blood. The soaring elation which sizzled along

every nerve as if lightning laced his entire body. His heart pounded, thinking of it, lusting for it.

The main body of the Hastur force had come forward, engaged with the center and left wing, leaving their flank relatively unguarded.

Yes! We have them! Exultation washed through every fiber of his body, more intoxicating than wine.

The Yellow Wolf's reserve troops surged forward. A noise rose up from them like no other. A thousand battle cries merged into a single roar. The lions which roamed the deserts beyond the Dry Towns might sound like that as they surrounded a gazelle.

For an instant, Belisar wondered what the Hastur men must be thinking as these fresh troops bore down on them, as they turned to fight, perhaps back-to-back with their brothers, knowing that at last they must fall. Would they curse the King who had led them into ruin? Or would they fight unthinking to the last?

Rumail had thrown his hood back from his face to scan the sky. His eyes narrowed and Belisar sensed his concentration, seeking to pierce the clouds.

"There!" Rumail cried, and pointed aloft.

A graceful V-shape shot into a patch of blue, wheeling, circling downward.

"What is it? A hawk? There was one earlier. Or *kyorebni* come to feast on what we leave?"

"Sentry-bird." Rumail's voice was grim.

No ordinary bird flew above them. Somewhere in the Hastur party, a *laranzu* or perhaps one of those accursed *leronis* women had linked telepathically with the bird and could see everything the bird saw.

Still, what did it matter? Seeing the jaws of the trap close shut about them would not save Rafael's forces. The Wolf's plan was unfolding brilliantly. His reserves would do their work and the Hastur men would be forced to retreat or be cut to ribbons. Either way, such a resounding defeat would demoralize the enemy and do as much damage as the loss of territory and fighting men. Belisar tasted victory, honey-sweet.

He would be magnanimous at the end. It was not necessary to destroy Hastur utterly at this time, only to beat him back so that he was no longer a threat, so that treaties and alliances could be dictated on King Damian's own terms. Eventually, the kingdom would be absorbed into Greater Ambervale. Then no other Domain would dare challenge them.

Horns sounded below, perhaps the signal to retreat. Belisar could not be sure, for the pattern was unfamiliar and distorted by the uproar of the battle.

Sure enough, the Hastur men began falling back. They were good soldiers, for instead of turning and running, they regrouped even as they gave way. From the manner in which they clustered together, he imagined their walking wounded in the center. He admired men with such discipline in the face of certain defeat.

Back and back the Hastur units crept, blue-and-silver pennants flying. Ambervale swept after them, closing, harrying. Belisar heard more horns, this time his own, giving the brassy signal to charge.

"The day is ours!" Belisar cried. He thrust his sword aloft. His horse leaped forward, eager enough for both of them. He hauled on the reins and circled back to his position.

In turning, he glimpsed Rumail's frown. Let him fret. Not all battles were won by wizardry, although it was good to hold such weapons in reserve.

As Belisar returned his attention to the fields below, something struck him as subtly odd. For a long instant, he could not put a name to it, then he saw. He had been so filled with the exultation of victory, that he had not noticed how deliberate the Hastur withdrawal had been.

They did not move like defeated men struggling to keep themselves and their wounded fellows alive. No, they moved too smoothly, in too tight an order. Their movements reminded him, in a bizarre way, of an exotic Dry Towns dancer enticing her patrons, skipping backward, smiling, gesturing for them to follow. . . .

The Ambervale troops, screaming in triumph, came flooding after their foe, flanks and rear ragged, all attention focused on their prey. They rushed down the open valley between the fog-shrouded hills.

Rumail stared at the sky once more, at the sentry-bird which was no longer visible in the haze. When he turned to Belisar, urgency twisted his features.

"Retreat! Call the retreat!"

"What are you talking about?" Belisar said.

More horns blared out, shrill and eerie, distorted. Their echoes filled the valley. Belisar's blood ran cold, hearing it. It took all his self-control not to clap his hands over his ears. If Zandru and all his horned demons had gone hunting on the face of the earth, surely they would sound like this.

Below, the Hastur forces continued to fall back, even faster now. Ambervale men paused in their attack and looked around, as if searching for the source of the sound.

Rumail seized Belisar's forearm in an iron grasp. His breath hissed through his teeth. "Send a rider to The Yellow Wolf. Now, before it is too late."

Belisar stared at him, uncomprehending.

"It is a trap!" Rumail screamed.

The horns fell silent and in that moment, Belisar realized the old *laranzu* was right. His men and those of Hastur were no longer engaged; a space had opened up between the two forces. Dust settled, leaving a clear view of the field. The battle cries died to silence.

Rumail looked up, eyes bleak. Before he could speak, a roaring went up from the hills. The fog blinked into nothingness, as if it had never existed.

The Ambervale forces were surrounded by an army twice their size, standing on the heights to either side . . . and behind them. Under the cover of the unnatural fog, their retreat had been cut off.

Those sandal-wearing nine-fathered dung eaters!

"Do something!" he roared at Rumail.

"They are too strong," the older man snapped. "And they are protected by *laran*. How else do you think they managed to stay hidden from *me*?"

On the field below, a rider spurred his mount from The Yellow Wolf's position toward the cluster of Hastur banners on the far hillside. He carried a white flag. A short time later, another Ambervale rider, or perhaps it was the same, approached Belisar's party.

The man's face was chalky, but he held himself proudly. He slipped from the saddle and lowered himself to one knee. "Your Highness, I bring the Hastur's terms for our surrender."

Belisar fought a spurt of anger. *He* had not given any word to offer surrender. His father would be furious, no matter what the outcome now, whether it be defeat or the decimation of his fighting troops. Either way meant the loss of territory and the failure of their objective. The only difference would be the cost. The Yellow Wolf was right to seek a way to save his men to fight again, to snatch some particle of remaining strength out of ruin.

"On your feet, soldier. Let us hear these terms."

The terms, although simple, were unexpectedly generous. The men would be free to return to their homes, even retaining their personal weapons, if they swore to never again take up those arms against Hastur. But Belisar himself was to surrender to King Rafael, to be taken back to Thendara.

"As what? As prisoner? As hostage?" Belisar said. "My father will never stand for this or bargain with this—this rabble!"

Belisar had never been so aware of his position as his father's only living son, his heir. Damian had been right to keep him out of the battle itself, but erred in underestimating the Hastur. With Belisar in their hands and at their mercy, the mission would come to a standstill. His entire plan of conquest would fail. Just as he had needed Acosta as a gateway to Hastur, now he needed Hastur as the key to larger unity.

Belisar called for the Hastur envoy to be brought out and instructed the boy to tell his masters that the Prince required time, four hours at least, to confer with his general and make preparations. Then he dismounted and waited impatiently for The Yellow Wolf to join him. Then he walked apart with Rumail and the general, keeping his voice low.

"I must not surrender, you know that," Belisar said. "We cannot let this happen, it's impossible!"

"They will not permit us to retreat without it," The Wolf said gravely.

Belisar fingered the edge of Rumail's sleeve. The hooded robe was full enough to disguise the shape of its wearer. Muffled in its ample folds, he could leave with the other *laranzu'in*.

But who would take his place? Could they fool the Hastur generals into thinking some subordinate was really Belisar himself? There must be a way! Quickly, he outlined his idea. The Yellow Wolf shook his head, saying, "They will know it is not you. Your appearance is too well known."

"Together we three could cast a glamour on some other man that would resemble your outward appearance," Rumail said. "He would have to resemble you in size, but that is not difficult. There are many soldiers who are close enough in height and build."

"How long could you hold such an illusion?" The Wolf asked. "And would not their own sorcerers suspect such a trick and examine the man closely? Can you truly hide all traces of the disguise from them?"

"It will not last long outside of our influence," Rumail admitted, "nor will it pass the close examination of anyone with trained *laran*."

"Hastur's generals are no fools, and as for his *laranzu'in*, we have already seen what they can do," The Yellow Wolf said, rubbing the old scar which slashed across one cheek. "They will suspect . . ."

"Ah!" Rumail said. "But we will plan for that."

◆

Over the next hour, envoys went back and forth, as Hastur offered one hour and Belisar demanded three. The armies held their positions, Hastur on the heights and Ambervale in the valley. Men from both sides attended to the dead and nursed the wounded.

Rumail and his colleagues from Tramontana went back to the prior night's camp, where they sequestered themselves in the quartermaster's tent. Just as Hastur's final deadline approached, Rumail sent word to Belisar.

The tent stank of the heat of the day, stale sweat, and the faint tang of wine. In the shadowed center, Belisar saw two men. They bowed to him, but neither spoke. One looked like any other young officer of about his own stature, but the other—it was *himself* he stared at. The imposter even spoke with his voice, a muttered, "Highness," as if he were afraid to open his mouth properly.

No, he thought, moving closer, it was no mirror he looked at, but a blurred copy of himself. The face was right, the bright sunlit hair, the curve of lip and line of jaw, but surely he carried his shoulders straighter and moved with a more assertive stride?

"And you say this illusion will fool the Hastur and his wizards?" Belisar asked Rumail.

"Oh, I fully intend it will not. As you can see, this spell is crude, as if hastily wrought." Rumail closed his hand around his starstone. The features of the counterfeit Belisar wavered like a mirage in a heat wave, and another man stood there, blinking. In the next moment, the illusion was restored. "Anyone who knows you well will detect the difference in a few moments."

"Then what—"

"The Hastur *laranzu'in* are competent. They will surely unmask this man as an impostor. We will admit our duplicity—your general and I—and reluctantly turn over this second man instead."

"But he looks nothing like me!"

Rumail gave an exasperated sigh. "He looks, to anyone with even a trace of *laran*, like a man whose true appearance has been disguised with a glamour. And his 'true appearance' . . ."

"Will be mine!" Belisar cried, delighted at the trick.

"Having discovered one disguise, they will not think to look deeper," Rumail said. "They may be skilled, but victory will make them arrogant as well."

"Uncle, you are indeed a crafty old fox!"

After the imposter mounted Belisar's red-gold horse and headed for the Hastur encampment and his formal surrender, Belisar and Rumail remained in the tent. Belisar removed his fine tunic, boots, and sword on its leather belt, and slipped into Rumail's cloak. Rumail himself put on ordinary clothing, shirt and breeches over worn boots. He looked like any middle-aged camp servant, a physician perhaps, but nothing more. As Belisar finished adjusting the cloth belt, Rumail gestured for him to approach.

Belisar stared into Rumail's starstone. Something behind his throat turned icy and *shifted.* For a long moment, his lungs locked. He seemed to be encased in blue ice.

"There." Rumail's word released him and Belisar could breathe again. "Now you can swear by anything you like, even under truthspell, that you are Beron, a novice matrix mechanic training with us at Ambervale, and no one will be able to gainsay you."

◆

During the inspection of the vanquished troops and the taking of their oaths, Belisar kept the hood well down over his face. He tried to stand with his hands folded meekly and remembered to keep his posture stooped. His ears strained for every syllable of the officers' conversations, particularly the surrender of "Prince Belisar."

The ordering of the armies to march out went smoothly. The first impostor was discovered, even as Rumail had foretold, and the second offered and accepted.

By the time the second exchange was complete, sweat covered Belisar's sides and his nerves were strained as taut as bowstrings. From the shadows of his hood, he watched The Yellow Wolf's impassive face as he led the retreat.

Although Belisar did not particularly like his uncle, the man clearly had his uses. When the Hastur lieutenant asked for his name and Belisar offered the alias, not even a flicker of doubt crossed the man's face.

Belisar mounted a mule, by its conformation and temper a pack animal completely unsuitable for riding, and followed Rumail and his *laranzu'in*, at a respectful distance behind The Yellow Wolf and his senior officers. The mule shook its head from time to time, long ears flapping away the flies. Belisar wondered irritably how long he was going to have to sit on its bony back before he could command a proper horse. He knew better than to draw attention to himself; he must act as he appeared, a very junior *laran* worker, a person of no special account.

Rumail rode hunched over, one hand cupped in front of him, the other loosely holding the reins. Suddenly, he straightened in the saddle. His mule jumped, ears flattening as he clapped his feet to its sides. Shouting, he headed straight for The Yellow Wolf.

Belisar could not see exactly what happened next. There was a flurry of activity in the general's party and officers spurred their mounts back toward the main force. Trumpets sounded retreat, with the emphasis on the sequence which meant *as fast as possible.* One of the lieutenants, the earnest young officer who was the special protege of The Yellow Wolf, slid his tall roan mare to a halt before Belisar and jumped from her back.

"Take the horse, my prince! General's orders!" he cried, grabbing the mule's reins.

Belisar kicked his feet from the mule's stirrups and landed lightly and gracefully. The hood flew back from his face. "What's happened?"

"The second imposter has been discovered. *Dom* Rumail saw it in his starstone. They know, Highness, *they know!*"

Already the foremost men passed them, footmen and archers running, cavalry moving to defend the rear. Rumail had returned to join the other *laranzu'in* away from the main trail. From his saddlebags, Rumail took out a small metal apparatus, unfolding its segmented wings. The belly of rounded glass glowed poisonous green, but otherwise it was shaped like a bird. A starstone chip glittered where its left eye should be.

So Rumail actually meant to deploy the accursed things. Belisar knew it was their only hope—*his* only hope—and yet his stomach kindled with frozen fire.

Belisar vaulted on the roan mare's back and dug his heels into her sides, whipping her with the ends of the reins for every last bit of speed.

28

Under a sky the color of slate, afternoon sat sullen over the hills surrounding Acosta Castle, Damian Deslucido's battle headquarters. Black-and-white pennants sagged from their moorings on the walls and the tents of the army encamped on the fields below. Now and again, a fight between two or three soldiers broke the lassitude of the day. No birds sang, although huge black flies sent the picketed horses stamping and biting at one another. Within the castle, a baby cried fitfully.

Damian Deslucido stood on the battlements, looking out over the far vinyards, and reflected on how easy it had been to ride through them on the way to victory and how unsatisfying that victory had become. The thrill of conquest evaporated in the reality that he now ruled such a vast land that he must sit here, waiting for news, while other men led his armies. So he had sent Belisar on what should have been an easy foray, to snatch and hold a few miles of useless borderland.

He pushed himself away from the stone parapet. Beginning a few days ago, men had been trickling into camp, some so exhausted they fell unconscious and died. What in Zandru's seventh frozen hell had gone wrong?

Rumor swept through Acosta of a resounding defeat in which Prince Belisar had run away to save his cowardly life. Some spoke of the demonic power of the Hastur lord, who used his sorcery to curse men from afar with lingering death. Damian's own guard caught a man spreading these tales and hanged him naked from the castle gates. After that, such things were spoken only in whispers.

Damian muttered curses under his breath. This sense of drifting was nothing more than the result of the weather. If only the clouds would gather and thunder break. He would welcome a lightning storm with all its glorious savageness.

Where was The Yellow Wolf? Where was that worthless sandal-wearing brother of his? And *where was Belisar?*

◆

The last Rumail had seen of his nephew was the rump of the roan mare, galloping for all she was worth. Belisar was leaning over her neck, pounding her slatted sides with his heels. Men scattered before him, watching him with eyes pale with consternation. Rumail caught their unvoiced words, *Why is our Prince and commander running away?* Within moments, Belisar disappeared into the throng of mounted men and foot soldiers.

Good, Rumail thought. With any luck and barring the nag breaking a leg, the royal heir should be well clear of the area to be contaminated.

A moment before Belisar's departure, Rumail had reined his mule apart from the main body of Ambervale men in their orderly withdrawal. He needed concentration to accomplish his next task, to keep the Hastur scum from harrying the Prince. From his saddlebags, he drew out three mechanical devices, fashioned in the size and shape of small hawks.

The thought flickered through Rumail's mind that if he delayed, if Belisar were caught and killed, then he, Rumail, might well be the heir to Ambervale and all its possessions. As quickly, he brushed aside the notion as unworthy. At one time, it might have seriously tempted him, but he had grown beyond the desire for simple kingship. Now he knew better. The key to ruling Darkover did not lie in the might of ordinary arms. This day's battle proved that decisively. Without their *laran*, the Hastur would have been easy prey.

Brows furrowed, Rumail studied the *laran*-powered devices. The bonewater dust which filled their fragile glass bellies was intended only as a last resort. If this was not a situation of last resort, with Belisar's freedom and perhaps his life at stake, then what was? Unchecked, the Hastur forces might well plunge on into Acosta. They had momentum, confidence and leadership on their side. With their *laranzu'in*, they might even lay a successful siege to Acosta Castle itself. And if Damian could take the castle, then so could Rafael Hastur.

They must be stopped, no matter what the price, or all might be lost, far more than Belisar's cowardly skin.

The bonewater dust, quiescent now, with only a faint greenish pinpoint radiance, had been purchased from the renegade circle in Temora at an obscene cost, since Tramontana insisted they were unable to produce it.

Unable? he'd wondered. *Or simply unwilling?* As soon as he could convince Damian, he meant to travel there and institute proper obedience. Since he could not train up his own circle, not in the time these momentous events demanded, he must take control of an established Tower. Being Keeper of a fully trained circle would be a very different affair than struggling to draw together such unsuitable, undisciplined novices. Tramontana and then Neskaya would fall into his hands like ripened plums.

He established a link with the small starstone guide chips set in each device and tossed them into the air. The guidance mechanisms were so simple, he effortlessly controlled all three of them. Mechanical wings whirred as they gained altitude. He followed them with his mind as they navigated the air currents, never drifting on thermals as would natural birds, but heading unerringly toward the sky above the oncoming Hastur force.

Not too high . . . He wanted a limited area of dispersal, so as little of the surrounding area as possible would be polluted. The poison would last for generations, rendering the Drycreek area impassable to all but suicidal fools.

Rumail brought the mechanical birds lower. He could not follow them with his physical eyes, only with his *laran* senses. He gave the *Release* signal. Glass cracked and shattered into myriad tiny shards.

Dust began its slow, inexorable fall toward the Hastur soldiers. Rumail looked up, squinting, as it caught the sunlight. It had never occurred to him that it might be so beautiful, sparkling and glowing in the sun. Men on both sides paused to look up.

With death drifting from the skies, those Hastur fools stood gaping at their doom. Suddenly a breeze sprang up, as if from the bellows of Zandru's forge.

It blew the unnatural poison back toward Rumail and his own men.

Rumail pulled his mule to a halt. Gesturing, he shouted and pointed in the direction of the retreat.

"Flee! Flee for your lives!"

Those closest to him took heed and bolted, some dropping their weapons and packs. Others paid no attention or looked to their own officers, if they could find them in the growing chaos. Ordinary dust billowed up, choking man and beast.

Taking out his starstone on its chain around his neck, Rumail focused on its depths, using its resonances to amplify his *laran*. He launched his mind aloft, into the currents of air, and felt a wash of relief. This was a natural wind and not one created by psychic meddling with weather patterns. The Aldarans were rumored to do this on a huge scale, and most circles could manipulate rain clouds to some degree. That is, when their Keepers allowed them, without the usual endless agonizing over disrupting natural patterns and causing unforeseen consequences elsewhere, a drought here or a flood there, all from moving a few little clouds around. These things doubtless would have happened anyway. Rumail possessed no special talent in controlling weather, but neither was he overly modest about his power as a *laranzu*. He knew enough to contain the breeze and even turn it back on the Hastur forces.

Rumail spread out his psychic senses, mapping out the areas of cooler and warmer air. Nudging the streams of different temperatures, he felt the pressures driving the breeze lessen. A moment more would reverse the air current, sending the deadly powder back toward its target.

"DEMON!"

A cry, so hoarse as to be barely human, burst through Rumail's concentration. Blinking, he snapped back to the material world to see a man in Hastur colors rush at him. In a single moment, his vision filled with sky, glowing dust and a reddened face, distorted with fury. The man stumbled, caught his balance, and lifted his arms. Sun flashed on the point of the man's halberd, aimed upward toward Rumail's belly.

Without thinking, Rumail jerked the mule's head and twisted in the saddle. Something struck him in the side, a heavy blow like the kick of a wild *oudrakhi* that sent him tumbling to the ground. The earth rose up to knock the breath from his lungs. Someone shrieked, rising above the shouting, neighing mass.

With a panicked bray, the mule reared up. Rumail tried to roll out of its path. His body felt leaden, unresponsive. Heavy blows battered him. He couldn't tell if he'd been kicked by the mule or the men rushing past him. His eyes caught the image of the mule's belly as it leaped over him. He pulled himself into a ball, covering his head with his hands.

Someone hooked him under the armpits and dragged him along the ground. Rocks bit through his clothing, scoring his skin. The pain receded, as if happening to someone else. Roaring filled his ears.

For a long moment, he lay still, tensed against the next blow of hoof or booted foot, but none came. Pain throbbed along his side, over the short ribs, so sudden and intense it took his breath away. He uncurled himself and tried to sit up. The slightest movement escalated the pain. His vision whirled, but he saw that he lay at the base of a little rocky mound, well out of the path of the army.

Gingerly, he reached over with the uninjured hand and brought away fingers sticky with blood.

Rumail lay back and closed his eyes, gathering his strength. Thank all the gods at once, he still had his starstone. The chain had not snapped in his fall. Moving carefully, he gathered it up.

He had only the most basic training as a monitor, lacking the empathy necessary to do the work really well. But now his life depended on his skill.

The pain would be a distraction, so he would have to deal with it, but if he numbed the area, he would not be able to determine the nature of his injuries. He lay very still, keeping his breathing shallow and high in his chest.

Go into the pain, he told himself. *Immerse yourself in it. Move through it to your goal.* For a moment, he remembered the transfixed expression on Ginevra's face as she drank in the pain of the young girl—what had her name been? It didn't matter.

The pain eased somewhat as he penetrated deeper into his own body. Within a few minutes, he knew that the tip of the halberd had slashed through his skin and one of his ribs splintered. The point had pierced his lung, collapsing one lobe. Blood quickly filled the surrounding tissues. Given time, he could heal himself. But if it pinned him here, the wound might nonetheless prove fatal.

Tightening his grasp on his starstone, he focused on the torn tissues—skin, muscle, capillaries, nerves. It would be a slow task to mend them enough so that he could travel.

The first particle of bonewater dust touched him.

In Rumail's state of heightened *laran* awareness, it burned like *cling-fire,* though it was neither hot nor caustic. Desperately, he threw up an energy barrier between himself and the particle and felt it lift, buoyed by the repulsion forces. He shifted his consciousness to sense thousands of them, millions perhaps, hovering in the breeze.

The breeze, he repeated bitterly to himself, which he'd been unable to stop. He wondered if his own death were a fitting payment for that failure.

But he still wanted very much to live. He had not finished all that he wanted to accomplish. In fact, he had just begun to figure out what those things were. Somehow, he had to find a way to survive.

Rumail drew his knees to his chest, making his body as small as he could, and drew upon his trained *laran* to create a shield between himself and the toxic dust.

As he sank into a deep trance, he realized that he had no strength to spare to heal himself. And without the ability to walk, he could not leave the contaminated area. No man alive, nor woman either, could teleport themselves without the aid of a circle and great artificial matrix screens. He might lie here undiscovered and undisturbed, locked behind the barriers set by his own mind, as his life energies dwindled and guttered out, cinders to ashes.

He was trapped.

Somewhere out there were the Hastur *laranzu'in,* the ones who had shielded themselves from him and masked the encirclement of the army. If he could reach them—

Beg for rescue from my brother's enemies?

But he must survive, he must. If not for his own sake, then for the vision which he had shared with Damian, and the far greater dream which was his alone.

His last conscious act was to disguise his mental thought pattern as he sent out a plea for help. . . .

29

A rider clattered into the Hastur encampment just as dusk was falling. Coryn heard shouting from the tent he shared with several of the junior officers. He had not planned on coming at all, but had agreed at the last moment, hoping for a chance to plead his case privately before Rafael. Surely the King would agree that whatever role *laran* weaponry might play, the Towers themselves must not become involved.

Here in the field, it all seemed a moot point. He had not realized the seriousness—or the desperation—of men in armed conflict. No sane king would throw away his most powerful weapon.

At the same time, Coryn felt sure that neither King Rafael nor his adversary truly understood the magnitude of the forces a Tower controlled. They had never delved miles beneath the surface to raise precious minerals, nor manipulated the energy binding the tiniest particles together, nor touched the vast magnetic and electrical fields of the planet itself. If *laran* could power an aircar or send messages across hundreds of miles, how much more was possible? Yet anything Coryn could say might only strengthen Rafael's resolve to use the Towers at his command in this or any other war.

Coryn, still biding his time, found the sentry-birds of interest, never having learned to fly one. Neither Tramontana nor Neskaya had any use

271

for the birds, which required the care of a skilled falconer. In this case, the handler was a stocky, middle-aged *laranzu* named Edric, who answered all of Coryn's questions with grunted monosyllables and kept his *laran* barriers so tightly raised that Coryn suspected he was comfortable only in the presence of his beasts. He, along with Lady Caitlin and the third worker, a shy young woman named Graciela, had ridden out with the main body of the army two days before.

Now the shouted hails and hoofbeats of the rider brought out everyone left in camp. The rider wore an officer's tunic in Hastur colors, torn and caked with sweat-streaked dust. His horse slid to a halt. Its sides heaved like bellows. Lather dripped from its muzzle and frothed the sides of its neck where the reins had rubbed. Its coat was so dark with sweat, it looked black.

The rider stumbled into the circle at the center of the encampment. Two of Rafael's personal guards ran to catch him or he would surely have fallen.

"Are you hurt, man?"

The rider shook his head. "I must—tell—the King."

"The battle—did it go against us, then?"

The rider only shook his head again and pulled free, toward the King's tent. Just then Rafael Hastur appeared, lifting the door flap aside. The reddening sunset flashed on the simple copper circlet on his brow. Coryn felt the aura of energy surrounding the king like a crackle of dry lightning.

"Your Majesty!" the rider cried. "We are undone!"

A stormy expression flickered across Rafael's eyes, as quickly gone. "Come with me," he told the rider, gesturing to his tent. He gave a string of orders, for food to be brought, for wine, for the camp physician, for his senior officers. Coryn felt the heat of his gaze. "You, too. You will hear and advise me."

Within minutes, the party gathered in the shadowed closeness of Rafael's tent. *Laran*-powered glows brightened at Edric's touch to fill the space with eerie radiance. The rider lowered himself to a canvas camp stool before the King's chair, gulping water. Coryn thought he would rather be on his knees, pleading outright.

"At first everything went as we had planned," the rider said. His name was Vincenzo or Vincento, Coryn didn't catch which, and he was a captain, a leader of men.

There was something subtly wrong with Vincento that went beyond the stress and urgency of the moment. The man was not only exhausted, he was ill in some way that Coryn could not pinpoint. Gareth or Liane would know.

"Deslucido advanced as we retreated, right into the trap. *Domna* Caitlin and the others held the illusion until the last moment. Then we lifted the fog and let them see us." Vincento stopped for more water. His skin looked dull, like unfired clay, and he was sweating visibly, although the tent was cool and night was falling. A flicker of pain crossed his face, deepening the lines of strain.

They all waited for him to continue. Rafael sat back in his chair, stroking his beard with one hand.

"We offered them your terms and they agreed."

One of the officers said. "Did they forswear themselves, then?"

Vincento shook his head. "Their men gave us the required oaths, and we permitted them to leave after Belisar Deslucido had given himself into our custody. But once he came into our camp, *Domna* Caitlin looked straight at him. The air shivered, and we saw we had been tricked. It was not young Deslucido, but an ordinary man, put under some kind of spell so as to resemble the Prince." He paused, mouth working, sweating even harder now.

Coryn reached out with his mind and tasted Vincento's sickness, felt the roil of nausea an instant before the man bolted for the back of the tent. They heard him retching outside. Rafael gestured for everyone to remain as they were except for the camp physician.

The physician came back a few minutes later, his face seamed with concern. The messenger followed him for a step or two before collapsing. Coryn caught the man before he fell and lowered him to a pile of folded blankets. The man curled on his side, body spasming with dry heaves. His skin felt hot and papery.

"This man is acutely ill, Highness," the physician said. "He must rest, or he may not live past the telling of his story."

"What is wrong with him?" Rafael asked.

"I . . . I am not sure."

Coryn heard the resonances in the physician's voice. If he did not know, he suspected, and that possibility terrified him.

The messenger flinched at the physician's touch as if the merest contact with his skin pained him. He struggled to sit upright. His retching had subsided enough for him to speak. Rafael, despite the physician's warning, came closer.

"Sire—" the voice, like the man's skin, sounded shriveled, whispery. "We pursued them—and they—they—" For a moment, his words were lost in labored breathing. Coryn heard the wheeze and rale of congested lungs. A shiver went through him as he remembered that horrifying moment of *being* Kristlin stricken with lungrot.

Yet another foul weapon . . .

"Bird-things—dropped—" the next word was indistinguishable. The man sagged back on the piled blankets. His chest rose and fell like the fluttering of wings. A shudder passed over his body and watery blood trickled from his mouth.

Coryn felt the sudden stillness, the weight of the man's flesh as the spirit left him. The old ache behind his breastbone, which he had thought healed and gone with his childhood nightmares, throbbed.

"What is it?" Rafael asked. "What did he say?"

"He said nothing, *vai dom,*" the physician said in a hollow voice.

"Out with it, man! What happened?" *And will others of my men die like this?*

Coryn heard the fury in Rafael's voice, the passionate concern for his people. Rafael raised one hand and Coryn saw his intention, to go to the aid of his men, to see the destruction with his own eyes. He would spare himself nothing.

"No, Highness!" the physician let out a cry. "You must not risk yourself. We must move this camp back and set up to tend to the survivors—"

"I will not abandon my men to die." Rafael barked out commands—to move the camp to a safer location, to set up facilities for nursing the wounded.

Within minutes, Coryn found himself on horseback, galloping in Rafael's wake in the midst of the King's hand-picked guard. Before long, night gathered inky shadows about them. Improvised torches wavered in the distance. Sometimes they heard rather than saw the oncoming soldiers.

Coryn called a sphere of cold blue light and held it aloft. They passed the retreating Hastur forces, cavalry bearing double or sometimes triple. Others jogged by on their own two feet, weapons and gear abandoned. Coryn saw how orderly their progress was, despite the darkness and the fear which burned in the air and glazed the eyes of the exhausted-looking men. There was no shoving, no disarray, no signs of panic.

A mounted officer held a torch aloft, shouting orders. He spotted Rafael's banner and spurred his horse toward it. At Rafael's command, he gave his report. The substitution of captive had been discovered, even as the dead messenger had said, and orders given to halt the retreat. An elite party of the fastest cavalry had ridden for the Ambervale vanguard where the real Prince Belisar must be hiding. The last third of the enemy foot soldiers, who had no notion of what had transpired, had halted. Somehow, word had gone forward, and the Ambervale forces had split in two. No one was sure what happened next in the dust and confusion, with riders going in both directions.

Something had exploded over the valley floor where the first ranks of the Hastur force surrounded the puzzled Ambervale foot soldiers. A hazy dust filled the air, each particle alight with green phosphorescence. Men on both sides had stood open-mouthed to watch its eerie, glittering fall. It billowed on even the faintest breeze as it slowly settled. And then, as if sent by the Lord of Light himself, a wind had sprung up, fitful gusts blowing the stuff toward the retreating Ambervale army. Within a few minutes, the air had grown unnaturally still, but not before the glowing mist had covered a good portion of Deslucido's men.

"Sweet mother of darkness," Rafael said, his voice gone suddenly hoarse. "Bonewater dust."

Bonewater dust. A *laran* weapon so horrible it poisoned the very land itself. No one knew how long its curse lasted, only that many who had been exposed and lived died later of burgeoning tumors, of falling-sickness with wasting and baldness, bloody diarrhea and madness.

"Deslucido must have dropped it to cover his retreat, but the wind betrayed him," Rafael said. "The messenger spoke of bird-things, did he not? I have heard of small, individually guided devices, like birds with bellies of hollow glass, used to deliver *clingfire.*"

Coryn, too, had heard of such small, *laran*-powered machines. They were costly. Deslucido must have been mad to order such a thing.

"Your Majesty," one of the officers said. "You *must* go back. The risk here is too great. Another shift in the wind, and Deslucido will have won."

For a long moment, Rafael said nothing. The officer's torch and Coryn's ball of blue-white light cast warring hues over Rafael's features.

His eyes glittered gold and blue-white, although his expression remained impassive.

An aura flickered around the King's head and shoulders, composed of energy rather than visible light, as if Aldones himself had touched the mortal man, turning him into something more. Something deep within Coryn shifted, opened. In that instant, he would have died for his King.

So this is what it means to be a son of the Lord of Light, Coryn thought. *To have no thought for your own desires, your own life, except as it serves your kingdom.* He thought of Taniquel with a shiver of inexpressible sadness.

"Majesty," he said. "Let me remain behind. I am a trained Tower worker. I am needed here."

✦

Nothing moved on that stretch of land where the earth itself now smoldered with a ghostly green fire. Not even a rat or bird broke the stillness, nor were there any *kyorebni,* carrion birds, to be seen aloft. Until he looked down on the contaminated land, Coryn had no direct experience of bonewater dust. It was worse than he'd ever imagined.

Dark mounds covered the field, in places blotting out the luminescence of the poisoned earth, so thick and numerous were they. Coryn knew he looked upon the piled bodies of dead men, hundreds of them, lying where they fell as the dust blew over them.

The Hali workers, Lady Caitlin, the sentry-bird handler, Edric, and the slender young woman, stood together on a hilltop. Their heads were bent and eyes closed in concentration.

Coryn slipped from his horse and approached them, careful not to disturb their linkage. He touched the starstone at his throat, using it as a focal point, and the ordinary world blurred.

They had created a *laran* boundary akin to the one used to separate out the particles of raw *clingfire.* Coryn immediately saw the sense in it. Circles of Tower workers often handled dangerous materials without harm, so long as their concentration held. Bernardo's experiments with the less-explosive detonated *clingfire* had used *laran* forces as a buffer. Coryn's hands had healed completely from his lapse while refining fire-fighting chemicals, but he remembered the shame of having been the one to break focus.

Whether this bonewater dust worked as waves of energy or bits of material, he realized, it had a signature resonance, and Caitlin and the others struggled to set up an interference pattern matched to it.

Caitlin had the skill of decades of Tower training, and the girl the raw power. But she was no Keeper and the merging was inherently unbalanced. Edric's mind bucked and pulled at the constraint of her iron-hard discipline.

Smoothly, firmly, he caught up and shaped their linked mental energies. Where Caitlin had striven to create a series of rigid shields, he imagined a huge, flexible bubble, shimmering blue with *laran* power, enclosing the entire contaminated zone. He made no attempt to interfere with the processes of the dust itself, though he sensed myriad bits of energy, mindless, doing only what their nature had created them to do. It was the malice of the men who shaped them which caused the destruction, not any inherent evil in the stuff. He thought of poisonous plants, which often made beautiful flowers and harmed no one unless eaten, or of herbs which could cure in one dosage and kill in another.

Let each thing keep to its natural place . . . He sent out the thought. The girl and the other man picked up it, amplified it.

Keep to its place . . .

The bits of energy whirled and darted within the bubble. Coryn softened the bubble's filmy layer, giving it flexibility. *The willow bends before the storm. The bird aloft shifts with the rising thermals . . .*

He felt a surge of response in Edric's mind as the man answered the image, envisioning the bubble as an airstream lifting a falcon's wings. The willow, that was the girl Graciela, slender and whipcord-tough. She gave a silent laugh like rippling bells that reminded him of Bronwyn's mental signature. Her bubble was a basket, thousands upon thousands of tendrils all woven together . . . *growing* together . . . so that not water, not wind, not the whirling bits of bonewater-dust could penetrate.

Keep to its place . . .

Caitlin, with her orderly, squared-off patterns, she was the rock on which they all stood. If she could not weave or bind, she could anchor them in any storm.

Minute by minute, the bubble grew stronger. It shifted and flexed minutely under the battering of the energy motes, but where it gave way in one place, it drew closer in another. It held, containing the polluted land and air.

Rapt in the unity of the circle, Coryn felt a distant tug at his mind, a resonance which seemed muffled by a powerful barrier as well. Could it be that out there in that wasteland of a battlefield, someone still lived, someone with enough *laran* to reach out, if feebly, to the circle's protective field?

Could it be Rumail?

Coryn flinched involuntarily at the thought. It took all his Tower discipline to instantly regain his focus, to hold and not to waver. Too much and too many lives depended upon his steadfastness.

Coryn, what is it? Caitlin had sensed his instant of distress.

Drawing upon her steadiness, he sent a thought questing out into the darkened fields. The life spark was dim, but not dying. It had been deliberately lowered, as the monks at Nevarsin did during the killing winters and as he himself had learned to do to conserve precious energy during the most demanding Tower work. He probed deeper.

An insulating blanket of *laran* . . .

An island of refuge in the midst of rampant poison . . .

Pain . . . A wound, no longer bleeding, but unhealed, enough to cripple any attempt at travel . . .

But no sense of identity.

The mind bore some resemblance to Rumail's, what Coryn remembered from his first contact as a boy. If it were one of the others, someone Rumail had trained and worked with, he might well bear the stamp of his teacher's personality. Should Coryn condemn him for that?

There is someone out there, he thought to Caitlin. *But I can't tell who.*

One of our own, she asked, *a latent talent?*

Mentally, he sent her a negative reply. Faint though the presence was, it could not have come from an untrained mind.

It is your decision, she said telepathically. *You are our Keeper.*

Should he risk letting an innocent man die for fear he might be the banished *laranzu*? And if it was Rumail, how could he let even such a man perish as he had seen so many others do, when he had the means to save him? Years ago, Rumail had been judged by his own Keeper at Neskaya. He had been punished according to that verdict. The fate of his soul was in the hands of the gods and not for any man to say.

Even if it was Rumail out there, even if there had been some bad feeling between them, it all lay in the past. And whatever else Rumail might have done, he had saved Verdanta during that terrible fire. He had tried to serve his brother-king and had dealt honorably with Coryn's family.

Deftly, Coryn shaped the *laran* of the circle to set up a resonant field around the injured man, sending the psychic energy he would need to pass, undamaged, from the field.

✦

Grayness seeped across Coryn's vision, so that for an instant he thought they had taken their force bubble into the Overworld. He blinked. The pale light disappeared and then returned, so that he knew he sensed it with his fleshly eyes.

Dawn.

He became aware of the chill running along his bones, the ache in joint and tendon from standing immobile for so long. Working as they did, they had no monitor to guard them against physical exhaustion. His clothing was damp on the inside with sweat and on the outside with moisture.

Dawn had come, and with it the gentle fall of rain. Water would wash the rest of the dust from the air. The earth was already contaminated; only time and Avarra's blessing could cleanse it now.

Coryn opened his hands, where he had clasped those of his circle, but he did not release the joining of their minds. The bubble still held, and must continue for a little while longer. He tested it, shaped it. Gently he thinned it overhead so that it opened to the heavens.

As he did so, he reached out his mind to the valley floor, to the surrounding hills. Where the earth glowed an unnatural shade of green, men and beasts huddled, dead or dying, beyond any human help. He could not tell which side they had fought for, nor did that matter. Every living thing which could escape already had. There was no trace of the dim *laran* presence from last night, but no residue of death either.

We must go, too, he sent to his circle. He felt a pulse of stony endurance from Edric, shuddering exhaustion from the girl. Caitlin, who had endured years of Tower training, and nights of work as exacting as this one, assented wearily.

Coryn knew he must go carefully, for an abrupt rupture of the circle might create a damaging backlash. Caitlin, sensing his caution, held the anchor point as they dropped out one by one.

Graciela whimpered, and her knees folded beneath her. She would have fallen, had not Edric caught her in his arms. "We must get her out of here," he said, scooping her up as if she weighed no more than Tani-quel's toddler son.

Caitlin met Coryn's eyes for a moment. The gray dawn bleached all color from her hair and face, yet softened the lines of age. She looked beautiful and eldritch as a *chieri*.

"You did not tell me you were a Keeper," she said.

He started to say, *I am not a Keeper, not yet.* Instead, he made a comment about what a pleasure it was to work with her. She brushed it aside, descending the hill with stiff dignity toward where their horses were tethered. Before they reached Rafael's camp, moved back another five miles, she swayed in the saddle, but never uttered a word of complaint.

Someone took Coryn's horse and someone else brought him food. Numbly, he spooned it into his mouth. He was too drained to feel hunger, but he knew the danger of not replenishing his physical energy. At one point, Rafael appeared. Coryn remembered saying something about the bubble shield, but wasn't sure he made sense. He was even more exhausted than when he'd fought fires across the Verdanta hills as a boy.

✦

The day had been a victory of sorts for Hastur, for when their scouts returned from surveying the battlefield, they brought news of the numbers of Ambervale dead. Terror snaked through the Hastur camp along with the news of the virulence of the bonewater dust. The King and as many men as could travel, whole or wounded or sick with fever, withdrew even further. Even so, the tents for those exposed to the dust were set up some distance from the rest of the camp, and few of the unaffected soldiers ventured very close.

Coryn and the Hali workers spent long hours in the infirmary tents, doing what they could to help the men exposed to the dust. Injury to skin and gut, if not too great, could be stemmed until the normal healing processes took place, but they all sensed how much deeper the damage ran, right down to the very germ stuff of cells.

More men died every day, first on march and in the encampment, and then fewer died, and then none. Many of those who had been sick began to recover their appetites. They'd all lost weight as well as the hair from their heads and beards, giving them the appearance of wizened, emaciated babies.

"None of these men ought to sire children," Coryn said quietly to Caitlin when he was sure none of their patients could overhear. They had gone walking along the perimeter of the camp in the cool of twilight.

Her eyes went gray and opaque. "I do not believe they still can."

"Why—how could any man use such a weapon?" Coryn cried. "It is not like attacking an enemy soldier with sword or even arrows. He is a fellow fighter, he can defend himself or attack you in return. The risk is equal, or almost so. They have each *chosen* to fight. Their unborn children have no part in it. But Deslucido or any other tyrant can give orders from some safe place and this land will be taboo for generations. Who knows how many innocents will suffer? How? How can he do such a thing?"

Caitlin looked away, her expression desolate beyond words. "Because he *can*. Because he gets what he wants—and there is no one to stop him. The Hasturs have tried for years now to contain the worst of these weapons. Sometimes I wonder if it has done any good at all." She gestured back in the direction of the contaminated valley.

"And yet," Caitlin went on, "perhaps without that restraint, this would be commonplace. Men would become inured to horror and no longer shrink from it. Who is to say?"

"Or perhaps war has not been horrible enough," Coryn said with sudden heat. "Perhaps the only way to end it is to make the price beyond bearing."

"What do you mean?"

"A friend of mine once argued that the only way for two small warring kingdoms to be safe was to arm each of them with a weapon the other dared not risk. In this case, it was *clingfire*. What if Deslucido had known that any use of *laran* weapons would be met with devastating retaliation? Would he have so readily spread this obscenity we see before us if the result would be the same on his own land?"

"I cannot believe any man would risk it," Caitlin answered. "There would be nothing left to fight over for either side. I cannot—I do not want to believe this is the only way, to arm every small kingdom with such terrible things. Sooner or later, some fool would release them upon his neighbor, perhaps for some imagined offense. Who is to say it would end there? Does *clingfire* or bonewater dust care whether it lands on friend or foe? Would the madness spread from one realm to another until all of Darkover is consumed? Is there no alternative?"

Coryn stared into the gathering night and prayed to whatever god would listen that there was some other way.

30

Belisar arrived at Acosta well in advance of the bulk of his retreating army, along with the handful of cavalry. Men who'd seen him ride from the border as if all of Zandru's scorpions were on his tail had followed and become his personal bodyguard. As they passed through the encampment outside the castle gates, dogs ran barking in their path. Soldiers stopped their preparations to stare at the panting horses flecked with yellow lather, legs coated with mud from the recent rainfall.

"Belisar! Belisar has returned!"

Bells rang out from the castle and cries echoed from the battlements. Belisar lifted his head, pleased at his reception. When one or two of the soldiers stepped forward to ask their fellows, *What has happened? Where is the army?* he waved them away. They would learn what they needed to when the time came.

Within the gates, servants ran forward to greet the prince and his guards. Ostlers led away the horses. Belisar mounted the steps leading to the stronghold. He recognized Gavriel, the old *coridom* who still ran the place with impeccable efficiency. The old man bowed.

"Where's my father?" Belisar strode past the opened doorway, his spurs jangling on the scrubbed stone.

"He is in his presence chamber, Your Highness. Your own is being readied for you." Gavriel's tone was in every way respectful. He turned, as if to lead the way.

"Later," Belisar said, and hurried on. He waved a dismissal.

The guard bowed and made no attempt to interfere as Belisar entered without knocking. Inside, he passed through the little anteroom and burst into his father's presence chamber. With its unlit fireplace, the place looked very much as it had in the first days at Acosta. King Damian sat at a table with two officers Belisar didn't recognize. He looked up, and the room fell still.

"Father, I'm here. I made it back alive."

"I see that you did." Damian, who had been leaning over an unrolled map, straightened up. His hair was freshly trimmed, his clothing neat, his hands clean. He nodded to the officers. "Leave us."

Damian sat back in his chair, staring, jaw set, waiting. Some dark emotion, one Belisar could not put a name to, flickered across his face. Belisar lifted his arms, then let them drop. His father had not, as he had imagined over the harried miles, been worried half to death about his fate. Instead, he was apparently carrying on as if nothing had happened. And he, Prince and heir, was expected to make his report, just as if he'd been an ordinary officer.

Belisar set his own jaw in unconscious imitation of his father. He squared his shoulders. His muscles trembled from the exertion of so many long hours at a gallop. Two horses had died under him and the third was near done in.

"Sire." He gave the word both honorific and familial inflection. "I wish to report that although I was unable to fulfill my mission of seizing control of the lands beyond the Drycreek border, it has been secured against Hastur aggression."

At that, the King's eyebrows lifted. His expression lightened. He listened with evident and growing interest as Belisar told his story, finishing with his departure from the border. Curious, how less frightening it seemed in the telling. His own deeds seemed bolder, the colors of the day brighter. Horns rang out brassy challenge behind his words. He could almost see the pennants shimmer in the sunlight. His legs grew steadier beneath him with each phrase.

It was a pity, he thought as he came to the end of his tale, that he had not stayed to see the bonewater dust sifting down from the sky. From everything he had been told, that would have been a sight indeed. He could only imagine its deadly beauty.

When he finished, Damian sat silent, brows drawn slightly together.

"Are—are you displeased with my command?" For the first time since his escape, Belisar felt unsure. "I assure you, there was no possible better outcome, not after the Hastur treachery—"

"Where is the army I entrusted you with? Where is The Yellow Wolf? And where is Rumail, my brother?"

"Oh, they are following. The orders to retreat had already been given. I could not, of course, allow myself to be captured once the second ruse was discovered, and so their slower pace afforded me some protection." The Hasturs would have had to push their way through the entire Ambervale army to get at him. It had all worked out rather nicely.

"Protection." A pause, the flicker of eyes gone suddenly cold. "And what protection did *you* afford *them?*"

"I don't understand." Belisar shifted from one foot to the other. "Against what? They already had safe passage home."

"Against the bonewater dust."

"Well, Rumail wasn't going to unleash the stuff over *them.* It's not as if the men were in any danger."

"But you did not stay to see to it yourself. To make sure there were no other . . . surprises."

Now Belisar's spine prickled with irritation. "I told you, the Hasturs had demanded my surrender. Should I have risked my freedom—*my* freedom, as the heir to Greater Ambervale? I don't understand your point. If you think I should have acted otherwise, stop dancing around and tell me."

"Yes, it is clear you don't understand." Belisar caught the growl of resignation in his father's voice. With a barely-disguised sigh, Damian heaved himself out of his seat. He crossed the distance between them with two strides. For an instant, Belisar was afraid Damian was going to strike him, or walk right by him, which would have been worse.

Damian grabbed him in a rough hug and pounded his back several times. "Ah, well," he said, half under his breath. "You cannot help it, I suppose. But you are still my son and heir. There is much good in you. I will have to teach you better."

◆

For days, soldiers poured into Acosta, weary in body from battle and flight, wearier still in spirit. They offered a patchwork tale of entrapment, surrender, and an orderly retreat turned into a rout. None of them knew exactly what had happened, only that they had bolted for their lives at the command of their officers.

The next men to arrive were already dying, their guts turning to water even as their hair fell in patches. In his presence chamber, Damian interviewed those who could still talk. He forced Belisar to listen, to face the human wreckage from his aborted command. To cover his escape, Rumail had indeed released the bonewater dust over the Hastur army. But something had gone wrong, so that the Ambervale forces had also been exposed.

Belisar left his own men to die while he saved his own skin . . .

A pang shot through Damian as he glanced at Belisar's uncomprehending expression. Perhaps the shortcomings of the son were the fault of the father. He had not spent much time with Belisar as a child, for that was during the long, difficult conquest of Linn. That was before the vision had come upon him. Then he had assumed Belisar would tread in his footsteps, be molded by that same vision. He thought of Belisar as a young man, hair like a cap of gold, Belisar out on the practice field, mastering a fiery horse, Belisar grinning at him across a banquet table with torchlight burnishing his skin, Belisar wooing that Hastur vixen, Belisar so tall and proud as he led out the army. . . .

Belisar the coward.

It was probably Damian's own fault. The boy was young, untried, idealistic. He had been fed on visions of victory and glory. He knew nothing about honor in defeat.

Damian dismissed the last of the soldiers and downed a goblet of wine, an exquisitely rich vintage even though well-watered, and set it down on the little inlaid table. The wine sloshed onto the polished surface.

This much sitting around waiting would drive Aldones himself mad. What he needed was action. The border skirmish was a minor setback, that was all. He still held Acosta and the mountain kingdoms, as well as his home territories of Ambervale and Linn. The better part of his army was intact.

Voices reached him from the outer room. Though the words were muffled, he recognized the baritone of his personal guard. A prickle swept up his spine as he heard the subtle rise in pitch of the guard's voice. He gestured to the page standing at the door to admit whoever it was.

The man had ridden long and hard, Damian saw at a glance. Travel grime darkened his leather-plate armor, the worn straps which once held sword and dagger. Sweat and dried blood etched the seamed scars on his face. What struck Damian as the man fell to his knees, trembling, was the mixture of horror and despair in the whitened eyes. So should a man look, who had seen defeat turned into disaster, and his own fellows die from bonewater dust. Yet the man before him was no raw recruit, but a battle-hardened veteran.

"It's all right," he said, gently gruff. "I already know."

The man's mouth opened and closed. A sound came from his throat, half gasp, half moan. He shook his head, and Damian saw the tears.

"*Vai dom*—Lord—!" The man passed one hand across his face, visibly struggling not to fall on his face. A moment later, he had control of himself, although he did not meet Damian's eyes. When he spoke, his voice sounded hollow, like an echo of the grave:

"The Yellow Wolf is dead."

For a long moment, Damian sat, uncomprehending. He was beginning to suspect, from all the reports, but the words carried a dreadful finality.

"The general, dead?" His voice seemed to belong to someone else, someone immune to grief.

"By the Lord of Light himself, I wish it were not true! He stayed behind to make sure we got safe away." Now the man's words came in a rush. "At first, I would not leave him, but he commanded me. I went with the others."

Now Damian recognized the man, one of The Yellow Wolf's most trusted captains. Battle and desperation had transformed his rugged features. His name was Ranald Vyandal and though his family was poor, his lineage was honorable. Strange that Damian should think of that now.

"We got well clear of the dust, then I waited for him while the others went on. And then those who came had blistered faces. Some could not run more than a few paces without puking out their guts." Ranald gulped, memory paling his face to the color of bleached bone. Damian saw death in his eyes, but whether his own or only a reflection of all he had seen, he could not tell.

Ranald went on as if desperate to tell his whole story while he could.

"Still I waited. Toward the very end, when I could see only a few still on their feet in the distance—four of them carried him. They could barely stand, and yet they would not leave him—" his voice broke, but only for a moment.

"He was still breathing when they laid him at my feet. His face was horribly burned, his lips blackened. He looked at me and did not know me. He—oh, Dark Lady Avarra! Have mercy on us!"

Ranald buried his face in his hands, choking down sobs. "He was a father to me. I should have—"

I should have died at his side. Or in his place.

Damian, unexpectedly moved, reached out to lay a hand on the man's shoulder. His fingers moved over leather stiff with filth, to feel the deep racking sobs.

I have lost my general, and maybe my brother, Damian thought. *My son is a fool who can command but not lead.*

"I will hear no more of this. Dying is the easy part!" Damian said. "You have done your duty, a far more difficult task. You have brought this news to me, your King."

"That's—that's what The Yellow Wolf said. That I must live, and tell you he did his best. He spoke those words with his last breath."

"And what of the *laranzu* Rumail?"

Ranald knew nothing of his fate. He had not seen or heard of any gray-robed wizards.

Damian called for servants to see to Ranald's needs, and a physician to assess his exposure to bonewater dust. As for The Yellow Wolf, there would be time enough to mourn, once the battle was won and Hastur ground into dust.

I will need another general. If this man lives, perhaps he might serve. He seems capable of both loyalty and initiative. And he has seen the worst of battle.

Damian sat for a long time in his war chamber, with his hatred for Rafael Hastur growing like a cancer in his heart.

With The Yellow Wolf's death, Damian had lost a friend as well as a brilliant war leader. Yet to give himself over to grieving now would mean throwing away whatever The Wolf had died for. He, Damian, was still king. He might have failed to gain the border territory, he might well have erred in giving Belisar so much responsibility or in underestimating that snake, Rafael, and his witch niece, but by all the gods he knew and any others who would listen, he was not finished yet.

✦

Rumail's first waking awareness was warmth and a deep sense of well-being, then movement. He drifted in and out of true consciousness with the swaying of his body. The wound in his side had faded to a tightness, like the drawing of a stiff, old scar. At first, he thought some soft thick blanket swathed his body, then he realized it was not a physical fabric but an encompassing field of *laran*. When he tried to open his eyes, he saw only a blurred swathe of blue and golden green. His energies were depleted, but he was moving, perhaps on a cart or sledge. Through the muffling shield, he felt neither jolt nor bumping.

Voices reached him distantly, the harsh tones of the poorer sort of foot soldier. From time to time, the swaying halted and then went on with hesitation. He continued moving by fits and starts away from the heart of the contamination. That much his *laran* senses told him.

In his desperation, he had reached out for help, and had been answered. It was best to keep quiet and let events take their course. With any luck, he would be out of the danger zone before the Hastur fools realized who they'd helped.

When he came to full consciousness, the protective, smothering blanket of *laran* had lifted. Rumail found he could lift his head. He was lying in the back of a cart, the sort used to transport provisions to the battlefield, and the cart had tipped half on its side. In place of a pair of mules, a single animal stood in harness, lazily shaking flies from its long ears.

By his thirst, days had gone by. Rumail sat fully upright, grasping the side of the cart for balance. The mule had come to a halt in the middle of a rutted, churned morass which might once have been a road. A man in a soldier's jacket slumped at a precarious angle in the driver's seat. Rumail's movement tipped the cart and sent the man tumbling facedown into the mud.

Cautiously, Rumail used his *laran* to taste the air for poison. It was clean, although some residue of bonewater dust clung to the wheels of the cart. He slid to the ground, sinking ankle-deep in the muck, and rolled the man over. The mule cocked one ear in his direction.

The soldier whose compassion or duty had gotten him this far was too far gone for even a trained monitor's skill, which Rumail did not have.

He bent closer as the man's lips moved. No sound came from the blistered mouth, but Rumail caught his dying thoughts.

For the King . . . save his wizard . . . tell my son . . .

And then nothing.

Rumail passed a hand over the staring eyes. It would have been decent to bury such a man and not leave his body for the *kyorebni*, assuming any would venture this close to bonewater-polluted land. But he could not delay. Taking the soldier's knife, he cut the mule free from its harness, shortened the reins to a manageable length, and clambered on. Its back bone made a ridge like a knife and it limped a little, but it moved off willingly enough.

✦

When Rumail was within view of Acosta Castle, his mule, which had been stumbling with exhaustion, lowered its head, set its hooves, and refused to take another step. Whipping the animal produced nothing beyond ears laid flat against the thin neck. He slid from the mule's back and took up the reins, clucking encouragement. The animal sighed and followed at an easy amble.

A pair of guards stopped him at the edge of the army encampment and demanded his business. When he gave his name and rank, *laranzu* and *nedestro* brother to the King, one laughed. Eyes flickered over his torn, mud-smeared breeches, his patched tunic. He knew what they saw, an exhausted civilian trying to pass himself off as his betters for a bed and hot meal.

"*Dom* Rumail perished in the battle of the border," the other snarled. "You should be torn apart by banshees for besmirching his memory."

Rumail was in no mood to explain himself to ordinary men, let alone such inferior ones. One hand crept upward to his starstone. His fingers touched its warmth. It would not do, he reminded himself, to kill or cripple. These men, coarse and ignorant as they were, belonged to his brother. Their lives belonged to Greater Ambervale. So the first guard, the one who had laughed, tumbled to the mud, clutching his throat but still alive.

"*Sorcerer!*" the other man cried, his eyes bulging in his weathered face.

Rumail lifted one eyebrow. "Precisely."

Casting bewildered glances at his hapless mate, the guard fell to his knees. Others in the outermost camp circles took notice and a few made their way over. An instant later, a dozen broke out at once, although they kept their distance.

"It is the King's brother—the sorcerer—he's alive!"

"Come back to us from the dead!"

Rumail smiled inwardly, enjoying the reaction.

"How do you know—I've never seen him before."

"Look how he witched Seamus!—Seamus man, can ye stand? Are ye all right?" cried a soldier, helping the choking guard to his feet.

"Quickly, send word to the castle!"

"No, bring him a horse!—a drink—a clean cloak!"

"*Vai dom*—" One of the soldiers dared to approach Rumail, hands outstretched in entreaty. "If it please you—we are but poor soldiers—"

Please don't curse us.

Rumail thought wistfully of commanding them to carry him on their shoulders up to the castle, for they would have eagerly done his bidding, but in the end, he settled for an escort and an easy-gaited horse.

By the time he approached the outer gates, they were already swinging open. There stood Damian, resplendent in golden brocade and white fur. His arms stretched out to meet Rumail and he embraced him with such fervor, pressing Rumail's filthy garments against his own costly ones without the least concern. Rumail caught the expression on his brother's face, far more than delight at discovering him alive.

He needs me. He is desperate. It was a good thing Damian had little *laran,* or he would surely have picked up Rumail's surge of exhilaration. *And I will use him to get what I most desire—to be Keeper of a Tower today and to rule all the Towers on Darkover tomorrow.*

31

Edric flew his sentry-birds several times more, following the path Deslucido's forces had taken. A small group of horsemen had broken away
from the rest, moving in the direction of Acosta Castle. Undoubtedly,
Prince Belisar was making a swift escape, using the confusion to cover
him. The ragged remnants of the army remained straggled over the increasingly hilly terrain.

Edric pointed out their location on the maps spread over the improvised war-room table in the command tent. Coryn had been included in
the planning. Caitlin, after sending word to Hali with her starstone, had
withdrawn to replenish her strength.

"It gripes me fierce to see them get away, when we could so easily
run them down," one of the generals said. "With the Drycreek border
fallen, Acosta's vulnerable from this direction."

"Or would be, without the bonewater dust," Rafael commented.
"Caitlin, who knows about such things, says it may be a generation or
more before the land is safe for passage." He looked grim. "To reach
Acosta, we'll have to backtrack and go through the Venza Hills, with all
the nightmare logistics that entails."

"Aye," said the senior of the officers, "the danger will be if he mobi-
lizes quickly enough to meet us in the middle of the Hills. The major pass

is shaped to even the odds for a smaller army and he'll be approaching with advantage of terrain. If I were Deslucido, I'd lie in wait right here—" he indicated the area on the map, "—where we'd have to charge uphill with no cover. If it rains, as it often does at this season, we'll be slogging through mud up to our knees."

"He's no fool," Rafael said. "And neither is his general, The Yellow Wolf. If we know about the pass, we must assume he does, too."

"About a half-day's march past the funnel, there's a wide valley," another officer said. "If we can force the battle there, we'll have room to maneuver."

"Our best chance is to get there before him," Rafael said. "Yes, I know we'd all have to sprout wings to do that. We must find a way to slow him down, keep him pinned at Acosta."

"How?" the first general asked. "The cub has sealed himself a very effective barrier. There's no way we can cross it."

But bird-things such as Rumail had used to launch the bonewater dust could cross the desolation. Aircars could rain *clingfire* down on Acosta Castle. Rafael had pledged himself to restrain such horrors. Would he now use them to further his own ends?

Aldones, Blessed Evanda, even you, St. Christopher, Holy Bearer of Burdens, show me another way!

Coryn bent over the map, trying to visualize the land as he had seen it in his travels, the land he knew like the inside of his own dreams. "*Vai dom*, there is no barrier. Look, there are passes all through this outcrop of the Hellers. Small groups of men could travel swiftly by forest roads here and here," he pointed to the map, "and then join into a larger unit. From this point, the way to Acosta is clear."

"How do you know this?" Rafael asked. "I see no passes marked on the map."

"Because I was born in Verdanta," Coryn said quietly. "It is my brother Eddard who rules there under Deslucido's heel."

"You will never cease to amaze me, lad, or to supply my every need!" Rafael exclaimed. "Here we are, thinking the Oathbreaker beyond our reach, while right in front of us sits a man who knows the very inside of these mountains."

"We may not catch them before they reach Acosta," Coryn said, "but they will not expect an attack on their stronghold so soon."

"Aye," said another of the generals. "They will think themselves safe, with us bottled up here. He won't expect a direct assault on Acosta Castle. If Deslucido can take it, then we can take it back from him."

Rafael turned to Coryn, and his grin had a wolfish edge. "What say you? Can you map out routes and guide a team yourself along these trails into Acosta?"

Coryn chose his next words carefully, keeping the surge of hope under tight rein. "Majesty, I am yours to command. But one of these routes leads through Verdanta. There I would be of greatest use to you. Given the men to capture the castle by surprise, we might be able to retake Verdanta. You would have an ally right on Deslucido's doorstep."

"An excellent idea!" Rafael's eyes lighted, clearly pleased at this new prospect. "You could organize a contingent from Verdanta to join us at Acosta."

The last thing Coryn had expected when he came to Thendara to plead for his Tower was to be given the chance to free his homeland. To see Eddard and Margarida and Tessa—but he must not imagine a simple, happy reunion. He had not seen what Deslucido had done to them. They might be lost beyond finding, or deeply scarred by what they had survived. He must be prepared for pain as well as joy.

"If you ask it, I will try, although I have no experience leading soldiers," Coryn said. "Verdantans may follow me from patriotism and family loyalty, but it would be better done by Eddard, if he is still capable of it, or even one of your own men. My people will see you as a liberator." He paused.

"Ah, there is something you wish in return?" Rafael's brow darkened minutely.

Coryn took a deep breath. "Afterward, I beg your leave to return to Neskaya. Majesty, I am no soldier. I have no skill at arms. I am a trained *laranzu*. My mission, which was to plead that we be left neutral, is clearly impossible. As long as Deslucido has *laran* weapons and is willing to use them, he must be met with equal force. I can offer you no greater service than continuing the work there."

◆

They were about a day's ride from Verdanta Castle, traveling along game trails through the densest part of the mountain forest, when Coryn became aware they were not alone. He had no fear of attack, not with the dozen men King Rafael had sent with him. He had seen the hard light in their eyes before, in the single eye of Rafe. Two of the men, silent and apart as brothers, were said to have once been Aldaran assassins, legendary for stealth and tenacity. Now one of them lifted his head, also sensing the change in the forest.

Coryn, in the lead, raised one hand to signal a halt. For a long moment, nothing stirred, not even the clink of shod hoof on stone, the swish of a restless tail, the whisper of leaves in the sun-tipped breeze. Not an insect buzzed, not a bird sang.

Too still, too silent.

He touched the silken pouch at his neck which held his starstone, felt the hard crystalline outline, drew it out. In a shaft of stray sunlight, blue-white facets sparkled. He felt the indrawn breath of the nearest men.

Laranzu! Wizard . . . sorcerer . . . Yes, that was how they thought of him, these battle-hardened men.

Coryn reached out with his *laran* in a widening circle. Living creatures glowed like iridescent jewels, waiting. Watching. Tiny hearts quivered. Squirrel, bird, tree-climber, serpent in its burrow . . .

Men. There—where the trail dipped across the stream bed, widened and curved around the rocky outcrop. The corner was blind and the open space brilliantly lit after the darkness of the tree-cast shade.

Coryn gestured for the men to remain behind. He nudged his horse and the animal ambled forward, then stopped at the stream bed. He had the positions of the men ahead clearly now, half a dozen in all. Their confidence bore the tinge of desperation.

Coryn took a deep breath, searching more deeply. These men did not feel like ordinary bandits, who would surely have sought easier prey than a force of armed men. The minds of the ambushers felt oddly familiar, but they were on Verdanta lands; he might have known some of them. The leader . . . yes, there he was . . .

Recognition flashed across Coryn's mind. His horse surged forward at his urging, splashing across the stream and up the opposite bank. In the wide space of the trail, he lifted the reins and halted.

"Petro! Petro, come out!"

A long silence answered him. Then leafy branches fluttered and a twig snapped. A man moved from the shadows, difficult to see in the dappled light. His vest and breeches were stitched together in shades of tan and green, like a harlequin woodsman.

"Who goes riding in this forest? Who asks for Petro of the Green?"

"I had rather give those answers to Petro himself."

"He stands before you."

Now Coryn laughed outright. "Petro, come out! It's Coryn!"

"*Coryn!*" A voice, familiar but roughened, called out from behind the rocky outcrop. Coryn jumped from his horse's back and caught his brother in his arms.

"You disappeared—I could not find you!" he cried, pounding Petro's back, then drawing back to look at him.

"I could hardly send word to Tramontana," Petro shot back. He called out the others of his band, mostly younger sons of smallholders, one minor noble who'd fled from Acosta, and a slender youth with rough-cropped red hair and a sprinkling of freckles across a snub nose, bow in hand and quiver across back . . .

"*Margarida!*"

All her girlish prettiness, her love of adornment, had been pared away, leaving a core as spare and supple as a whip. She grabbed him in a quick embrace, her body taut. As the bare skin of his cheek brushed hers, Coryn sensed how she had woven her *laran* in something akin to the shield Coryn had created to contain the bonewater dust. From more than a few yards away, she and anyone close to her became telepathically invisible. Her barriers were like a mat of fibers, each weak and flexible, but so tightly intertwined that nothing could penetrate. No wonder he had been unable to sense her or Petro, who had never had much *laran*.

He remembered the sweet, playful sister who had taught him to stitch a silken bag for his starstone out of scraps she'd pilfered from the patchwork basket. Perhaps with the return of peace and order, that young girl would emerge once more.

By this time, Coryn's men had come to investigate, and for a long while everyone shouted and exclaimed and hugged each other. Petro's band was part of a larger group which mostly ranged along trade roads, doing what damage they could to the Ambervale occupiers, burning what supplies they could not carry off.

"And a rough life it's been, too," Petro said. His voice sounded different, hoarse around the edges as if it had been damaged. His manner, too, betrayed a wariness masked by his bantering words.

"But you didn't come all this way merely to see to our ease," Petro said.

As Coryn told the story of the border battle and Belisar Deslucido's defeat, Petro's face contorted in a black, triumphant rictus. Several of his men cheered. Only Margarida did not smile, but continued to stare at Coryn and Rafael's men. She'd lost all the modesty of a gently-reared woman of a minor noble house.

Petro eyed Coryn's band, measuring them. "But perhaps your coming is just what we need. We've been waiting for the time to strike. Deslucido's grown complacent, thinking we no longer pose any real threat to his rule here." He glanced at Rafael's men. "Now we have a real chance."

"What about Eddard? Could he rally men from inside?"

Margarida, who had been listening silently, shook her head. "It's said he's still alive, though none have seen him for this last half-year. Deslucido's left a watchdog here, a snake-brain named Lotrell, Eddard's 'chief councillor' and jailer. He gives orders in Eddard's name."

Coryn described his mission. "King Rafael means to harry Deslucido to the ground, whether it be in Acosta or Ambervale, should the Oathbreaker flee there. To this end, he has sent these men to restore Verdanta to us."

Petro took Coryn's arm. "Walk with me apart. We must discuss this further."

They went back up the trail, far enough to not be so easily overheard.

"You have been talking about using King Rafael's men to free Verdanta," said Petro, "and for this we all will be grateful. But what will he demand in return? Are we to become a vassal state to Hastur as the price of our freedom?"

Coryn paused, taking in a deep breath. The smell and texture of these woods stirred memories. There was no other place which tasted so strongly of home. A thought whispered through him, that after he had restored his family, he would have a home again, a place he could always return to, a place he need never leave.

"I can't speak for Rafael Hastur or anyone else," Coryn said. "I do know that he is a man of strong principles. I have never seen him betray a promise or turn against a friend. I believe him when he says that all he expects is for those battle-worthy men who can be spared to join on the assault on Acosta."

"Ah, but how can you know that for certain?" Petro's eyes glittered. "Has it occurred to you that doing so will strip us bare, open to anyone who wants easy prey? Or have you switched your allegiances so thoroughly that you cannot see the danger? Have you become a pet and lackey of this lowland King?"

"I serve Neskaya Tower, and Neskaya answers to Hastur," Coryn answered with quiet dignity. He looked back to where Margarida and the men waited in the pools of shade and sunlight. "Help us get into the castle. Together we will oust Deslucido. After that—"

"After that, we are free men and beholden to no one," Petro said in that bitter-edged voice. "Or you could order these men to stay and strengthen our defense."

"I have no authority to command these men except in their master's cause. For now, let us fight together, side by side as brothers should, for Eddard and our sisters. For Verdanta."

"For Verdanta."

◆

Petro was better than his word. He broke the parties into small groups, each with a different entry route into the castle, each with a different objective. Once inside, Rafael's men captured or disabled the captain of the guards and all five chief Ambervale officers. Margarida led a smaller force to seize the armory and stables. Coryn, flanked by the two assassin brothers and one of Petro's men, began a search of the family apartments. They encountered and as quickly dispatched anyone in white and black who challenged them. A couple of older servants recognized Coryn and ran to spread the news.

Alarms sounded, as if from a distance. Coryn and the others made their way to his father's suite of rooms, guarded by four armed Ambervale soldiers. Coryn hung back to let Rafael's men do their work. Within moments, two lay dead, one winded and hamstrung, and the last had fled, bleeding. Coryn set his hand to the door latch.

"Who is it? What do you want?" came a quavering voice from inside.

The door swung open. One of the assassin brothers gestured for silence. He slipped through the opening, his mate covering him with drawn steel.

"Who is there?" came the voice again. A man's voice, old and frail. It tugged at Coryn's memory. Wild hope flared within him—*his father, still alive?* Had the reports been a hoax, set to mislead and sow despair? No, he had felt the black emptiness in place of his father's life energies.

Coryn stepped into the room. It was empty. The voice, mumbling now, came from the inner chamber. Coryn rushed ahead, past Rafael's men.

White of hair and skin, swathed in the same color, an old man stood beside the bed, frozen in midstride. Sheets wound around his hips and trailed on the floor. Two servants, a dumpy, middle-aged woman and a half-grown boy, cowered in the far corner.

No, not his father.

Eddard.

Eddard, old before his time, shrunken from a sturdy, vigorous young man to a wraith. One emaciated hand reached out, trembling.

"Speak! If you have any mercy in you, speak!" Eyes gleamed in their sockets like twin orbs of pale marble, without any hint of pupil or iris.

Merciful Avarra! No wonder Deslucido let him live! Pity swept through Coryn, pity for his brother's shame.

"Eddard," Coryn said softly. He touched the bony fingers, clasped them in his hand. "It's me, Coryn."

"Coryn? Oh no, he's safe, far from here . . . Coryn?" Eddard turned his head, but not before Coryn had caught the glint of tears.

"Sir," said one of the assassin brothers. The other had disappeared to check the rest of the suit and returned. "We cannot stay here, not until the castle is properly secured."

"In a moment," Coryn said. "Eddard—" Quickly, he outlined the situation. "The people will need a Leynier to lead them, to tell them Verdanta is free."

Eddard lifted his arms, wasted even through the folds of his night shirt.

Coryn grasped one shoulder. "I'll be back once we've secured the castle and grounds." Petro's man indicated he would stay with Eddard. Coryn turned to follow the assassin brothers.

"Wait!" Eddard cried. "My wife and son! My Adrian! They're under guard—Lotrell—Damian's jailer—he has orders to kill them—"

"Where are they?"

"Servants' quarters—if he hasn't moved them."

The servants' quarters were at the far end of the east hall. To detour there would take them well out of the areas they needed to sweep clear to secure the castle. "Go on!" he told Rafael's men. And then, to Eddard, "I'll find them!"

He started down the hallway toward the east wing. Margarida appeared like a shadow at the branching. She held a knife as long as her forearm, poised as if she knew how to use it. Knees bent, body turned to present the smallest target, she glided toward him, hugging the wall. When she saw him, she lowered the tip of the sword.

"Eddard?" she asked.

"He's alive, but we've got to find his wife and child before they're used as hostages or killed outright."

"Lotrell." Her voice was tight, clipped.

She hates him to hide her fear. Something had happened to her—the *laran* armor, the set mouth, the eyes like stone.

Margarida lifted her chin. "There is no need to search. I know where he is. Before we could secure the armory, Lotrell snuck in, carrying a sack. It could easily have held a small child. He barred himself inside before we could cut him off. Well, he's not going anywhere. If we can't get in, he can't get out."

Without need for further words, they walked down the corridor together and down the broad stairs. Margarida's stride was as free and strong as any man's. She had, Coryn reminded himself, lived and fought among men in the forest as one of them.

The armory was a long, stone-walled extension to the castle, more shed than fortress. It was used for storing things besides arms, the picks and shovels used to fight fires, livestock equipment, straw for archery practice. Narrow, unglassed windows let in light but kept out the worst of the weather. The inner door had been barricaded so that the only entrance was the outside door facing the stables.

A handful of castle servants had gathered a distance from the door. A few carried makeshift weapons, one old woman a broom. There was no doubt that Lotrell held a hostage. Shrieks of childish terror issued from the armory. One of Petro's archers stood on a makeshift platform of barrels and planks, bow drawn and arrow aimed through one of the windows into the dark interior.

"Call off your dog! I see him at the window!" roared a voice from inside. "Or the brat dies! By Zandru's bloody hell, I swear it!"

The man lowered his bow and glanced at Margarida. "He's holding the child above an old rack of swords. They've been turned and fixed point-up. Even I can't aim that well."

If he falls, so does the child.

Touching the starstone at his throat, Coryn reached out with his *laran*.

He caught the harmonics in the archer's gruff voice, followed by a wave of renewed panic from the boy. From the man inside, desperation. He was no longer thinking but acting on instinct. Margarida's analogy of a snake fitted him perfectly. His mind twisted and darted, wily and devious as he sought a means of escape.

There must be a way out of this, one without bloodshed.

"He can't keep it up forever," one of the other men said.

A woman raced around the castle wing, sobbing, "Adrian! My baby!" Coryn barely recognized the sweet-faced woman who was his sister-in-law. Once rosy-plump, she'd grown thin, but not decrepit like her husband. Although her flat breasts swayed beneath her loose gown, she moved with vigor. She rushed for the armory door.

Coryn, sensing her goal, moved to cross her path. He caught her in his arms. For a moment, she fought him, pushing mindlessly onward, flailing at him with her fists.

"Shhh . . ." He enveloped her mind with his, as if catching a falling rainbird fledgling in a cushioned nest. Her eyes cleared as she looked up at him. Her lids were red and puffy, underlined with circles the color of bruises, and her skin had a pasty roughness.

"That monster has him—he's only three!"

"If we force his hand, he might hurt the boy." Coryn used his *laran* to underscore his words.

She drew back, hands hugging her sides, but recovering visibly. "What—what must we do? We can't just leave him in there!" Underneath, he felt her resilience. She was a decent woman, strong but not unbreakable. Whole and in command of her resources, she would do more for Eddard than a score of physicians.

Coryn turned from her and approached the armory door. "You in there! Lotrell—Deslucido's man! This is Coryn Leynier."

"I don't know you. What do you want?"

"Put down the child. I want to parley. We can come to an agreement and end this stalemate."

"That's easy!" A laugh like a bark. "Give me your fastest horse, food and water, and two hours' lead. The kid comes with me. I'll let him go once I'm well away. You can pick him up—if you can find him."

"The child stays here. I give you my word that if he is unharmed, so will you be."

"Ha! What kind of fool do you think I am, to trust any man's word?"

The voice escalated in pitch, still crafty but now edging toward madness. The boy's wailing subsided into hiccoughing sobs. "This mewling brat is my guarantee."

"Be reasonable. If you kill him—" the child's mother smothered a shriek, "—there will be nothing to stop us from rushing you. Your own life won't be worth a pile of stable sweepings then. Think, Lotrell. The castle is ours again." *Or will be shortly.* "The only way out is through us. No man can hold out against so many forever. You have no choice."

"If I have no choice, then neither do you. This babe is Eddard's only son. If you've taken back the castle, you've seen the father. Do you think he can sire others? No, my fancy talker. I hold Verdanta's heir and right now he's a hair away from being spitted like a *chervine* kid at Midwinter feast."

Margarida stirred, shifting from one foot to the other. Her eyes had gone dark, like slate. In a low voice that would not carry within, she said, "This talk is useless. You might as well argue with one of the dogs in the kennel. With every word, he becomes more fixed in his position. Let me bargain with him."

"You?" Eddard's wife said, "what can you, a woman, do?"

Margarida gave no notice she'd heard. Coryn could not read her intentions through her *laran* barriers. Before he could reply, she called out.

"Lotrell! This is Margarida! Do you remember me? I'm still alive! Since you must have a hostage, take me instead of the boy!"

"Mar—"

She hushed Coryn with a look so fierce that not for the world would he have been in Lotrell's boots. "Get the horse," she said, loud enough for Lotrell to hear. "Give him what he asked for." Two of the castle servants ran off, a man to the stables and the old woman with the broom to the kitchens.

There was no immediate answer from the armory, only the continued soft whimpering of the boy. Tension gathered, a palpable weight. Eddard's wife had pressed both hands over her mouth. Tears streamed over her fingers, but she had command of herself.

Without conscious intention, Coryn deepened his *laran* contact with the man inside the armory. His own vision went blank as he sank into Lotrell's mind. He slipped below the surface emotions. Darkness lapped at him. His senses shifted; he caught the tang of urine where the boy had wet himself, mingled smells of metal oil and leather, trembling muscles in shoulder and arm from the boy's weight, cold sweat trickling down the sides of his neck, dull squeezing just behind his breastbone.

Threadlike tendrils, tangled and pulsing ugly red, wound through Lotrell's chest, down his belly. He clamped down on his lower lip with his teeth, feeling the gap where his left eyetooth had been until it was pulled last winter.

The pain will pass . . .

The man's thoughts sounded like the clanging of distant, discordant gongs. Coryn assessed the unhealthy congestion of the life forces, heard the laboring of the heart, felt the pain of starving cells. The body around him wavered. The man's free hand groped for his chest, kneading the muscles.

Pass, damn you, pass! I can't afford to be weak now!

All it would take was a nudge. As a monitor, he'd learned to clear both physical and *laran* channels. With a single movement of his mind, he could ease the heart-pain . . . or tip the man into a fatal seizure. This Lotrell had a diseased heart which would have given out anyway. Who could say the seizure wasn't natural, wouldn't have happened in the next few moments?

It would be so easy . . .

The boy, Eddard's son, Verdanta's heir, would be saved, as would his mother and Margarida. No one would know . . .

But he, Coryn, would know. He would live the rest of his life knowing that he had broken the most solemn vows of a *laranzu*, that he had committed the one unforgivable crime of the Towers, the forceful violation of another man's mind. He would be forever unfit to be a Keeper.

In a shiver, half-remembered memory swept over him, leaving nausea in its wake. He knew he had never done this, and yet the vision of it seemed hideously familiar. Loathing rose up in him. The next moment, he found himself back in his own body, hands tearing at the shirt over his abdomen.

Not more than a heartbeat or two had passed. Margarida still stood, legs braced, one hand resting on the hilt of the knife she'd thrust under her belt. Her head cocked slightly to one side, as if listening. Coryn took a deep breath and the muscles of his belly unlocked.

The door to the armory swung open a crack. There were sounds of a scuffle and more childish sobbing. A man slipped through the door, one arm pinning a red-faced toddler tight against his chest, the other hand gripping a dagger. The child's struggles threatened to dig the tip into the side of his own neck.

"Put the boy down," Margarida said in a low voice. "I'll go willingly."

"Get rid of that knife."

Margarida lowered the blade to the ground and pushed it away with one foot. She held her hands away from her body, slowly approaching Lotrell. When Margarida was within a pace of him, he lowered the child, grabbed her arm, and spun her around, holding her with the dagger at her throat. The child scuttled away. His mother darted forward and scooped him up in her arms. Without a backward glance, she sprinted for the castle. No one else moved.

Although Margarida had made no effort to resist, Lotrell held her awkwardly. He shifted his grasp on her, drawing blood. The archer beside the armory moved to draw his bow, but Coryn waved him back.

"Where's that horse?" Lotrell growled.

The servant trotted up a saddled horse from the stables. Coryn didn't recognize the animal. It wasn't nearly as good as his father's stallion or the black Armida mare he'd been given, but it looked fit enough. Lotrell had the horse placed beside the mounting block the *coridom* had made for Tessa so many years ago. He ordered Margarida on the horse's back. He settled himself behind her. His face had gone gray, his lips dark. The hand holding the dagger shook visibly.

A man came running from the kitchen with two sacks, tied together to fit behind the saddle. It was one of the assassin brothers, taking the chance Lotrell would not recognize he did not belong to the castle. To Coryn's eyes, his shambling gait could not hide the taut control, the fighter's balance.

Snarling, Lotrell hauled on the reins, wheeling the horse. "Treachery! Stop where you are, or she dies!"

Blood flowed in a dark red thread down the side of Margarida's neck. She betrayed no trace of either pain or fear, simply waiting.

Waiting . . .

At Lotrell's command, Rafael's man handed the sacks to one of the women. Timidly she approached the horse, which was lashing its tail in discomfort, mouthing the heavy bit. Lotrell shifted in the saddle, reaching down for the sacks. The horse danced beneath him and the woman shied away, then sidled nearer, holding her burden to keep the most distance between her and the nervous, prancing animal.

Coryn read the surge of exultation even through Margarida's tight *laran* barriers.

In a single movement, she twisted in Lotrell's grasp. She threw the power of her shoulders against his grasp, opening a space between her flesh and the dagger point. At the same time, her weight unbalanced him. Even before they hit the ground, her fingers closed around the hilt.

Two entangled bodies slammed into the bare earth. Lotrell was on top for an instant before they rolled, clutching and grappling. Coryn and the assassin brother dashed in.

The fight stopped abruptly. Lotrell lay across Margarida's body. For an awful moment, neither moved. Blood, bright and pungent, pooled beneath the bodies. The woman who'd carried the sacks of food screamed. Then Lotrell slid to the side and lay sprawled half on his side.

Red-faced and gasping with effort, Margarida pulled herself out from under him. She refused the proffered hands, getting to her feet under her own power. Her shirt was drenched in blood, but Coryn knew that very little of it was hers. As she limped past him, he met her eyes once and could not read what he saw there. Her barriers were once more in place.

Chiya, *what has happened to you?*

As if in answer to his question, she paused, shoulders sagging. "It is finished," she murmured. "Now I can be free."

He watched her go with an ache in his heart for the sister he had found and lost again.

32

They had struck just after dawn and by the time the Bloody Sun stood straight overhead, Verdanta Castle was theirs. What was left of the Ambervale guard had thrown down their arms, their situation hopeless. There would be much work to do, sweeping the borders and smallholds for others who had escaped or been stationed afield.

Everyone who could hear the summons of the alarms gathered in the courtyard. Eddard stood on the threshold, with Padraic at one elbow and Petro at the other. Coryn watched them, acutely aware of the vast gulf which had grown between himself and his family. With Verdanta free, he could no longer justify lingering here, no matter how much he might desire it. His mission for King Rafael had come to an end.

Eddard's face flushed with effort, but his back was straight. Despite his thinness, he radiated energy. As he began to speak, even the toddler in Tessa's arms grew quiet, for his voice, although unwavering, was far from powerful. Coryn imagined him repeating these very words of triumph to himself, hour after hour in the dark, drawing courage and hope from them.

"Verdanta is ours, and we are free. We will never permit her to be taken from us again. Every man who has fought in this cause will be venerated for the rest of his days, and the family of every man who has died be cared for with

*that same honor. Let all who would strive against us know our vengeance, and
all who would lay down their weapons and swear peace between us depart
unmolested. If any man who was once our enemy would stay and pledge fealty
to this house of Leynier . . . if he submits to our judgment, he may have a new
life with us. And this we say to our brothers of Storn and Hawksflight and all
the other lands which groan under the Ambervale yoke: Join with us! Lend
your strength to ours! Seize back our own kingdoms and drive the tyrant from
the face of the earth!"*

Before he had finished, the men who had been sitting in the dust,
exhausted and confused, had risen to their feet. Ambervale prisoner and
Verdantan alike clapped and cheered so that whatever more Eddard had
to say was lost in the revelry.

Petro grinned, a flash of his old merriment, and looked as if he would
have hugged Eddard, if not for the solemnity of the occasion. One of his
men grabbed Margarida around the waist and spun her, laughing. Tessa
ran to where the little knot of men in Ambervale colors stood, under
guard, and reached out her hand to one of them.

One of King Rafael's men drew Coryn aside and said, "We cannot
linger here, no matter how useful we might be to these people. They will
have to fight their own battles in restoring order. We were never intended
as an occupation force. You must make arrangements for the men who
are to come with us."

That night, there was feasting in the great hall. Coryn did not recognize half the people seated around the great table. Eddard sat in their
father's place, flanked by Petro and his wife. The boy, exhausted but
uninjured, would not leave his mother, so she held him on her lap, feeding him bits from her own plate until he fell asleep. Margarida had gone
down with Rafael's men, a little apart, but listening intently to their talk.

Tessa came forward with her own toddler in her arms. Coryn scarcely
recognized her. Lines bracketed her mouth and eyes, but motherhood
had softened the curves of her body. She'd been prepared, she said, to
plead for the life of her husband or else accept exile with him, explaining
that although the marriage had not been of her choosing, it was as good
as any other and with one child, a lusty son, born and another on the way,
she would stay with what she had. Eddard promised to hear her husband's case the next morning and added that he hoped the man knew
what was good for him.

Singers performed their new ballads of the liberation of Verdanta, and exhausted, half-drunken men staggered off to sleep. As the wine flowed freely, the brothers exchanged stories. Petro and Margarida had both had mild cases of the lungrot and had escaped through the kitchen cellars. They'd hidden in the forest by day and traveled by night, seeking shelter in the caves they'd explored as children and living like outlaws. Once, they became separated and it had been days before he'd found her, too badly beaten to talk. Eventually, the hunt for them had died down enough for them to gather others.

"It was Margarida who insisted we stay and fight," Petro said, his eyes flickering in her direction. "Me, I would have kept running from here to Shainsa."

Look at her now, his thought echoed in Coryn's mind. *What has she done? What has she* become?

Coryn shifted uneasily. He turned to Eddard and asked for his story.

"Deslucido's estimation of my weakness was somewhat exaggerated," Eddard said with a flicker of a smile. "At first, perhaps, I could do little. The lungrot left me blind and barely alive. I was told he took my family as hostages. Orders went out under my name. From time to time, men came, dressed me up, sat me in that big chair Father hated so much, and made speeches in my name. When I realized what they were saying, I spoke up. Oh, that was a mighty scene. I'd scrambled to my feet, screaming to whoever could hear that I did not countenance the things they said, that all true Verdanta men must resist the Ambervale rule. They beat me senseless and when I recovered, they told me they had killed my eldest son."

Coryn could think of nothing to say. Petro laid down his knife and listened, eyes dark and mouth set. They waited while Eddard regained his composure.

"They had not," Eddard went on. "Although he had died of some childhood fever. I did not learn that until later when they allowed my wife and second son to join me here. By then, they believed me broken . . . and I suppose for a time that was true. They brought her, she said, because they feared I was willing myself to die and they still needed me as a figurehead. . . ."

Eddard's voice trailed off; his sightless eyes reflected nothing. His wife, who had been rocking their young son, fast asleep in her arms, reached out to gently touch his hand. He came immediately to himself.

"I lay there with darkness filling my heart," he said in a voice resonant with passion, "and all I could see was fire. I thought of that big one—you know, Coryn, the one when *Dom* Rumail arrived and summoned the fliers from Tramontana. The one which began all these troubles. I told myself I wouldn't let that fire win, so many years afterward. Over and over I told myself that."

Coryn nodded. He could well see Eddard's anger simmering over the months, keeping him alive.

"After that," Eddard said with a wry twist to his mouth, "I recovered somewhat more quickly than I allowed them to see. Somehow, I knew the time would come when I might have another chance to act." He fumbled for Petro's hand, clasped it. "I never dreamed my baby brothers would come riding to the rescue!" His head swung in Coryn's direction. "You will stay and help us rebuild, won't you, Coryn? Verdanta needs all her sons now."

"I cannot stay, Eddard," Coryn said quietly. "My greater duty is to the Tower I serve and the King who commands us."

"You would leave your own family to go fight Rafael's war?" Eddard said, gray-white brows drawing together.

Petro tightened his grasp on Eddard's hand, drawing his attention. "It is Rafael's war that brought us this victory, my brother. Until now, my men and I could do no more than harass and delay. We had not the means or the skill to strike directly until Coryn and these men arrived."

Eddard's stormy expression softened. "Then I suppose you must go where duty commands. Remember the old proverb, *Bare is the brotherless back.* We will always be here if you need us."

As much as he loved his country, Neskaya was his home now. His father had been right, so many years ago, when he said that Coryn might not want to return after seeing the wide world. It was not a matter of wishes, but where he truly belonged, what he had become, who he was now. For today, it would be enough to see Verdanta free and his family safe.

"We may defeat Deslucido, but that will hardly put an end to men's lust for power or their abuse of it," Petro said with a spark of his old cynicism. "As long as we are small and weak, there will be others to prey upon us. Verdanta has never been able to support much of an army, not compared to what Ambervale can raise, or the lowland kingdoms. We stayed free for a long time simply because we had nothing they wanted." His dark eyes met Coryn's defiantly.

"We cannot rely on our continued insignificance," Eddard said. "Sooner or later, someone else will come along who wants what we have, even if we're just a step to some place else." He shifted his head in Coryn's direction, as if to say, *You are a Tower-trained* laranzu. *Can't you protect your own family?*

What? Coryn thought with a flare of heat, *by arming you with* cling-fire?

And yet that was exactly what Liane had urged when her own home-land was under attack by their shared enemy.

If we had clingfire, *someone like Deslucido would only use it in greater quantities against us, or worse, and then turn our own stockpiles against us as well.* But what if the mountain kingdoms had stood together against him—Verdanta and Storn and Hawksflight—even Taniquel's Acosta?

Verdanta allied with Storn . . . Coryn could imagine Petro's response to that idea, but so much had changed in all their lives. Coryn and Liane had forged a bond deeper than friendship.

Only a heartbeat of conversation had passed. Petro was still staring at Coryn, as if challenging him for answers.

"You are right, my brother," Coryn said in his most temperate voice, "as long as we are small and isolated, we are vulnerable to ambitious, unscrupulous men like Deslucido. I think Father had the right idea in seeking formal connections, but he looked in the wrong place."

"Where should we look for allies, then?" Eddard asked, genuinely interested. "You have been among the powerful kings beyond these mountains. Which of the great Domains would consider us, except as vassals for their own purposes?"

"Not a great one," Coryn replied, "but an equal. There is power in numbers, just as a single reed becomes unbreakable when joined to its fellows."

"You're thinking of *Storn?*" Petro asked incredulously. Eddard's fea-tures darkened. "I'd as soon trust a fox to guard a coop of chicks!"

"And yet," Coryn went on, "Liane Storn, who loves her homeland as much as we love ours, has held my life in her hands when we worked in a *laran* circle together and never once failed me. She had been taught to hate me, that I came from a line of despicable villains, just as I learned to think the same of her. As we came to understand each other, we saw that what we had in common far outweighed old quarrels and petty differences."

"But—*Storn!*"

"Think on it," Eddard said, rubbing his face with one hand. "They have been under the Oathbreaker's boot even as we have been. It would not be the first time that a common enemy made strange comrades."

"You speak from the past," Coryn added, thinking of Petro's mission to High Kinnally during the great fire. "But we are none of us who we were then. Look at Eddard, at Tessa, Margarida—me." *Yourself.* "Don't you think the Storns might have changed, too—especially with a daughter held hostage at Linn."

"My—my wife was held there at first," Eddard said. "She spoke of a Liane, a *leronis*, though she did not know the girl's family. She—she said Liane nursed the baby through a fever, as tenderly as if he were her own."

"I see you are in league against me," Petro said, "and I still say no good will come of this. I suppose next you'll be wanting to send me as ambassador to High Kinnally."

They all laughed while Eddard said, "It *is* a thought."

"Seriously," Eddard went on, "there could be no better way to open discussion than to help the Storns win back their freedom. I cannot send fighting men, not and honor our debt to Rafael Hastur. A small group of your foresters, Petro, those skilled in stealth and hiding, might bring news of our victory here and give them the heart to rise up on their own."

"That I will do." Petro's smile held more than a trace of ferocity, and Coryn saw that nothing would please him more than to strike back at Deslucido, even if it meant aiding their old enemies.

✦

King Rafael's men stayed to organize as many men as wished to go with them, and most of the good horses. Petro had already melted into the forests on his way to High Kinnally, but he left two of his best trackers to guide the Hastur men through Verdanta lands.

Coryn stood watching Padraic count heads and horses in the court-yard, knowing that he, too, ought to be going. The war would not wait for him, and Aldones alone knew what new strategy Deslucido might be hatching.

Margarida came up to him, so silent that he barely heard her approach. She still wore her forest garb, her hair short as a boy's, with the long knife strapped in a sheath to one thigh.

"Last night, I spoke with the men who came with you," she said without inflection.

"Yes," Coryn answered, since a comment seemed to be called for. "I wondered what they were saying of such interest."

She shook her head and went down the steps, heading for the stables and inviting him by her posture to join her. "Not so much what they said as how they said it. The silences between the words, the things they didn't say.

"I know what people are saying about me," she said, "that now no husband will take me to wife, dowry or no. Husband! Well, where was he when Father and Kristlin sickened with lungrot? Where was he when the Oathbreaker's hounds came pouring through the gap? Where was he when Lotrell and his men caught me in the forest and left me for dead?"

Her pain seeped through her tightly woven barriers. Coryn ached to reach out, soothe it away. He brushed the back of her wrist with his fingertips, Tower-style, but she shrugged off the touch.

"I survived those things, me alone. I don't know—" she lifted one hand, palm callused and fingernails ragged, "—I don't know how all this would have turned out differently if Deslucido had not come."

He did not need *laran* to read the rest of her thought, *How I would have been different.*

"I had no husband to take care of me, and after this, I do not want one. Nor can I live on here like Great-aunt Ysabet, weaving tapestries until I'm ninety. King Rafael's men have told me of the Sisterhood of the Sword. I mean to join them."

Coryn had heard of such, women who trained in weapons and hired themselves out as soldiers, fiercely loyal where they had pledged themselves but knowing no law but their own. He had even seen a few, moving through the streets of Thendara in pairs or threes, grim and aloof in their blood-colored vests. Gold earrings gleamed in their ears, visible below short-cropped hair. He began to say something about how improper they were, and then realized how well his sister fit their description. But for the earring, token of whatever oath they gave one another, and their distinctive garb, she might already be one of them.

"I believe there is a house of such women in Thendara," he said. "I can ask Rafael's men to escort you there, if that is truly what you wish."

She laughed, an unexpectedly merry sound. "Dear brother, I do not need an escort, any more than I need a husband. I have asked these men if I may travel as one of them. It may be a long while before they return to Thendara, but meanwhile I will be learning the skills I will need to earn my bread."

"You can fight that well?" True, she'd taken Lotrell by surprise, but how could she match a man's strength?

"I can *shoot* that well. As for swordskill, I have years to make up for, when I was playing at flower decorations and sewing, while these boys were hacking at each other with wooden swords. I don't expect I will ever be as powerful as a man, but stealth and speed can do much to even the odds."

Coryn could not help grinning at her. "I can see you have much to teach me. When you have pierced your ear and become a fearsome warrior, will you still allow me to call you *little sister?*"

"You blockhead, of course! And you will always be my bossy brother." She threw her arms around his neck and for an instant, her barriers went transparent and he saw the sister he loved, tempered by a fire he could not imagine, but still a sweet and gentle spirit. He wished for all the world he could undo what had been done to her, but he realized that to even speak of it would take away from what she had achieved.

They spoke no more of these matters, but parted amicably, he toward Neskaya and she with a contingent of armed men for Hastur.

BOOK 4

33

Coryn's second arrival at Neskaya was as unlike his first as night to day. His horse was as footsore and his own body as weary, for he had pressed both of them hard over the miles. Those miles had been uneventful except for the growing impatience within him. As his horse clattered down the last slope, the spires of pale translucent blue stone rose before him with their faintly luminescent glow. As before, his breath caught in his throat at the beauty of each pure line, the arched entrance, the windows ablaze with reflected sunset. Now his heart warmed to the familiar sight.

One of the younger novices called out, "Coryn's home!" and ran to spread the news.

Yes, he thought, *home.* More than Verdanta, more even than Tramontana, this place was now his home. He had earned his place here.

Within minutes, those workers who were awake and not sleeping off a night on the relays came out to welcome him. Few did more than touch his sleeve, yet the warmth of their welcome washed through him. As he greeted each one, his mind brushed theirs with the lightest touch. Had he not been bound by hard-won Tower discipline, he would have taken them in his arms. As it was, his eyes stung with tears. He knew these people as he did not, could not, had never known his own family. Their respect and love for him was evident in each gesture, even their restraint. In that vision behind his eyes, he felt them all clasp invisible hands.

Bernardo, eyes tinged with red, came hurrying down after a few minutes. His face had shrunken in on itself, although his step was as firm as ever, his voice as certain.

"Do you bring us news from Thendara? Were you successful?"

"Yes, there is news, and whether I was successful remains to be judged," Coryn answered somberly.

"Come, then, and let us hear it." Bernardo led the way to his private quarters. Mac, as senior technician, and Demiana, the slender gray-eyed woman who was the Tower's most skilled monitor, attended the conference.

They sat for hours, listening to Coryn's story. Because he was lightly linked to Bernardo and the others, their shock rippled through his own body as he told of the battle with Belisar Deslucido's forces.

"Bonewater dust . . ." Demiana whispered, so low and tremulous that Coryn felt it as a quivering along his spine. He could not be sure if he had heard the words spoken aloud or who had said them. She sat before him, head bowed so that shadows hid her face, shoulders rigid with tension.

"We thought—" Mac stumbled, then burst forth. *"Clingfire* is horrible enough, but it is akin to natural fire. We make it from elements which we find deep in the earth. It burns through flesh and bone, eating away until there is nothing left to consume. But then, once it has done its worst, it goes out like any other fire. The ground is safe to walk upon. *Clingfire* will not spring up anew to torment the innocent in years to come. When it is over, it is over. Not so this bonewater plague, or so those who have dealt with it tell us."

"They do not lie," Coryn said. "For so Caitlin of Hali, one I have every reason to trust, has told me."

"She would know," Bernardo said. "For if there were a woman anywhere capable of a Keeper's work, it is Caitlin Elhalyn. Bonewater dust poisons the land itself, so that for generations afterward, no man may travel there in safety or eat anything which has grown or grazed on it. There may be more horrors in years to come. We can only pray we never find out what they are."

"But this Deslucido used it . . . on his own men, on land he claimed as his own . . ." Demiana said in a small, thin voice. She lifted her head, eyes swimming with tears. "Why? How could he do such a thing?"

"Because," Coryn found himself repeating Caitlin's words with unexpected vehemence, "because *he can.* Because there is no one to stop him, and no consequence beyond the loss of troops which can be replaced."

"Surely his own people will rise up against him once they learn of this," she said. "A king is sworn to protect those who serve him, is he not?"

Coryn, who had never thought of himself as particularly knowledgeable in the ways of the world, was struck by her naivete. He had grown up believing the same, for his father had been a just ruler, acutely aware of his responsibilities. Since then, he had learned that power too often came without accountability.

"Who knows if the truth will be told in lands which Deslucido controls?" Coryn said. "He may well place the blame on the Hastur lord, with none to gainsay him."

"But Verdanta is independent once again," Mac said, looking at Coryn. "And other conquered kingdoms may follow."

"They will have to sort out their own fates," Bernardo said with an air of finality.

"I disagree," Coryn said. "We will be drawn into the conflict one way or another. I went to Thendara to plead for neutrality, and I learned that was neither possible nor desirable. For how can we sit up here in our Tower while Darkover burns? Even if we were not bound to Hastur, I would urge us to join his cause. The only way to stop Deslucido and others like him is to make the price of using such terrible weapons so high that not even a madman will risk it."

"What?" Demiana asked in a voice whispery as paper. "Would you have us make worse things?"

"Not a weapon to be used for attack, no." Coryn raked the fingers of one hand through his hair. "What if we could make a weapon—no, let's not call it a weapon, but a shield. Something which, when triggered by an attack would annihilate the attacker. What if we could do that?"

All through the journey back to Neskaya, he had pondered the idea. The only way to stop Deslucido or others like him from using whatever horrible weapon they liked with impunity was to create an immediate and overwhelming backlash. He kept thinking of Bernardo's idea of modifying *clingfire* so that it would require detonation. What if it could made to burn only when triggered by an attack, perhaps incorporated into a covering for a shield or castle wall? But that type of defense would react only to physical impact. *Laran* weapons came in many forms, from compulsion spells to poisoned dust. Their only common element was the use of *laran*, either in their manufacture or delivery. Even if there was no longer any direct *laran* involved, such as the case of ordinary men shooting arrows tipped with *clingfire,* there always remained a residue, a vibration signature.

He explained his ideas to the others, adding, "Those *laran* traces could then become our detonator, as well as the target our defense will focus on."

Bernardo stared at him for a long moment. "Before you came to us, Kieran of Tramontana said you were not afraid to try something new, that vision and courage were your particular strengths. I thought I was taking on an apprentice, someone with whom I could share my innovations. I had no idea how quickly you would take the lead."

Coryn bowed his head. "I do not know if it is even possible. I only know that we must do something, before all of us are drawn into the maelstrom."

Mac stirred, his brows drawn together. "I wonder if the principles underlying a trap-matrix might not be used for the trigger."

"I don't understand," Demiana said. "A trap-matrix is keyed to the mental signature of a specific individual, which is why they have so few usages which are not illegal."

"But it's activated by whatever it's keyed to," Mac said. "The Veil at Arilinn involves a trap-matrix attuned to the presence of *laran*, not any one particular person. We could design one to be so broad as to respond to any trace of *laran* or so narrow that only a certain weapon or a certain origin would set it off."

"Even if we could make the detonator or trigger or whatever it is," Demiana said, heat rising in her voice. "What happens then? How will we avoid destroying ourselves as well as our enemy?"

Coryn hesitated. He had tried several approaches as he had ridden along, all with the idea of taking the energy of the incoming attack and reflecting it back to the sender. But so far, no specific plan had come clear.

"These are worthy questions and call for discussion by the entire Tower," Bernardo said, getting to his feet. "Let us take our time in consideration, not only how to proceed but whether we *should.* We will need the wisdom and talents of everyone here if we are to make wise decisions in this matter."

Demiana shook her head. "I only hope we are doing the right thing, if we do choose to build such a thing. I fear we may be creating what we most wish to avoid, an even more terrible weapon."

"May Aldones light our path," Bernardo murmured. "We can only do our best. The rest is in the hands of the gods."

✦

Sitting in the center of the laboratory, the matrix glittered in shades of blue from the palest aqua to a deep azure that sent up a peculiar buzzing behind Coryn's eyes. He'd worked with artificial matrices before, first at Tramontana and now here at Neskaya, but he had never seen one constructed like this. The dark blue tint, he knew, resulted from a series of channels within the linked stones, designed to redirect incoming energy. This was the third of five layers, Mac explained. The first was the activation device, the "trigger" they had spoken of so many weeks ago. The second concentrated and harmonized energy. The fourth and fifth layers connected the device to banks of *laran* batteries which would amplify the counterattack and target its origin.

"It's something like a ninth-order matrix in complexity, although not in usage," Mac said, and went on into a technical explanation. Normally, it took a complete circle to safely use anything above a fourth- or fifth-level stone, but this one had been designed to be inert until triggered.

"How long before it's finished?" Coryn asked. He'd been working as Keeper in a healing team for the past tenday. Several families from Hastur lands had been exposed to the bonewater dust contamination blown by the winds, and King Rafael had sent them to Neskaya for treatment. Coryn had not slept for more than a few hours every day, struggling to repair the damage to the children's bone marrow cells.

"We've just finished the linkages between the first and second layers," the technician replied. "We'll need the full circle for the next step. Bernardo wants us to wait until things quiet down." He pulled the three layers of insulating silk over the matrix. The light in the laboratory dimmed, and the nagging ache in Coryn's temples eased.

Mac met Coryn's gaze, as if catching the flare of concern for the long period of secrecy. If word of their shield reached Deslucido or any other enemy of Hastur, it might provoke a pre-emptive strike. Deslucido might well decide it was better to destroy the thing now, before it was completed. Coryn had not thought how vulnerable they would be, especially with the influx of strangers.

Coryn's stomach growled, reminding him that he had been working all night. He'd have to replenish the energy he used, and soon. He bade good morning to Mac and went downstairs, where everyone on a regular schedule was enjoying breakfast. The tables were laden with the kind of food Tower workers most needed, dried fruits and honey for a quick lift, nuts and hearty wholemeal porridge, eggs and soft creamy cheeses for sustaining protein. There was no meat for this meal and he wondered if that were because the cooks were once again experimenting or the disorder of the region had made cattle harder to come by. He stirred thick cream into his porridge and poured himself a mug of *jaco.* Across the table, Amalie was spreading her third slice of nut bread with cheese. She ate with a child's appetite, although she was actually a few years older than he.

"I'll be glad when this war is over," she said in between tiny bites. "I can't remember when I've been so tired."

"You never fought on the fire-lines," Coryn said.

She shook her head, tossing back her frothy halo of straw-pale hair. "No. Have you?"

He grinned. "I grew up in Verdanta. Of course I did. Now, that's *really* tired."

"Well . . ." She stretched, her spine popping audibly. "It always seems that whatever crisis of the moment is the worst. That is, until the next one comes along."

Coryn shivered in the sudden thought that the time of war would never end, that the Ages of Chaos would return again and again, no matter what any man did. The only hope was to hold the worst at bay, even as the Hasturs tried to do. An image sprang unbidden to his mind, the flash of Tani's mind in the garden. Whoever she had been, the spirited young girl with all her life before her, would never be again. Even if peace could be hammered out, it might be too late for her—for them both.

His fingers closed around the copper hair pin which he carried in the inner pocket of his robe, in place of his mother's handkerchief.

I had never hoped to see her again, he told himself, echoing her words. *That time was a gift, something to remember. Nothing more.*

34

Taniquel bent over her desk, with the morning sun slanting through the mullioned windows of her sitting room in Hastur Castle, and ran one hand through her hair in exasperation. Two hair pins went flying and a tightly-wound curl dangled free. She'd spent the better part of an hour trying to make sense of her uncle's battered copy of Roald McInery's *Military Tactics,* and her eyes burned with the effort. Unlike most gently-reared young women, she'd been taught to read, although with difficulty. Whoever had written this copy, though, must have had yardfowl scratchings for a model. In a moment of temper, she'd ordered all her ladies to be about their tasks, except one, a demure soul who sat stitching pillow cases with the silver tree emblem of the Hasturs.

With some gratitude, Taniquel looked up at the sound of footsteps in the outer chamber. It was Bruno Reyes, one of the *laranzu'in* from Hali Tower, a kindly-eyed older man with a reserved manner. She knew him slightly from social functions, and suspected he might be Caitlin's special friend.

Taniquel jumped to her feet and greeted him, remembering hastily that Tower folk did not like to be touched casually. She caught the flare of emotion beneath Bruno's serene surface, although she could not name it. "Why, what has happened?"

"News has come from Hali. Caitlin Elhalyn, who serves with the King's army, was able to send a message to them. The Ambervale army is routed—"

Taniquel felt a rush of elation, quickly suppressed.

"—but at great cost."

Now she heard the quiver in his voice. "Please," she said, gesturing to the chairs drawn up around the unlit fireplace. "Sit and tell me the story."

He told it, with a calm dispassion which amazed her. *Bonewater dust!* And Coryn—her heart tripped over itself—Coryn had been there, in danger! She forced herself to listen. The Hastur casualties were relatively light, though many would require care for years to come. Of the *laran* workers, none had taken harm. Now that she could breathe more easily, the rest of the story fell into place.

Clearly, the war continued. Neither her uncle nor that demon Deslucido would be content with one border battle, no matter how dire. She fumed at the prospect of more months sitting here in Thendara, while the fate of her kingdom, her son's inheritance, was decided by others.

"King Rafael wishes you to know that he now marches on Deslucido's headquarters at Acosta. He cannot go directly there, not across the Drycreek area. That will be forbidden for a generation or more to come."

"He goes to free Acosta?" *Without me?* She felt as if she'd suddenly been plunged into fire.

One look at the *laranzu's* face told her that he had caught her emotion, even if he could not read her thoughts. Quickly she collected herself. She thanked him with all the graciousness she could muster and dismissed him.

There was nothing to discuss with anyone, only orders to be given. She was Queen Regent of Acosta, she had given her oath to restore her son and her kingdom, and if her uncle was going to march on Deslucido there in her name, she was going to be at the head of that army.

Roald McInery had described the uses of symbolic gesture to either hearten or demoralize a fighting force. Her strength lay not in arms but in moral right—and perhaps a touch of legend. She remembered the ballad recounting her escape from Deslucido's clutches. By the last rousing choruses, it wouldn't have taken much to drive the listening courtiers into battle for her sake. She would have to speak with the *coridom*, the

Hastur cousin acting in Rafael's stead, and the captain of the guard. But first, she would have a word with the minstrels. . . .

✦

"Majesty?"

Damian's new general, Ranald Vyandal, paused just inside the door to the presence chamber, now the war room, and bowed a shade more deeply than usual. Damian, who had retreated to his private chambers along with Belisar after the memorial for The Yellow Wolf, beckoned him forward.

"Majesty, I bring news— A rider from Verdanta. It has fallen."

"What do you mean, *fallen?*" Damian snapped. He heard the stridency in his own voice.

I'm off my stride. It's this damnable waiting. I need to be out there, seeing and doing for myself.

"Exactly that, *vai dom.*" Vyandal bowed again, still keeping his eyes on Damian. "The castle has been captured and our men there killed or taken prisoner. We think the Leyniers have regained power, but we cannot be sure. The messenger did not stay for the details. He barely escaped as it was. My man is still questioning him."

"Verdanta," Damian murmured, his eyes playing over the maps unrolled on the table and weighted on four corners with the hilts of swords taken in battle. "Why Verdanta?"

"Desperate men are unpredictable, sire," Ranald replied. "However, I don't see them as posing any current threat. They will have their hands full, restoring their own rule."

"Verdanta might be retaken," Belisar suggested. "She is as vulnerable as ever in armed strength, and the man who now leads her, this Eddard, is a blind cripple."

"There remains the question of outside forces, how many and what kind," Ranald said.

Belisar scowled at him. "What do you mean?"

"They didn't free themselves," Damian pointed out patiently. "If they had the power, they would have done so long ago. And please remember, the goal is to conquer Hastur, not a pack of insignificant mountain kingdoms. They are the means, not the end. If someone's going about fomenting rebellion in our provinces, we need to know who . . . and why."

"From our information, Verdanta did have help," said the general. "A small, highly skilled team could have done it. Perhaps they found the means to hire mercenaries, even Aldaran assassins."

It must have been Hastur's doing. Damian's right hand curled into a fist and as quickly released it. Now was not the time to let emotions dictate strategy. He still had scattered outposts throughout Verdanta as well as forces in High Kinnally. He did not think the Leyniers, no matter how foolish, would dare turn their backs on their old enemies.

Let them go, then. As he had pointed out to Belisar, they were valuable only as a means to Acosta, and Acosta he already had.

Outside, thunder crackled. The atmosphere shifted from the sullen brooding of the last few weeks to potential danger. Storm weather, this, flash flood weather, a time when anything could sweep away the plans of men.

Damian went to the windows and threw them open. A fitful breeze carried the metallic tang of lightning. He knew the storm as if it were a fellow creature, a twin. Inhaling great gulps of air, he drew its energy into himself. In his vision, he saw Verdanta and Kinnally, even Hastur itself, as bits of storm-wrack caught up in the looming tempest. *His* tempest, which he would ride to a victory so complete it would, like its earthly namesake, transform the world beyond recognition.

It was time to carry the battle home to Hastur himself, to make him pay for what he had done.

There must be a way to snatch victory from the situation. The army which Belisar had taken was in tatters, with more men ailing every day, draining the resources of the others to care for them. True, there were squadrons of battle-worthy men here at Acosta, and more could be summoned from Ambervale and Linn. But that would take time.

The instinct in Damian's guts told him time was a thing he did not have. Events were moving forward with a momentum all of their own. Like his father's yellow stallion so many years ago, he must either ride this elemental chaos or be trampled by it.

Where sheer might could not prevail, vision and cunning must. The first step was to know the enemy. Rafael had shown his true cowardice at the *Comyn* Council, with his endless arguments about not using *laran* weapons. He was so pompous, telling everyone else how to live, little dreaming his words would come back to him. *His* lands were vast, he had no need for greater territory, *he* could afford to prattle about balance and restraint. What chance did anyone else have, except to use whatever weapons the gods had placed within reach?

Rumail . . . the Deslucido Gift . . . Tramontana Tower . . . and his own army in place when they struck.

Damian began to pace, thinking hard. He could not cross the disputed lands any more than Hastur could, not until the contamination had subsided. But there was more than one route to attack King Rafael. This time, Belisar would be right where he could keep an eye on him. There would be no surprises. A plan took shape in Damian's mind, one which went beyond anything he had so far attempted.

He dismissed the others, saying, "We can retake Verdanta at our leisure, once we have dealt with the greater threat. Strengthen the patrols along those borders. And make sure we leave a sufficient contingent here so that Acosta will still be ours . . . when we return."

Then he summoned Rumail to his chamber. As the *laranzu* listened to his plan, a look of sheer exultation passed over his features.

◆

Damian rode out to the music of pennants snapping in the breeze and harness rings jingling, shod hooves on dust and stone, the rhythmic tread of marching men. His horse, a lanky, mud-colored gelding with a mouth like leather but the strength of ten ordinary mounts, shook its bony head and pranced beneath him, eager to run. Sun glittered on spear points, for the morning was sweet and mild. He inhaled the freshness of the day, his spirits lifting.

As the day wore on, the army settled into a traveling pace. Somewhere behind Damian, a chant sprang up. This far ahead, he could not make out the words and it did not matter. They had the heart for the battle to come. No king could ask for more.

And yet . . . he had ridden from Acosta with a smaller army than he had hoped. As soon as he had formulated his plan, orders had gone out to the minor lords for levies of footmen and remount horses. Far fewer had returned than he had expected, and of those, most had sent only a handful of men, not the number required. He would deal with such disobedience later. He had enough for now, or would soon.

Damian's route took him past two of the largest holdings from whom he had no answer. They would make up what their neighbors failed to supply. He would have his full planned strength when he arrived at the Venza Hills.

The Drycreek border would be closed for a generation or more, due to the residue of the bonewater dust. Even a quick passage across its poisoned length might mean a man's death for years to come. Damian had chosen it as his first battlefield with Hastur because of its history of disputed ownership. Now he needed no such legal justification. He meant to fight the war on Hastur's own holdings. Perhaps, should fortune and Rumail's powers favor him so much, he might even press on to Thendara itself.

Ah, the glory of conquering Darkover's greatest city! From there, he could truly bring about a golden era of peace. But to do that he needed an avalanche of victories.

✦

As his army neared Vairhaven, Damian sent heralds ahead so that a proper welcome could be prepared. He would, he thought with some satisfaction, stay there while the levies were made ready. Supplying his men and their animals with food, drink, and shelter would teach the lord, whatever his name was, his place.

He signaled for Belisar, who had ridden a respectful distance behind, to draw even with him. In every particular, his son's behavior since the aborted border invasion had been obedient, if at times sullen. There had not even been the boy's usual high spirits. He wanted to grab Belisar and shake him, though he sensed that would do no good. Perhaps the boy's confidence had been troubled by defeat; perhaps he had been given too great a command, had outreached his abilities. Well, he would learn, given smaller responsibilities and closer supervision.

They had not gone much farther when one of the heralds spurred his horse back down the road. "Majesty!" He jumped from the saddle and made to kneel in the dust.

"Oh, get up!" Damian snapped. It was no small thing to halt an entire army and certainly not worth it just to mollify one fainthearted messenger.

The man scrambled back into the saddle. "Majesty, they would not receive us! When we arrived, we found the gates shut and when we told them who we were, they shot arrows at us! Teale's horse took one in the shoulder."

How dare they shoot at my herald! How dare they refuse!

"And—and they sent a message."

Anger, hot and silvery, pulsed through Damian. He sat very still in the saddle, his fingers tight on the reins. "What did they say?"

"They said," the man ducked his head, stammering, "they said—"

"Out with it, man!" Damian roared. Belisar flinched visibly. The mud-colored gelding reared on its hind legs for an instant.

The herald's words came in a rush. "They said they would no longer bow to an unlawful usurper and that even now, their rightful king, Julian Acosta, is on the way to take back the throne which is rightfully his."

"Julian Acosta? Who in Zandru's name is he?"

The herald flushed darkly and stammered something incoherent. Belisar said tightly, "The son of Taniquel Hastur-Acosta, the one born after her escape."

"The bastard infant?"

"She claims him to be the legitimate son of King Padrik Acosta," Belisar said.

"I don't give a scorpion-ant's nit what she claims!" Damian snorted. "Where is this boy wonder and his mighty army now? It will be a satisfaction to smear out his paltry existence. Never mind."

Damian turned to his son. "Belisar, be my counselor in this. How would you advise me to deal with this insolence?"

For an instant, some unreadable emotion played across Belisar's features. "I think—I think such rebellion must be crushed. If we allow this one small holding to defy us, then word will quickly spread that we have gone soft as Dry Towns traders, and we will have a dozen Verdantas to deal with."

The senior quartermaster, who had ridden a little to the side, motioned for permission to speak. "In addition, we cannot afford to pass up such a rich resource. The farther into Hastur territory we extend, the more serious the problems of supply lines will become. The lands are rich . . ."

Belisar's chin shot up. "The Hasturs would have no scruples about taking whatever they want. Look at how they tricked us at the border! They have no honor on the battlefield—or in the bedroom. Father, we must use every weapon to defeat them. We cannot afford to diminish our strength when we go up against such an enemy."

He has the right of it. The dream of uniting Darkover will never come to a man who is weak or irresolute. Yet Damian paused, for he had never before permitted his men to loot from field or holding.

Perhaps I have been too soft, as Belisar says.

Nodding in satisfaction, Damian signaled for the trumpeter to call a halt. "We will camp here this night. Tell the captains they may forage from field and village. Seize whatever you need. The best way to handle even the smallest hint of rebellion is to make the price too high. Tomorrow we will take this upstart castle and let the baby king do his worst!"

✦

Vairhaven, little more than a fortified manor house, fell the same day, despite a heated skirmish at the front door. It sat atop a knoll with a view of the wheat fields and a river sparkling below. Heartleaf ivy covered its walls and ferns crowded the riverbanks, giving the place the air of a green bower, cool and inviting after the dusty road. Within minutes of their arrival, the thirsty horses had waded out into the river, churning mud and trampling the delicate purple water-flowers.

It was, Damian thought, a perfect location, with forage and water for the horses, space enough to establish a proper encampment. He put Belisar in charge of setting up the latrines and burying the few dead.

Comfortably ensconced in the one good chair in the central hall, Damian had the Vair lordling brought forth. Vair was a man of middle years, dressed as if he intended to join the fight himself. Now his face was dusky, congested, eyes never still. The loose skin along his jaw and neck quivered. He refused to kneel until Damian's guards forced him down.

I should have him hamstrung so that he can never stand before his betters again, Damian thought, and then gave the order to hang him and any sons. *The price of resistance must be seen by all to be too high.*

Vair blustered and made threats as they dragged him out. Damian, eyeing the crowd which gathered at the gates, hoped word would spread quickly. It would make his job that much easier.

By the time the Ambervale forces marched out of Vairhaven, the *kyorebni* had picked the lordling's corpse almost clean. So too were the fields and most of the surrounding orchards. When a party of farmers had approached to complain, saying they had done nothing to deserve such treatment, Damian snorted and ordered the right hand of their headman cut off. Then he conscripted all the men between the ages of fifteen and fifty to the ranks of his foot soldiers.

"It is the way of war," he said to Belisar once they were on the trail.

For the next tenday, no one could doubt Damian's victory as one petty lordship after the other surrendered bloodlessly to his forces. Yet, too frequently, the lord turned out to be some aged grandfather, half blind and palsied, and once, a woman. Pock-faced, simpering, and none too clean in her personal habits, she offered to share Damian's bed as a conquest of war. He declined. Conscripts were few and either too old or too crippled to be of any use. No decent horses could be found.

✦

Scouts brought news to Damian's army as it made its way toward the Venza Hills which rose like the backbone of an ancient monster along the eastern horizon. Rumors of Queen Taniquel's return reached them daily. Some said she had a thousand men, ten thousand; others that the very beasts of the field bowed down before her; still others that Aldones himself had come down and blessed her cause.

> *"And where is the tyrant*
> *Who fights with treachery and lies?*
> *Darkness falls, honor dies*
> *At his foul approach.*
> *But up from the ashes*
> *A bird of unquenchable fire,*
> *She comes to us, she comes to us,*
> *Blessed by Aldones' everlasting light . . .*
> *Lift up your head, O Acosta,*
> *Bound in sorrows and blood—*
> *The new day is coming!*
> *Lift up your voice, O Acosta,*
> *Lift it up in every land.*
> *Huzzah! Huzzah!*
> *Weep with joyful heart!*
> *Lift up your arms, O Acosta!*
> *Every man's hand*
> *A blow for freedom!"*

Damian rained curses upon Taniquel Hastur-Acosta and also on himself, for not pursuing her or finding some way of forcing the *Comyn*

Council to turn her over when he had her within sight. But upon reflection, he realized that the result would have been the same. Hastur would have found some other excuse to get involved, once his own interests were threatened. Sooner or later, they must meet on the battlefield. This time, it would be on his own terms.

News came also of armed bands making their way through the Hellers foothills. One of the men Damian had left behind at Vairhaven clattered into camp on an old farm horse, his head shaved bald and painted blue. His hands had been lashed to the saddle and a note pinned to his tunic,

So shall we deal with all tyrants!

It was signed, "The Free Men of Acosta."

When the note was brought before the war tent, Belisar roared out that such rebellion must be put down immediately, but Damian managed to calm him down.

"They pose no real threat to us. They do these things only to slow our progress. If we take the time to deal with them, we give Hastur that same time to advance even further, to meet us closer to our own territory instead of his own. Our advantage lies in our speed, our ability to choose our own battlefield. Meanwhile, I will have General Vyandal double the scouting patrols and night watch. We may have a few skirmishes here and there, but we will not be delayed."

The next day, the vanguard of his army approached the Greenstone River, a minor tributary of the Valeron. Trees clustered along the banks on either side, narrow ribbons of green. To avoid a long detour to the treacherous fords downstream, General Vyandal had suggested the easier route over the stone bridge, even though to cross it, the men could march only four abreast on foot or two on horse. This would leave them strung out and vulnerable. Moreover, the brushy trees gave excellent cover for an ambush.

Damian ordered a slow, careful reconnaissance. He sent mounted scouts up and down the river, but they saw no sign of any body of rebels. When they approached the bridge, however, they gave a warning.

Damian spurred his horse to the front, followed closely by Vyandal and his personal guard. The Ambervale soldiers halted an arrow's flight away from the bridge. On the far side, a party of men raised their bows and shouted for them to halt. Some of them stood on the stone railings. They wore woodsmen's clothing in shades of brown and green, difficult to see in the dappled shade. An arrow quivered in the matted grasses in front of the hooves of the foremost horseman. He was still struggling for control of his white-eyed, snorting mount.

"That was a warning!" One of the ruffians, a man with a full black beard, called out. "Come no closer! Go back to where you belong!"

The man atop the left side railing drew his bow and sighted along the arrow. He was more boy than man with his slender build and cropped russet hair, but Damian had no doubt that his was the arrow and that he had placed it exactly where he meant to.

"What do they think they're doing?" he asked aloud, caught between irritation and bemusement. "Trying to become the stuff of legends?"

"Dead legends, sire," said Vyandal. "But not stupid ones. We can charge them over the bridge, but not fast enough to prevent them from shooting down the first rows of horses and creating a nice hurdle for the rest of us to cross."

For a flicker, Damian wished he had not sent Rumail on his mission. It would be satisfying, and so much simpler, to boil the brains of these miscreants in their skulls or turn their arrows into venomous snakes.

"We'll have to make a wall of shields," Vyandal said.

Damian nodded assent. It would be slower, and there would undoubtedly be a mess of hand-to-hand fighting at the end of it. As the first ranks of foot soldiers inched across the bridge with their shields forming a barrier, the archers let loose a half-hearted volley and retreated beyond the trees, where their own horses were picketed.

Once a foothold was established on the far bank to cover the slow passage of the army, Vyandal called forth a unit of his own archers. In the field beyond the river, the bandits circled, aiming when they could and occasionally hitting a target. One of them, the red-haired youth, was wounded in the thigh, but not badly enough to take him from the fight. They began taunting Deslucido's men, hooting at them and daring them to follow. Once a horseman rushed them for a few paces before a rain of arrows sent his mount rearing in panic. Whenever the Ambervale bowmen would move into position, they would retreat to a safe distance and continue their obscene calls.

"They're making fools of us!" Belisar cried. "Get rid of them!"

Damian, who had been watching the action, shook his head. The archers were an annoyance, true. Their major power was to sting, not to harm. It would be easy to send out enough men to chase them away or run them down. But that would take time, and their harm was their ability to slow him down. Some of these ruffians might even have been the ones who retook Verdanta. Yes, that would make sense—small bands of men, preferably the pick of the seasoned veterans, making their way through the Hellers foothills and into Acosta.

They hoped to pin me down before I could mobilize another attack, but I stole the march on them, Damian thought. *Like a spear, like an arrow, I will outrun them.*

The crossing took hours, for the rest of the day. The archers melted away with the gathering shadows of nightfall.

◆

Damian pushed his forces across the remaining stretch of Acosta fields and into the Venza Hills. As they came into the funnel pass, the heavens seemed to gather themselves for the battle. Clouds swept white and gleaming, the sky a sheet of polished silver. Radiance saturated the air. No breeze stirred, but the army made its own storm. Damian poised on its crest, glorying in the sense of vast, unstoppable power. He had not only men and swords, but the rightness of the day, that vision which made victory inevitable. Darkover *must* be united and these petty bickering squabbles put to an end.

A mote of blackness broke the brilliant sky, no—two. Squinting, Damian made them out to be birds. Large hawks, he thought, or scavenger *kyorebni*, scenting the battle to come. They descended, hovered, then dropped even farther so that he could make out their pinions outstretched to catch the air currents. For a long moment, they hardly seemed to move. He held his breath, remembering his own boyhood dreams of flying. Then one plunged to begin a sweeping arc over the army.

The bird's smooth flight broke, as if it staggered. Wings folded, it plummeted to earth. Damian wheeled his horse in the direction of its fall.

Ranald Vyandal stood holding the bird, a huge ugly thing with mottled naked skin over its head and neck. An arrow jutted from its breast. It must have died instantly.

"It's a sentry-bird." Vyandal's voice came thick and dark. He looked up, to the now-empty sky. "The Hasturs know where we are. They cannot be more than a day or two away."

Belisar's horse, catching his surge of excitement, danced beneath him. "Then we will meet them all the sooner!"

"We go no farther today." Damian reined in his prancing mount, yanking the horse's head up and back. "We make camp here. It is time for the second part of our plan."

That dusk, Damian sat in conference with Ranald Vyandal and his senior lieutenants. Camp chairs were drawn up in his tent and guards posted to prevent any eavesdropping. Belisar sat in one corner, face unreadable in the shadows.

"We had hoped for a larger army at this point," Ranald said.

Damian propped his elbow on one arm of his chair, leaning his chin on his cupped hand, eyes absently following the pattern of the travel-stained Ardcarran carpet. "Our numbers will be enough. We will attack from a quarter Hastur is *not* expecting." He had kept his true plans secret until now, even from his general. He could not chance any word of it leaking to the Hasturs or even his own men. The time had come to let his officers know what a glorious victory awaited them.

"Sire?" Ranald Vyandal blinked.

"I bet it has something to do with Uncle Rumail," said Belisar.

"Indeed, before we left Acosta, I dispatched *Dom* Rumail for Tramontana Tower with a picked escort, a sort of enforcement team, if you will. Just to make sure there is no problem of obedience to our will. And our will is that he be placed as Keeper there, with absolute authority to issue orders in my name."

Vyandal, however, went pale. "Majesty, you do not mean to bring the Towers into this war?" In his eyes, Damian read the barely-healed memories of his last battle with *laran* weapons.

"I do not mean to use bonewater dust," Damian reassured him. "But a far more powerful strategy. Before, we could only use those armaments which the Towers could physically produce. Yes, I plan to bring Tramontana into this conflict, but in a very different way. A way that will blind the Hasturs' advantage and turn the battle with far fewer of our own men lost."

He watched the shifting expressions on their faces as he outlined the plan, astonishment and consternation giving way to devotion. These men would follow him anywhere, die at his slightest word, for he had handed them a victory such as the world had never known.

What he proposed had been done before, but on a very limited basis, only by small *laran* circles who traveled with their armies. Their powers were limited by their numbers and distance from their targets. Rumail's genius showed how the strength of an entire, fully functional Tower circle could be brought into battle, no matter how far away. For in the Overworld, that vast mental plane, the power of the mind reigned supreme. It was from that bizarre and terrible place Deslucido would launch his true assault.

"As soon as we are in position, it will not matter what the Hasturs know or how many more men they have. They will fall like ripened wheat beneath our scythe. Nothing they do can stop us now."

35

Rafael Hastur's army made its way along the circuitous route from the Drycreek area to the Venza Hills and the border with Acosta. It moved slowly as supply lines were reestablished and the sick men tended to. About halfway there, Taniquel joined him with her heavily-armed escort. This was no longer a simple border dispute, she pointed out in her missive, informing him that she was coming. The goal was now the liberation of Acosta and she, as its Queen Regent, had every right to be in the forefront.

When she went to greet her uncle the morning after her arrival in camp, she found him scowling as he sat in his favorite camp chair. In front of him, two men knelt while a handful of others, subordinates by their bowed heads and awkward hands, stood a respectful distance away. Their scabbards hung empty from their belts.

As Taniquel approached, Rafael looked up, his expression lightening. The kneeling men turned, and she recognized the elder of them. Esteban—Esteban of Greenhills.

A little shock went through her. It had been Esteban who led the expedition to Thendara to plead for relief against Damian's rule. He and the other Acosta lords had been so desperate, they determined to pledge themselves to a foreign king rather than continue to see their land pillaged by Delucido's tyranny. But Rafael had refused to hear them, and in his place, they had found her.

I swore to them I would return and free Acosta. That was the day my life truly ceased to be mine.

Joy blazed across the old man's face. "My Queen! We have found you at last! We all heard the rumors, but dared not hope at first. Then came word that you yourself had taken to the field." He bowed his head, eyes gleaming, and reached for the hem of her gown. "Lead us! We are yours!"

Taniquel gently pulled her skirts away. "Please, good sir. Get up. This groveling is not seemly before the Hastur lord." She turned to her uncle, eyes questioning.

"It seems," Rafael said in a dry voice, "that your reputation has outsped you. These men have been searching for you. They wish to enlist in your cause."

Taniquel had no armies of her own, let alone any grasp of how to command one effectively. But how could she say so to these men who looked to her with eyes brimming with hope?

She was Queen Regent of Acosta, mother of the one true heir, and she had been Queen in her own right before that, Taniquel reminded herself. She was kin to Kings and gods. The blood of Hastur, Son of Aldones, Lord of Light flowed in her veins.

She drew herself up, head high, shoulders squared. "How many men do you bring me?"

Esteban named a number, men from his own province and more from his neighbors. Some, she guessed, had been fugitives under Deslucido. All would be sorely missed come harvest time. She had half a mind to send them all back where they would do the most good. But she could not throw away the gift of such loyalty or expose them to Deslucido's retaliation.

Taniquel inclined her head toward where Rafael lounged in his chair like a throne, amusement playing across his eyes. "There sits my uncle, who is my champion in this war. In this campaign, I am guided by him. Are you willing to place yourselves under his orders, to march with his own soldiers against the tyrant of Ambervale?"

Esteban glanced from her to Rafael. Emotion twisted his features, though he held himself proudly. "Your Majesty, *vai domna,* we are yours to command."

"And you, Uncle," Taniquel said, raising her voice. "Will you accept the loan of these fighting men, to lead and care for as your own, for the duration of this campaign and without any commitment of future fealty?"

He nodded almost invisibly and she felt the flush of his approval. "I will, my niece."

"Then," she turned back to Esteban and the others, "I command you to go with King Rafael's officers and do as they bid you. I commend you for your service." With her eyes, she dismissed them.

In a few minutes, the tent was cleared, the Acosta men directed to their new units. After that, there was no discussion of her going back.

As the army got underway again, Taniquel found herself subject to restrictions. It was one thing to travel alone or in command of a small armed party, and quite another to be in the midst of such a large body of soldiers. She knew nothing of the routines and discipline of a traveling army, and she did not want to take men away from their necessary duties to dance attendance on her. Since there was little for her to do except sit quietly while generals discussed things, she spent most of her days with the *laran* workers.

Trailed by two bodyguards, Taniquel and Graciela followed Edric, who was mounted, a short distance from the main army encampment, watching him fly the sentry-birds from a little grassy knoll. The two women chatted comfortably as they stretched their legs in the morning sunshine, each happy to have found a friend. Caitlin had returned to Thendara to oversee the care of those sickened by the bonewater dust. Her place had been taken by two men from Hali whom Taniquel did not know.

Graciela's initial shyness was wearing off, revealing a surprisingly self-confident young woman. She was the fourth out of seven daughters of an impoverished but noble family, and her family had been only too happy to send her off for Tower training at the slightest hint of talent.

"I had thought I might become a Priestess of Avarra," she'd confided to Taniquel, "but I would miss the fellowship of men. This is much better."

For the last hour, Edric had described the location and arrangement of Deslucido's forces with a detail that she could not have imagined. Had anyone cared to enquire, even the number of latrine ditches and cooking pots could be known. Rafael's aide, a huge blond man whose skin had sunburned badly and was now peeling away over new pink skin, had taken notes and consulted his maps, then ridden back to deliver the news.

"Aaieeeh!" With a cry, Edric jerked as if struck. His limbs stiffened. The horse beneath him flinched and jigged sideways.

"Catch him!" Graciela cried, as Edric swayed in the saddle.

Taniquel, who was on foot, rushed to the *laranzu's* horse, holding out her arms. He fell slowly, as if through honey. His weight dropped onto her. For an instant she staggered, then caught her balance and braced herself to lower him to the ground.

Graciela knelt at Edric's side. His face had gone pasty, his body inert. Taniquel could not see any movement in his chest.

"Is he breathing?" she asked anxiously. *And what happened?*

The younger woman's face went slack, her eyes losing their focus. Her hands skimmed the air just above his body. With that odd *laran* sense of hers, Taniquel felt Graciela sink into rapport.

Graciela kept one hand, fingers spread wide, bare inches over Edric's chest. The other twisted the neckline of her gown where it covered a pendant on a heavy silver chain. Power crackled through the air between the girl's hand and the man's body. Taniquel imagined tiny blue lightnings crossing the narrow space.

Edric gave a convulsive shudder. He gasped for air. The long muscles in his neck stood out like cords.

Sighing loudly, Graciela sat back. "The parting—" she said, her voice reedy with tension, "—it was so sudden."

Then, seeing the look of puzzlement on Taniquel's face, Graciela added, "He was linked to the sentry-bird when it was killed. An archer from King Damian's army must have spotted it. It is bad enough for a handler to lose a bird he has worked with. But when his mind is linked to it, he *becomes* the bird—do you understand?—and if the tie is severed then, it is like being wrenched from his own life. I have heard of *leroni* who have suffered such a shock and become lost in the Overworld, so disoriented they could not find their way back to their own bodies." She brushed Edric's tousled hair back from his forehead.

"Edric . . ." At her touch and the sound of her voice, his eyes opened. Blinking, his mouth rounded into an "O" of surprise. He seemed not to know either of them, glancing from one to the other. Then he came to himself, eyes softening. He reached out to grasp Graciela's hand.

"It was fortunate I was at hand," she said briskly.

"Will he be all right?" Taniquel asked.

"He must rest," the girl's voice turned clinical. "And he must not fly the other bird for several days, perhaps as much as a tenday. That he recovered consciousness so quickly is a good sign."

And I thought her a simple country girl because of her age and lineage! Taniquel scolded herself. In her own time, she suspected, Graciela would be as intimidating as Lady Caitlin.

"If the bird was recognized by one of Damian's men and killed for it . . ." Taniquel murmured to herself. She got to her feet, not bothering to brush the grass and tawny seeds from her skirts. "My uncle must know of this."

She hurried away, back toward her uncle's tent.

✦

A knot of men, including Rafael's personal bodyguard, waited outside the royal tent. Rafael, as usual, had drawn back the door drape and sides, leaving little more than a pavilion.

By their expressions, the bodyguards recognized Taniquel as she approached. Their posture remained wary, hands resting on the hilts of their swords, eyes restless. Since Rafael had declared her Queen Regent of Acosta, they had treated her with additional deference, so they did not challenge her now.

"Please conduct me to the King," she said politely.

The bodyguard sketched a half-bow and stepped back for her to approach. She dropped all decorum and darted to her uncle's side.

"I come from Edric, where he has been flying the sentry-birds."

"Yes," he nodded, composed and somewhat distracted. "My aide's been bringing me reports all morning."

"Not ten minutes ago, Edric's bird was shot and killed by Deslucido's archers. Without Graciela's prompt aid, he would have perished along with it."

"I am sorry. The bird is a great loss."

"The bird is nothing! He *knows!* Deslucido knows we have been spying on him!"

Rafael got to his feet in a burst of energy. "We must act at once, before he can regroup, or everything we have learned will be useless." His eyes glittered like those of a cloud leopard which has scented its prey.

"We will attack and we will keep attacking until he has nowhere left to run. And then we will put a final end to this menace."

✦

Taniquel had not realized an army could move as swiftly as Rafael's did now. Everything seemed to be happening at once. Officers shouted orders as messengers darted throughout the camp, horses were saddled, tents taken down, gear laden, and bows and spears prepared. The first units of horsemen, Rafael's vanguard, formed up even before the last carts were loaded.

After the sowing of the bonewater dust, Rafael had good reason to fear another trap. Edric, as senior *laranzu,* must therefore ride at the head of the army to scout out signs of *laran* weaponry. He looked pale but able to ride. Muscles made iron ripples along his jaw.

Edric left the remaining sentry-bird behind with Graciela. Taniquel thought that whatever reason Edric might have once had to hate Deslucido, he had a greater one now. She nodded to him as they rode together to the vanguard.

Rafael had not argued with Taniquel's demand to ride with the army, and for this, she was grateful. By his own command, her colors flew at the forefront, a reminder that their mission was to restore her son as rightful king of Acosta.

Now as she cantered her easy-gaited white mare past the assembled men, Taniquel caught their expressions, snatches of words. Since they'd left Thendara, whispers had flown through the camp and across the countryside. *Queen Taniquel, come to fulfill her promise, come to free us all!* She had already become a legend, larger than life. Let them think what they liked, so long as they fought bravely.

Rafael gave the signal to advance. Trumpets sounded, and the first ranks surged forward. Taniquel's horse leaped beneath her. Miles sped by, trot and canter, keeping the horses fresh.

Deslucido's army had withdrawn from the funnel pass where the sentry-bird had last reported it, but the Hastur forces made their way uphill, just beyond the pass, to close with them. As the Ambervale army came into sight, Rafael ordered Taniquel to a safer position, to the side and up a little rise. Edric came with her, along with a team of hand-picked bodyguards. She couldn't see much after the first few minutes for all the dust and confusion. From one instant to the next, she could make out the individual war cries of men, some of them yelling *Acosta! Acosta!*, horses neighing, hooves pounding, swords clashing.

"Can you see anything?" she shouted to Edric, although she could hardly hear her own voice.

He shook his head. As she watched, a pattern of movement gradually emerged. The black-and-white banners drew back while her uncle's colors surged forward. Screams grew fewer. They must be giving way, on the run. What if it were a trap?

She glanced at Edric, who had closed his eyes in concentration. Something prickled the nape of her neck like a half-remembered thought. She felt his mind spreading out, questing. Finding nothing.

As one minute melted into the next, she knew she'd seen rightly. The Ambervale forces no longer fought to hold ground but only to cover their retreat. They moved in an orderly way, without any trace of panic. It was a calculated move, not a rout. Taniquel did not know *how* she knew this, unless she were picking it up from Edric's mind. She had expected more fear, less organization, from Deslucido's men, but what did she know of warfare? Perhaps all retreating armies were so deliberate.

Yet . . . she had studied the reports of the border battle, how the Hastur units had done exactly the same thing, withdrawing in order to lure their enemies along the valley where they could be surrounded.

Hastur trumpets sounded the advance. Despite her misgivings, exhilaration swept through Taniquel. She wanted to shout, to draw a sword and brandish it. It was all she could do to keep to her place instead of charging along with her uncle's men. Shortly afterward, word came for her to proceed along with the army. It felt wonderful to be moving again, to be doing something.

Deslucido's forces seemed to melt in front of the advancing Hastur forces. Rafael's generals kept their men in check to prevent an outright chase. A trap was still possible, even with Edric clearing every step of the way. It would be too risky, one of the lieutenants explained to Taniquel, to spread their forces over miles of territory, unable to draw up in any decent formation. Their rear guard, wagons and foot soldiers, followed behind. By the time they made camp, their enemy had outstripped them.

The pass opened into a flat, rough valley ringed by the remnants of badly eroded canyon walls. A stream made its way along a wash that must turn into a flood in bad weather. There was a little forage for the horses.

The cooling air awoke the pungent smell of crushed grass. Rainbirds called from a bedraggled copse.

The camp settled into the familiar nighttime routine. Horses stamped and nickered along the picket lines. Taniquel handed her mount to the grooms and made her way to the tent which she shared with Graciela. It had, like Rafael's own, come ahead of the rest on its own luggage cart. Her servants were already unpacking the small comforts afforded by her rank, a pallet bed, two cushions, a strip of carpet and a narrow leather chest containing a change of underclothing, cosmetics, hairbrushes, basin, and scented soaps for bathing. The water had not yet been carried in.

Taniquel paced the length of the tent, restless with a dull pressure in her head. She massaged her temples and the back of her neck, but found no relief. Despite the excitement of the day, she itched with inactivity. There was nothing for her to do. The grooms would tend to her horse. Rafael would plan the next strategy with his officers. Graciela was off with Edric and the sentry-bird.

It was improper for her to stroll through the camp, chatting with her own men, the way Rafael might do. In Acosta, she would have given propriety scant notice, but her uncle had spoken sharply to her about the necessity of royal dignity.

"Your name and the legend which is growing up about you is essential to your cause," he said. Grudgingly, she'd admitted she could not throw away such an advantage for an evening's diversion, and until now she had not regretted her promise.

Two moons shone in the sky where more stars appeared every passing minute. Taniquel followed her escort to her uncle's tent. He had invited her to dine with him, as was their custom so far. Now, Rafael looked tired as he gave her his usual courteous greeting. The lantern light deepened the lines around his mouth and eyes.

He is no longer a young man. How much he had changed since she was a girl playing hoyden in his castle. The campaign had been harder on him than she realized. The years, or perhaps the recent stresses, had pared him to wiry leanness. His hair and neatly trimmed beard were more silver than red.

With a pang of guilt, she thought, *He could have stayed safely in Thendara and left me to my fate.* But he had not gone to war or even sent one of his sons merely to save Acosta. He went because Damian Deslucido was a threat to all of Darkover.

"Uncle," she said impulsively, "will we truly be able to put an end to him? What if he keeps running? What if he locks himself up in Acosta?"

Rafael did not answer immediately. He dismissed his servant and took up the trencher of stew, a soldier's mixture of grain, parched and then simmered with dried meat and whatever vegetables could be obtained locally. In this case, chunks of something yellow like carrots laced the mixture. It smelled sour, but when she took a bite, the mixture tasted sweet and slightly spicy. Warmth spread through her body and filled her head, easing the ache.

After they had eaten, Rafael said, "Now, then. The first rule of campaigning is that things change, often much faster than any of us would like. You never know what's going to happen until you get there. The second rule is that no plan, no matter how carefully made, survives the first battle."

At the tone of his voice, Taniquel relaxed; he was in a good humor.

"I have pledged to follow Deslucido wherever he goes, to—as you phrase it—put a final end to him. I did not specify how or when. Such things are not given to us to know. Here, have some more wine." He refilled her glass. She could not remember having drunk the first one, but the garnet red was a good vintage and went down smoothly. Her belly felt full and warm. With every sip, the headache became easier to ignore.

The lanterns burned softly. Outside, men's voices muted to a drone. From time to time, they raised in song and she found herself humming along to a tune whose words she should not, as a gently brought up lady, know. Sprawled in his chair, Rafael began a long rambling story about three Dry Towners and a *leronis*. Taniquel had heard it, or rather overheard it, in the armory at Acosta when the men had not known she was there. It was obscene, of course, but there was something *wrong* about her uncle, her mother's brother, telling it to her. The prohibition against sexual relations, even jokes, between generations, still ran strong, a remembrance of the time of group marriages when any man of her father's age could have actually been her father.

She put her goblet down on the little folding table with such force that the wine sloshed over the sides. The goblet tilted and then, before she could grab for it, fell over. Wine splashed across Rafael's lap. He straightened up as if stung.

Taniquel clapped both hands over her mouth. What was wrong with them? Why were they acting this way? Whatever had possessed them to get *drunk?*

Humiliated, she dashed to the door flap, which had been tied back to admit the evening breezes. She ran a few steps into the camp before coming to a halt.

Night air lay thick and cool over the camp. In all directions, tents and firepits stretched out in the familiar pattern. Gone was the peaceful hum of conversation, the snatches of song. A man's voice growled out a curse and a short distance away, another let out an inarticulate howl.

How dare they? How dare they? Fury pounded through her brain.

White-hot pain lanced through her temples. She staggered under its impact. Her breath came hot and ragged between clenched teeth. An invisible weight, crushing and inexorable, pressed in on her, brought her to her knees. Fingers digging into her scalp, she rocked back and forth. "Avarra—Dark Lady—help me!"

As if in response, memory flooded her. She had felt this searing pain in her skull once before, when Deslucido's sorcerer led the attack on Acosta Castle. All that morning, the sensation of urgency had built and built. It ended at last in the compulsion spell to keep the gates locked. Until she realized what was happening, she had been as ensorceled as any of them.

Laran attack!

Now as she clambered to her feet, she remembered the hours of restlessness through the afternoon, the vague aching which escalated into this headache. Wine had dulled it, but only for a time. Or perhaps that sense of well-being was part of the attack, designed to lull them all into complacency.

Tell . . . Uncle Rafael . . . He must . . . take action . . . be ready . . . for whatever follows . . .

Another jolt sent her stumbling, tripping over the hem of her gown, clutching the tent pole to steady herself. She grabbed fistfuls of skirt and yanked them up, out of the way. Anger rushed through her—at Rafael, at Edric, at everyone in this loathsome camp. Her fingers twisted the fabric into knots. Adrenaline sizzled through her veins.

No! Fight the spell, not your own people! That's what they want—for us all to be at each other's throats!

Taniquel bit down hard on her lower lip, using the pain to keep her thoughts clear. From inside the tent came a cry of inarticulate rage. There, within the pool of lantern light, Rafael and his paxman, Gerolamo, wrestled. They strained against each other, grappling, fists pounding. One of them bellowed curses—she could not be sure which, the voice was so distorted.

She dashed toward them, resisting the urge to snatch up an eating knife from the table and plunge it into the back of the nearer man.

"Stop it!" she screamed, but their roaring drowned her words. They were beyond hearing, beyond all reason.

The struggling men pivoted, scrambling for leverage and clawing at each other. As the light fell across them, she saw Gerolamo clench one huge hand around Rafael's throat. The tendons of his fingers stood out with effort. Rafael's face contorted. No sounds issued from his opened mouth. He staggered, arms flailing, eyes bulging.

Taniquel still held her skirts high off the ground. With all the power she could muster, she aimed a kick at Gerolamo's back at kidney level.

"Yaaah!" Gerolamo howled. His back arched spasmodically. As his body tipped backward, his knees buckled slightly.

In a flash, Taniquel saw his hand loosen on Rafael's neck. She pivoted and stamped down on the back of one bent knee just as Padrik had taught her, using her weight to drive downward. The knee gave way. Gerolamo's body slammed into her, and she lost her balance, going down in a flurry of skirts.

Something struck the side of her head. Gerolamo's fist, she thought. Her vision whirled sickeningly. She tried to sit up. His heavy body pinned her legs. For a moment, she thought he had shifted his attack to her. Then he rolled free and lunged once more at Rafael.

Taniquel scrambled to her feet, tangled in yards of silk but managing to stay upright. A hem ripped.

Rafael crouched in a fighter's stance, sword held at ready. The lantern light burnished the steel to molten gold.

"Have done, traitor!" he rumbled.

"No!" Taniquel cried. "Uncle, no! It's not Gero! This is Deslucido's doing, this anger!"

He turned his face to her, his features congested with dark, wild light. "And as for you, little minx—"

Gerolamo rushed at him, unheeding the blade aimed at his heart. Taniquel threw herself at Gerolamo. She knocked him sideways. They both went down again. Gerolamo rolled on the carpet, clutching one shoulder, bellowing.

Taniquel rolled free. She must have shoved him safely out of the way. No mortally wounded man could make so much noise.

Gerolamo hauled himself to his feet, still holding his arm. Dark blood flowed over his fingers and down Rafael's bright blade. Its pungent smell filled the tent.

"By all the gods, what have I done?" Rafael's voice shook. His eyes blinked, like a man emerging from a nightmare. The sword dipped.

Gerolamo toppled to his knees in front of Rafael. "*Vai dom,* kill me now, I beg you. I do not deserve to live—to have laid hands on you—I tried to—"

"Oh, stop it, both of you!" Taniquel snapped. "We don't have time for this! We've got to pull ourselves together. It was some kind of *laran* attack, don't you see, that made us turn on each other. Who knows what Deslucido will try next?"

As if in reply, another invisible wave of the mental energy swept through the tent. This time, Taniquel felt it as a physical blow. She wavered on her feet. The men's faces hardened, eyes gone cold. Before she could summon words, could remind them again that whatever they were feeling wasn't real but only a sending from Deslucido's sorcerers, Rafael shook his head and raised one hand. The starstone hidden in the folds of his shirt glimmered. He seemed to grow taller, straighter. She remembered that like all Hasturs, he had been tested for *laran* as a youth, and had trained, at least minimally, at a Tower.

Gerolamo fastened his eyes upon his lord as a drowning man toward the shore. His face paled and colored, but he held firm.

"Gero, get that arm bound up. Then find me. I will have need of you shortly," Rafael said.

The glittery panic in Gerolamo's eyes vanished. He did not flinch when Rafael turned and plunged into the night.

Gerolamo glanced down at the blood-smeared hand over his wound. "By the time I've knotted a kerchief over this, he'll have half the camp organized."

"Sit down. This will take only a moment." Taniquel took the eating knife and slashed a long strip from her ripped hem. A few strokes cut away the worst of the bloodied shirt. Luckily, the cut was not deep and had bled freely at first. The blood was already beginning to clot. She poured the rest of the wine over it.

"Yow! Woman, that stings!"

"If you were a *cristoforo*, it would be just penance for your sins." Taniquel wrapped the hem strip twice around his arm and knotted the ends, making it tight enough to compress the wound edges together and yet loose enough not to cut off circulation. "Off with you!" When he turned to say something, whether thanks or yet another apology, she shoved him bodily out of the tent.

36

Taniquel stood alone in the tent. While she'd had something to do, some focus for her thoughts, she had been able to resist the relentless pressure. Now thoughts crowded in on her, pounded through her mind.

He would seize your throne, he has betrayed you . . . None of them can be trusted . . . They deserve to die . . . Kill them all . . . Kill . . .

"NO!" A voice cried out, distorted but still recognizably a woman's. She lowered her hands from her ears, with no memory of having covered them. It was her own voice.

Take a knife . . . Kill . . . Kill . . .

"Merciful Evanda, mother of life, protect me!"

The cry, torn from her soul, brought a measure of respite. But in the end, she knew, as long as she had no better defense than her own weak prayers, the voices would win. She must fight the spell with action, just as she had at the gates of Acosta. Only this time, she must not be too late.

She strode to the opening of the tent and grasped the door flap. Outside, she heard the sounds of men struggling, steel clashing, screams and war cries. The darkness seethed with blood lust.

Her fingers dug into the canvas and for a heartbeat she could not move. Every instinct urged her to stay hidden, a rabbit-horn in a pack of

wolves gone mad. What could she hope to accomplish out there? She
had no weapon and poor skills to use any she might find. Would an
attacker recognize her and hold his hand? There were men out there who
had no loyalty to her, only to Rafael. They might well see her as the
enemy, the way this spell warped men's minds.

I am afraid, the thought came to her, to be answered, *When has that
made a difference? You were afraid when Deslucido cut down Padrik. You
were afraid on the trail, in the frozen river. You were afraid to face Deslucido
at the Comyn Council. Yet you did all these things and more. Do you claim
to be a Queen? Then go out there and act like one!*

Taniquel took a deep breath and stepped into the night. A stench like
burning copper hung in the air. For an instant, she thought Deslucido's
men had already fallen upon the camp, catching them unawares. Tents
had fallen into misshapen heaps between those which still stood like decrepit sentinels. Here and there, bodies lay in clumps of shadow, as if
dead. She feared some of them were. Between them, in the aisles and
around the campfires, men fought with anything they could lay hands on,
whether rock or steel and their own bare fists. In mindless frenzy, they
swung and stabbed, or grappled each other. She hurried past knots of
soldiers where two or more cornered a single man, then turned on one
another.

Where Rafael had passed, however, order prevailed, frenzy held in
abeyance for the moment. Men were already setting the camp to rights,
pulling apart those who were still fighting. A few sat groaning, heads in
their hands. Aides ran along the aisles, shouting orders.

In a few moments, she reached the tent she shared with Graciela, but
it was empty, undisturbed. She made her way to Edric's tent, a short ways
distant. It too looked untouched. Inside, however, she found Edric and
the others. They stood in a huddle, hands joined. Graciela, recognizable
as the only woman, swayed on her feet like a willow in a storm.

Taniquel closed her eyes, trying to envision what she could not physically see. They'd linked somehow, forming a single unit with their minds.
Wave after wave of madness battered the camp, but now she sensed a
shield arising from the joined minds of the workers. It was thin, more veil
than armor, but they were able to keep out the worst of it.

She stood irresolute for a time, wondering what she could do to help.
Domna Caitlin had told her long ago that she had not enough *laran* to be
worth training, but she no longer believed that. Had she not resisted

Deslucido's spells, first at Acosta Castle gates and now this night? Surely that must be of some value. But she did not know how to join with the others. She feared that if she spoke or touched one of them, disturbed their concentration, then the protective circle might shatter, leaving the entire camp vulnerable. Not even Rafael's leadership could draw the men back together.

And no one knew when Deslucido's armies would strike in earnest . . . They had to be ready.

Sounds came from outside the tent, toward the back—shouts, scuffling. Light flared, penetrating the canvas walls. In a moment of brightness, Taniquel saw the faces of the other workers, set with concentration. Blood trickled from a gash in one man's forehead.

More lights from outside, more shouting. The voices sounded closer, almost on top of them. Still the *laran* workers stood, eyes closed, focused inwardly. Taniquel moved toward the door. As unthinking as the men under the spell were, they might smash into this tent as they had others. She must stop them. Maybe if she taunted them, lured them away . . .

A circle of fire points appeared on the tent fabric, low down. The dry cloth ignited instantly. Fire exploded up the wall, leaving gaping holes. Clumps of orange coals came hurling inside. Whatever they touched— carpet, furnishings—burst into flames. The tent wall blackened and fell away. The robe of one of the men burst into eye-searing white-yellow flames. He screamed and so did Graciela.

Taniquel grabbed the screaming man by both shoulders. It was Edric, his eyes wide and unfocused. He struggled in her grasp. Years of childhood scuffles with Padrik came back to her. She hooked one foot around the back of his knee, kicked back hard, and twisted his shoulders to break his balance. He went down heavily.

She snatched the carpet, praying she was near an edge, but could not get a hold. Her fingers touched something soft and loose—a blanket from one of the sleeping pallets. She pulled it over him, wrapping it as best she could. Her eyes streamed tears, half-blinding her.

The whole tent was on fire now. Within moments, it filled with smoke, dense and acrid. She could see only a few feet. ·

"Come on!" One of the other men, the one with the gash on his forehead, grabbed Taniquel's arm and hauled her to her feet.

Together they dragged Edric through the tent door and let him fall on the bare earth beyond. Graciela knelt beside him, her starstone in her hand. It glowed with an eldritch blue light.

Two men in uniform appeared with buckets of water, which they threw over the collapsing tent. Their lips were drawn back over their teeth hard and tight, caught in a terrible rictus of effort. Taniquel shuddered, sensing how that awful pressure was even now shredding their self-control.

"We can't face this!" she cried. "We must get the circle back!"

"Are you crazy?" In the last flickers of the tent fire, Graciela's face contorted. "Edric's burned too badly to focus. And we cannot do it without him. We barely held them as it was!"

Taniquel's temper broke. She grabbed the younger woman's arm and with a strength that surprised her, lifted her to her feet and shoved her in the direction of the two *laranzu'in*.

"To Zandru's icy hell with your *cannots!* You *will* do it! You will do it now!"

"*Vai domna*—" one of the men began. His shoulders sagged. "You do not understand. It is no use. The Ambervale army is but an hour away."

"Did you send word to my uncle?" Seeing him shrug and shake his head with an expression of *In this madness?* Taniquel took a step closer. Her hands curled into fists and the physical act of restraining herself from striking him sent jagged lightnings of pain up her forearms. "Then you must give us that hour!"

"Even if we could . . ." Graciela lifted her hands in a gesture of helplessness. "We are too few to stand against a Tower . . ."

"A Tower? What Tower?"

"Tramontana," one of the men said wearily. "Only a full circle could cast a spell of this magnitude over such an area and control so many minds at once."

"Graciela's right," the other said. "We don't have enough strength."

A Tower pitted against an army of men unable to defend themselves in the slightest? It wasn't fair!

"Can you not reach them through your starstone?" Taniquel had heard of such things. Caitlin, who was a telepath like many in the Towers, could speak mentally with her friends at Hali, if the distance were not too great. She had done so, in sending word of the Drycreek disaster.

"You must convince them to break off the attack so it will be sword against sword, unhindered!"

"We tried that, when the attack first began," Graciela said. "They are barricaded against us. Nor can we contact Hali, to ask them to restrain Tramontana. There is too much—you wouldn't understand the exact term—psychic static."

Taniquel's thoughts raced like wildfire. "There must be another way!"

"What do you want of us?" Graciela cried. "We are not enough to defend the camp as it is, and now you want one of us to go wandering through the Overworld on such a fool's quest."

"I ask only that we do what we can—all of us," Taniquel said, putting all the command she could muster into those few words.

In response, they took up positions in a triangle, lightly joining hands. "It will do little good," one of the men said, "but we will try our best."

"I must go to my uncle now. He is—*I* am—counting on you to do your part."

There was no reply, which Taniquel supposed was good. She hurried in the direction Rafael had gone. After a couple of steps, she cursed her own folly in not asking one of the *laranzu'in* to locate him. But she could not go back now and ask. That would surely start another debate all over again. She tried to make out those channels of order in the seething darkness of the camp which had marked where Rafael had spoken to his men, gathered them back into sanity. Minutes slipped away as she searched, while the awareness pulsed through her veins, *Only an hour away!*

✦

Almost by accident, she met Gerolamo giving orders to a group of younger officers. She heard his voice before she saw him, rough-edged but firm, and caught the gleam of ivory silk tied like a badge around one arm. He held a naked sword in one hand and looked ready to use it. The officers dispersed even as she approached.

"Where is King Rafael?" she said without preliminary.

"He's taken those men still fit to fight to the field beyond," Gerolamo said.

At least, there were some. She dared not think how many or what had happened to them when the circle broke. "I must speak to him right away!"

Gerolamo said it was not safe for her to be wandering the camp, even as he took her arm to escort her himself. Once an armed man rushed at them from the darkness. Moonlight glinted off the whites of his bulging eyes and the dagger he jabbed at Taniquel. He screamed, "Witch-hag! Your kind killed my father! You poisoned him in his sleep!"

Gerolamo deflected the thrust and sent the dagger skidding into the dust. The soldier stared at Gerolamo's sword, then sprinted away. Gerolamo handed the dagger to Taniquel.

"Use this only if you must," he told her, "but use it to kill."

Nodding, she took the dagger. Rank and reason would avail her nothing tonight. If she needed to use the dagger, she would get only one chance.

In a pool of torchlight, Rafael was talking to his soldiers in quiet, even tones. She felt them drinking in his words. The pressure of the *laran* spell still resonated through her. Yet these armed men resisted its command, each in his own way. Until that moment, she had not understood how loyalty could override even the most deeply-rooted hatred.

"Each of us carries the seeds of war and the seeds of peace," Rafael's voice rang out. "We make a choice every day of our lives, every moment. To kill, to preserve. To grow a tree, to chop it down. To stand with law and right, to let loose the outlaw within us."

And every moment he talked, they chose. They chose to stand, hands unmoving on their weapons, eyes fixed upon their king.

They are worth more than all the gold in Shainsa, these men, she thought. *They must not fall beneath Deslucido's swords!*

Rafael, seeing her approach, paused in his speech and drew her aside. "*Chiya,* you should not be here—"

"Edric and the others have been screening us from the worst of the *laran* attack," she said, brushing his words aside. "It comes from Tramontana. Now Edric is hurt and our own defenses crippled. We have less than an hour before the Ambervale forces arrive."

"An hour . . ." he said, drawing in a breath, "and we cannot withdraw with the men in such disorder. The hills will force us to scatter where they could hunt us down one by one." *Or,* he thought but did not add aloud, *fight like this.*

"Uncle, there must be something we can do!" Desperation rose in her, closed icy fingers around her throat. By the torches, she caught the shift in Rafael's expression. He meant to order her from the camp, into what fragile safety lay beyond. He thought her useless at best, to be protected at the cost of his pitifully thin resources.

"No, do not spare a man for me," she said as briskly as she could. "I can resist this spell, don't you remember?" She lifted the dagger Gerolamo had thrust into her hands. "And I am armed. I will see what aid I can bring to Edric and the others."

This might be the last time she saw Rafael Hastur alive and she wanted to throw her arms around him, thank him for his kindness and his vision. But she dared not. She had to pretend that they had a chance.

Less than an hour!

◆

As Taniquel rushed back to her tent, the *laran* attack seemed to intensify. There was less active fighting among the soldiers, but more sitting with their heads bowed, sobbing or hiding their faces. In the eyes of the men who looked up as she passed, she saw not only lurking madness, but desperation. There must be *something* she could do.

Taniquel lowered the tent flap behind her, sat on her sleeping pallet, and buried her head on her folded arms. Not for the first time, she wished she had a starstone and the training to use it. Then she could join Graciela and the others and strengthen their resistance. She wished she could send visions of flaming scorpions upon Deslucido's men in return. Perhaps she could even go out into that nebulous place apart from normal time and space called the Overworld and find help.

Help. Where would she go, whom would she ask? Except for Caitlin, she had only a passing acquaintance with the folk at Hali.

But Hali was not the only Tower beholden to her uncle. Neskaya Tower also owed allegiance to Hastur, and Coryn was at Neskaya.

Coryn . . .

Taniquel lifted her head. Memory flooded her senses—the warmth of dappled sun in the garden that magical afternoon, the sweet softness of his lips on hers, the smell of flowers and his skin. His hair, loose to his shoulders, had brushed her face when he turned; she could feel that light, silken touch even now. Shadows delineated the curve of his ear, the strong line of his jaw. In her mind, he turned back to her with those eyes so full of light that she felt herself falling into them . . .

She lay back on the pallet, clasping her hands.

Coryn . . .

Even as she spoke his name in her thoughts, her heart called out. Longing pierced her.

Through water you have come to me; through fire I must come to you. But where was the water? Where the fire?

Fire . . . and once again, as in her dreams, she saw the impossible blue flames. Now she stood in the very heart of the blaze, in the heart of a sparkling matrix. For a moment she could not move, dared not even breathe lest she sear her lungs. But the flames burned without heat or smoke. They consumed nothing, arose from nowhere. Her hands passed through the shimmering walls, untouched.

Drawing courage, she took a step and then another. As she emerged from the blue fire, she felt solid ground beneath her feet. She blinked, clearing her vision.

She stood on a plain of unbroken gray beneath an equally featureless sky. No wind stirred the air, nor did any sound reach her ears. It seemed to go on forever, gray ground, gray sky, gray horizon.

Although she breathed, she had only the haziest sense of her own body. When she looked down, she saw the ghostly outlines of gauze-draped limbs. She had, by some eldritch magic, become a wraith in this strange colorless world. Yet she felt solid enough with her heart hammering against the inside of her chest.

Tramontana! Where in this monotone world would she find the Tower? She did not even know in which direction to begin her search. She pivoted slowly, scanning the horizon.

In the distance, Taniquel made out a building, squat and lit from within with lambent white. She made her way toward it. It grew larger much more quickly than it should have, given her own speed. Perhaps distances here did not mean the same thing as they did in the ordinary world.

It was, she saw as she drew nearer, a sort of tower, but of no architectural style she had ever seen. It seemed more theater dressing, as in the plays she had seen performed in Thendara, than any real place where people might work and live. Jagged lines of brilliance coruscated over its surface. The air bore a slight metallic tang which reminded her of summer lightning. Within its flickering aura, nothing human stirred.

"What is this place?" she called out. Her voice sounded tinny and weak to her own ears. She took in a breath and tried again, louder. "Show yourselves! Where am I?"

When minutes passed without an answer, she began to circle the tower. What she discovered on the far side startled her. Instead of a glistening surface, featureless except for the darting lines of brightness, she found a huge round piece of blue-tinted glass, twice the height of a man and mounted in a frame of silvery metal. As she gazed upon it, watched it swivel on its mountings as if turned by an invisible hand, she was reminded of a giant lens. She'd seen their kind used to concentrate the sun's energy to start a fire.

By squinting, she could almost see the rays of invisible power streaming from inside the tower through lens . . . and disappearing from the Overworld. With a shudder, she realized that she stood before the psychic manifestation of Tramontana Tower even as it rained down madness upon her uncle's camp. Here was the source. Here she must stop it.

With an inarticulate cry, she hurled herself at the lens, thinking only to point it elsewhere. Even as her fingertips touched the silvery mountings and the blue glass, jolts of electric energy leaped out to sting her with a thousand points of pain. Her body jerked away of its own accord, her arms reflexively pulling back.

She reached out a second time. Again, it was like trying to grasp a stalk of lightning or thrust a naked arm into a nest of scorpion-ants. She fell back, stumbling to her knees. Goosebumps covered her skin and every nerve shrilled. Too furious to think straight, she picked herself up, marched around to the smooth side of the Tower, and kicked it.

To Taniquel's surprise, her foot did not meet solid rock. Something slowed the blow, but did not stop it. She had expected an unyielding surface and when her foot kept going, she almost lost her balance. She pulled her foot free without difficulty and aimed another kick.

Kick! Recover . . . kick!

"Who is that down below, playing children's games at our gates?" The voice was sepulchral, echoing. And familiar.

"Tramontana!" she called out with all her strength. "Listen to me! I am Taniquel, Queen of Acosta! In the name of King Rafael Hastur, I demand that you break off this abominable spell! Let ordinary soldiers fight their battles without interference!"

A surge of energy passed over the surface of the Tower, blinding in intensity. Taniquel threw her arms over her face to shield her eyes. Her breath, white hot, caught in her throat. A voice sizzled through her mind.

The Hastur bitch! Seize her, that her spirit may wander here until her body withers and dies!

Now she knew where she had heard that voice. Rumail—Damian Deslucido's sorcerer brother!

Her muscles tensed to flee, but for an awful moment, she found she could not move. She could not even see clearly. Rumail held her fast in his mental grip. She could neither defend herself nor escape.

No! It must not end like this! Coryn, help me!

But no answer came. She was alone with her folly. And she had come so far, been so close to her goal! Tears of pain and frustration smeared her vision.

The Tower wavered, mirage-like. A human figure took shape inside the blur, as if someone were swimming underwater toward her. A corona of silver fire framed the woman's ageless face. As if blown by an unfelt wind, a gown of luminescent gray swirled about her slender frame. Her voice whispered through Taniquel's mind, each syllable ringing like tiny bells.

"Kinswoman, you are in grave danger here in the Overworld. You must withdraw!"

Kinswoman?

Taniquel found that she could move again. Stepping closer, she recognized the familiar cast of the woman's features. She had seen that faint elven tilt of the eyes, the shape of the nose and curve of the hairline in her uncle, in her own mirror. This stranger must be of Hastur blood.

"Cousin! Please help me!" Taniquel said. "You must stop this attack—"

"There is no time for discussion! I cannot hold the breach for more than a few moments. Go now, with the grace of the gods!"

As if propelled by the other woman's cry, Taniquel sprinted away. She ran faster than she imagined possible. Her feet skimmed the smooth gray floor. Her face burned with the wind of her passing.

Once or twice, she glanced over one shoulder to see Tramontana shrunken to a fraction of its former size. The second time, she dared to slow her pace. From the light which pulsated over the distant Tower, she guessed it had taken up the attack on her uncle's men once more.

Were Deslucido's forces even now bearing down on them? How

much more could the Hastur army stand before it turned upon itself like a rabid beast, or fell, unable to act in its own defense?

No, Taniquel murmured to herself. It could not end this way. It *must* not.

Her body turned thick and heavy, like unfired clay. Unable to walk any further, she drew in a deep, sobbing breath. Her legs buckled beneath her.

Coryn . . . Oh, sweet love, where are you?

37

"Taniquel?"

Coryn sat up bolt upright, blinking away sleep. He had just fallen into a drowse after working the better part of the night charging the immense ranges of *laran* batteries. The complex matrix device which made up the weapon of ultimate defense—*his* weapon—were complete, awaiting only the reservoir of power. They had all been working extra shifts these past ten days, sharing the painstaking work. Some mornings, Coryn had barely enough energy to haul his aching body up the stairs to the part of Neskaya Tower reserved for senior technicians, Bernardo, and himself as under-Keeper.

This night, though, he had called an early halt. Mac's focus had gone patchy after the first few hours, as if he were a novice and not a highly experienced technician. Even Amalie, usually as steadfast as the Wall Around the World, had fidgeted, twice nearly breaking the link. As for his own performance as Keeper of this circle, that was nothing to be proud of. He had held them together perhaps longer than was wise, for his own judgment had been none too rational.

Since late the previous afternoon, something had niggled at his nerves, never coming clear enough to identify. He'd meant to speak with Bernardo about it, to try to differentiate what was natural fatigue from a

359

demanding task, and what perhaps stray psychic tension. He knew that he'd become much more sensitive since his return to Neskaya. Bernardo had noticed, and suggested that perhaps his bonding with Taniquel, given her empathy and sensitivity to him, had awakened deeper levels of his *laran* talent.

Taniquel!

Now the unmistakable stamp of her personality, that sweet wildness which was so much the core of who she was, resonated through his mind. Linked as they were, she was never far from his thoughts. In the hypna-gogic state of near-sleep, after long hours in psychic linkage with a circle, he was even more open to her.

Somehow she had managed to reach him across the miles.

He swung his legs over the side of his bed and went to the window, open in this mild season. A nuance of light touched the sky toward the east, little more than a mist of gold at this hour. His back and shoulders ached from the hours of immobility.

Taniquel had *laran*, yes, but she was untrained in its use. As far as he knew, she did not even possess a starstone. He considered this nothing short of criminal. But the family which saw her primary value as a bearer of sons would think such schooling a waste.

She must have been desperate to reach him, even in his receptive state. What had happened? Had Deslucido's forces achieved a military victory? Was she now a prisoner? His heart stuttered at the thought of her in the hands of the Ambervale king and his brother. Gently, he tapped one fist against the pale blue stone of the windowsill. There was only one way to find out.

Coryn returned to his bed and pulled the light summer blanket up to his chest. From the quilted silken pouch in which he carried his matrix stone, he drew out the hairs once tangled in the copper pin she'd given him in the garden. The pin itself was stored in his chest along with a cloak brooch which Rafael had given him and a few other small items of no value to anyone but himself. The filigreed metal still retained the imprint of her energy, but the hair, which had once been part of her living body, resonated even more strongly. He twisted the hairs through his fingers. They curled around him as if they recognized his touch.

He arranged his body on the bed in a posture of minimum stress, a pillow beneath his knees and a smaller one supporting the curve in his neck, just as Gareth had taught him so long ago, when he had first come to Tramontana. Closing his eyes, he used the twined hairs as a talisman and sent his thoughts outward, questing for that evanescent contact.

Tani!

As effortlessly as if he had stepped through his own doorway, he found himself in the Overworld. He had been here many times before, from his days as a novice at Tramontana, but that had been with hours of preparation under the careful guidance of his Keeper. This was the second time in as many minutes he'd thought of Tramontana.

The Overworld, for all its unchanging stillness, was a dangerous, even lethal place for the unprepared. There were few landmarks here, and those could change with the speed of thought. Time and distance lost their usual meaning. Even a skilled matrix worker could wander, lost or trapped, unable to tear himself free, until at last his physical body perished of starvation. Had Taniquel been thrust here unawares—was that why she'd reached out to him in panic?

Tani!

Now fear fueled his own cry, fear for her sanity as well as her life.

But he would do her no good if he himself became lost. With a few practiced strokes, he summoned the thought-shape of Neskaya which its workers used as an anchoring place. Like the original Tower, it glowed with a soft blue light. But this version was taller and more slender, designed more as a beacon than anything solid enough to withstand Darkover's fierce winter storms. Satisfied that he would be able to find his way back, Coryn turned to scan the horizon.

Tani! Like a fisherman casting nets, he sent out his thoughts once more.

Coryn?

Faint and far away the answer came, as much whisper as word, but undeniably Taniquel. Coryn knew better than to race toward it, although at that moment there was nothing he wanted more. Instead, he imagined a thick silken cord running from the astral Tower along the sound of her voice. Slowly, with a firm even pull, he drew the far end of the cord toward him. For what seemed like an eternity, he gathered it in, seamless gray fibers. He felt a slight tug, a resistance at the far end, and his heart leapt. There, where the cord seemed to end, he made out a shape. As he hurried toward it, the cord vanished.

He came upon her in only a few minutes. She'd fallen in a heap of gauzy draperies, head bowed, arms wrapped tight around her body, knuckles pale. Her hair, unbound, fell forward over her shoulders like a cascade of spun jet. He knelt at her side and gathered her in his arms.

"Sweet love, it's all right, I'm here," he murmured into the soft cloud of her hair.

Taniquel looked up at him, face shining with tears. Although people's forms often altered in the Overworld, she looked exactly as he remembered her. Perhaps that was because, since the day he'd met her in the travel shelter, he had seen through the beautiful outer body to the even more precious person within. He kissed her eyelids and tasted salt.

"Is it my Coryn and not yet another false vision? Are you really here?" With a wondering expression, she touched his face.

He drew her closer, sending confidence—*I am real and solid and here, beloved.*

My heart. Her arms tightened hard around him. After a moment, she drew a deep, shuddering breath and pulled back. When she looked at him this time, her eyes shone like hard-polished marble.

"Coryn, there is no time to lose." In terse, direct terms which would have done a general proud, she outlined what had happened, how Tramontana launched their psychic attack at Deslucido's command, the desperation of Rafael Hastur's situation.

"Edric said King Damian's army was but an hour away, and most of that time has already passed," she added. She lowered her eyes, for the first time sounding uncertain. "I don't know how long I've been wandering here."

"In the outer world, it is near sunrise," he said, helping her to her feet. "Doubtless, Deslucido plans to follow the night's confusion with a dawn offensive. Whatever can be done to even the battle odds will be done, I swear it. But you cannot linger here." He did not want to alarm her with words of her grave danger. The longer she remained in the Overworld, the slimmer any chance of her successful return to her body.

"Oh, no . . . I'm all right. Please, get help. I'll just . . . just sit here."

He looked into her face and when he saw the vagueness in her eyes, his heart failed for a moment. This was a warning sign that the wanderer was losing touch with her physical body. Unless recalled, the tie would wither, leaving only a breathing husk on the material plane and the wisp of a ghost here.

All the fire, the determination which had brought Taniquel so far drained from her as Coryn watched. Under his hands, her body grew airy, almost as insubstantial as the filmy gown her mind had created.

Coryn took her hands between his, as if he could warm her back to life. Laced between his fingers were two strands of ebony hair. He brought them to his lips.

"Find yourself," he said. "Close your eyes, hold on to who you are, think of nothing else. You are Taniquel—Queen—mother—lover."

A smile flashed across her face, a moment of brilliance. Color brightened in her cheeks and the outlines of her form steadied. She clasped both hands over the entwined hairs, eyes closed, lashes dark on pale-rose cheeks, head tilted slightly back as if awaiting a kiss. His body moved without his will to bend and touch her lips with his, but he restrained himself. For her life's sake, he must make no move to hold her here.

Coryn . . . beloved . . . until we meet again . . .

Taniquel's words, unspoken, shivered through him. Then, as if she had never been, she vanished.

✦

Coryn paced the length of the matrix laboratory where he waited with the members of his circle. Quickly assembled, they lacked only their Keeper to begin. Bernardo himself had gone into the relays in an attempt to negotiate with Tramontana. Coryn studied the faces of his circle, from Mac, whom he knew as well as the back of his own hand, to fragile-looking, vivacious Amalie to serious Demiana to silver-haired Gerell, who had trained first as a *cristoforo* monk at Nevarsin and then at Dalereuth. They were seven in all, plus Bernardo. Although the First Circle at Tramontana was larger, Coryn did not think there was any working group on Darkover he trusted more, not since Kieran had died.

They came alert as one, without any need for words, as Bernardo's footsteps sounded on the stone corridor outside. Amalie raked her fingers through her pale frizzy hair, a gesture of impatience. Demiana placed two fingertips on the back of her wrist, caught her gaze, and held her. She closed her eyes and then slowly opened them as tension left her jaw.

Bernardo slipped into the room with barely a whisper of his crimson Keeper's robes. "They refuse to alter their course," he said. They all knew, of course, but hearing the words spoken aloud brought a certain finality.

"This is the word of Tomas, Keeper of the First Circle?" Coryn asked.

"Tomas no longer speaks for Tramontana," Bernardo said, his voice rumbling. "Rumail commands there in Deslucido's name. He is now Keeper as well as voice of the King."

Coryn flinched under the reflex sizzle of energy around the circle. These people had known Rumail, had worked with him . . . had made the painful decision to set him aside no longer one of them, when they expelled him from their company.

"There is no hope of any further discussion, then," Mac said. A statement, not a question.

"It was a small chance," Bernardo said. "We are no worse off now than before. Come," he held out his hands for them to take their seats. Gerell, whose back had been bothering him, joints stiff from too many long Hellers winters as a younger man, arranged the cushions on his chair. "Let us begin."

Coryn went to the low bench he preferred. A thin pillow softened the wood surface. He crossed his legs loosely and settled his body. A wave of relaxation passed through his muscles. It was a posture he could hold for hours, head balanced on a straight neck, chest lifted, back long and easy.

He closed his eyes and dropped into the circle. Bernardo began weaving them into a unified whole. As they attuned to one another, Coryn saw them as an ever-changing rainbow, then heard them as voices settling into harmony, then sparkling dots of sun reflected on a clear pool of water. Bernardo's touch dropped a stone into the water, creating ripples. Energy surged through each ring, out and then in again—in to the center point, where Bernardo gathered it together.

Once again, Coryn found himself standing outside the Overworld manifestation of Neskaya. Bernardo moved them to the topmost spire, looking down. Deftly, he began to reshape the psychic substance of the tower. Walls thickened and grew battlements, windows narrowed. A tracing of lace-ivy burgeoned into a covering of sword-edged thorn vines. From a landmark of grace and beauty, Neskaya drew in on itself, now a fortress.

"Tramontana!" Bernardo's psychic voice rang like a gong, reverberating from ground and sky alike.

With the speed of thought, they now faced the other Tower. Here in the Overworld, it was as easy to move an edifice as a game token.

Although the Tramontana circle must surely be aware of their appearance, there was no reaction. For a moment, Coryn did not recognize his former home. This squat edifice, encased in constant electrical discharge and dwarfed by the huge lenslike structure, bore no resemblance to either its physical reality or the airy, graceful form Kieran had designed, reminiscent of a grove of willowy goldenbark trees.

A beam of thought-energy, invisible but readily discernible to Coryn's *laran* senses, emanated from the lens and disappeared through the seamless ground. This, he knew, was the source of the spell which held the Hastur army in shambles. He felt Demiana's shiver of disgust, Gerell's stony loathing of the thing. From Mac came a simple, almost mechanical suggestion.

Why not block the accursed thing?

With precise control, Bernardo shifted the position of the astral Neskaya to take the full impact of the lens beam. Atop the tallest battlement, Coryn reached out his hands. Strength flowed around the circle. The walls, resilient as living things, flexed and held.

Coryn caught a fleeting glimpse of soldiers in Hastur colors scrambling to their feet, of officers waving them forward, hands clutching sword and bow, men mounting and spurring their horses into formation, eyes glowing like white-hot coals. Then a ferocious shout from Tramontana brought his attention back to the present.

"NESKAYA SCUM! GET OUT OF THE WAY OR WE WILL BLAST YOU ALL TO ZANDRU'S COLDEST HELL!"

He had almost forgotten that voice, though he had dreamed of it enough times in his early years at Tramontana. Just as some people had different bodily appearances in the Overworld, so did their voices sound different, although still recognizable. They sounded more like themselves, their true selves. This voice, though, had not changed since the first time he'd heard it as a child.

By what right does Rumail of Ambervale speak for Tramontana? The thought flamed within him.

Coryn held back his mental challenge, for it was Bernardo's place, as Keeper of Neskaya, to speak for all of them. Bernardo simply waited.

Slowly, silently, the lens swelled even larger. It tilted on its bearings so that it faced Neskaya directly. Scintillating particles of blue and poison-green appeared in the colorless beam. At first, there were only a few, drifting outward like so many colored dust motes. They moved almost lazily, coming to rest on the outer surface of Neskaya's wall. Tiny explosions blossomed into pinpoints of brightness where they touched. They reminded Coryn of the stinging flies of Verdanta summers.

Within moments, the colored specks multiplied, not tens but hundreds, thousands, even more. The beam swarmed with them. Several struck at once, so that the combined impacts grew ever larger and brighter. Fire lingered in the wake of each explosion. Coryn felt the heat on his face. He sensed the flames burrowing through the substance of the wall, searching for what it could feed on, like some demonic mental *clingfire.*

Even as a roar of denial rose in his throat, he felt Bernardo's sure guidance. From Neskaya's slitted windows came a flurry of wings—feathers in every hue of the dawn or skin stretched over long, delicate bones. Hunting cries filled the air, sweet and high. The beam disintegrated into shards of brilliance as birds and tiny bats dove and fed on the light-motes.

Laughter bubbled up in Amalie, spreading through the circle. Minutes seeped by and the flying hunters slowed as fewer of the motes appeared. Soon only a cluster here and there remained, quickly snatched on the wing. Moving as one, the flocks circled Neskaya and rose skyward.

Somewhere below, in the material world, steel clashed against steel, sweat ran with blood, war cries rent the air . . .

"Hastur! Hastur! Permanedal!*"* The Hastur motto, *I shall remain.*

A figure appeared on top of Tramontana's manifestation, arms raised. Red robes whipped in unseen winds. The hood had been pulled far down to shadow the face, but Coryn would have known Rumail anywhere.

The winds died, leaving an island of crystalline calm. As clearly as if they faced each other across a sparring square, the Tramontana circle appeared. Coryn knew that Bernardo and the others were equally visible. He recognized each one who stood to the side and behind Rumail—Cathal, Garreth . . . Aran. Aran, once so filled with life, now bore the appearance of an old, gray man. He stared past Coryn with white, unseeing eyes.

Only Tomas and Bronwyn were missing from the Tramontana circle, though Coryn sensed their presences elsewhere in the Tower. Rumail had taken Tomas' place as senior Keeper.

Rumail lifted the hood back from his face. He looked younger than the last time Coryn had seen him, his skin unlined over arching bone.

With an impassive expression, he surveyed the Neskaya circle. His gaze rested on each one in turn, as if none of them were worthy of further notice. When he came to Coryn, however, he lingered for a heartbeat. His eyes glinted red in the reflected color of his Keeper's robes, as if they glowed with their own inner fire.

Burning . . . probing . . . the light in those eyes shifted with recognition.

Deep within Coryn's body, something roused, uneasy as the memory of a half-healed wound. He told himself he had nothing to fear. Whatever had happened was a long time ago, and he was no longer a child. He was a grown man, a trained *laranzu,* and he stood in the midst of his own circle.

Dark patches swirled across the gray Overworld sky. Coryn licked his lips, tasting ozone. A gust of chill, moist air lifted his hair. He tightened his hold of Demiana on one side and Bernardo on the other and took a deep breath, steeling himself for what he feared would come next.

Rumail reached up with one arm. He cried out, though Coryn could not make out the words. Lightning, a jagged tree of eye-searing white, burst from the sky and came to his hand. For an instant, he poised there, though whether he held it or hung from it, Coryn could not be sure. He remembered the old proverb about the perils of chaining a dragon to roast one's meat. Surely dragon-fire could be no less brilliant . . . or deadly.

Rumail shifted, gathering himself beneath the pulsing lightning.

"Here it comes!" Mac cried.

With an odd, puppetlike jerk, Rumail hurled the bolt toward them.

38

Even as the lightning bolt left Rumail's hand, Coryn felt a terrible pull, a drawing of energy from his own Keeper. He channeled all his strength into his response. He felt the skill of Bernardo's mental shaping and saw instantly what the Keeper was doing.

Bernardo acted the instant before the lightning struck. Instead of stone and thorn-vine, it crashed into a sheet of impenetrable mind-stuff, smoothly curved, a mirror to the other tower's lens. White heat reflected back. For a long moment, the backlash played over Tramontana's walls, smoothing out the crazed energy patterns. Then it vanished in a sizzle and a fall of fine black powder. Atop the tower, Rumail slumped. The sky cleared.

"Coryn," came Bernardo's voice. "We have a moment of respite before he can try again. But there is great danger here. He is using forces he cannot control, forces that span both worlds. Should we take a direct hit here in the Overworld, I fear the result would break through into the physical plane."

Coryn's thoughts raced ahead. *And that would be equivalent to an actual* laran *attack. The doomsday device—*

"Yes!" Bernardo agreed. "You must go quickly and disarm it, lest we destroy Tramontana in truth."

It would put an end to Rumail Deslucido, Coryn thought hotly. Then, with a rush of shame, he remembered—*Aran is in that Tower, and Bronwyn, and Gareth, people I love.* As quickly as he could, without disrupting the linkage, he dropped from the circle and into his physical body.

✦

To reach the laboratory where the *laran* shield had been assembled, Coryn had to descend one staircase and cross to another. As he went down, he missed a step. His legs gave way beneath him so that he had to grasp the rope support which had been strung along the stone wall. He stood there, gulping acid, fingers curled around the coarse twisted fibers, and sweated hard in the cool of the stairwell.

He was not alone. Something—*someone*—rode within him, no longer quiescent but aroused.

Rumail . . .

When the two circles faced one another in the Overworld, Rumail had known him. And what of that? Rumail knew them all, from Bernardo the Keeper to Amalie, from his years of service here. The man had gone mad with power now, unfit for the robes he had taken on. Any fool could see that.

Then what had he, Coryn, to fear? Why did he tremble like an orphaned *chervine* kid in the shadow of a banshee?

Suddenly, Coryn's fingers opened, nerveless upon the rope railing. Without support, he crumpled on the stairs. Stone, hard and cold as ice, bit into his flesh. As if an invisible hand turned a key in a lock, something opened inside him, no mere physical wrenching of the gut, but an even deeper, more profound ripping at his very essence.

Memories filled his vision, blinding him to the shadowed walls. As it had so many years ago, a corridor appeared before him, composed of the featureless gray substance of the Overworld. He had been here before, had sought refuge from a shadowy figure. The memory shifted, dissolving as quickly as it arose. Cold, more than marrow-deep, shivered through him and for a moment, he was a child, painfully poised on the brink of manhood, tortured with the changes racking his body as his *laran* awoke. Wordless terror jolted through him, stripping thought. He bolted down the corridor.

No escape this way . . . The words came slowly, pale and thin He struggled to remember more. There had been a talisman, something which would guard him. Darting this way and that, he searched for it. His hands were empty, the gray corridor featureless. There was no help there, or anywhere.

Walls surrounded him, drawing closer until he could no longer run. Coryn tried to brace one shoulder and shove it aside, to kick out. Each time, the substance of the walls gave way, elastic, only to constrict even more. He was trapped, like a rabbit-horn in the coils of a snake. Knowing this, he tried to calm himself, to gather his resources. There must be some way to escape.

The walls pressed closer with each passing heartbeat, squeezing the air from Coryn's lungs. Panic drove him like a whip, but he could not move his arms or legs. His vision went dark, streaked with red. Pain lanced through his lungs. His muscles turned to water as his strength flowed out of him. Unable to resist any longer, he sank down into the gray floor. It covered him in its muffling blanket. Silence and numbness bathed him. He could fight no longer.

NOW YOU ARE MINE.

That voice, that hated voice!

For the first time in his life, Coryn prayed to Avarra, Dark Lady of night and death. *Take me!* he begged. His only answer was a resurgence of despair.

There is no hope.

His physical body righted itself, stood, continued down the stairs. He seemed to be watching its movement across a great distance.

No hope . . .

Like a white bird piercing the darkest stormcloud, a thought came to him, the image of his mother's handkerchief. He remembered holding it in his hands the morning after Rumail had examined him, remembered the softness of the worn fabric between his fingers, the relief soaring in his heart.

Remembered giving it to Taniquel.

That part of me is safe. Rumail can never have all of me.

In his darkened mind, her eyes glimmered, her chin lifted proudly. Blue flames surged up to surround her, and yet she walked on, untouched. Free.

And yet, the body moved, more surely now with every passing step. It hurried across the adjoining corridor and up the flight leading to the second laboratory.

Glow-globes placed at either end filled the room with a soft illumination. One of the novices, a boy from the Alton border who had not got his full growth yet, bent over the battery ranges, making notations on a pad. He looked up at Coryn's approach, his broken complexion flushing. Normally, checking the charges of the batteries would fall to a more experienced worker, a mechanic, but everyone else was either aloft with Bernardo or resting, drained from the night's work.

"I require isolation for this task." Coryn picked up a tray of tools sct with starstone chips and went to the shrouded device. Setting down his pad, the child darted from the room.

Coryn approached the great matrix screens which formed the device itself. He pulled away the triple layers of insulating silk and felt the familiar buzzing between his temples. Blue light shimmered through the room in every hue from palest bird's-egg to deep azure. Each layer of the device gave off its own unique color and because of the way the artificial crystals were linked, they interpenetrated one another. When he and Mac worked on the device, they used the signature tone of that particular element as a focus point.

The trigger lay in the first layer, the lightest shade of blue. As he had practiced so many hours while working on the screens, Coryn let his eyesight soften and then blur. He envisioned himself floating down a river. In some places, sunlight glared off the water's surface, in others lay pools of shadow.

Light . . . gather the light . . .

His hands moved over the tray of instruments, fingertips skimming their shapes.

WHAT ARE YOU DOING? The words whispered through his mind in a voice that was his and yet not his.

What am I doing? he wondered, momentarily puzzled. His vision cleared enough for him to look down at the tool in his hand, poised over the great glittering screen.

I am disarming . . . disarming the trigger . . .

WHAT WEAPON?

The motes of sunlight flashed hot and white, blinding him. He flung up one hand to shield his eyes. The movement sent sprays of brilliance in all direction. They encircled him so that he stood in the center of a glowing ring. The ring hummed with its own energy, sending reverberations through his body.

Dimly, he felt the clash of thunder and the rattling of steel. Sparks flew as shields raised against a volley of psychic arrows. Coryn tensed, then relaxed as the deadly barrage fell away.

Before his sightless eyes, his hands took up a different tool. He circled the screens, moving through their scintillating colors like a fish in that river he had imagined.

Dark blue . . . dark and darkest . . . that was what he sought. Yes, there it was! The third layer, keyed to redirect incoming *laran* energy, rose into clear view. The tool interrupted the energon link connections. Strand after severed strand fell away.

At last it was done.

◆

Coryn stood looking down at the great matrix screens, momentarily unsure how he had gotten here. In one hand, he held a slender metal tool which he could not remember having picked up. A fine trembling vibrated along his jaw and forearms. He rubbed the muscles, feeling the whipcord tension there.

But there was no time to rest. Tramontana might resume the attack at any moment. Bernardo needed him back in the circle. He had accomplished his mission here. He paused only long enough to replace the tool on its tray.

Coryn sensed the disturbance in the Overworld even as he climbed the stairs back to the laboratory where the others waited. He had just set foot on the landing between the two stages of stairs, beside the tall narrow windows, when the sky above flashed into brilliance. Ozone and the unmistakable reek of *clingfire* filled the air. The sudden percussion almost knocked him from his feet.

Grasping his starstone where it hung on a chain about his neck, he set his mind aloft to the laboratory chamber. He found the circle there, intact but locked against him. They had formed an impenetrable link, an unbroken sphere of power. To allow him to join them, they would have to relax their concentration and reconfigure the pattern. It would be like cracking a window open, and Rumail might seize upon the moment of weakness. Coryn would have to wait until another lull in the battle, if there was one. He watched while lightnings of pure mental energy rained down upon them.

Across the flat gray Overworld sky, patterns of brightness shimmering with rainbow edges exploded and then blurred into darkness. The stones of the mental projection of Neskaya Tower quivered under the onslaught. Dimly Coryn felt the real Tower shudder under the energy lash as if it were a living thing.

Hold! He sent the thought to his own circle. There was not much chance it would get through, that his Keeper might be able to draw upon his strength, even for an instant. Coryn dropped back into the physical world, strode over to the windows on the stair landing, and stared out.

The fight raging above him had very much the feel of a stalemate, and a stalemate meant success for the Hastur army. Already, they had interrupted the barrage of fear-spells from Tramontana. Taniquel's forces would win or lose on their own, steel against steel, unhampered by any interference.

Perhaps all that was needed now was to remain firm until Rumail had expended his anger.

It would not end here, Coryn thought. Not as long as Damian Deslucido ruled with Rumail as his right hand. Taniquel had been right. The Deslucidos must be stopped by whatever means—sword or *laran* spell— necessary.

More of that bizarre silent lightning jagged across the sky outside the windows. He winced. It reminded him of the storm which had swept across the mountains during his journey to Tramontana. Only luck and Rafe's skill had kept him alive. Rafe had mentioned the Aldaran ability to work weather-magic, and there had been real fear in his voice. This flashing turbulence lacked the pattern of normal weather. When he opened his *laran* senses to it, he felt other differences. The Aldaran storm had been an attempt to replicate natural processes for human purposes. Perhaps those who shaped it desired rain in one place and not another, and directed air and wind and cloud to that end.

The lightning now overhead felt *focused*, aimed like a spear point. With a shiver, Coryn realized that what he saw was no accidental bleed-through, no overflow of energy from the Overworld. It was a deliberate attempt to bring the battle to the physical plane, to use the elastic space of the Overworld to span the miles between the two Towers. It carried a sense of determination bordering on obsession. He wondered what drove Rumail. Did he hate the Tower which had rejected him so very much, that he would now seek its destruction? It was fortunate he'd disarmed the *laran* shield to protect his friends at Tramontana from the devastating backlash. Neskaya would stand, if a little singed, and Rafael Hastur would triumph on the battlefield.

As Coryn watched, the diffuse brilliance overhead condensed into a single line, not branched like ordinary lightning, but straight as an arrow. It hung for an awful instant, entire, filling the sky with its whitened glare, spanning from near the horizon to somewhere directly above him.

A *crack!* resounded through the Tower. Beneath Coryn's feet, the building shuddered like a stricken living thing. He fell to his knees. Pain lanced through his temples. He clapped his hands over both ears to ease the pain and drew them away covered with blood. The next sound also came from higher in the Tower, piercing the cloud of deafness, a sound like nothing he had ever heard. Coryn felt it through all his *laran* senses. It was as if the stones themselves cried out, as if each tiny particle were suddenly wrenched from its place.

Screams now echoed through the corridors. With his ears still deadened and his head spinning, Coryn could not make out their direction. For a terrifying moment, he feared they came from aloft. He must be sure, he thought as he clambered to his feet.

He had not climbed more than a step or two when the Tower shuddered again, rocked by an explosion so massive, the air burst from his lungs. Balance lost, he tumbled down to the landing. One elbow smacked hard against a step. Nerve pain and then numbness seized his entire arm. His eyes watered, blurring his sight. Before him, the pale blue stone rippled, as if seen through currents of rising heat. He blinked, struggling to focus. The wavering shapes elongated to take on the form of flame.

Fire . . . Blue fire . . .

Coryn's mind raced ahead, up the stairs.

Bernardo! Mac! Amalie!

The circle's concentration shattered, the interwoven strands of mental energy unraveling like badly ripped silk. The anchor which was Mac's place was nothing more than a pit of darkness. Demiana's mind twisted like a fistful of storm-blown streamers, shrieking in agony.

Coryn touched Bernardo, felt the searing shock, the desperation as the Keeper struggled to gather the circle together again. Like two hands clasping, Coryn linked with the older man. Pain racked Bernardo's body. Coryn scanned the astral image of Bernardo's physical form and saw the great laboring wound of his heart.

Demiana! Coryn called.

In an instant, the monitor scanned Bernardo's astral form, analyzing the energy flows and their correlations in his physical body.

At the same time, Coryn drew together what was left of the circle. There was no sign of Mac except the pit of oozing darkness. Coryn feared he was dead, but there was no time to make sure, or to grieve. That would come later . . . if any of them survived.

Here, as in the corridor, flames of blue so pale as to be colorless, leaped higher with every passing moment. Eagerly they seized on any fuel—the stones themselves.

Gerell was the next to recover, to answer Coryn's call. He dropped into the linkage and his strength flowed out to Demiana and the others.

Moments later, Demiana's clear mental voice spoke. *Bernardo cannot take more strain. One of the vessels which carries blood to the heart muscle is blocked. I have eased it, but it will take time to repair the damage. If he is to live, he must rest.*

We cannot break the circle! Gerell said. *Rumail will not let up the attack just because we have wounded.*

A circle without a Keeper— Coryn began in protest.

You are *our Keeper now,* Amalie replied. *What have you trained with Bernardo for, if not this?*

Another explosion rocked both realms, physical and psychic. This time it did not come from overhead. All around them, beneath and above them, raged a far greater storm. Blue flames, fiercer than any ordinary fire, raced along the bare walls and flooring. Stone cracked under its unearthly heat and splintered away.

Even as Coryn tensed, he realized that they were no longer under outside attack. Not from Tramontana. Rumail's circle had taken no action since the fatal lightning bolt. This assault arose from within Neskaya itself.

Break the circle! Get everyone out! he roared. *NOW!*

Forcibly, he thrust the others out of the Overworld. They glanced with dazed eyes from their own pale faces to the burgeoning flames. Gerell moved to lift Bernardo's limp body.

Coryn dropped back into his own body, huddled against the stairwell wall. His ears still rang and his muscles trembled, but he forced himself to stand, to turn back down and across the corridor. He hauled himself up the far steps, shaking now with anger. Rumail's face shone behind his eyes, Rumail who had done this foul, obscene thing to him.

In the next moment, Coryn reached the laboratory which housed the weapon that should have been Neskaya's defense. The huge screens burned as brightly as the sun, all color washed to incandescence. The glare left him half-blind, but he did not need his fleshly eyes to see what had happened. Powered by its fully-charged *laran* batteries, the matrix spewed forth a barrage of incinerating blasts.

And he, Coryn, had done this thing.

The last assault had penetrated Neskaya's psychic defense, as it had been intended to do. It had left the Overworld battleground and had struck the physical Tower. Bernardo, fearing such a possibility, had already dispatched Coryn to disarm the trigger, to prevent any counterattack. Instead, Coryn had set the *laran* shield to blast his own Tower.

How could he have made such a mistake? He knew the device thoroughly. It had been designed to prevent such an error.

If not by mistake, then deliberately? How? How?

The voice echoed in his mind, *YOU ARE MINE.*

The corridor . . . The shadowy visitor, the knife slashing open his belly . . . the soul-sickness whenever he thought of—*Rumail.*

Rumail had implanted some kind of *laran* trap in his mind, that day so many years ago when he had taken a trusting boy into a linen closet under the guise of testing his talent. Coryn saw it all in a flash—his nightmares, his suspicion of the Deslucido *laranzu.* He had sensed the wrongness of what happened, but had no clue as to what it was.

As clearly, Coryn remembered coming to this chamber only a fraction of an hour ago. His hands had picked up a tool, then another, had moved across the huge artificial crystals. But he had not disarmed the trigger, as he had intended. He had not rendered the weapon inert. Instead, he had disarmed the third layer, the one which would have taken the energy of the incoming attack and redirected it, amplified a thousandfold, against the attacker.

Tramontana's lightning bolt had triggered the device, which had then unleashed its stored power here, at Neskaya. And he, Coryn, had been Rumail's agent to do this thing.

Coryn stilled the impulse to hurl himself into the flaming screens. There would be an instant of agony as the unearthly fires shunted through his own body before they killed him. But Rumail would go free . . . and for that reason alone, he must live. Live and avenge Neskaya.

Until that moment, he had not known it was possible to hate another man so much.

If we go down, Rumail goes down with us.

His face set in an unconscious rictus, Coryn strode to the bank of screens. Blue fire washed his face. He breathed it in, drawing pain to himself as a rudder. The tray of tools lay as he had left it. His fingers curled around metal already heated to the point of pain, but he did not flinch. He plunged his hand into the inferno.

The glare was so intense, Coryn could not make out any shapes or colors. He did not need to. He knew the device, its layers and connections, the flow and check of power, as the movements of his own hand.

The last time he reached into its depths, it had been to separate, to cleave. Another's will had guided him. Now it was his own bone-deep fury which pulsed through every movement as he rejoined severed connections. He did not need to plan, to consult, to consider. A new pattern emerged from his will as he reshaped the device from reflexive defense to outright retaliation.

To retribution.

As he worked, the stone floor began to burn, lines of pale flames seeping up through the hairline cracks. Smoldering wood, furniture, and carpets gave off acrid smoke. He coughed, his throat scoured raw.

Flames licked his booted feet. Leather sizzled as heat seared through to his skin. A voice cried out, wordless, unrecognizable. Beyond the open door came the thunder of walls crashing. His hands did not waver.

With the final connection, the immense power stored over weeks and months in the *laran* batteries flowed into a new course, following the path left by the incoming energy. To Tramontana . . . and Rumail.

In an instant, the flames diminished but continued to burn. Its brilliance shifted, colors reemerging. Voices called from the corridor outside. More stones shattered.

Gasping, Coryn drew back from the crystalline arrays. Distantly, in far Tramontana, he felt the awful explosions, the leaping flames, the splinter and crash of stone walls, the screams torn from human throats as flesh crisped or ripped under a hail of rocky shards. Images burst upon his mind—

—Rumail shrieking orders as the floor beneath him heaved and collapsed—

—Tomas' colorless cheeks flecked with blood—

—Aran contorted in wordless agony, his lower body pinned beneath a huge granite slab—

Aran! No! Coryn's heart stuttered within his chest. Horror washed over him. *Aran!*

Lord of Light, what have I done?

"Coryn!" Amalie stood in the doorway, one arm slick with blood. Behind her, dust billowed. "You've got to get out!" Her words disappeared as a hail of loose stone cascaded from the roof above. One struck her. She fell like a hamstrung deer.

The doorframe collapsed, falling in on itself. The long flat stone of the lintel crashed sideways to the floor, covering Amalie.

Coryn rushed forward and tried to lift the stone. Its upper end had landed on another, thicker chunk, or he would not have been able to move it at all. With a heave that wrenched his back muscles, he rolled it to one side, enough to make out Amalie's curled form. One arm was outflung, near enough for him to reach. He grabbed her wrist and pulled. She slid toward him, at first inert, then struggling, drawing herself toward him. Kneeling, he wrapped her in his arms. Half-sobbing, half-coughing, she laid her face against his chest. Her fingers dug into his arms.

All around them, the Tower was burning, falling. And he knew as certainly as he knew the beating of his own heart that the same thing was happening at Tramontana. Both Towers had been caught in the same wave of destruction.

I—I unleashed it. The thought came with deadly calm to Coryn's mind. *And I must put an end to it, no matter what the cost.*

39

Coryn lifted Amalie to her feet. For all her outward appearance of frailty, she wasn't light, but wiry with muscle. "Get out," he said, adding the weight of a mental command. "Don't stop, not for me, not for anyone."

Amalie opened her mouth to protest, then nodded. She might be strong for her size, but she could not drag an unwilling man to safety, not with the Tower collapsing every moment around them. The best way she could serve Neskaya now was to stay alive and whole, to be ready to help those who escaped. To her credit, she did not linger to ask questions. She raised herself to her tiptoes, kissed him lightly, and left without a word. He watched her crawl over the tilted stone and disappear into smoke and flames.

Back at the borderlands, when Deslucido loosed the horror of bone-water dust, Lady Caitlin and the others had formed a sphere of *laran* energy to protect the retreating Hastur troops. Now he must do the same, only this time he would be keeping the destruction *in* rather than *out*, and he would be acting alone.

Once more, Coryn bent over the immense matrix screens. He clenched the starstone at his throat with one hand and held the other out, skimming the glittering halo. This time, he needed no metal tools as intermediaries. He himself would enter into the heart of the crystalline array. He closed his eyes and dove.

Shock jolted through him, neither searing heat nor paralyzing cold, but the worst of both. Immensely powerful streams of energy flowed from the batteries and outward. A moment's effort disconnected the source, and yet the energy surged on, no longer growing but with a life of its own.

Instantly, Coryn was caught up, buffeted, the merest bit of flotsam on a torrential flood. The edges of his mental form dissolved. For an awful moment, he lost all sense of himself as a separate entity. Nothing existed but the tempest.

Fool! a distant voice cried. *Fool and triple fool, to think you can control a matrix of this level!*

What hope had he? The onslaught swept away all purpose but its own. Despairing, he gave himself over to it.

Power surged around and through him. He was no more a man, but a river of blue fire, endlessly burning, endlessly hungry. It carried him in widening circles, engulfing the two mirrored towers. His body—his form—his essence, for he no longer had any words for what he was— stretched out upon its vastness like a fisher's net spread upon the sea.

Here, in this world that was stranger still than the Overworld, distance and size meant nothing. Blue flames burned on the earthly plane in two separated locations, but there was only one firestorm. The only reality was the single maelstrom upon which he rode.

He rode it . . . and by degrees he saw the pattern of its mindless devastation. It existed in both planes, straddling them, just as it burned in both places. In the physical world, he saw the shapes of men and women struggling to escape as the walls about them flared and shattered. He heard their screams, smelled singed flesh and powdered blood and stone. He felt the heat of the pallid blue flames.

In the Overworld, the fires leaped even higher. Whatever had been touched by *laran*—stone or human mind—fed it, fueled it.

His mission was even harder than he'd imagined, for he must battle this monstrous storm on both levels. In human form, even here on the psychic plane, he could never contain it alone. Even a full-strength circle might not be able to. It would have been like trying to scoop up a river in flood with his two arms. By surrendering to it, he had allowed it to carry him, to shape him, and so he had become part of it.

Once he had used a cord of mind-stuff to lead him to Taniquel here in the Overworld. It was an image he trusted. Concentrating now, he envisioned himself as a network of tiny fibers stretched across the outside of the storm. At first no more than a film of gauze, he watched the strands thicken. Webs grew between the fibers. At first they were delicate, pliable. But just as the most slender waterweed stems create eddies in a stream, he sensed the building effect. At a hundred minute points, the energy-flood swirled and slowed.

He tensed, drawing himself smaller. The strands of the net coalesced. Moment by moment, the storm shrank in size, but not ferocity. In its core it still raged, far beyond his strength. This must be what it is like to hold a dragon by the tail, he thought, or to ride a banshee. One false move and it would blast clear through him. Without any hope of directly con-trolling it, he must guide, direct, channel its force . . .

In the real world, Bronwyn knelt over Aran, screaming orders at two men Coryn could not see. Her hair was singed half away, and blood streaked her arms. Aran's face, under the dust, was ashen. The massive stone shifted. She hooked her hands under his shoulders and slid him free . . .

. . . Bernardo, leaning heavily on Gerell's arm, limped down the stair-way, pausing at each barrier of fallen stone, breathing hoarsely . . .

I must hold on, Coryn thought. *I must give them time.*

He could not dissipate the storm. Hundreds of hours of *laran* energy, concentrated in the batteries and flowing through the device, was now loosed beyond control. He must move it to where it would do the least harm, where no human mind would ever venture. Already he was growing weary . . .

With a burst of effort, he launched himself back into the Overworld, but not where he had last been, between the manifestations of the two Towers. Once more in human form, he stood on a plain so gray and featureless that he could not distinguish the ground beneath his feet or any roof or sky overhead.

His teachers had told him that often the dead hovered between one world and the next, especially those who had been torn from life without any preparation. One of the dangers of the Overworld was that some-times their loved ones, gifted with enough *laran* to venture there, would see them at a distance, would call to them, run toward them. But no matter how fast or far the person traveled, the beloved would retreat in an endless and futile chase. On a few sad occasions, the person would

himself become lost, his mind wandering forever as his fleshly body with-
ered and died.

Coryn had brought himself, tied to the energy-storm, to the very
brink of the land of the dead. It was even more empty than he had
envisioned it. Were he not so desperate, he would have wept for its desolation.

His hands grasped a thousand cords, woven into an impenetrable
whole and rooted in the deepest core of his being. The strands spread
out, spanning time and psychic space. He tugged, and the resulting coun-
tershock almost knocked him from his feet.

Coryn tightened his grip and leaned his weight against the net. For a
long moment, nothing happened. The ropes might have been attached to
a mountain. Then he sensed a slight give. When he tried to take a step
backward, the mass rebounded, pulling him forward again.

He could not simply draw the thing into this empty world, like a draft
horse dragging a fallen log. Though he shuddered at the notion, he knew
what he must do. And quickly, too, for though time did not flow in the
Overworld as it did on Darkover, every passing moment narrowed the
chances for his friends' safe escape.

Coryn loosened his fingers, keeping only a guiding touch on the net
strands. Bending all his strength, he began to shorten the strands, to
draw them into himself. They slid easily, though the effort was enormous.
Nothing he had done before in his life, not climbing the tallest peak in
the Hellers or battling a forest fire, had been this difficult, this close to
impossible. Pain shrieked through his body, along every nerve and muscle, bone and sinew.

Moment by moment, heartbeat by heartbeat, he drew the storm into
himself. He was the net, he held the net. He was the storm, he held the
storm. When he contained it fully, he, Coryn, would cease to exist.

With trained senses, he felt his own energon channels swell as more
and more power surged through him. But unlike riverbeds in flood, where
the water could overflow, there was no place for the extra power to go.

He had heard stories of the Aldaran clan and their experiments with
weather control, how on occasion one or the other had channeled lightning or even the magnetic forces of the planet through their own bodies
and had died horribly as the result. Now he realized the true folly of what
he had done. He had taken into himself the stored *laran* energies of the
entire battery array, concentrated and magnified through a ninth-level

matrix. He, one single man, had bonded himself to this thing and now there was no escape.

He would die, he knew that now. With each passing moment, with each sliding of the thought-cables into his astral body, he felt delicate channels bursting, nodes swelling with congestion. His energy-body systems had already begun shutting down in a desperate, reflexive attempt to contain the forces surging through him. Soon even the minimum necessary for self-survival would degrade under the pressure.

And yet he must hold on, hold on until the Towers below were evacuated, the workers safe.

Blue flames crept along the nerves from fingertips to shoulders. It crisped the skin on his hands. Like *clingfire*, it burned even more brightly as layers of flesh fell away in cinders. The air shuddered with his silent screams as the fire reached for his heart.

Taniquel!

Without thinking, he cried out to her. Once he had promised her that he would come to her across fire. Now he had become that fire. His words were as ash upon the wind.

Coryn had no hands to hold the skeins of thought-stuff, but that no longer mattered. Nothing remained to grasp. He had taken it all into himself. Of the form that was his body, only a few shards of charred bone remained. Bone and the shrieking echoes of pain.

CORYN!

A voice called somewhere in the distance, called a name which was no longer his. The sound reverberated through the air, fracturing the tenuous bonds which held what remained of his consciousness.

Far away, in a room high in the ruins of a mighty Tower, a man toppled across banked arrays of artificial crystals. The weight of his inert body collapsed the metal frames, warping them past repair. It fractured the larger gems and sent others skidding into the crevices which had opened up in the stone floor.

Dust sifted to the floor, only to billow up again as the Tower trembled. From above, walls gave way. Structural stones tumbled earthward, corridors and stairwells caved in.

The translucent *laran* form of a woman shimmered above the prostrate man, eyes brimming with emotion. Her mouth moved softly, but no sound came, only the thunder of the falling stones.

A moment later, two men pushed their way past the fallen doorframe. The head of one was bound with a bloodstained cloth, ripped hastily from a woman's shift. His companion knelt beside the ruin of the matrix and reached one hand toward the fallen man.

"Aldones spare us! He's not breathing!"

BOOK 5

40

Taniquel swayed with weariness in the saddle. Her mount, a raw-boned sorrel mare which one of Rafael's officers had lent her after her own had fallen with an arrow through its throat, trotted on in silent endurance. She had been riding toward Acosta for what seemed a tenday, but was only a night and the better part of the next day. Dust scoured her throat and coated her skin. Her hair had come loose after the first hours and now fell in a tangled mop almost to her waist. Her eyes burned and the tracks of dried wind-tears on her cheeks itched. With one hand she clutched both the mare's reins and the pommel of the saddle. The other held the dagger Gerolamo had given her, although she no longer feared she would have to use it. It was enough to keep her seat as the war cries died and the last of the fleeing enemy surrendered.

The Ambervale forces had swept into the Hastur camp expecting an easy victory. Expecting, she reminded herself, that her uncle and all his men would be still paralyzed by mindless fury. But the spell lifted in enough time for Rafael and his officers to gather them together. The defenders, released from their madness, had leaped to follow their orders.

Never had she seen her uncle's genius for military strategy so clearly.

With a few orders, simple enough for men still dazed and quick enough to carry out in the little time granted them, he had prepared an ambush.

Deslucido, gloating with triumph, had ridden headlong into it.

As the great Bloody Sun cleared the horizon, it illuminated a field stained the same color. The armies of Hastur and Acosta fell upon their tormentors like captive dragons suddenly unchained. After the first few minutes, the battlefield disappeared into a hurricane of dust, of flying hooves and striking steel, flights of arrows and the screams of men and beasts. Taniquel had yelled herself hoarse from where she watched, shoved hastily aside with the *laranzu'in* and a handful of her own Acosta men, who'd appointed themselves her bodyguard.

At one point, the fighting swept in her direction, a sudden shift that happened too quickly for her guards to pull her away. A huge red-gold stallion reared straight up, above the billows of dust. For a moment it seemed to hover there, forefeet pawing air, eyes whitened, ears pinned to its neck. Yellow froth streaked with blood covered the bit of its bridle. Its rider, twisting away to slash at some unseen foot soldier, jerked hard on the reins. The horse lost its balance and went over backward. Foot soldiers, many of them in Hastur colors, swarmed out of the melee toward it.

A Hastur aide came by a few moments later to see how she fared. Taniquel shouted above the din, indicating the Acosta men who encircled her, spears and swords pointing outward.

Suddenly, trumpet calls blasted above the noise of the battle. The aide turned back, face quickening. "Stay here, *vai domna!*"

For a few long minutes, the fighting continued as before. Then Taniquel heard a new rhythm to the shouting, "Hastur! Hastur!" taken up and repeated. One of her bodyguard pointed, "Look there! They're runnin' like rabbit-horns!"

Within an hour, the field was swept clear. The Ambervale retreat turned rapidly into outright rout into the hills. Taniquel's bodyguards insisted that she stay toward the rear as the Hastur army, organized now and euphoric with victory, charged after them. Much as she resisted restraint, she agreed with them. Desperate men acted in desperate ways, and she had no right to risk herself more than could be helped.

As the dust settled, she spotted the fallen red-gold horse. The beast lay unmoving, its neck twisted in an unnatural angle. Something appeared to be pinned beneath its body, perhaps a man. She urged her own mount forward, gesturing for her bodyguard to follow. Little moved upon the field except for the wounded and a few Hastur men.

As she circled the fallen horse, she recognized its rider. Belisar Deslucido lay there, twisted half on his side. Both legs disappeared beneath the bulk of his dead mount. He grasped one thigh with his hands, his face twisted in agony. As she halted, the rising sun cast her shadow across him. His eyes squinted open.

"You are my prisoner," she said.

He nodded with a grace she had not expected of him. At her signal, men rolled the horse to pull the prince free. Belisar cried out once, then bit his lip.

Taniquel looked down at her enemy without any recognizable feeling, not even joy in his pain. She ought to hate him with a fiery, consuming hate. She ought to hold every memory of him, from that last vision of Padrik falling to Belisar's insolent grin as he talked about bedding her lady companion to the endless moments of terror on the trail. But she could not summon the feeling.

Something ran like ice within her veins. In the dust and blood, all personal hatred had fallen away. What remained, colder and far more implacable, was the fact that the secret of lying under truthspell—and everyone who knew it—must be obliterated. She supposed this was what it meant to be a Queen, to have no purpose of her own, no duty save that of her caste and country.

One of the Acosta men examined both of Belisar's legs quickly, carefully, pressing here, moving the hip and knee joints. All the while, Belisar made no sound except for the hiss of his breath through clenched teeth.

"His leg is broken," the soldier said, pointing to Belisar's thigh. The other leg was, by some miracle, whole. There might be internal abdominal injuries from a blow by the saddle horn, but the soldier could not be sure.

The thin, supple leather of the prince's breeches was stained by seeping blood. His face was already turning white under the coating of dust and sweat. Taniquel slipped from her horse and knelt beside him. His pupils dilated as she bent over him. For a moment, she thought he might already be slipping away from her, but then his eyes cleared.

Taniquel brushed one hand over the break. Although her fingers barely touched the leather, she felt the waves of pain shooting through him. "I want to know one thing only." She pitched her voice low, so that only he could hear. "This—ability of your father's. To lie under truthspell. How did he come by it?"

His mouth worked, cracked lips twisting. He looked as if he were about to spit at her. Then he shook his head.

With a slow, deliberate movement, Taniquel placed her hand on his shattered thigh, placed and leaned her weight. His body spasmed, eyes rolling up in their sockets. For a long moment, he did not breathe. The muscles of his torso quivered. She released the pressure and waited. She took no joy in his pain, nor had there been any sense of punishment in her callous action, only of necessity.

"I ask you again." The words which came from her throat were as cold as steel from Zandru's forge. "How did he come by this ability?"

"It—it is a family Gift."

"And you—do you have this Gift also?"

Blue eyes widened, and she had her answer. What was more, she knew the history of the old *laran* breeding programs. It was a genetic trait. And it bred true.

Taniquel bade the men splint Belisar's thigh and tie him to a litter, guarded so that he might not speak with anyone. He could not get far on his own, and from the look of him, he had not long to live. In the event he survived until the battle was over, she would decide what to do with him. How she would ensure, once and for all, that Darkover was safe from this threat.

Horns sounded. Voices raised in a triumphant cheer. "Hastur! Hastur! *Permanedal!*" The senior of her Acosta bodyguards, riding in front of her, slowed his mount, turned in the saddle, and grinned. They halted in a knot, she in the center of her guards. Her horse lowered its head, gulping air.

She gestured to the senior guard. "Find out—do they have the Oath-breaker? Has Deslucido surrendered?"

He nudged his tired horse forward, into the dust and melee. Taniquel closed her eyes, trying to slow her pulse and quiet the wild sick excitement running like a fever through her veins. In a moment, word would come, whether she had them both, father and son. Without him and his armies, the castle there would be easy prey. There still might be *nedestro* offspring to be searched and tested. That would come later, once this diseased root was uprooted. That would—

TANIQUEL!

She rocked in the saddle and only her grip on the pommel kept her from falling. Dry lips moved of their own volition, forming a name, *Coryn!*

His voice echoed through her mind, raw and yet honey-sweet, as if all the longing and tenderness of their few brief hours together were distilled in that single cry. Again she called to him in her mind, but there was no response. When she opened her eyes to the now-familiar scene of men and horses, spear points rising above the dust and the Venza Hills like the broken spine of a dragon, she wondered if she had imagined it.

✦

They camped in the open that night. By the time Rafael's officers had restored some semblance of order, disarming the defeated Ambervale soldiers and cordoning off areas for prisoners, the light had seeped from the sky. But the night was mild, and Taniquel content with the prospect of a pallet of blankets.

Two moons glimmered in the sky, mauve Idriel and the tiny pearl of Mormallor, still low on the horizon. Taniquel made her way to the area where her uncle had set up his command center, marked by pennants curling in the evening breeze. A few men called out to her as they sat around their cookfires, hailing her as Queen. She heard the admiration in their voices bordering on reverence, scant recompense for the questions roiling inside her.

Coryn—what could have happened to him? No matter how many times she told herself she had her own work to do—the matter she must discuss with her uncle—and even if Coryn were in trouble, there was nothing she could do, she could not drive the memory of that anguished cry from her mind.

A meal had been laid out on a folding table, along with a flagon of wine from the same mysterious stores which had produced the tent and scrap of carpet. Rafael Hastur himself was nowhere in sight, although a young aide busied himself about the tent. She recognized him, although she'd forgotten his name. When he saw her, he bowed and stammered greetings.

Outside, Taniquel lowered herself to the smaller of the two camp stools and composed herself to wait. Her stomach rumbled, for she had not eaten since breaking her fast that morning, but she wanted sleep more than anything else. Or rest, for she feared that on this night of all nights, sleep would elude her. Not yet. Once this night's business was finished, maybe then.

The sky darkened and more stars became visible. The aide lit torches. The moons swung in their silent dances. Mormallor set and Kyrrdis rose to shimmer like a blue-green jewel.

Rafael Hastur strode up to his tent, talking in quiet tones with Gerolamo. Taniquel rose and bowed, the restrained salute of one monarch to another. In the flickering orange light, the lines of his face, etched deep by the strain of the past year, ran like gullies through the landscape of his flesh. He filled both goblets with wine, handed the flagon to Gerolamo with a nod to go off and enjoy it, and downed his own. As he settled on his own stool, his dark eyes glinted.

"What a day's work," he said in a voice roughened by exhaustion. "What I really want is to fill my belly and get more than halfway drunk." He reached for a chunk of bread. "But I don't think you'll let me."

"I am not your Keeper," she replied, smiling despite herself. "And if any man deserved it, you do."

Rafael gestured to the meal laid out. "Break bread with me and then we will talk."

They ate in quiet. The camp food, although better than anything the men would receive, was dry and tasteless. After they finished, Rafael sat stroking his beard. "What is on your mind? You would not be sitting there so primly without a reason."

She met his gaze, levelly. "Damian Deslucido and his son."

"They are both in chains. Neither of them is going anywhere to-night."

"Except to Zandru's coldest hell."

"Lord of Light, woman!" he cried with such force that the two swordsmen standing guard turned to see what was the matter. "What do you want of me—to just cut their heads off and be done with it? Without a trial?"

"What purpose would that serve?" she plunged on, hating what she must do. "Except to buy them a slim chance of escape or rescue. Uncle," she leaned forward, thought of touching his arm for emphasis, then held back, "that must not happen. If we are to wipe out the whole nest of scorpion-ants, we must do so at once. Deslucido and his son are within our grasp. We must finish what we have begun. We will never get a better chance."

Rafael sighed deeply. She felt, like a shimmer along her bones, how much he wanted this whole bloody business to be over with. He was exhausted in spirit as well as body, tired of slaughter, tired of hard pounding days in the field. Tired of the endless struggle to hold something of value together in a time where every force split the land apart. Compassion whispered through her and she wished there were some other way.

He has his own burden, one I cannot share without surrendering my own.

"Perhaps you are right," he said, straightening his shoulders, "and it must be done quickly, before the heat of battle has faded. The people will accept a swift execution as the natural outcome of defeat. Deslucido gambled on easy conquest—and he lost. Such is the way of the world."

When he met her gaze once more, the light in his eyes glinted. Jaw muscles tightened, visible along his temples. With a word, he summoned his aide and gave orders for Deslucido and his son to be brought.

"But first," Rafael answered Taniquel's objection, "I will hear him."

"He is not to be trusted," she cried. "You know he will swear anything if it serves him."

"I will hear them both." His voice deepened in pitch and he sat even straighter. "Deslucido faced his test and chose tyranny, but we must not answer him with the same. Do you see, it is not enough to defeat him by force of arms or superior strategy? If we follow our passions and do as we please, without any regard for justice, then we are no better."

"But he *lied*—"

He hushed her with a gesture, and she saw him torn between his own ideals and the absolute necessity of preserving Darkover's fragile progress from chaos. With a shiver, she realized he would not retreat. He would insist on justice as well as peace.

Deslucido and Belisar were brought to the tent, the father hobbling as best he could with ankles as well as wrists in irons, the son carried on a stretcher. One leg had been bandaged and lashed to a makeshift splint. His eyes, dull with endurance, flashed briefly as he recognized her.

Deslucido, too, seemed subdued, his fire quenched. He lifted his head and glared directly at Rafael.

"Vai dom," he said, without the slightest incline of his head. "You have won the day. Our people will be eager for our safe return. What are your terms for our ransom?"

"That depends," Rafael answered, "upon how you explain certain irregularities of conduct."

One eyebrow twitched upward. "Irregularities? This is war, my most worthy opponent, not a game of battledores with a code of regulations."

"I am not referring to our present conflict, but to the events which preceded it. The meeting of the *Comyn* Council."

"Oh." Deslucido's eyes widened minutely, and Taniquel could almost hear his thoughts scattering, scrambling. "Are you holding me responsible for the Council's failure to achieve an amicable resolution and avoid all this? May I remind you that the Council sided with *my* arguments and that *you* were the one to defy them. I thought you supported the Council."

"I do." Rafael's quiet tone sent shivers up Taniquel's spine. "So much so," he continued, "that I take special offense of any action which undermines its most basic principles." He paused, as if waiting for a reaction.

Deslucido's expression did not change, that mixture of battle weariness, noble acceptance of defeat, and implacable arrogance. After a long moment, he said, "Are you accusing *me* of undermining the Council?" He lifted his manacled hands in a gesture of disbelief. "However could I have done that? I, a newcomer presenting my first petition? Why, I barely know the other lords. Are you suggesting I found a way to *suborn* the Council? *Vai dom,* surely you realize how foolish and unnecessary these charges are. We were at war, and you won. You have no need to prove your righteousness or my own culpability."

Deslucido made as if to kneel before Rafael, but the shackles on his legs prevented a graceful movement. "You have triumphed on the field of battle," he said, his voice eloquent in surrender. "I am your prisoner, at least until we settle upon honorable terms. What more do you want of me?"

"Something I fear you are incapable of offering." Rafael's own voice turned steely. "The truth."

"I honestly don't know what you're talking about. At the meeting, we all testified under truthspell. You were there. You heard me. You saw the light on my face."

"I heard what I heard," Rafael said. "And I saw what I saw. What I want from you now, to answer your question, is an explanation of how you were able to do it."

"Do what?"

"Tell a deliberate falsehood under truthspell."

Deslucido blinked, the picture of innocent consternation. He opened his mouth as if to speak, but no words came.

Deslucido glanced about the tent, as if searching for escape. His eyes lit on Taniquel, and it was all she could do to hold steady, so hate-filled was his glare. His mouth twisted, his cheeks flushing an angry red. "This—this monstrous charge is all your doing!"

He turned back to Rafael. "I don't know what she's told you, but she's nothing by a spoiled, manipulative little hellcat! She cares for nothing but her own whims! She'll say or do anything to cause trouble—even cast ridiculous accusations upon her betters."

His voice sank to a velvety purr. "You are a man of discernment and experience, Rafael. You must have seen through her spite by now. Surely you would not put her insinuations before the word of a fellow King! I will swear by anything you hold sacred that whatever she's told you about me is a lie!"

Taniquel trembled with the effort of remaining silent. Her uncle was letting him go on and on, spinning a web of the most reasonable-sounding deceit. She remembered how he had swayed the *Comyn* Council with his honeyed words. In another five minutes, she thought, he'd have all of them, even her uncle, believing he was an honorable man with only the best intentions.

"Tell me, Deslucido," Rafael said with that slow, infuriatingly patient tone, "why I should trust any of your vows, made under truthspell or not? How can I believe that you will keep any conditions of parole?"

"Because we are both men of the world," Deslucido went on, his voice like soft golden thunder. "We understand how things have always gone, how they always will. These women have no notion of anything beyond their own apron strings. But we—we share a vision of what Darkover can become. A world of unity and peace."

"Your peace," Rafael returned. "But for anyone who opposes you, the peace of the yoke. The peace of the grave."

"You mistake me entirely. I have never desired anything other than the highest good for all our people. I promise you—"

Taniquel's nerves had been frayed to the breaking point by the *laran* attack, her journey through the Overworld, the exhaustion of battle and then that single heart-rending mental cry from Coryn. If Deslucido uttered one more soothing reassurance, she would break his neck with her own hands.

"That's enough!" It was the same tone she'd used to snap Rafael and Gerolamo out of their confusion under the Tramontana madness. "We can debate this all night and be no closer to the truth." She stroke over to Deslucido, but still beyond the reach of a sudden lunge. She came close enough to see his eyes in the torchlight.

"You," she pointed at him, "kept me from a proper vigil for Padrik. You pawned me off with a bunch of excuses—"

"If I've offended you—" Deslucido began, clearly thinking her outburst due to frustrated womanly feeling.

"What offends me," she cut him off, "is that you told the *Comyn* Council you *had* given me leave." She paused to let that sink in. *"Under truthspell."*

For a long moment, no one moved. Outside the tent came the usual camp noises, a whinny from the picket lines, a snatch of a ballad, men talking.

Deslucido closed his mouth, visibly gathering himself. Rafael glanced from his captives to Taniquel and back again. His expression remained impassive.

"A thousand regrets, my lady," Deslucido said, "for the distress you've suffered from this simple misunderstanding. Let me explain what really happened—"

"Don't even try!" Now she whirled on Belisar, who blanched as she approached his stretcher. "Tell them what you told me—the ability to lie under truthspell is a family trait. What did you call it? The Deslucido Gift? You have it, just like your father—"

"No! No!" Deslucido yelled. "It's all a mistake!"

"Oh, give it up, Father," came a voice from the stretcher. Belisar strained to lift his head, his features distorted with loathing. "It's no use, don't you see? *They know!*"

"You fool! Shut up!" Deslucido turned as quickly as the shackles would permit. Had he not been bound, Taniquel thought, he would have struck the boy, wounded or not. She caught the flicker of an image, a weasel twisting and turning in a trap. She remembered that some animals would rend their own flesh, even chew off a paw, to escape.

Belisar shouted again, "It's all over! They know!"

Deslucido threw himself at the stretcher, manacled hands outstretched. Rafael leaped from his chair to pull Deslucido back. A heartbeat later, his men came in and wrestled Deslucido under control. The very air of the tent swirled restlessly after he and his son were removed.

"I cannot let them live." Rafael stood, his chest rising and falling. "You were right, niece."

"You had no choice." Tears of relief stung Taniquel's eyes. She sniffed, tasting dust and the rank sweat of fear. Deslucido's, Belisar's. Her own.

We alone will know the truth, she thought with a strange hot sadness, *that Deslucido and his son died not for their aggression in war but for their deceit in peace.*

She sent a silent prayer to whatever god would listen that this horrible secret would end with them.

41

Taniquel watched, numb and dry-eyed, as the bodies of Damian Deslucido, once King of Ambervale and Linn, then Acosta and Verdanta and a handful of other conquests, along with his firstborn son and heir, were cut down from the trees. *Hanged at dawn* sounded like something from an old ballad, and doubtless one would be made about this one, but the reality had been quite different and she was glad she had not had the stomach for breakfast.

Word of the execution had spread through the camp. She felt the whispers rather than heard them, saw the whitened cheeks and tight jaws of the Ambervale prisoners. Yet there was no hint of censure and more than a little of relief. Rafael Hastur might be seen as a harsh victor, but also a just one. And from her own Acosta men came the exhilaration of liberation, even in their exhaustion.

"Bury them on the battlefield," Rafael ordered, "but in unmarked graves, so that no man can say who was the loyal soldier and who the King who led him into defeat."

He gave other orders, too. An elite cavalry force under his most experienced general would press on to Ambervale Castle while he himself returned to Thendara. Taniquel would go with her own men to Acosta.

Rafael had offered a squadron of his own men in addition, in case any remaining Deslucido forces put up a fight. She accepted.

Later that morning, as she sat with her uncle in his tent, one of the Tower workers approached, looking uncomfortable. No, she decided with a glance at his impassive face, *feeling* uncomfortable. The skin over her spine prickled.

"*Vai dom.*" The man bobbed his head to Rafael as if he were unused to speaking in the presence of a king. What was wrong with him? He was a trained *laranzu*.

"Word has come from Hali. *Damisela* Graciela reached them through her starstone. They have lost all—all contact with Neskaya." The slight stumble betrayed him. Taniquel heard the shudder of fear behind his throat, felt the effort it took to keep his voice and eyes steady. "We fear something dreadful has happened."

Oh, sweet Evanda, Coryn!

"What? What has happened?" She stepped forward, halfway afraid to see the answer in his eyes.

"Perhaps *you* could tell us." His eyes flashed and his mouth went tight. "You were the one who bade us bring them into this fight. You were the one who said they had found a way to block the *laran* spells from Tramontana."

"Thank you for your message," Rafael said in a voice that brooked no protest. "Your concern for your fellows is most laudable. Let me know if you receive any further word."

The *laranzu* bowed again and retreated. When he was out of earshot, Taniquel said, "Will you send to Neskaya?"

Rafael looked thoughtful, but he shook his head. "I have only so many men, and we are already split with one group to Ambervale, another with me back to Thendara, and yet another to hold Acosta for you. We do not know what we will find at Ambervale, so I must divide my *laranzu'in*. I cannot weaken my forces any further on a fool's mission."

"Why a fool's mission?" she demanded hotly. "Do you not owe Neskaya protection?"

He turned to her, eyes hooded like a falcon's. "It is a fool's mission because the thing which is mostly likely to have befallen them is confrontation with Tramontana, so there is nothing we can do with ordinary means to help them. Thus, we would diminish ourselves for no good purpose."

It would be no use arguing further. She had seen the look on his face before, gauging whether a horse was strong enough to run the distance, whether a sword might break in the heat of battle, whether a messenger might be trusted. Whether she were truly worthy of being *comynara* and Queen.

She inclined her head. "Uncle, I am deeply grateful for everything you have done in my behalf and Acosta's. As always, you speak with wisdom and act with generosity. You know far more of military strategy than I, so I will be guided by you."

"You have been an apt student," he said, a bit stiffly, then softened. "And I am pleased to be able to help you. I have done what was needful for the future of all Darkover. If any of us is to survive this terrible time, we must curtail the worst abuses of *laran* warfare, find our way to a less destructive way of settling differences and . . . preserve the basis of integrity in our dealings with one another. In this, our purposes are one. *Adelandeyo,*" he added, giving her a short bow. *Go with the gods.*

◆

As Taniquel took her leave of him, she realized how true this was. Rafael Hastur could well have stayed safe and secure in Thendara. He could have compelled her to remain with him, dependent and powerless. Deslucido's territorial expansion might eventually have provoked Rafael to forcibly defend his own boundaries.

It was the misuse of *laran* which had spurred Rafael into immediate action. Releasing bonewater dust at the borderlands was bad enough, though others before had done so and would probably do so again. But to lie under truthspell . . . that had shaken him to the point where he would hazard everything, even his own Domain, to eliminate it.

As he had said to her one night at Arilinn's Hidden City, "*If a man's oath cannot be trusted, then there is nothing left but force, and men will use any weapon available. Then there will be no consideration or holding back, for words and reason will become as dust. The only defense will be even more powerful weapons. Zandru alone knows when that will stop, perhaps when there is no one left to fight and nothing left to fight over.*"

For that cause alone, Rafael would set aside everything—his own life, his kingdom, his honor. He would expect Taniquel to do the same.

Taniquel's blood ran cold, and she remembered the way her voice had rung all through her when she questioned Belisar. Her duty called her to leave Coryn to his fate, as if he were no more to her than any other useful tool. She wondered what she had become, that she could even think this way. The answer came, a blending of a dozen voices—her uncle's, Lady Caitlin's, Padrik's father's.

You are what you have always been, a true daughter to your family and caste.

And am I never to have a life and will of my own?

If the gods had set that as your fate, you would not have been born comynara.

At the back of her mind came a faint, wild keening, a cry of pain beyond words, beyond bearing.

So it had come this, she thought, that as Queen she must tend only to her duties, thinking only of bringing her son safely to his majority and the throne. Eventually, of course, she would learn what happened at Neskaya. News would come to Hali and then to her uncle and finally to Acosta. It was doubtless some consequence of their intervention, for they had succeeded in blocking Tramontana's spells. Perhaps some temporary drain of psychic energy kept them silent for a time.

Within the coiled chambers of her heart, she knew this was not true. Coryn would not have called out to her like that—would not have reached her with her paltry insignificant *laran*—if there had not been the direst need. What was perhaps the worst uncertainty was that she did not know if he had reached out to her for help or in farewell.

A Queen such as she had been raised to be would not even think of riding to Neskaya with Ambervale and Acosta uncertain. But she had already paid that price over and again.

Taniquel paused, her feet tangling in her now-ragged skirts. Esteban, shadowing her half a pace behind, looked around, startled. He slipped his sword from its scabbard and glanced around as if he had missed some oncoming threat. Absently, she laid her hand on his arm and then walked on, relying on him to guide her. His back straightened.

She felt like a blind woman, as if she had already left some essential part of herself behind in Rafael's tent. The body which walked slowly, proudly, fingertips resting lightly on the muscled arm of her paxman, was that of a stranger. On some cell-deep level she realized that if she rode to Acosta now, if she abandoned Neskaya, she would indeed become only a blinded shell of herself.

Was she fooling herself, telling lies at the urging of her heart? Coryn had stirred her with dreams and longings she had never imagined. They were for characters out of song and legend, for Hastur Son of Light and his beloved, Cassilda, for whose love he put off his godhood and took on mortal flesh. *She* was not meant for any such love. *She* had been born for something else, for the duty of her blood.

The *cristoforos* might pray to the Holy Bearer of Burdens to ease their own sorrows, but they took up their tasks of their own free will. None were promised from before their births to follow that path. Nor were there, as far as she had ever heard, any women monks among them. She had heard of women pledged to serve the Dark Lady, Avarra, but knew little of them save that they had no dealings with men.

Coryn might die, and with him such passion and tenderness that came but once in a lifetime. If she held back now, she closed her heart forever.

He might already be dead, she told herself. She might sacrifice everything she had struggled for in vain.

I will not know. I cannot know until I go and see for myself. Going to Neskaya meant looking within herself.

It seemed that for this moment, her life parted like a crossroads. She knew the path she had followed all her life.

I will not be that kind of Queen, who breaks faith with those who have given everything in her cause. I will not be a Queen who has no heart.

She came to a halt outside her own camping place, the sleeping pallet which was little more than a pile of blankets, many of them none too clean. Esteban looked at her, a question in his eyes.

"If you would be so kind," she said, "pack food and my clothing into saddlebags and ready the sorrel mare."

He faced her full on. "May I know where we are going, *vai domna?*"

"Not *we*, my loyal Esteban. I do not—cannot—ask anyone to come with me."

Esteban's expression turned stubborn. "The camp is safe enough, but not the roads. There are stragglers from the Oathbreaker's army, not to mention the less savory sort of person you'd come across in troubled times where a lord's reach is short and coin scarce."

Taniquel raised her hands in a little gesture of surrender. He was coming with her, whether she wanted him to or not, and the only graceful thing to do at this point was to accept his help. Rafael was also less apt to send a party after her if she had her own personal bodyguards.

"We ride to Neskaya," she said, "to see why the Tower has fallen silent. To offer what aid we can, if need be."

"We ride in honor, then."

Taniquel thought about that for a moment, then nodded gravely. She said the word *honor*, mostly to herself, as if she had never truly spoken it before and now knew its meaning for the first time.

✦

In the end, it was not just Esteban who accompanied Taniquel, but about thirty mounted Acosta men, a miniature army emerging from the larger force with its own colors and allegiances. She sent the rest, along with Rafael's and an experienced captain, on to Acosta.

Pennants bearing the eagle emblem appeared and supplies were packed, including a tent for Taniquel. Graciela somewhat diffidently offered herself as chaperone, for it was not proper for a woman, even a Queen guarded by her own sworn men, to travel unaccompanied. Taniquel accepted, not only for the sake of a propriety she no longer cared about, but because Graciela's skills might be useful once they arrived at Neskaya.

The miles passed with infuriating slowness, for the larger force moved slowly on their battle-weary horses. One night they camped beneath the stars and Taniquel fell asleep almost as soon as she stretched out. The next day, they came upon a little trading village by a river. Taniquel went with Esteban to bargain with a farmer for bread and grain for their mounts. She asked news of the road ahead.

"I wouldn't go in that direction," the farmer said, eyeing them with escalating suspicion. He'd refused to speak directly with Taniquel and clearly regarded her as an immodest woman and Esteban a sandal-wearing fool for not beating her properly. "M'cousin two farms over said a tinker came through, told him there'd been witchy wars out Neskaya way. Stone buildings set afire, like they had over to Valeron in olden days. My grandsire, he told of it, how the wizards can make rocks bleed and rivers speak. Me, I think it's likely Aldaran doings, and I won't have none of it."

Esteban thanked the man, paid him, and they went on.

Stone buildings set afire . . . The words echoed in Taniquel's mind as she nibbled the bread, laced generously with coarse-ground nuts and tiny sweet seeds. Esteban sat on his own mount, staring fixedly ahead, giving her what measure of privacy he could.

Through water you have come to me. Through fire I will come to you.

Had he tried, and called out, and failed because she could not answer? She wanted to dig her heels in the sorrel mare's sides and ride headlong for Neskaya.

42

The cloudy day muffled the town of Neskaya and its environs in a strange blue-gray haze. Although small compared to Thendara, the town was far older. It was said to be one of the very first human habitations, its origins shrouded by time and legend.

As Taniquel rode through the outskirts, with Graciela on one side and Esteban on the other, she felt as if she were going backward through history, passing a strange jumble of old and new, of patched-together buildings, wide boulevards suddenly narrowing, walled gardens and houses so old they seemed to be standing only because they were packed so tightly against their neighbors. Few of the buildings were more than two stories, so that she expected to see a Tower rising above them, but even from a distance, there had only been the town.

Shopkeepers and inn landlords emerged to watch their passage. Children, considerably less ragged and better fed than the street urchins of Thendara, ran alongside. Unlike their Thendara counterparts, they did not beg, only shouted in excitement.

Taniquel had halted at one of the outermost establishments, an inn and stables. The innkeeper eyed her and the armed men she rode with.

"Is there any news of Neskaya Tower?" she asked after a few preliminary comments on the weather, the road, and the oat harvest.

His eyes had darted to the Acosta pennants. There was little enough breeze, so that the eagle emblem remained hidden, but they were clearly not the Hastur blue and silver. "The Tower? What of it?" he said rudely. "Who wants to know?"

Esteban gestured for them to move on. They'd find out soon enough.

They had not gone far into the town itself when a pair of stern-looking guards greeted them with drawn swords. Their eyes shifted from Esteban, who by his position and dress was clearly the leader, to the body of Acosta soldiers, to Taniquel. They were wondering what sort of expedition this was, a group of grim-faced armed men in unfamiliar colors, too many for a lady's honor guard, and with the smell and dried blood of battle still on them.

The center guard stepped forward and asked their business. Esteban glanced back at Taniquel, for the decision to reveal her name and rank was not his to make. Hers would be the risk of being taken hostage or becoming a target for Ambervale sympathizers.

Taniquel took in the guard's bearing, the subtle tensions in his face. *Something* has *happened here.* And she had not come this far to shrink from her mission, to hide behind some subterfuge.

"We have come from the army of Rafael Hastur, second of that name, to enquire of the welfare of Neskaya Tower and to offer any assistance we may on the occasion of need." Her formal inflection gave her words a stilted character, as was her intention.

The man's mouth opened slightly, his gaze flickered from Taniquel to Graciela, sitting with almost inhuman stillness on her horse, as if seeing the two women for the first time. In that moment, the Acosta expedition changed from a military force to a proper escort. Gulping, he bowed.

"My pardons, *vai leroni,*" he said, bowing. He gestured for his men to put up their weapons.

He had mistaken her for a *leronis,* Taniquel realized. Neither she nor Graciela wore robes which would identify them as Tower workers, but they had clearly ridden long and hard. Even the most dignified *leronis* could be expected to look trailworn. Gathering her wits, she set her chin and modulated her voice as she had seen Caitlin do innumerable times.

"What is the current situation?"

"It is even worse than we thought when the Tower first fell." The edges of the man's voice cracked. "The stones keep burning and burning, so that rescue workers cannot reach buried survivors. Not that we expect any. There are so many dire wounded, it was a miracle any made it out alive.

"Lady," he looked up at her with fear shining from his eyes, "I have seen what a sword can do to a man's body and I have heard of *clingfire,* how anything it touches must be cut away or it burns flesh and bone until there is nothing left. But these flames . . . they feed on stone itself. And . . . I do not know, I am only an ordinary man, I should not have said as much. You are wise women and know more than I."

"Take us there."

✦

Taniquel could not think even one moment ahead, must not let herself imagine what she would find. They went along one street through an open area where women sold vegetables and flowers from carts, past prosperous-looking houses. Gardens sloped down to a winding stream and on the other side sat an enormous pile of tumbled stone. Graciela gave a small cry and covered her mouth.

In places, the stones burned, even as the guard had said. It was diffi-cult to tell their natural color, for the flames which flickered over their jagged surfaces or sprang from crevices between them were an eerie blue. Here and there, a robed figure moved about the rubble. A pavilion had been set up on the bank, lined with swathed bodies, and several more on this side of the stream. Two figures in ordinary clothing hurried in oppo-site directions across the bridge.

"Who—" Taniquel shaped the word, and for an anguished moment no sound came. "Who is in charge? Where is the Keeper?"

"Come," said the guard captain. "I will take you to him."

He led the way to one of the nearer pavilions. A woman in a white monitor's robe, torn and smeared with dried bloodstains across one thigh and both sleeves, straightened up from where she bent over a pallet. With eyes so dark they looked bruised, she glanced over Taniquel to Graciela, who slipped from her horse and darted forward.

"Demiana!"

"Is it Graciela of Hali?" the monitor woman cried. She reached out and brushed Graciela's outstretched fingertips with her own. "How—how—did word somehow get through? Is help on the way?"

With a start, Taniquel realized that this slight flame-haired woman was in charge, the senior of all the Tower workers. *Where is Coryn?*

Graciela shook her head. "No, we only heard that Hali could not reach you. Edric and Buthold and Jerred and I were in the field with King Rafael."

"The attack from Tramontana—"

"Was stopped in time. We carried the day, for which we will ever remain in your debt." Taniquel dismounted and walked the few paces to the Neskaya *leronis.*

Demiana looked in question to Graciela.

"I am Taniquel Hastur-Acosta, niece to King Rafael and friend to Coryn of Neskaya."

Demiana's eyes widened. "Coryn's Taniquel?"

"The same," Taniquel said. "Where is he? Is he—"

Dark, unrecognizable emotion flickered across Demiana's face. "He lives still, if you call it life. For the moment, anyway." She gestured behind her. "Here we have those we could safely transport, both our own people and those townsmen who were near enough to be injured." Her eyes went to the pavilion on the far side of the river. "Coryn is there, along with Bernardo and three others we dared not move."

"Bernardo—?" Graciela's voice held real fear, the first Taniquel had ever heard in her.

"A seizure of the heart," Demiana said. "He should recover with rest and care. If I thought he would fare better, I would have had him carried into town, for many have opened their homes to us. But he would only fret worse, so I have left him where he is." She sighed. "Come with me, Lady Taniquel. I will take you to your Coryn."

Although every fiber shrieked to hurry, Taniquel stayed for a moment to ask Esteban to contact the city elders for an assessment of the civilian problems and offer of help. Then she hurried after Demiana and Graciela across the river.

Drawing closer to the rubble which had once been a marvel of soaring grace, Taniquel shivered inwardly. This close, the fires gave off no heat. For a moment, she thought it was the pale blue translucency of the stone which gave the flames their tint. Here and there, where the rocks burned from underneath like chunks of wood thrown upon embers, their surfaces glowed so bright it hurt to look too long at them.

Demiana introduced Taniquel briefly to Bernardo, Keeper of Neskaya Tower. He bore the unmistakable stamp of authority on features drawn thin and ashen around haunted eyes. To Taniquel's relief, he made no attempt to rise, although his hands stirred on the unbleached muslin sheets.

When Demiana said, "This is Coryn's Taniquel," Bernardo smiled. On impulse, Taniquel knelt beside his pallet and took one of his hands in hers. Despite the pallor of his skin, it felt warm, a good sign, she thought.

"Do not despair, my child, or blame yourself," he said in a whisper.

"What do you mean?" Taniquel asked above a suddenly pounding heart.

"That's enough," Demiana said. "He needs his strength for himself," with a pointed look down at the older man, "not for conversation."

Rising, Taniquel asked Demiana, "What did he mean?"

"Coryn is there. What is left of him." The *leronis* pointed to the far corner, which had been cordoned off with thin sheets strung over ropes. Something cast lambent shadows over the draped fabric. Demiana made no attempt to impede Taniquel as she slipped between the curtains.

The air in the little chamber was still and warm, catching in Taniquel's throat. A man lay on a pallet of folded sheets, feet toward her. His arms had been arranged at his sides, legs outstretched in the graceless sprawl of unconsciousness. A strip of spotless linex had been tucked around his hips, but he was otherwise naked. His face was hidden from her, turned away under a tousle of bright russet hair. Only the chest moved, rising hesitantly in shallow, irregular breaths.

For a long heartbeat and then another, Taniquel stood immobile, staring at the glowing blue-white patches which covered the man's exposed body. She shuddered and inhaled the faint smell of burned copper.

"Coryn?" Taniquel fell to her knees alongside the pallet. She stared down at the nearest patch. It was like looking into the depths of an oven where embers still clung to life. When she held out the flat of one hand and gently touched his unmarked skin, it was smooth and resilient. She thought of *clingfire,* how it kept burning until it was cut away or else there was nothing left to consume. But this was something else, perhaps a kind of *laran clingfire.* Blue was the color of starstones, of the stone fire which had felled an entire Tower.

She turned her head slightly at a rustle of cloth from behind. Demiana.

"What is wrong with him? Can't you—put the fires out?"

"We have tried," the *leronis* said in a hollow, distant voice.

What had Bernardo said, *"Do not despair . . ."*? Demiana, if not in actual despair, wavered perilously close.

"We have tried," Demiana repeated heavily. "What you see—this fire—cannot be extinguished from outside. In the battle, he took the backlash through the energy channels of his body. He transported it somewhere, beyond all the known reaches of the Overworld." She paused, visibly struggling for self-control. "We think he is still out there or perhaps he has already perished and all we see is the body's automatic reflexes, the way the heart may go on beating for a time, even when the spirit has gone."

"And you—what do you think?" Taniquel demanded.

"If you must know, I think it is too late. I think he died to save us. I am the strongest *leronis* here," Demiana said without boasting, stating a simple fact, "and I cannot reach him in the least." She pulled the curtain aside. "I have already said my farewells. I leave you to say yours."

✦

Afraid to change Coryn's position, even the angle of his head and yet wanting—*needing*—to see his face, Taniquel moved to the other side of the pallet. His face was unmarked, skin clear and firm, eyes closed in an expression of peace. At once, she was struck by how familiar and yet how strange he looked. There was so much she did not know about him. So much she wanted to say.

She wondered if she spoke, if he would hear her. Caitlin had once said that people could hear and see even in their sleep, though they might not remember. Everything which a person experienced was imprinted in the energy body, but most especially the words of someone greatly loved. She and Taniquel had been sitting in the solar in the Hidden City, and she had been talking about her own father, how he had slipped into a coma after a series of strokes, and how she had sat at his bedside, telling him what she had become, what she had made of the life he gave her.

"And when I was finished, when I had said everything there was in my heart to say, he died." Yet there had been no self-accusation in Caitlin's words, only a sense of completion and acceptance.

But I have not said everything there is in my heart to say to you, Coryn, Taniquel thought. *I have not even begun to. Where have you gone? Where must I follow, to reach you?*

She took his hand between hers. Though his body had been bathed, dust still clung to his hair and grit beneath his fingernails. There were a few half-healed abrasions on palm and knuckles. The patch on his shoulder flickered lightly.

On impulse, she bent to press her lips against his. She thought, quite irrationally she knew, that if she could only put enough passion, enough tenderness into that kiss, he would somehow respond. Wherever he was, he wanted to come back to her, or he would if he knew she was here. Of that she was absolutely certain.

There was not the faintest answer as she straightened up, no movement of his own lips under hers, no deepening of those too-shallow breaths, no flutter of eyelids. She sat there for what seemed hours, wondering what to do next. It *must* be possible to reach him. She dared not believe otherwise.

As if in a dream, her hand moved to the neckline of her dress and slipped between her breasts, where she carried the handkerchief he had given her. She shivered, remembering the warnings she had been given, the stories of people wandering lost until their fleshly bodies perished. Did she have any right to risk herself, when the future of Acosta depended on her?

But for this moment, she had set aside her crown. She was no longer Taniquel Hastur-Acosta, Queen and Regent of Acosta, niece to Rafael Hastur, second of that name. She was simply Tani, who had been lost and then found in more ways than one.

"*Vai domna?*" came a soft voice.

Taniquel straightened up to see a woman barely out of girlhood, thin face haloed in frizzy yellow hair, slip between the curtains. She wore the white robe of a monitor. With a dancer's floating grace, she came over and knelt beside Coryn. Level gray eyes met Taniquel's. On closer inspection, she was not so much young as almost sexless, with only the narrowness of her chin and her mane of straw-pale hair suggesting femininity.

"So you are Coryn's lady," she said. "Demiana said you had come, but not that you were so beautiful."

"I'm sorry," Taniquel said. "I don't know you."

"Oh! It is I who should apologize. I'm Amalie, matrix mechanic at Neskaya, or I should say I *was*. I'm doing monitor's work again, for there are so many wounded." She glanced down at Coryn's body in such a way that Taniquel knew she had been the one to bathe him and lay him out like this.

"If I were to touch that," Taniquel pointed to the patch of smoldering blue, "would it spread to me? Are they changing, getting bigger?"

Amalie pushed back her hair with one hand and shook her head. "No. What you see is an outward projection of an event which is essentially energetic, not material. The—fires, if you will—are most concentrated over the energon nodes, which function as capacitance sites—" she broke off. "Again, I am sorry. That is not what you need to hear."

How can you know that? Taniquel wondered as she searched the other woman's eyes. She felt a feathery brush of fingertips on the back of her wrist.

"He is gone where none of us can follow." Amalie's words were slow, like a funeral chant.

"Into the Overworld? But you know—you are trained—" Taniquel stammered.

Amalie shook her head. "We have searched as far as we dare go."

"Then you must dare beyond that. Or if you cannot—" Taniquel swallowed. "Once I went into the Overworld because I was desperate, and I knew that only Coryn could help me. Now, he needs me just as much. I have to try. I cannot do any less for him. Will you help me?"

Gray eyes widened minutely. "You will not succeed."

"Why, because I am a woman and therefore weak? Because I have no training, no talent?" Taniquel fumed.

"No," Amalie said, raising her hands in a calming gesture. "Because no one can."

"But I am not no one!" Taniquel's words hung in the air like a challenge. She gathered herself, smoothing her voice. "I ask you to help me into the Overworld. I have been there once before. I know how frightening and disorienting it is. You may be right, I may not succeed. I may not even survive." Tears brimmed, quickly blinked away. "Please. Let me try."

After a long moment, Amalie said with a tiny shake of her head, "I must be as mad as Durraman's donkey to even consider such a thing. But I owe Coryn my life, and if there is any small thing I have not yet done to help him, I will."

She returned after a few minutes with an armful of bedding, which she laid out in a pallet alongside Coryn's. Taniquel was secretly relieved that she would not have to be parted physically from him. She lay down as Amalie folded and tucked blankets under her knees and the small of her back.

"I will go with you into the known part of the Overworld," Amalie said. "You know that distance has no meaning there, nor time. We think that Coryn may have strayed—or gone deliberately—into the shadow of the dead."

Taniquel nodded, gulping. Amalie adjusted the pillow beneath her head.

"You may meet people or catch a glimpse of them from afar."

The monitor's lips pressed together, almost bloodless. "Some of them may be dead, wandering shades who have not yet accepted their passing. This is especially true when their deaths were sudden or violent. They may seem frightening, but they have no power over you. They can harm you only if you believe they can. One thing you must not do, no matter who you see, is to run after them. That is the one thing which will truly doom you."

"You mean—anyone but Coryn."

Amalie shook her head. "*Especially* Coryn."

"I don't understand." Taniquel pushed herself up on to her elbows. "If I don't go to him, how will I ever—" Amalie pushed her back down.

"I told you that distance is not important in the Overworld, but love is. Truth is. We could not contact him with our minds, no matter how well trained and powerful. You—" with a fingertip laid gentle as butterfly wings on Taniquel's lips "—you may be the only one who can reach him."

43

Before she closed her eyes, Taniquel reached into the folds of her bodice and closed her fingers around the much-folded handkerchief which Coryn had given her. She had held it like this, close to her heart, many times since Coryn gave it to her in the garden. The fabric had once been very fine, the embroidery done with skill and delicacy. Its age and wear suggested it had come from mother or grandmother. Sometimes she almost caught a hint of a scent, sweet and spicy like strawflowers. But more than that, she sensed—no, she *knew*, with all the wordless certainty of her empathic *laran*—that with this scrap of cloth, Coryn had entrusted her with a piece of his soul. There was nowhere he could go that she could not follow him, if only she had the courage.

Taniquel drifted on Amalie's rhythmic murmurs and silky touch between her brows. Her body felt heavy, sinking into the cradle of blankets and pillows. At the same time, some other part of her felt light, like a bird eager for flight.

Amalie's words became a muffled echo, as if heard through a long tunnel. Taniquel could no longer feel the bedding beneath her, the folds of her gown, the pressure of her boots against toe and arch.

In a heartbeat, she was back in the Overworld. She sensed the place, as clear as the metallic taint in the air before a thunderstorm. She opened her eyes to grayness. Flat, featureless sky and unending horizon greeted her. A day or a century could have passed with no perceptible difference. Only she had changed, although her body and gown looked exactly as they had before.

"Taniquel." Amalie stood a few feet away, her hair blown into a solar aureole. She wore a filmy green dress which seemed in constant motion. As Taniquel got to her feet, Amalie pointed behind her.

Taniquel turned to see a Tower made of glass, barely discernible against the ashen sky. Only a faint rippling, like air rising from the earth on Midsummer Day, indicated anything at all was there.

"Neskaya Tower," Amalie said, "or all that's left of what we created here." She sounded weary with sadness. "Now it's more memory than anything else."

"Where do I go from here? What do I do?"

Amalie shook her head. "Go where you are led, or stay here, it makes no difference. I—" her voice caught for an instant, "I wish you success. You are not the only one who loves Coryn, but you are our only hope." Then she vanished.

Taniquel shivered, remembering her last foray here and the shadowy figures she had seen before Coryn rescued her. She'd been so frightened then. Now she had some idea what to expect, some warning that distance meant nothing, only intention did. And if she did not find Coryn, if he could not return with her, she was not sure what she would do.

She held the handkerchief, which had somehow retained its original form. Pressing it between her hands, she called his name and waited.

At first, nothing seemed to happen. Sky and ground gave no hint of passing time. After a while, she noticed that the Tower had disappeared, or at least gone so invisible, she could no longer make out any hint of its contours. The air turned a shade cooler.

On the horizon to her right, an ill-defined shape appeared, quickly growing in size as if it rushed toward her. It was, she saw, a group of people. As they drew closer, their number varied, sometimes half a dozen individuals, sometimes four, sometimes twice ten. They wore flowing gray robes and hoods which hid their faces, or perhaps it was her own urgency which muted her sight. Forgetting Amalie's warning, she called out Coryn's name again and rushed toward them.

The faster she ran and the faster the people seemed to come toward her, the farther away they seemed. If she only ran more swiftly, she would surely catch them.

Just a little longer—

She could almost feel the wind of their passing. Every muscle strained for more speed. Her hair whipped behind her and her feet skimmed the ground, smooth and cool like a single, unbroken slab of polished slate.

Suddenly, one of the figures sped past her as if she were standing still. She barely glimpsed it, only enough to make out a woman's face, eyes white and staring, mouth distended in a soundless howl. The rest— body swathed in shapeless gauze, limbs, hair like rent clouds—blurred.

The expression of utter despair on the woman's face shocked Taniquel. She stumbled to a halt, barely keeping her balance. She could not think what the figure was—a dead person, eternally lost in confusion, or a living person like herself? Until that moment, she had not realized the terrible risk of coming here, how ignorant she was of this place and its perils.

"Oh, Coryn, Coryn . . ."

His name came like a sob. Taniquel wanted to throw herself down and give herself over to grief. Once he had found her in this eternal gray wilderness. He had come to her rescue. Now it was she who must find him.

But how? She lifted her head, tightened her grip on the handkerchief, and waited.

Two more figures approached, one in robes which might have been crimson but were so thin and diaphanous as to be the faintest rose. The face of the man who wore them was all but transparent, yet he seemed to see her. He slowed his pace, eyes searching hers. She did not know him, though he seemed to be pleading for some recognition. Shaking his head, he went on. A few paces behind a woman followed. Her face shone with tears and she lifted her arms toward him. Her lips moved in sound- less pleading.

Now the mass of figures drew visibly closer and more numerous. More of them parted from the group and passed by Taniquel. Many of these gave no sign they even noticed her. One man, though, paused. The colors of his hair and face were stronger than any of the others, as if he burned with an inner fire. He wore a Keeper's crimson robe, the fabric dusted with soot. When he saw her, his face darkened, brows drawing together over flashing eyes.

She *knew* that face—

Rumail! Damian Deslucido's *nedestro* brother, the renegade *laranzu!* For an awful instant, Taniquel wanted to run, to hide. His was the voice which had threatened her outside the Overworld Tramontana, and his had been the mind which probed her when she was a captive in her own home.

She lifted her chin a fraction higher as she remembered Amalie's words. The dead had no power to harm her unless she permitted it. Still, she flinched when he spat at her and called her a word so obscene she had never heard it spoken before, not even in the Acosta armory when no one knew she was listening.

"You!" He made a broad, sweeping gesture to indicate the surroundings and for an instant, Taniquel saw the hazy outlines of rubble. "This is your doing! Upstart chit from an insignificant little dirt-hole! We should have slaughtered you along with your worthless husband, or else tracked you down like an animal. You thought you could stand up to us, to strike back—a rabbit-horn who thinks she's a dragon! Luck and the Hastur lord have been on your side for the day. But in the end, he too will fall. He cannot stand against us. My brother's vision will prevail. King Damian—"

"—King Damian is dead!" she snapped. "Have you not seen his shade wandering here in the Overworld?"

"You lie, hell-bitch!"

"I saw him hanged, and his lecher son at his side."

Rumail burst out in another round of profanity, then broke off and threw back his head in peals of insane laughter. "I leave you with this curse—the Deslucido curse—that you and yours will never know a moment's peace. I will take my revenge —"

"Then you will have to do it from hell!" she cried. "Get you gone, shade of a dead man, to whichever of Zandru's frozen levels will have you!"

"Dead? You think I'm dead?" For the merest instant, Rumail looked startled rather than enraged. "I will show you what it is to die!"

He moved closer, hands raised with fingers spread as if to close around her throat. As he bore down on her, she felt his hot breath on her skin, smelled the rank odor of his sweat. She had not realized the dead could be so vivid.

He cannot harm me, she repeated to herself, but with each passing instant, her words carried less and less credibility. Just as he was about to grasp her, she broke, whirled, and ran headlong in the opposite direction.

"Go on, little bitch! You cannot hide from me! And after I hunt you down, I will come for your precious son!"

Raucous laughter trailed her, escalating in pitch until it no longer sounded human.

✦

Taniquel ran and ran, sometimes stumbling over her own feet, sometimes rushing so effortlessly that the only thing she was aware of was her own speed. She lost all sense of time passing. The immediate cause of her flight quickly disappeared from view and from mind. She ran, and that was all. Without visible landmarks, even variations of the flat gray sky and ground, one place looked the same as any other. Only the absence of her enemy marked any difference. He might be one mile behind her, or a hundred.

Her footsteps slowed as she realized that she had also lost sight of the crowd of shadowy figures. Regret slashed through her. She had disobeyed Amalie's most important instruction and had lost what little bearing she had. Now, as she came to a halt, she looked around, seeing nothing but unchanging grayness in every direction. She was no closer to finding Coryn, and now her chances were even dimmer.

Yet . . . Amalie had said that distance didn't matter in the Overworld. Only love did.

Taniquel held out the spectral handkerchief and pressed it between her breasts.

Coryn . . . Coryn, wherever you are, hear me! Answer me! She could not tell if she had spoken the words aloud. They reverberated through her mind, through the core of her body.

Hear me! Answer me!

No, that was not going to work. He could not answer, he could not come to her. Suddenly, she had an image of him, standing on the other side of a wall of blue flame. Words whispered through her mind, resonant with his voice.

. . . through fire I must come to you . . .

Fire! I must find fire! She tightened her grip on the handkerchief and put all her will into the thought. Eyes narrowed in concentration, she scanned the horizon for any trace of brightness. Though at first she saw nothing, she had the sense of flexing an unused muscle, of holding something between imaginary hands—something huge and dense—and drawing it toward her.

Out of the corner of her eyes, brightness glimmered. She turned, half-afraid that it would vanish once she faced it, but there it shone, a mote on the horizon like a fallen star. Every fiber urged her to run to it, but somehow she held firm. She could not cross this distance with her own feet. She had summoned the fire with her mind, with the *laran* she had been told she had so little of. And it was this talent she must use now to bring it even closer.

Once more, Taniquel imagined herself pulling on that heavy weight, drawing it to her. Again, she had the sensation of solidity, of inertial resistance. But as she pulled, it seemed to slide more smoothly as if, once uprooted, it had no fixed place. She wondered if she were actually moving the fire or somehow folding the space between.

Within minutes, the flickering grew larger and brighter. Her heart leaped when she made out a figure standing in its heart. For a moment of soaring hope, she forgot everything else. The sense of holding an invisible weight subsided. She had to close her eyes, concentrating, before it became quite solid again. When she opened them again, the fire appeared to be only a few paces away, as high as she could reach and twice as wide.

A man stood inside.

Taniquel crossed to the fire with outstretched hands. Her fingers brushed the outermost flames and she drew back, for although the fire gave off no heat from a distance, it burned as hot and fierce as any earthly blaze. She cried out, shoving her singed fingertips into her mouth like a child. Her eyes watered.

Within the flickering depths, the figure stirred. Somehow she knew that he had felt her pain, heard her cry. The flames thinned in places, becoming more transparent so that she saw Coryn standing there. His pale skin reflected the ghostly blue of the fire. At first, his eyes were white but as she watched, they darkened and she knew that he could see her.

"Taniquel . . ." His voice was no more than a papery whisper, yet it filled her with a rush of absurd joy. ". . . what are you doing here? Are you . . . have you . . . died, too?"

She wanted to shout, to dance, to hurl herself into the fire to be with him. "No, I am not dead. And neither are you. My body lies beside yours

just outside of what is left of Neskaya Tower. I came to bring you back."
She added, "Amalie helped me."

"You should not have come," he said hollowly. "This is the land of
the dead, or as close to it as any in the Overworld."

"Amalie warned me I might encounter dead people, but that they
could not harm me. She was right on both counts. And if I should not be
here, neither should you."

He shook his head, slowly, with an infuriating lassitude. When he
spoke, she made out only isolated phrases. "I put myself here . . . brought
the backlash where it could harm no one . . . anchored . . . sacrifice . . .
my responsibility."

"Coryn," she said firmly, "you were very noble in what you did, but
you serve no one by lingering here. Back—home," she said, for want of
a better word, "your body is on fire from within, and they cannot help
without your active participation. I have not come all these miles and
waited all these years and given up everything I thought I was—" her
words came in a tumble between sobbing gasps, "—everything I had
believed in, only to forsake you now.

"Beloved," she said the word aloud for the first time, "we may not
have much of a life together, but I will not give you up. I will stay here
with you. I will find a way to join you in the fire if I must. But do not ask
me to leave you. Loving you is who I am."

"Oh, sweet gods." He hung his head so that his hair, dark as clotted
blood in the eerie light, fell across his face. "I do not deserve this love."

"Coryn, come to me. Through this fire, come to me."

"I cannot. The fire—I am what binds it here, where it can do no
harm. I cannot let it go, or allow it back into the material world."

This is the Overworld, she thought. *Towers appear out of thought, space
folds on itself at a command. Dead people go rushing about their own business.
Anything can happen. Distance doesn't matter, only love.*

"Then let go of whatever you must," she said. "Just so the rest of
you comes back with me."

"It is my *laran* that holds the fire."

She wanted to stamp her foot and scream that she didn't care about
his *laran*. She had been judged by hers, found wanting, and valued at no
more than what bloodlines and alliance she could bring. His love had
given her value in her own right.

"Then leave it," she said. "I care as much for it as you do for my kingdom."

For a long moment, he hesitated. Perhaps he was weighing her words, trying to decide it she meant it. His doubts shivered over her skin. For a *laranzu* of his rank, such a choice must be agonizing. Who would he be without his Gift? Where would he go? What would he do?

No, as the moments passed, she realized it was more than that. It was choosing to live blind and deaf, or in a world without taste or color. There was no way she could make it up to him, no matter how much she loved him. She had not thought any of this through. Perhaps she had wronged both of them in asking.

But she had asked, with her heart rather than her reason. It was all she had to give him.

The flames parted, and he stepped through, a man of fire and flesh. The fire died, leaving only a pale man collapsing in her arms.

44

Taniquel stayed in Neskaya for the rest of the season, a guest along with Coryn in one of the richer houses, until falling night temperatures threatened an early winter. As it was, she stayed longer than she should. Word had come that Acosta's occupiers surrendered after only a brief siege. She was needed there. Julian was still in her uncle's castle, safe but growing into a sturdy boy without her. Their separation ached like a wound in her heart. Sometimes in the middle of the night, she would look out toward Thendara and feel as if she were being torn in three different directions at once. Then she would look down at Coryn, sleeping, the few remaining patches of blue fire casting a pale illumination across his features, and know that she would not for all the world have chosen differently.

Coryn would not be able to travel for some time. After he had tumbled into her arms in the Overworld, she awoke beside his physical body to find him regaining consciousness. For many tendays after that, he drifted in and out of sleep. Each time he awoke, Demiana and the others were able to reduce the luminous patches further and strengthen his ravaged energy channels. Often it took all his stamina to eat, meditate, and take the small amount of exercise allowed him. Demiana had absolutely forbidden him to leave Neskaya until the fiery patches had disappeared.

Now Taniquel had to accept that would not be until the spring thaws, but she could not wait that long.

As Taniquel prepared for the journey to Acosta, sitting with Coryn in the chamber they shared and going over the lists of supplies while he dozed, a commotion from below drew her attention. Exclamations from their host's adolescent daughter blended with men's voices, indistinct but recognizable as belonging to her Acosta guards. Taniquel got to her feet, the papers sliding off her lap. Coryn's eyes opened.

"It's all right, beloved. I'll see to it," she said, then paused as she noticed his smile. He did not smile very often, the lines etched deep crevasses into the landscape of his face. She had been afraid it was news from Tramontana, where the devastation had been even worse. Several of his closest friends, including a man named Aran, had been badly hurt in body and mind. It was the nature of the *laran* injuries that sometimes improvement was followed by an abrupt turn for the worse.

"No," he said. "Let her come."

Her?

Footsteps clattered down the corridor, heavy boots and a lighter tread, then a knock sounded. Taniquel drew herself up and lifted the door latch. Outside stood Esteban's nephew and another Acosta man, little Raquella, and a woman with startling green eyes and straw-pale hair, disheveled as if she'd just come from a long and windy journey. She wore a half-length cloak over a jacket and a skirt split for riding, all of thick soft *chervine* wool, dyed dark blue and edged with snowflake embroidery, the sort of warm, beautiful clothing Taniquel would have chosen for travel at this season.

"Excuse me, *vai domna,*" the woman said without the slightest trace of deference, and slipped through the door. Only the hem of her cloak brushed against Taniquel. Her unselfconscious poise reminded Taniquel of Lady Caitlin.

The next instant, Taniquel recovered herself. Who did this woman think she was, *comynara* or commoner, to enter here without leave? She glared at Esteban's nephew and drew breath to command the woman's removal.

But the green-eyed woman had rushed to Coryn's side and taken him in her arms. Over her shoulder, Taniquel glimpsed his face, eyes closed in an expression of uncomplicated joy. He hugged her with equal fervor, rocking gently. She murmured something Taniquel did not catch.

Regaining her composure, Taniquel dismissed the guards and closed the door on the host's inquisitive daughter. In a matter of minutes, the story would be through half of Neskaya and all the old busybodies of both sexes would want to know who this stranger was. A sister, perhaps? She frowned, for none of them that he'd mentioned fit this description. Especially not the one who had gone off with her uncle's men to join the Sisterhood of the Sword.

"I never thought—" Coryn murmured.

"Of course, I had to come," the woman said, then drew back, regarding him with a practical and unabashedly fond expression. "Even at Linn, we heard what happened." Her eyes flickered to Taniquel's flushed cheeks. "You should introduce us, you know."

"I'm sorry. Tani, may I present Liane, *leronis* of Tramontana Tower, once my enemy and now my oldest friend."

Taniquel felt giddy with relief. She inclined her head. She barely heard Coryn's next words, only the gentleness in his voice as he called her *my beloved*. Liane gave her a smile so radiant and without jealousy that Taniquel immediately began to like her.

Liane, it seemed, was Liane Storn. High Kinnally, her home, had fallen to Deslucido even as Coryn's had, and like Verdanta had thrown off its oppressors in the wake of the Hastur victory. She'd spent the last few years at Linn, a hostage against her family's good behavior. When word had come of the fall of King Damian, she had taken back her parole. No sooner had a contingent of Rafael Hastur's men crossed the border between Linn and Ambervale than the vassal lords rose up in a body and ousted their wardens. She'd departed the next day, with Lady Linn's best horse and traveling clothes.

"Ah, you were much better prepared than I," Taniquel said, laughing.

They told stories and compared journeys until Coryn tired. Taniquel went with Liane to see her settled with the other *laran* workers. "I am not here to gawk at the ruins," Liane said, her eyes hardening, "but to work. I am a trained monitor and needed here."

Taniquel felt a surge of sisterly understanding for this determined woman. They had each been blessed with useful work beyond the alliances or sons they could produce. Of Liane's devotion to Coryn, she had no doubt, and she was heartened when Liane insisted on nursing him herself.

She left them on a frosty morning. Liane had let Coryn have the last meat bun, having argued with him in a ruse to tempt his uncertain appetite. She walked to the door with Taniquel and brushed her lips against her cheek.

"I will keep him safe and make him as whole as I can," Liane said. "But he is wounded in ways I cannot, with all my monitor's skill, heal. I can only pray that time and your love will do the rest."

✦

Coryn waited for Liane's visit, dressed for walking. He'd decided that as long as the weather permitted, he would exercise. Movement helped him regain his physical balance. His eyes still saw the sun and the brightness of the day, his ears still brought him the laughter of children and the harmonies of the *rryl*, he could still form coherent words, and yet some part of him had gone blind, deaf, and dumb.

He strolled with Liane through the streets of Neskaya, limping a little from muscles damaged by the inward erosion of the flame patches. She tilted her head toward him, as if catching his thought but too tactful to ask him. They'd discussed his condition, monitor to patient, so many times, they'd worn out the words. He knew what had happened to him, the damage from the massive overload to his energon channels and nodes. He also knew that it was too soon to know how much had been burned out, or if there might be some slow recovery over time. Neither one of them had spoken aloud the truth that hung between them, which was that he would never again be capable of a Keeper's work, or in all likelihood of any capacity in a Tower.

My life will be with Taniquel, at Acosta.

Now, as they skirted the area from which the jumbled ruins of Neskaya Tower could be seen, he realized he had never asked Liane what she meant to do.

"I am not sure," she said. "At first, I thought to help out here with monitoring and healing, for that was the most pressing need. But, after this winter, there will be only you and Bernardo who need more care, and his kin at Armida have asked him to join them."

"I can't see him retiring," Coryn said. "Dreaming away the rest of his life at someone else's hearth."

She shook her head. "Neither can I, but his heart cannot take the strain of circle work. He could do much good as a teacher of novices, but where would he go? Any place another Tower might offer him would be charity, and he's too proud for that." She sighed. "It's as if Neskaya and Tramontana, everything we built and dreamed, is being scattered to the winds. I suppose after you've left I will go home and make my family happy with a marriage."

"Is that what you truly want?" Coryn searched her wide green eyes for her reaction.

"You asked me that once before, at Tramontana," she said, laughing a little ruefully. "And no, then as now, what I want is to do the work I was trained for. But the world goes as it will, and not as you or I would wish it."

"Perhaps a place could be found for you at another Tower." His right side had begun a slow, crawling burn, and he was forced to pause. Beyond the river, the piled rubble of Neskaya still smoldered.

"Ah, how simple things are for you men. I am doubly beholden to my family, both as a woman and as a daughter of Storn."

Coryn heard the quiet acceptance in her voice. She, too, had changed in the last few years. The captivity in Linn had sobered her, even if it could not steal her dreams.

His eyes rested on the pale blue stone that had once been a tower of such soaring beauty. In his imagination, he saw the blue fires lighting it from within. It would take a generation and the will of a Hastur lord to rebuild it, if ever. Meanwhile, Darkover would lose all that precious *laran*, those finely trained minds. Women like Liane and Demiana would tend babies instead of matrix circles. People would die because there were no skilled healers or not enough workers to keep the relays going or make enough fire-fighting chemicals.

He and Taniquel shared a dream, and more than a dream. *There must be a way to make our lives whole,* she'd said on their last night, lying in his arms.

Coryn turned to Liane and saw reflected in her face his own dawning hope. "Perhaps there is another choice . . ."

✦

Taniquel rode along the narrow spit of land and through the front gates of Acosta to a hero's welcome. Despite the dusting of snow, people lined the roadside as if they'd been waiting for her for days. Men and women, babies and stripling youths stood red-cheeked in the cold, cheering wildly.

At first, she smiled and waved, caught a nosegay of dried flowers. The crowd went on and on.

Waves of adoration battered her. Her jaw muscles ached with smiling. By the time she reached the courtyard, her face was wet with tears.

It is too much, she thought numbly. How could one person receive so much concentrated gratitude, as if all their pain and hope were poured into her at once?

To them, I am not a person. I am a Queen. Yet, for those blissful ten-days back in Neskaya, she had been only a woman in love. She would forever hold those memories in her heart, no matter what happened now.

Gavriel and the *coridom,* as well as Rafael's officers and senior staff, waited for her below the steps leading to the castle. The Hastur captain bowed, but Gavriel bent his old knees to kneel before her. She saw from the way he moved and the wetness in his age-rheumed eyes how difficult it was for him. Although she wanted nothing more than to run to her old chambers, shut the door behind her and bury her face in the comforter she'd had as a child, she held herself immobile as she listened to his formal welcome.

She stooped to raise him and say in a voice only he could hear, "Old friend, the past is forgiven. I want no shadows of Deslucido between us."

In slow procession, she greeted each of the people who had taken back her home and held it for her. Many had waited for her return before starting back to their own homes.

"There is not one among you," she told them, "who has not earned a place here, for himself and his family, whenever there is need. Acosta will forever honor those who have served so faithfully in such desperate times."

As I make a home for Coryn, I will make a home for them all. This, too, was what it meant to be a Queen, to have sovereignty over her own kingdom.

In the days that followed, she had many occasions to make good on that promise. One man, a grape farmer, had lost a leg to a festering wound in the retaking of the castle. Another brought forward his brother's widow. Still others had lost the goodly portion of their farms or livestock to Deslucido's army. Taniquel, working with Gavriel and the *coridom*, found a way to help them all. There was enough work to fill her days and send her into exhausted sleep each night.

Each morning, she watched the path of the sun as the days grew shorter. With the turning of the seasons would come new calves and foals, crops of fine grapes, wheat and barley, and perhaps of babies. With spring, too, would come Coryn.

Julian arrived before the first deep snow, brought by his nurse and a small entourage. After he was asleep, she walked the now-empty castle halls, remembering the sound of children's laughter. But whether it was an echo of her own or a promise of children yet to come, she could never be sure.

✦

After everyone else had fallen asleep, Coryn Leynier, once *laranzu* and under-Keeper of Neskaya Tower, now consort to Queen-Regent Taniquel Hastur-Acosta, stood on the battlements of Acosta Castle. Below, new spring green glimmered in the moonlight. Absently, he rubbed the nubbled scar along his right side where the last of the blue fires had had to be cut away. It had been five years since the disaster at Neskaya and sensation was slow returning to the thickened tissue, but it *was* returning. Still, at times like this when he awoke sweating from half-formed terrors, he could not help running his fingers over it, a fleshly symbol of how he was forever changed.

He was struck once more at the contrast between the timeless stillness of such nights and the ebullience of the days. From dawn until well past dusk, Acosta Castle hummed with activity, not restricted to the reordering of the kingdom. Almost independently, he and Taniquel had conceived the idea of opening Acosta to the workers from Neskaya or Tramontana, a place where they could continue their studies as they healed. One of the soldiers' barracks had become an infirmary ward and workshops set up for retraining. An outlying building was still in use for *laran* practice for those whose talents were not completely burned out.

Bernardo had been the first to come, accompanied by Liane, but he had died in his sleep the first winter. She had been preparing to return home when news of a marriage had arrived from Verdanta. Her elder brother, now Lord Storn, and Eddard had hesitantly agreed to explore the possibility of an alliance and taken to matchmaking like two gossipy old women. They had first thought of marrying Liane to Petro, but after a few visits back and forth, Petro had fallen in love with her acid-tongued younger sister and the bargain sealed in that way.

Liane, now an extraneous elder daughter happily destined to become a spinster aunt, had just been offered a place at Dalereuth and would be leaving in a few months. Bronwyn had never come to Acosta, but had taken a post at Hali as soon as she could travel.

Of the old circle from Tramontana, only Aran remained. He would bear the deformity of his shattered leg bones to his grave, but still rode like a centaur. Only this afternoon, he had ridden out with young Julian, teaching the boy to master his new pony. Julian, now seven, had taken a particular liking to Tessa's firstborn, sent here for fostering, and for his "auntie" Liane, who was utterly charmed by him. In less than a decade, the boy would be giving them all heartaches and early gray hairs.

"I will not leave you, *bredu*," Aran had said when it was clear his own psychic abilities had survived, although in lesser degree than before. He remained adamant in his belief that someday Coryn's *laran* would recover. Perhaps he had something of a catalyst telepath in him, for sometimes Coryn could almost sense his thoughts when they were together.

As for Coryn himself, he could not complain he was adrift. Five seasons flew by, filled with rewarding work. The skills he had absorbed along with his mother's milk, the management of an estate, supervision of staff and smallholder, training and care of livestock, all these things now came into daily use. He was as much Taniquel's paxman as he was her consort.

Taniquel . . .

He sensed her presence on the stairs behind him, although she moved soundlessly. He did not know, dared not hope, that this meant some portion of his *laran* had returned. Perhaps that was why he ran his fingers over the physical scar, testing that faint return of sensation as proof that healing could occur.

With a rustle of skirts and the kiss of breath on his skin, Taniquel slipped her arms around his waist. Lips brushed against the base of his neck, where the neckline of unlaced summer shirt lay open. The tension lacing his nerves softened, as it always did in her presence.

"Bad dreams?" she murmured.

"Rumail again."

She turned him to face her. Her eyes shone like polished steel. "He is dead, love. I saw his shade in the Overworld, remember? They are all dead. And the dead cannot harm us, not a single one of that whole nest of scorpion-ants."

He wondered, not for the first time, if she were right, if that disquieting sense of Rumail's presence were no more than lingering memory. It was natural to have such fears, the healers had told him, as the mind accepted what had happened, made order of tragedy and prepared to move on. But the image and the gut-wrenching reaction had seemed so real . . . He shook his head as if to clear it, and his hand went unconsciously to the invisible wound over his belly.

"We have won, truly won," she went on, her voice a shade strident now. "You can see that every day in the eyes of our people. Deslucido's terrible secrets died with him, and that is the end to it. Darkover is safe, thanks to all of us. Now we have the future ahead of us. We are together, which I never dreamed possible. Isn't that enough?"

Coryn lifted his arms and she came into them. When she talked like this, his life seemed an unfolding miracle. Even the loss of his talent could not negate the soaring joy he felt every time she enfolded him in her sweetness. The nightmares would fade, he told himself.

Taniquel pressed against him. Her belly and breasts had rounded these past few tendays and her skin felt hot, almost velvety, with early pregnancy. Sometimes he thought he felt—or perhaps only remembered—the golden glow deep inside her.

Our daughter, he thought. *Our future.* They'd decided to name her Felicia, as a token of their own happiness.

EPILOGUE

A ragged man rode into a small town along the Kadarin River, a town where no one inquired of any business past the color of a man's money. His mule limped, ribs staring out of a dull, dust-choked coat. The man himself was wild-haired and taciturn, his face seamed like worn leather. Even these rough folk who lived on the edge of bandit country looked away quickly, not wanting to meet his eyes.

The man shuffled into the single inn, hunched down at a table, and ordered hot food. It came, a bowl of steaming gray stew with a fist-sized lump of soda bread. He bent over it, staring into its opaque depths as if to read some secret there. The stew, though bland and greasy, warmed his belly. He would live, he repeated to himself. He might be too old to carry out his revenge during his own lifetime, but he was not beyond fathering sons to carry on. And someday, he swore to himself yet again, the Hastur bitch and her issue would pay for what they had done.